Countryside

The TEARS OF ADINA

J. T. Cope IV

Tiner

Tiner Press

Fort Worth, Texas

ISBNs:
Hardcover 978-0-9960500-6-7
ePUB 978-0-9960500-4-3
Kindle 978-0-9960500-5-0

This book is a work of fiction. Names, characters, places and incidents either are products of the author's imagination or are used fictitiously. Any resemblance to actual events or locales or persons, living or dead, is entirely coincidental.

Cover art and design and illustrations by Mark Korsak
Book design by Christopher Fisher

This edition was prepared for printing by The Editorial Department
7650 E. Broadway, #308, Tucson, Arizona 85710
www.editorialdepartment.com

To T, EK, and Car, the best story I've ever helped write.

CONTENTS

The TEARS OF ADINA

ONE

❖

The Messenger

A cool wind blew over the ocean waves and onto the little island of Shalloke a few miles off the coast of the Carolinas. Winding through a mix of palm, cedar, and dogwood trees, the wind slipped into a sleeping village known by the same name. Wooden signs swayed and lights flickered to life in windows above the shops. A man walked along with a bucket in hand and poles slung over his shoulder, a young boy skipping beside him. They waved to a woman leaning out the first-floor window of a two-story house across the street. Near the center of town a water fountain bubbled into the air, the wind toying with droplets of water as they fell back to the ground. It swirled around the fountain, over a stone bench beside it, and continued down the lane. The town passed behind, and a wooden boardwalk snaked its way toward a row of cottages beside the beach. Slipping over marsh grasses and sand dunes, the wind gusted past the farthest building and around three children running along the beach.

Another boy of some twelve years shuffled away from the children, shoving his rust-brown hair to the side, and plopped down beside a dune. The wind rushed on toward the north end of the island and past a dark shadow as the sun slipped behind the grass-covered dunes. An egret stared down from the bare branches of a bramble tree, and behind the boy, lights shone from the picture window framing the dining room of a white-walled beach house. Smoke curved into the sky as the boy glanced at the three children chasing each other back and forth along the beach. He reached into the cargo pocket of his canvas shorts and pulled out two folded and worn pieces of paper. Peeking again at the children, he unfolded one of the letters. The page was blank, marked only by creases. The boy leaned closer and blew gently across the paper. Light swirled over the page and glowing yellow letters formed under the fading sunlight.

Hey man,

I still can't believe you figured out how to make the letters disappear when someone else was around. Anyway, how's life on an island? Have you still not seen any nymphs or mermaids? Mom says they walk the beach most often in the evening as the sun is going down, so try then. Life is still kinda crazy here. They had another breach in the wards last night. ~~Mr. Rayburn~~ *Captain Rayburn is constantly out at night. The Guard has patrols roving the entire holding. We haven't had anybody else get hurt, but the Elder Council is all up in arms about the dark creatures getting in. I overheard your grandpa say something about Mr. Thompson arguing selfishly about patrols and money, but it didn't make any sense to me honestly. He didn't seem real happy. Oh well, have fun. Hurry up and get back. Samantha won't shut up about you, it's kinda making me sick! Bring me back something cool. We'll talk to you soon.*

Matt

15 July

Luke folded the letter and glanced around the empty dune. The egret squawked and took flight as Luke unfolded the second letter. Letters glowed dark red as he blew across it.

July 22

Luke,

I hope you're enjoying the island. Things here in Countryside are OK. Father spends a great deal of time with the Council and seems more upset each day. We've had two more attacks since I wrote you last. Your uncle and the Guard beat the darkmen back soundly both times, and no one was hurt, but people talking around town say it's disturbing that they're coming more frequently ... and that they're getting past the wards. So far we haven't had another soulless get into the holding ... Jeremy is recovering from his wounds, but the Council is still not sure how that last one got in.

The most interesting thing happened a few days ago, though. A group of kids were playing in the peach orchards near Sandy Island and suddenly a couple of dryads appeared. They seemed very agitated. Then almost immediately these dark little creatures popped out of a hole in the ground and took off running in the opposite direction of the dryads. They ran toward the children who of course ran screaming into town. It turns out the little creatures were gnomes! Can you believe it, gnomes. We haven't had gnomes since ... I haven't even ever seen a gnome! They're perfectly harmless to people it seems, well unless they catch you alone, but now the holding is covered with "hunting parties" of children. There's some grumbling on the Elder Council about why they're in Countryside, but I don't know anything about that, maybe Matt does.

Anyway, write when you can. I am sure you are having a blast and don't have much time though. We are all looking forward to you coming back.

Sam

Sam ...

Luke's mouth curled into a smile. He folded the letter back and ran his finger over the symbol pressed into the outside of the paper: the arch, tower, and teardrop-shaped flame indicating the letter originated in Holding Countryside. Luke thought of the cloaked riders who ferried mail between the holdings and the "outside."

I wonder if one of them will come tonight?

"Luke ... Luke!"

Luke started and shoved the letter back into his pocket. He looked toward the house, where his father stood waving to him in the fading light. Shadows crept toward the sea as the sun faded pink below the horizon. Trent, Jon, and Amy scampered up the boardwalk to the back of the house.

"Coming, Dad." Luke stood and dusted off his pants, then froze.

Grrrrrrrrr ...

He jumped around in a circle. A shadow flitted between two of the dunes. "Hello?" He squinted and stepped toward a large dune where the shadow had disappeared. The wind picked up again, howling past him inland as he padded forward on bare feet.

Grrrrrrrrr ...

He stopped in his tracks as the sound deepened and the pendant on his chest warmed. Glancing at his feet, he noticed a print of some kind and leaned down.

Grrrrrrrrr ...

Luke straightened back up. His eyes widened as a hulking shadow moved behind the dune. Green light burst into the sky from behind the dune, and he ducked his head.

Arr! Arr! Arr!

The light faded and Luke found himself alone. He took a step toward the dune but then stopped.

Maybe instead of staying out here and playing hide-and-seek with growling shadows, you should go in to dinner like you said you would, huh Rayburn?

Luke turned around and jogged toward the boardwalk under the gray of twilight.

Luke stood in the surf the next morning holding his hands over his head. Sweat poured off his forehead as the waves washed over the footprints that marked his run down the beach. Coach Williams's "suggested" workout list had arrived a couple of weeks before, and Luke's dad had offered him a glimpse of what opting out would feel like.

"… took it easy on you last year … this year will be kinda like having the wind knocked out of you and then someone telling you to run some more sprints …"

Luke sucked in his breath and shook his head as his father's smiling face flashed through his mind.

"Luke! … Luke, are you ready to go fishin'?"

Jon came running down the beach in rolled-up pants and a T-shirt. Luke laughed as his brother bounded into the water, splashing him. Luke picked him up and tossed him into a shallow wave rolling up the beach. "Ha, ha, ha!"

Jon stood up spluttering and laughing and ran at Luke. He tackled him into the water and they splashed back and forth until their father and Trent reached the edge of the water.

"How was your run?" his father asked.

Luke snorted as he stood up under the cloudless blue sky. "Brutal. I thought my heart was going to explode. If two-a-days are still hard after this, I'm gonna quit." Dragging Jon up out of the water, he turned and looked at his father. "I mean, seriously, Dad, Jon David's gonna have a heart attack!"

"Luke …" His father frowned down at him, but the corners of his lips twitched as he tried to hold in a laugh. "Well, maybe a little fishing will help boost your spirits."

Luke smiled.

"Where are we going anyway, Dad?" Trent said.

"You'll see."

Thirty minutes later, Luke stepped over the low-lying, bent trunk of a live oak and stopped. A cove opened up in front of him. Live oaks and dogwoods surrounded the north and east sides, sand and rocks formed the south side, and in the distance rose the towering spire of a lighthouse. A yellow warbler flitted across his field of vision as Trent and Jon raced barefoot toward the blue-gray water. Luke's father grinned and patted Luke on the shoulder as he stepped past.

"Thought you might like it."

Luke smiled and followed his father to the edge of the water. He pulled out a pole and began casting into the water as his father helped Trent and Jon toss a net into the small waves. As egrets took flight off the bare branches of some still-standing dead trees, the sun rose out of the ocean and warmed the morning air, drying Luke's clothes. One of the white birds flapped its wings, gliding out over the cove before turning back inland. As Luke followed the bird's flight, his eyes turned to the water and his heart jumped. Two feet from where his father, Jon, and Trent stood casting nets, a pillar of water grew. Reaching just above Trent's head, water flowed up the center of the pillar and cascaded down the sides, sea-green light flashing in the middle.

Then the water formed into a woman in a glistening blue dress.

"Joseph Rayburn?"

Luke's body filled with warmth at the sound of her voice rising and falling with the waves. His father grimaced and nodded, pulling the net and the boys out of the water. "Yes, ma'am."

The woman dipped her head. "Greetings, I am Josephine. Your father sends a message to you." She raised her hand to the side and another pillar of water rose. Luke gasped as the pillar morphed into Grandpa Rayburn.

"Is that really—"

The woman smiled. "No, youngling, this is a mere projection of the man, to give the recipient a clearer understanding of the message."

Luke stared back at his grandfather's face. He leaned forward, squinting as water flowed into the cove.

"You may touch it if you wish."

He brushed his hand against the water, distorting the figure of his grandfather. The water parted around his fingers just as if it were flowing around rocks in a stream. The water was cool, and as he removed his fingers, the figure returned to its previous shape.

"Wow."

Jon jumped up and down. "I wanna try, I wanna try."

Josephine nodded and Trent and Jon repeated Luke's experiment. Jon grinned and laughed as the water flowed over his hand. "Amy is gonna be sooo jealous!"

Luke's father pursed his lips. "I think that's enough for now, boys. You mentioned a message, ma'am?"

Josephine flicked her wrist toward the watery form of Grandpa Rayburn. Luke jumped as his grandfather's voice boomed.

"Joe, I hope y'all are having a good time. I'm sorry to bother you and the family, but we've come across some information I felt you should know." A smile crept onto Grandpa Rayburn's shimmering face. "Actually, I don't think it's anything that will affect you where you are, but … it was either this or your mother was going to turn me out with the dogs and get on a train and come there. She still might, knowing her."

Luke's father chuckled.

"At any rate, as I'm sure you know from Landon, we've had quite a few attempted breaches this summer, some successful, most not. A couple of days ago, however, the Guard came across some tracks outside the wards." The watery Grandpa Rayburn sighed. "The tracks appear to be those of a pack of bane wolves … and they appear to be following the direction of a man."

Luke's father mumbled a curse under his breath.

"We aren't certain yet, but … you know the possible implication. There were also boot prints leading from inside the holding out. Again, I can hardly imagine this affecting you on the island, but … There's no reason for you to come back early or any nonsense like that. Just be careful. Tell the kids and Sara we love them and are very much looking forward to seeing them again. Take care of yourself, son. I love you."

"You, too, Dad," Luke heard his father whisper as the form of Grandpa Rayburn cascaded back into the cove. The sun stood overhead as Josephine turned her gaze back to Luke's father.

"Have you any reply?"

Luke's father stared down at the sand. Gulls called in the distance, and wind whistled through the rocks at the entrance to the cove. After a few moments, he raised his head and frowned at Josephine. "Dad, we'll return if necessary and will send word if we learn of anything here. Be careful, and make sure that knucklehead of a brother of mine stays that way, too. We love you." He paused. "That should do it. Thank you, ma'am."

Josephine nodded. "He will hear, Joseph Rayburn."

With a twist, Josephine dropped back into the water, and the lapping waves of the cove swallowed her.

Carrying an armload of tackle, Luke dodged around the trunk of a sable palm as his father strode down the path to the beach house.

"Luke, when we get back, help your brothers get y'all's room picked up."

Luke frowned. "Yes, sir. Dad, what was that ... lady back there?"

His father climbed over a dune and helped Jon scramble up beside him. "That was an ocean nymph."

"Well, how did she get a message from Grandpa?"

"Probably from the dryads in Countryside. Flame creatures will often carry messages for those who are kind to them, or who they feel have the need. Your grandfather has been among the few people of Countryside who've consistently helped and fought alongside them. They would do a great deal for him" — he watched Luke as they stepped up onto the boardwalk — "and for anyone associated with him. There may have been other motivations, but I suspect your encounters last year with dryads resulted from your relationship to him as much as from your need."

Luke frowned. "Oh ..."

"Don't get too down in the mouth, Luke. They seem to like you well enough on your own merits."

Luke smiled again as his father chuckled.

"Joe!"

Luke stopped with his foot on the beach house's bottom step at the sound of his mother's voice. Looking to the south, he saw her walking along the boardwalk. A half-mile behind her, a bell tower and a steeple rose above storefronts of the seaside village. She held Jodi's hand and carried bulging canvas bags with her other hand. Amy skipped along in front of them in a white summer dress to match her mother's, carrying two bags of her own.

Luke's father closed his eyes for a moment. "Well, boys, do you think they left anything in the stores?"

Luke and his brothers laughed. Their father waved back at his mother and shook his head with a smile. "I guess we oughta go help th—"

"Dad, what kinda animal makes this print?"

Luke looked where Trent was pointing beside the boardwalk. Half a print was visible in a spot where beach sand mingled with dirt.

"I can put my whole hand in here, Dad." Trent grinned as he placed his hand within the outline of the print and looked up at his father.

Luke peered at the print as his father knelt beside it. A dark look passed over his face.

"Hmmm … I don't know, Trent, maybe someone's dog around here. What do you think?"

"I don't know, Dad, that looks awful big for a dog."

That would've been a huge dog—and it looks like the same kind of print from last night!

"Boys, if it's not too much to ask, do you think you could stare at the sand later?!"

Luke jerked his head up as his mother struggled with her bags a few feet away. Trent and Jon bolted over.

"Mom, Mom, guess what …"

"… at the cove …"

"… and Grandpa talked to us …"

They jumped up and down as they told their mom about the nymph. Amy's eyes grew to the size of saucers, her mouth dropping open. "And I missed it!" she said, stamping her foot.

Luke felt a hand on his shoulder. "Let's go save your mother," his father said with a grin before stepping onto the boardwalk. He walked over to Luke's mother, took her bags, and gave her a kiss. "Sorry, hon."

As Luke stepped onto the boardwalk, he looked back down,

but this time he didn't see the print—it was gone, sand brushed over it.

The fire burned brightly on the sand under the light of shining stars and the waning crescent of the moon. Jon and Amy played a game of stones, or damk'or, sitting across from each other on a blanket while Jodi tried to eat the smooth rocks. Trent held an empty glass training sphere in his hand. His grandmother had sent it from Countryside, and Trent sat staring at it. Every few seconds, a spark of light would flash in the sphere and fade. Trent would sigh, blink his eyes, and stare at the orb again.

Luke watched the flames and sparks dance up into the night sky as his parents leaned against a piece of driftwood beside him. He gazed at the red light to the north.

Seems higher this year ... Only six years left, according to Mr. Roberts. Luke watched the star float in the darkness above the waves. *He may not think it means the end of the world like the prophecy says, but I bet it's still not a good sign. I've gotta get my hands on the Book of the Wise again ... Maybe I can figure something else out, since apparently reading Ancient is one of my talents now.*

Luke screwed a marshmallow onto the end of the stick in his hand and studied the flames. He closed his eyes and a picture of Samech and a fire in an open field flashed by. Opening his eyes again, he grinned. Little flames jumped from the logs to roll over the marshmallow, turning it from white to black. After a few seconds, he leaned forward and blew the flames out. To his side, Trent glared up at him.

"Show-off."

"You'll get there someday, little brother, and probably be better at it than I ever will be."

Trent feigned a smile and turned back to his sphere. He glared at it and a spark exploded into a flame in its center. Trent jumped and the flame vanished. He gaped at Luke.

"See, I told you, just keep—" Luke froze as his chest warmed and movement caught the corner of his eye. "Dad ..."

Grrrrrrrr ...

That's the same sound!

Luke looked to his right and felt his blood run cold. Ten feet away, his father crouched with a silver-and-red blade lifted in front of his face. On the other side of the blade stood a wolf almost as tall as his father, with fur the color of the night sky between the stars. The wolf eased forward, tongue lolling to one side. It looked around the circle as Luke's mother pulled everyone except Luke to her side.

"Sara, as soon as it moves, get the children inside."

The wolf cocked its head and looked at Luke's dad, then up at the sky.

Ahoooooooooo!!!

Shivers ran up Luke's arms and he covered his ears as he took a step back.

"Momma," Jon whimpered, and Amy pulled closer to their mother.

Another howl answered in the distance, and another. Luke lost count of them.

"Luke, take Jodi," his mom said. "When I run, you and Trent run, too. Get inside the house no matter what. Do you understand?"

"Yes, ma'am," Luke said, never taking his eyes off the wolf.

The wolf turned and eyed Luke as he moved. His gums pulled back, and that was the last warning they had. The wolf leaped forward. Luke grabbed Jodi and took off after his mother and Trent, with Jon and Amy in front of them. He slipped in the sand as he climbed up the first dune, falling and losing his grip on Jodi.

Grrrrrrr ...

Luke cringed at the wolf's growl and jerked his head over his shoulder. The animal snarled but circled in the opposite direction from Luke and Jodi. Silver-blue light surrounded his father. A dark red streak marked the wolf's left side.

Jodi's crying filled Luke's ears, and heat bubbled up in his chest.

If I surrounded the wolf with darkness ...

The voice of Josiah, Luke's Fundamentals of Light teacher, sounded in his head: *... only with regard to how to defeat it or defend against it.*

Luke ground his teeth. *I am* trying *to defend against it!*

As he stared at the wolf, blackness darker than ink surrounded it. The creature snarled and snapped at the cloud. Luke poured in more darkness and the wolf shook its head, rearing up off the sand.

Luke's father jerked his head around. "Luke, the house, now!"

Luke shivered and the darkness vanished. He turned toward Jodi as the wolf lunged at his father.

What were you thinking, Rayburn?!

He picked himself up, snatched Jodi back into his arms and dashed away.

Ahoooooooooo!!!

The howls were closer now. Luke bounded up the stairs and into the dining room, where his mother and siblings stared out the window.

"Luke, what happened? Are you two all right? Where's Dad?"

He slammed the door behind him and shook his head. Jodi clung to his shoulder, clasping his shirt and his skin in her fists.

"I don't know, Mom. The wolf jumped for us, but Dad sliced a pretty good gash in its side. And … he told me to get to the house and … I don't know."

His mother turned back to the window. Orange light flared past the dunes and disappeared. Nothing moved in the darkness. In the distance, a dim glimmer of the moon reflected off the surface of the ocean.

Luke's mother gasped. "Joe!" She dashed toward the door and out onto the porch. His father stumbled up from the shadows and into her embrace. Blood covered most of his clothes as he stepped inside.

"It's OK, Sara, it's not from me. I'm fine, hardly a scratch."

Luke saw light glisten in his mother's eyes.

His father looked around at each of the five faces staring up at him. "We'll be fine in here, OK?"

Heads bobbed up and down.

"Dad, what're we gonna do?" Luke said.

"Tonight we're going to go to sleep, Luke. Everyone can bed down here in the living room. The wolves won't be able to get in tonight and they'll be gone by morning. Tomorrow, we're going back to Countryside."

With that, he pulled the door shut and ran his hands over it. A blue light cascaded down from the roof of the house to the sand below, and then the darkness of night rushed back in.

Luke rubbed his eyes and raised his head off the pillow. Pain throbbed in his right leg and he turned to see Trent's head resting on it, drool soaking the blanket.

"Ugh."

Luke shook his leg and pushed the blanket off. Trent's head smacked down on the tile floor and Luke winced.

"Mmmmm." Trent turned his head and lay still again.

Luke sighed and walked over to where his father sat staring out the back window in a dining-room chair. A pink sky covered the horizon out across the ocean as waves rolled in. Gulls soared through the air, and in the distance ships inched across the water.

"Mornin', Dad ... You OK?"

His father turned red eyes up at Luke. A tan ceramic mug sat beside him, filled with black liquid. A half-smile grew on his father's face, wrinkles forming around his eyes.

"I've had worse nights ... Did you get any sleep?"

"Oh, yes, sir. I slept great, after I put a pillow over my head."

His father chuckled. "Jon does seem to be able to out-snore even your mother."

Luke's eyes widened, and his father gave him a sly smile.

"If you tell her I said that, I'll deny it."

Luke shook his head and then froze as he noticed dark stains on his father's jeans. "Dad, did ... anything else come by last night?"

His father grimaced and looked back out the window toward the beach. "We had a few visitors ... but none ventured to come inside." His eyes narrowed as he looked at Luke. "We need to talk about something else though, Luke."

"What, sir?"

"Last night, when you stumbled on the way to the house, you did something I don't want to ever see you do again."

Luke swallowed.

"You used darkness."

"But Dad I ... I think it would've worked. And I was just trying to help stop that wolf."

"I know, Luke. I know my son, and I know you were only trying to help, but never ... *never* with darkness. You can't control it no matter what you think, and you see what it does to those who use it. Darkness only hurts; it never helps, son. It twists your senses and it scars your soul. No matter how good your intentions, it's never worth it. Do you understand me, son?"

Luke felt his throat tighten and he dropped his head. "Yes, sir."

"Luke ..." He saw his father's legs shift and felt calloused hands lift his face. A smile spread across his father's weathered face, and his eyes pulled Luke in. "Son, you make me so proud, and I love you so much. You were very brave last night, and I'm not mad at you ... I'm concerned for you. I haven't done a good enough job teaching you about this world you've been thrown into, but I'll fix that, I promise. You must trust me on some things, though, until you're old enough to understand them. This is one of those things."

Luke nodded and wiped away tears with the back of his hand. His father embraced him, and Luke stood quietly with his eyes closed.

When his father stepped back, he arched his eyebrows. "You OK?"

"Yes, sir."

"Good." His father winked at him and then looked at the floor where his wife and children slept among a mountain of blankets. "I hate to wake them up, but ... I guess we'd better. Lord only knows what else will come searching for us if we're still here tonight."

Luke swallowed as his father stood and stretched. *That doesn't sound good.*

"Get dressed and I'll get them rolling. We need to be out of here early if we're going to make it to the tunnel. The train from Chesterton is the only one I know of traveling to Countryside today, and I'd just as soon not have to hump all this luggage back home on foot."

"Yes, sir."

An hour later, Luke stood on the front porch in leather boots, jeans, and a long-sleeved work shirt. Jon and Amy sat on top of a pile of bags and a couple of suitcases next to a flat cart.

"All right, Rayburns, we're gonna go home a bit differently than how we got here. Because, Trent,"—Luke's father sighed and held up his hand to head off Trent's question—"I don't want anything out there waiting on us." Trent snapped his mouth shut. "We're gonna walk down to the dock and the ferry landing in town. Once we get on the mainland, we'll ride a bus back a few minutes toward Holding Chesterton and then take the train there through the tunnel back to Countryside … OK, everybody ready?"

Heads bobbed as Luke and Trent helped pick up bags and stack them on the cart. Jon and Amy followed their mother and Jodi down the stairs and to the north. Trent stepped off after them, but as Luke's foot hit the first stair, his father grabbed his arm and leaned down inches from his ear.

"Luke, when your chest gets warm today, I need to know, immediately."

"Yes, sir."

His father nodded and clapped him on the back.

I know that isn't good.

A few hours later, Luke stood on a train platform as a black locomotive puffed toward him from behind a screen of ash and oak trees. Its brakes screeched as it rolled to a stop. He

craned his neck, staring from person to person as they boarded the blue-and-black passenger car. He grasped his pendant as a couple of darkmen walked past, oblivious to him; the sphere warmed almost imperceptibly. A centaur strode down a ramp from a few cars behind him. Men in blue-and-green holding-guard uniforms stood in position around the station. His father helped his mother gather the children and herd them toward the second car. As Luke bent over to pick up suitcases, he felt heat radiate from his pendant. A man in a gray duster bumped into him as Luke jerked his head up. "Dad."

His father stopped and looked over his shoulder. His eyes narrowed and he nodded as Luke grabbed the pendant through his shirt. Nudging Luke's mother and siblings toward the conductor punching tickets, he stepped back toward Luke. "Did you notice anything?"

"Just a couple darkmen a minute or so ago," Luke said, "but the pendant hardly warmed up at all."

"All right, let's ease toward the car, but scan the crowd."

Men and women jostled up the stairs and across the platform, most of them looking down at their feet. Turning in a circle, Luke searched the crowd. Halfway through his turn, he stopped. The man in the gray duster stood staring at him. He had wiry black hair and weeks of growth on his unshaven face. Yellowed, feral eyes and a smile that was more of a snarl bore into Luke. His heart hammered in his chest and his arms trembled. He stood rooted to the spot, unable to move or think until a woman wearing a large feathered hat walked in front of him, blocking his view of the man. Luke blinked, shaking himself free of the gaze. "Dad!"

His father stopped his own searching and darted over to Luke.

"Dad, that man, there …" He pointed, but then his arm sagged. The man was gone.

"Where?"

Luke shook his head. "He's gone."

Pursing his lips, Luke's father pulled him back toward the train car. "Let's get on board."

Luke followed his father, looking around them as they climbed the stairs. They walked down the aisle and squeezed into one of the compartments, his father sliding the door shut behind them. Luke walked to the window and stared down into the crowd as his father's shadow slipped over him. "Luke, what did the man look like?"

"Like he hadn't bathed in a month. Half-grown beard. Nasty teeth and … yellow eyes."

His father grimaced. "Yellow eyes—you're sure, son?"

"Yes, sir. They seemed almost like they were … glowing. Why, Dad? What does that mean?"

"What makes you think he was the one causing the pendant to warm?"

Luke stared off into the distance. "The way he stared at me … He made me afraid … I couldn't move. It was almost like I was trapped … but I don't know, the pendant didn't actually feel too warm when he was looking at me, and now it feels a little warm again." Luke shrugged.

"The pendant won't tell you everything, at least in my experience. It's more like a guide." His father stared out the window with him as the train rocked forward. After a few moments, he clapped his hand on Luke's shoulder. "There's nothing wrong with fear, Luke. It's often what keeps us alive in dangerous situations. Anyone who says they've never tasted fear is lying … to you or to themselves. The trick is to not let the feeling overwhelm you—to learn to control it." He eased back into his seat, lifting Jodi to his lap.

The train trundled down the tracks and past the shadows of the pine forest. A few clouds dotted the sky, and red birds flitted through the air. Warmth spread across Luke's chest, and he grabbed the pendant hanging there, but as the train rounded the first corner, the warmth faded. He turned away from the window to see his father tickling Jodi. Jon and Amy pulled out a fist-size globe that Grandma Rayburn had given them and watched blue flowers bloom and petals fall. Every time they touched the globe, the process began anew. Trent sat in a corner and flipped a page of Gottfried's *On War and the Holdings,* which Uncle Landon had mailed him. Luke plopped down in his seat and pulled out the clear practice globe Trent had worked with the day before. A flame appeared in the globe and the color changed from red to orange to yellow. Luke let the flame vanish, but yellow eyes filled his mind as the blue-white light and the stones of the traveling tunnel enveloped the train and sent it toward Countryside.

TWO

Fire in the Orchard

Luke's heart soared as the Countryside Limited rolled across the southern half of the valley, smoke puffing up out of its chimney. Looking out the windows, he saw the Old Hargrove Forest in the northeast, the shimmer of Granite Lake to the north, and the Sandy Hills to the west, with Countryside nestled in the heart of the valley next to the Algid River. Pastureland spotted with cattle, horses, and sheep slipped past them on one side of the train while row upon row of corn and cotton slipped past on the other. A set of tracks merged from the west with the mainline before it turned to the northeast, guiding the train toward the Algid. Houses grew closer together as the train neared town, and children ran and waved as it chugged past and on toward the southern bridge. Jon and Amy pointed and exclaimed as a great gray heron glided over the passenger car to land in the shallows along the bank of the river.

Luke watched the loading docks go by and the train station come into view. As the train stopped, he grabbed suitcases with his father. A young boy chased a sparkling comet down the aisle and Luke grinned.

His father smiled. "Glad to be off vacation, son?"

"No, sir. Glad to be home."

His father dipped his head and followed Luke past the conductor and down the steps. People bustled to and fro across the station platform, and as Luke scanned the crowd, the tall figure of Mr. Acharon strode across to meet him. He grinned, patting Luke on the back and shaking his father's hand as Luke's grandparents walked up beside him. "Joe, Mrs. Rayburn, it's good to see you all back."

"Good to see you, too, Q. Mom ... Dad."

Luke's parents gave quick hugs to his grandparents as Trent, Jon, and Amy surrounded them, bombarding them with stories of the summer vacation. Luke looked past his grandparents and Mr. Acharon toward the crowd.

"I wouldn't be upset, Luke," his mom said. "Your father only sent word of our early return to Grandpa and Grandma Rayburn. I doubt your friends even know you're back."

Luke jumped, looking over his shoulder at his mother. "What ... oh, I was just ... I wasn't looking for anyone, Mom."

His mother smiled knowingly and squeezed his arm as she walked past to hand off Jodi to Grandma Rayburn. The women turned and walked toward the train station as his grandmother discussed a few new servants at the house.

Luke sighed. *Well, it's still great to be home.*

"Luke, you and Trent pick up those bags and bring them along," his father said.

"Yes, sir."

Luke and Trent snatched up the bags and followed their parents. They walked over wooden planks and under the eaves of the train station, where blue orbs hovered in the air. As they walked, weaving between long dresses, dusters, and business suits, Luke caught snippets of the men's conversations.

"... broke through the wards ..."

Luke dodged around a man in a top hat.

"The council has no idea ... inside ..."

A blue heeler barked as it dashed after a squealing girl whose mother tried to catch them both.

"... destroyed part of the west orchards ... dryads ... stopped ..."

Luke caught up with the men as they stopped beside his grandparents' carriage at the west end of the platform. His father stood in front of the brighthawk symbol engraved into the door. "Sounds like we have a good bit of work to do ... Luke, Trent, hand Ricardo those bags on the back, please."

Luke nodded toward Mr. Acharon and stepped toward the back, where a man with walnut-brown skin and even darker hair stood waiting to load the suitcases onto the back of the carriage. *He's so different than James. I wonder if Grandpa and Mr. Acharon will keep him, or find someone else from outside the staff; I wonder if he even wants the job?* The man who had recently taken over the job of assistant estate manager nodded his thanks and gave Luke a reserved smile.

As Luke and Trent walked back to the open door, Grandpa Rayburn looked down from the saddle of his horse toward their father. "I've got to get home and see if the boys have had any luck chasing the little beggars out of the pecan orchard." He wheeled his mount around in a tight circle. "I'd give my right arm to have a colony of tree sprites back in Countryside now."

Luke's father and Mr. Acharon chuckled at Grandpa Rayburn's dark scowl.

What are they talking about? And why does Grandpa want a colony of tree sprites?

Luke looked at Trent, who shrugged as he put his foot up on the folding step.

Never a dull moment …

The carriage rolled across the valley and toward Westcliffe Forest, and Luke soaked in the sights of the estate as they rode through it. His mother and grandmother talked of shopping and some kind of painting while his father sat silently across from them. As the stands of cedar and oak trees grew thicker, Luke and his siblings waved at men driving wagons filled with barbed wire, wooden posts, and loads of black soil. Luke grinned at Trent as the carriage turned the corner onto their grandparents' road and Rayburn Manor came into view. Stone fountains filled with water infused with blue-white light splashed in the front lawn. The carriage crunched over the crushed limestone as it pulled up to the front steps, where Ms. Lucy and Uncle Landon stood waiting. Luke's smile grew even broader as Matt appeared with his mother beside Uncle Landon.

"Matt!"

Servants bustled down the stairs to pick up bags as the boys raced toward one another.

"Man, it's good to be back."

Matt smiled, patting Luke on the back and turning to walk up the stairs with him and Trent. "It's good to see y'all back. How was it?"

"Pretty good. We had a great time at the beach and there were a lot of fun shops in the little town near us." Luke scrunched his face up. "But it's kinda weird now, to be around people that don't think centaurs or dryads are real, or don't know anything about the Flame."

Matt nodded, a twinge of incredulity in his voice. "That's still hard for me to believe, man; I mean everything is *made* of the Flame. I know you said it was like that back where you lived in your apartment, but"—he shook his head, pausing at the top step—"to not know about the Flame, to not be able to see the disciplines, or even worse to pretend they don't exist; that's just …" He looked at Luke. "It's like volunteering to wear a blindfold, *forever*."

Luke snorted and continued on, crossing the Entrance Hall and heading up the staircase on the far side. "I know. Although I guess I *kinda* get it. Most of them have never seen the disciplines, at least not the way we see them. I mean I've still never seen the Flame. I've never seen how the different disciplines come from it. I've just seen the disciplines, and I *live* in a holding."

"Maybe, but still you'd think they would know *something*."

Trent piped in. "I thought it was boring, especially the shops, I mean they don't even have any cool candles, or rocks or anything."

Luke frowned as they reached the second story. "Whatever, Trent. We didn't know about any of that stuff a year ago either. And, I mean, it's nothing compared to Countryside, but the beach was a lot of fun. We got to fish and play in the ocean, which we'd never been to before. Running Coach Wilson's 'suggested' workout on the beach was brutal, though."

Matt groaned. "I know. Two-a-days are going to kill me this year for sure."

"And we did get to see that nymph at the cove!" Trent said, changing his attitude. "And the wolf last night!"

"What? An ocean nymph! And what wolf? You didn't say anything about a wolf!"

Luke grimaced as a wide-eyed girl walked by carrying an armful of sheets. "Shh. Would you two keep it down? I'm not sure how much Dad wants everyone to know. And I didn't exactly have time to sit down and write a letter since last night, now did I? We can talk about it after we get upstairs."

The boys climbed up a couple floors and walked down the hallway to the door leading into the suite of family rooms. When they reached it, Luke projected a thought: *Open*. Light blossomed on the door, and a handle in the shape of a lion's head formed and turned with a click. The door swung open as the boys walked through.

As the door swung closed behind them and the light faded from it, Matt crossed his arms and looked at Luke. "All right, now out with it, Rayburn. What about this wolf?"

The boys sat in the north sitting area of the common room, and between Luke and Trent, they piecemealed the story together, from Luke's hearing the growling on the beach to the wolf's appearance on that last night and their father's battle with him and finally to the man who appeared at the Chesterton train station as they departed. By the time they finished, the family was all gathered in the room and Matt's eyes were almost as round as the setting sun. Uncle Landon's stern look and Ms. Nichols's gasp from the couch at the far end of the room made Luke think they were having the same conversation with Luke's parents and grandparents.

Guess they don't like what they're hearing any more than we liked seeing it.

"Man, I can't believe that," Matt said. "And you think that was what you saw the night before, too?"

"It fits," Luke said, "but I still don't understand what made the wolf run away, and what that green light was"—he fingered the pendant under his shirt—"or who that man was at the train station."

Matt sighed, a worried look clouding his face. "Well, I've pieced together enough over the past couple weeks that I *think* I might be able to sorta answer that."

Trent's eyes widened.

"Really?" Luke said. "How? I mean—"

"Well, I'm not positive, but it sounds like something I heard Captain Rayburn describe a few nights ago. Everyone in town knows about the few darkmen and soulless break-ins throughout the summer, and even the little gnomes—"

"Which you still haven't told me about."

"But what no one outside of the Elder Council and the Guard knows about are the things that haven't made it in yet, or *hadn't* until recently."

Luke sat forward on the couch. "What things?"

Matt looked across the room. "I'm not sure about everything. I wasn't exactly supposed to attend these meetings."

Luke snorted.

"Some of the things they described"—Matt shivered—"didn't even make sense, but about a week ago I heard them talking about wolves and something called a hunter. I didn't hear anything else, so I decided to check it out. One of the books my mom has—"

"Wait, *you* read a book?!"

Matt smirked. "Yes, smarty, I can read, I just usually have better things to do besides sitting in a dark closet smelling aging paper. Anyway, the book that had the information in it talked about this hunter, and it sounds like what you just told me about a man and a group of wolves. The hunter is a man or sometimes, more rarely, a woman. He used to be human, kinda like the soulless, but now is more animal than man. He controls the pack of bane wolves by killing and replacing their leader and giving each of them part of his soul." Trent's mouth dropped open. "And he makes them even more powerful than normal by using different disciplines, and darkness. But the reason I really think that's what you were describing is that one of the main features a hunter develops after some time with the wolves is their yellowed, almost gold eyes."

Luke sat back. "That would pretty much explain it."

Trent wrinkled his nose. "But what do they do? I mean, why would they have been on the island where we were on vacation?"

"I don't know," Matt said, "but the book did say that hunters were generally used by darkness as scouts … or sometimes even assassins."

Luke swallowed as the door to the family room glowed and the shape of a tulip formed in its center. The door swung inward and Ms. Lucy marched in ahead of a couple of footmen balancing silver platters on their shoulders. Jon and Amy bounded toward the table, laughing. The footmen set plates down until the table was lined with roast pork, warm yeast rolls, mashed potatoes, casseroles of mushrooms and green beans, and sauce boats with brown gravy. For the next hour, Luke's heart and mind were filled with the laughter and conversation among the family, and his stomach was filled with Mr. Robinson's cooking.

By the time he turned his fork over on an empty plate, pinks and oranges filled the partially cloud-covered sky. Luke's parents and grandparents and Ms. Nichols and Uncle Landon returned to the sitting area on the south side of the room with coffee. Luke motioned toward Trent and Matt, and they walked out onto the balcony overlooking the valley. A pair of doves flew below them, followed by a warm breeze under the shade of the manor. A hundred yards to the east, workers led a team of horses pulling a wagon filled with branches and debris out of the pecan orchard.

"So you didn't hear anything about what Uncle Landon or the Guard thinks about the hunter showing up?"

Matt sighed. "Nope. I got the distinct impression they weren't happy about it. But then, I also got the distinct impression they weren't happy with my eavesdropping on the conversation either." He rubbed his neck. "Captain Rayburn and Mr. Acharon aren't the gentlest people when they're mad."

Luke and Trent laughed as Matt winced.

"We really need to hurry up and learn some of that stuff Jennifer talks about her brother knowing, like how to twist the wind so it carries voices farther. *That* would be nice. Or at least learn some way to sneak around without everyone finding out about it."

Luke opened his mouth and then snapped it shut as shouts broke out across the north road on the far side of the pecan orchard. He peered into the fading light as people raced across the road. Fire appeared in the branches of one of the trees near the east side of the orchard and a shriek split the evening air, sending birds exploding out of the trees and chills racing up Luke's arms.

Eeeeeeiiiiiiiieeeeeee!

"What was that!?"

Matt jerked on Luke's arm. "A dryad. The gnomes are attacking. Come on, man!"

Luke and Trent stumbled away from the banister and raced into the room behind Matt. "Gnomes?! But I thought they were harmless ..."

Luke's mother and grandmother hurried to the east windows

and looked down on the orchard as Luke ran past them. Uncle Landon, Luke's father, and Mr. Acharon were already out the door. Luke's mother shouted something at them, but Luke and Trent were down the hallway after Matt and the door had closed behind them, muffling her voice.

"They *are* harmless ... unless they're in big numbers ... or a bunch of them catch you alone," Matt said.

They darted around a corner and down a flight of stairs.

"Then they're deadly."

Racing down a hallway, they wove between maids and a butler who were rushing about.

"And they're especially vicious when it comes to fighting other creatures of the Flame ... creatures that don't serve darkness ... like they do ..."

Luke took steps two at a time down one more flight of stairs and flew out a door on the east side of the manor as Matt huffed beside him.

"... like dryads," Matt finished.

Men ran into the orchard, but Matt veered toward the stables.

"Where are we going?" Luke gasped.

Matt darted into the stables with Luke hot on his heels and Trent a few steps behind. Blue light filled the stables and Matt skidded to a halt in front of one of the water troughs.

"What ... are we doing ... in here?"

Matt shoved a wooden bucket at Luke and a smaller one at Trent. He dunked his own in the trough and filled it to overflowing. "Gnomes hate anything clean ... but most of all light ... and water. Come on."

Luke filled his bucket and waddled after Matt toward the back of the stable and into the orchard, where the shouting had intensified. Matt slow-jogged down one of the rows toward where black smoke and flames obscured part of the evening sky. Luke followed, water splashing onto his shirt and jeans and soaking his socks and tennis shoes.

Eeeeeeeiiiiiiiiiieeeeeee!

A boy and girl in clothing made of leaves raced past them with grim faces. Luke glanced over his shoulder at Trent. "Stay close," he said and then shuffled up beside Matt. "What do we do?"

Matt nodded down at the bucket and then looked into dusk's shadows to his sides. "Just throw it on them. It's like someone throwing burning coals on us. They can't stand it."

"And when we run out of water?"

"Then go back and get some more. Use the light to chase them away. It won't hurt them as much, because they can counter it some, but it will scare them."

Ahead, figures of men raced back and forth alongside figures of dryads, whose skin glowed varying shades of brown and green. Little black shadows darted in and out of trees, and light flashed throughout the orchard. As they got closer, Luke heard strange grunts and squeals mingled with the shouts and curses of the men and the occasional shrieking he'd heard from the balcony.

Just ahead, between two towering pecan trees, a pair of shadows raced out. The creatures were no taller than Luke's knees, and under the light of the flames Luke noticed brown, wrinkled skin covered by random bits of mismatched cloth. Tufts of wiry black hair puffed out of large ears and bulbous noses. Round black eyes glared up at the boys in shock. Matt leaped forward and threw water from his bucket at the gnomes, pulling the bucket back so that only a small amount flew toward the creatures. Water splashed onto them and they shrieked and squealed with tiny voices.

"Cruel, cruel! ... mean big ones ... ah, killed us, you have, killed us ... dust-lickers ... light bloods ... cruel, cruel!"

Despite the shrieks, the burning trees and all the hollering, Luke stood and started to laugh as the little creatures scrambled in circles, rubbing their skin and knocking each other over, before careening away into the night. "That's hilarious!"

Trent laughed beside him and Matt grinned up at them. "I never can tell that the water actually hurts them any, but they think it does something fierce. It *is* pretty funny."

Eeeeeeeiiiiiiiiieeeeeee!

Luke and Trent cringed, and the smile slipped off Matt's face.

"That isn't so funny," Luke said.

Matt shook his head. "No. It's not."

"Let's keep moving."

Matt stepped forward, and Luke and Trent fell in behind him. They moved on through the trees toward the fire, throwing water on dark darting shadows until their buckets were empty. Luke noticed that the flashes lighting the orchard were softball-size orbs of light the dryads were throwing at the gnomes. Wherever the light hit, it exploded, globs of it sticking to anything it landed on—gnome, tree, dirt, man—and seeping in. On trees and dirt, the light simply faded away, but the gnomes howled as they had when the boys doused them with water. One glob of light landed on Luke and he winced, expecting it to burn. Instead, he felt a tingle in his arm, and warmth spread from the spot before it faded. "Hey, it doesn't hurt. It ... it feels warm and ... good."

"It only hurts dark creatures," Matt said over his shoulder, "particularly those of the Flame. For us it will just feel like warm water, and it gives you a little energy. Still not sure how they make them."

Luke watched as a dryad shot an orb of light toward one of the gnomes. It erupted, covering everything for a few feet and sending the creature squalling into the darkness.

I bet I could do that. Maybe light combined with another discipline? Maybe earth? Maybe if I pictured it breaking like glass, or exploding like a water balloon …

Luke's smile faded with the light as he looked ahead toward the east end of the orchard. In the last row, two of the pecan trees stood smoldering, their trunks blackened and their leaves and branches withered or turned to ash. Nearby, a tight cluster of dryads stood beside the trees. Only a few dark shadows appeared, and men from the estate quickly dropped them to the ground or sent them scurrying. Luke noticed his father standing next to his uncle outside the circle of dryads. He glanced up and his eyes tightened upon recognizing Luke. He jerked his head sideways and mouthed something to Uncle Landon. Uncle Landon glanced up and his expression hardened before he gave a curt nod.

"Um, Matt, I don't think they're very happy to see us." Luke turned to see that Matt's face was pale under the light of the torches and the floating orbs that were appearing with greater and greater frequency throughout the orchard.

"Matt … Matt, what's going on?"

Matt's eyes remained fixed on the dryads as he spoke. "I think … I think the dryads are dying."

"What … all of them?"

Matt shook his head as Luke's father stomped away from the cluster of childish looking creatures. "Just the two that were attacked. I've only seen this once before … It's horrible."

When Luke's father reached them, his face was grim.

"Dad, what's—"

"You boys will leave, now."

Luke swallowed at the quiet power of his father's voice and looked back at the dryads. As he did, the tight knot of dryads shifted and Luke's breath caught. He faltered backward a step. On the ground, two forms lay still, skin black and smoldering like the trees beside them. The glimpse lasted only a few seconds and then was blocked. Luke looked up wide-eyed at his father. "Dad! Dad, was that ... Can't you do anything?"

"Not this time. You don't need to see this, any of you. You will go back to the estate and stay there. We'll talk when I get back." He turned away. "Randy!"

A young man jogged over from his place beside one of the orchard trees. "Sir?"

"Take the boys back to the house. All the way to the family quarters" —he looked down at the boys— "and *only* to the family quarters."

The man touched his fingers to the cowboy hat on his head. "Sir." As he turned toward Luke, his eyes widened at something in the distance. Luke turned, too, and his heart leaped.

No! Trent, look out!

Luke's mind raced. Trent had wandered over to a tree about twenty feet away, obviously trying to get a better look at what was going on with the dryads. Behind him a trio of the dark little creatures crept slowly toward him, with glowing gray-black blades in grimy doll-size hands. Luke leapt forward.

"Trent, run! Get away from my brother!"

Red light seared his vision, and thoughts of the dryads throwing light across the orchard flooded his mind. Time slowed and sound faded. Three pinched faces turned toward Luke, wicked grins transforming into fear.

Light ... and water! Just like the dryads.

A sphere of light formed in Luke's hand and he threw it sidearm across the distance as he raced toward the gnomes.

The light slammed into one of the three dark creatures, knocking it backward and exploding. Globs of light splattered onto the other two. Luke fired another one as the gnomes scrambled blindly away. Thunder roared in Luke's ears. He thought and another ball streaked toward the creatures. He'd fired two more and chased them past Trent when he felt his arm jerked around and his body following it. His father's face appeared, his embrace crushing him, and then sound and time rushed forward like a river breaking through a dam.

"Luke. Luke." His father's voice whispered in his ears.

Luke gulped in air and looked up. Concern filled his father's eyes.

"It's all right, son, it's OK."

Luke glanced around, shaking. He'd run past Trent by about ten steps. The first gnome he'd hit lay senseless on the ground, its body sizzling. Matt and some of the other men eased forward and watched him with round eyes. Turning around as his father loosened his grip, Luke watched the two other gnomes continue to cry out and stumble into the distance. Trent stood with his arms limp at his sides and his mouth open, his body illuminated by the quickly fading glow of light from Luke's spheres. Luke sucked air into his lungs, his shoulders heaving.

What happened? Something's wrong. Why are they looking at me like that?

"Dad? What ... what's wrong?"

His father frowned down at him. "You ... you did it again, son."

Luke wrinkled his brow. "W-what do you mean? Did what again? I was just t-t-trying to warn Trent about the gnomes, and I've never thrown those ... those balls before." He looked around the circle and noticed the confusion on Trent's face mirrored in the faces of others.

Matt stepped up beside him and put his arm around his shoulder, shaking his head with a grin. "You went all Ancient on us again, man. Didn't make a lick of sense. Although I think the little beasties got your point well enough. I'm assuming you said something like 'go away'?"

Luke felt tension seep from his body and sighed as a few of the men guffawed and even his father grinned. A couple of the dryads nodded and smiled before walking away. Matt patted him on the back, and Luke took a deep breath.

"Ah ..." *Great, now everyone is going to think I'm crazy ... if they didn't already.*

Later that night, Luke sat on the couch back in the family quarters. Moonlight streamed in through the east windows as his parents and grandparents, Mr. Acharon, Ms. Nichols, and Uncle Landon talked at the south end of the room.

"You aren't even back for a day yet and the whole town will be talking about you by tomorrow," Matt said.

Luke sighed. "It's not like I'm talking crazy on purpose, you know."

Matt snorted. "You do know that by telling people you aren't trying to talk crazy, that makes them think you're even more crazy. That's like telling Ms. Lisantii that you got the wrong answer on your test because you copied Marti. It just doesn't help."

Trent giggled.

"Whatever."

"How did you figure out how to make the kad_ur anyway?"

"Kad_ur?"

"Yeah, that's what the dryads call those balls of light they throw at the gnomes." Matt cocked his head with a half-smile.

"Figured you'd know what it means, being able to speak the Ancient language and all."

Luke grimaced. "I can't do it on call. It just … happens. I don't even know I'm doing it. And I don't know, I just … I thought I could make one of them when I saw the dryads doing it, but …" He looked across the room.

"What? What is it, man?"

Luke looked back at Matt and Trent. "It's just … every time I've spoken the … Ancient language, I've seen these red eyes in my mind." Luke paused and then finished in a rush. "Like the eyes of the demon from the Westcliffe Forest." Luke winced as Matt and Trent sat back, their mouths forming large Os. "I didn't say anything to my parents, because I didn't want to freak them out." Matt and Trent nodded dumbly. "You know, kinda like y'all are doing to me right now."

Matt snapped his mouth shut. "Sorry. I just … Do you think that thing is … in your head or something?"

Luke shivered. "I don't know. Father Woods said something about it giving part of itself to me, but …"

Matt bit his lower lip. "Seems awful strange that it would help you fight off other dark creatures like gnomes if it was in your head, though, huh?"

Luke raised his eyebrows. "Yeah, I hadn't thought of *that*."

Matt smiled. "See, Trent, you *don't* have to read books to be smart!"

Luke smiled and chuckled, and for a few minutes they teased back and forth about whether Matt could really read and whether Luke was turning into a bookworm like Marti. At one point one of the housemaids, a girl named Kim, brought in glasses and a decanter filled with caramel colored liquid, coffee, and frozen hot chocolate and blueberry muffins from the kitchen. As the boys thanked her and grabbed their share of frozen hot chocolate and muffins off the platter, Luke heard his father's voice from the corner of the room.

"… make any sense to attack Trent. … so many people around … almost like they were hunting …"

Luke slowed his walk back over to the north end of the room, but his father's voice was drowned out by others' exclamations. Luke sat down, still looking across the room. His father and his uncle were staring toward them, but particularly toward Trent.

"What is it, man?" Matt said.

Luke tore his gaze away. "Is it strange that the gnomes were going to attack Trent?"

"I don't know. Why?"

Luke motioned over his shoulder. "I just heard Dad say that, and something about them hunting."

"Hunting … for *me*?" Trent swallowed and his face paled.

Matt frowned. "I doubt that, Trent. Mom has told me that gnomes don't usually attack people … but not that they *never* do. Besides that, they aren't the brightest creatures, clever but not very bright. Why would they be hunting for Trent anyway?"

"I don't know," Luke said. "Has there been anything else unusual this summer?"

Matt smirked. "Besides gnomes, darkmen, and bane wolves? Hmm … nope, nothing I can think of."

"I mean have you heard anyone else talking about the gnomes or other dark creatures hunting something or being here for any reason other than just to destroy stuff?"

"Not really. I mean, I heard Captain Rayburn talking about them helping the darkmen get into the holding a few times, and he said that cooperation was unusual, but …" A smile grew on Matt's face. "He did stop by for a while a few weeks ago with a funny story after an Elder Council meeting. Apparently, Mr. Thompson has hired Jon David and some of his knuckleheads to keep the little pests out of his orchards. Well, the league of misfits had chased a group of gnomes into one of his peach orchards beside the river. They lost the gnomes in a clump of rose hedge and decided to hide and wait to see if they would come back out. Dusk had set in by that point and they couldn't see very well. A few minutes later, they heard some rustling and saw a dark shadow next to the bushes. They started hollering and throwing their water onto the gnomes." He snickered. "Turns out it was Mr. Thompson and Mr. Jefferson out checking on the orchards, too. Captain Rayburn said a team of guardsmen had been on patrol and rode over when they heard all the commotion. Mr. Thompson and Mr. Jefferson ran by them wild-eyed and soaked, chasing the boys halfway back into town and yelling at them, they were so mad."

Trent laughed and Luke smiled at the thought of the two men chasing Jon David and his gang across one of the bridges back into town. "That sounds more entertaining even than watching the gnomes bumble into each other."

"Your uncle says it serves them right. He said that Mr. Thompson was the only councilman not willing to support the request by people in the holding for increased patrols … at least not until the gnomes attacked his orchard, then all of a sudden he was all in for more patrols. He also said that Mr. Thompson never seemed very surprised by the attacks until his orchard."

"He doesn't mean that Mr. Thompson knew about it, does he?"

"Don't know. Just said he didn't seem very surprised and then Mom shushed him and he wouldn't say anything else about it, at least not around me."

THREE

✦

Mayeem

A couple of days later, Luke walked along Main Street in town. Midday sun beat down on him and a hot breeze swept dust along the cobblestone street. People paused in their walks and sat under the shade offered by pecan and oak trees. Across the street, children ran through thick clouds of mist. Mr. Jacobs, the gardener who cared for the plants and bushes around the courtyard square, formed the clouds using water and air so that they hung a few feet above the grass. The clouds shifted and swirled, sometimes thick enough for droplets of water to stick to the children.

Matt grinned beside Luke. "Don't suppose Coach Wilson would let Mr. Jacobs set up some of those over the practice fields for two-a-days?"

Luke snorted as they stepped into H&C's Bookstore. "More likely he'd have us practice in an oven if he could."

"Hello, boys! Good first day of practice?" Ms. Morehouse waved the boys over and pulled two iced-tea glasses down from the back of the bar.

"We're still alive, ma'am," Matt said.

Ms. Morehouse rolled her eyes at him and set lemonades on the counter. "Pshaw. Now don't go tryin' to get any sympathy here. I know ya too well."

Matt feigned a hurt look. Luke chuckled and thanked her, picking up his glass.

"Hey, Matt, Luke." Jennifer walked across the room from the stairwell.

Matt turned and grinned. "Jenn! Y'all *did* survive Coach Engleton."

Jennifer's smile evaporated. "You mean the heartless minotaur that pretends to be our coach? Ugh! I think my legs are going to just stay one big cramp for the next two weeks." She paused and turned toward the counter. "Ms. Morehouse, I need another couple lemonades for me and Samantha."

Luke's ears perked up. Sam was upstairs.

He slipped away and walked toward the spiral staircase in the back of the store as Jennifer complained about volleyball practice. He half-ran across the second story past shelves and study tables and out onto the balcony. As he stepped through the doors, his heart leaped.

"Luke!"

A smile lighted Samantha's face as she jumped up. Luke stepped toward her, arms outstretched, but stopped as she raised her hand to shake his. Heat flooded Luke's face.

Stupid ... Nice, Rayburn, real nice.

He dropped his arms, trying not to spill his lemonade, and then jerked his right hand out, but Samantha smiled and stepped forward to hug him. "It's good to see you. We ... we missed you."

Luke swallowed and returned the hug haltingly before

Samantha stepped back. Round green eyes stared at him, and Luke's tongue stuck to the roof of his mouth.

Say something, Luke … anything! Tell her you missed her!

"Sam, I-I …"

"And then Karlie wouldn't keep her big fat mouth shut and we had to …" Luke and Samantha stepped away from each other as the French doors to the balcony swung open and Matt and Jennifer stepped through. Luke felt his face heat up and saw red bloom on Samantha's.

Jeez, they couldn't have stayed away for just one more minute?

He heard Jennifer snicker beside him. Matt looked away, pretending to study the children running around the courtyard lawn across Main Street. Luke's cheeks were still on fire as Matt turned around and coughed. "So, Jenn, uh, Jenn says practice was pretty brutal for y'all today, huh, Samantha?"

Luke's shoulders loosened as Jennifer shifted her gaze from him. Samantha let out a long breath. "Yeah, I can see why she's not married. No man would be able to keep up with her. She's like one of those car thingies from outside, except she never runs out of fuel."

Matt laughed and sat at the table. "That bad for you, too, huh?"

Samantha nodded. "What about y'all's?"

Luke dropped into one of the metal chairs beside Matt and set his glass on the table. "I didn't think football was that bad this morning, except for getting sat on by Jon David for the hundredth time. I think Coach Wilson thinks I like it."

As Matt laughed, Luke thought he saw the girls twitching and darting glances at each other.

"Whatever, man. If that was the worst part of your practice, you were at a different one than me. Just be glad you didn't have to be one of the dummies in Coach Jackson's dummy drills for the JV."

The four sat around the table talking for the next hour or so. Luke listened to tales of gnomes and darkmen again, and he and Matt told the girls the story of the gnomes' recent attack on the manor. Luke filled in the gaps in what he'd written to Samantha about the summer, not having to explain the details to Jennifer, because whatever Samantha knew, Jennifer knew. The girls were especially interested to hear about the ocean nymph.

"I wish I would have gotten to see her. I've always wanted to go to the ocean and talk to one." Samantha sighed, smiling. "My dad says they have quite a treat for us this year with our Fundamentals of Water class, though."

Luke sat forward. "Really, like what?"

Samantha smirked, but her eyes danced with delight. "He won't tell me. Just smiles and laughs and says, 'You'll see,' every time I ask him."

"I wonder if it'll be a new teacher, maybe another of the Reeshon like last year."

Jennifer shook her head. "I hope not. That Reeshon gave me the creeps. Besides, they don't come around very often." She narrowed her eyes at Luke. "Have y'all found anything else out from the ... the *Book of the Wise*? ... Like, did it tell you something else to do, or look for or anything?"

Luke looked around the balcony to make sure they were alone. "No, nothing. Why?"

Jennifer dropped her gaze to the table, her hands fidgeting. "No reason. Just wondered ... You know, it seems like such a big deal. I mean, you and Matt find it after, like, a thousand years when no one else can, y'all almost die fighting those soulless and that demon, and you discover some Starblood or whatever prophecy that talks about the end of the world, but no one has talked about it all summer. It's like the book just disappeared. I mean … doesn't anybody think that might be why there have been so many break-in attempts and the gnomes and everything? Like maybe they're trying to find it, to get it back or something?"

Luke sighed. Samantha sat back and bit her finger. Matt tucked his tongue inside his cheek and after a few moments shook his head. "I don't think the gnomes are searching for much of anything. I think they're just here to cause havoc and fight the dryads. As for the other attacks by the darkmen, I don't know … it seems like they're almost just looking to fight the Guard. I mean, from what I heard, one attack was all the way over by the Sandy Hills and another was up by Granite Lake on the edge of the Old Hargrove Forest and another was down south outside of Cedar Hills. No one seems to live in the areas, and as far as I know, there aren't buildings or ruins or anything in any of those places, right? I mean, if they're searching for something, it sure seems to be randomly."

The wind blew across the balcony and the subject changed to school, football, and volleyball schedules and a dozen other things. After some time, Luke noticed his dry throat and empty glass. *Maybe Sam will come with me if I go get something to drink.* He pushed his chair back and stood up. "I'm gonna, um, go get some water. Does anyone want anything?"

"Lemonade."

"Water."

"Tea."

Luke stared around at the three faces.

"You should know better than to ask," Matt said. "I'll come help."

"No, no, don't trouble yourself." He held the empty glasses

precariously as he backed through the doors. "I'll manage ... sheesh." *See if I can do this without dropping these or killing myself.* He weaved his way back to the stairs.

Perhaps you should ask for some help.

He jumped—that hadn't been his voice he'd heard in his head. He bobbled two of the glasses and held another with his fingertips. The fourth one fell to the stone floor and shattered. A second later, the one in his fingertips got away from him and shattered as well. He waited for the shouts from below, but none came. He felt a chill run up his spine and his chest warm as he turned around. His heart hammered and he backed up a step, the shattered glass forgotten. A man in a black suit with a cordoba in hand stood smiling at him. *Saul.* Memories of meetings in a streetlight-lit park and darkened gardens from the past year flashed through Luke's head.

"Hello, Luke."

Luke swallowed. "Hello, sir." Glancing past Saul, Luke noticed sunlight still streaming down on the courtyard square, but something seemed off. After a moment, his breath caught and he realized what it was: Matt, Samantha, and Jennifer weren't moving.

"They're fine. I merely wanted to ensure we could speak privately. They will catch up to us quickly enough once we are through." A look of concern slid across Saul's face. "Although I would suggest we hurry. Time is *such* a tricky discipline."

Luke pulled his stare away from his friends and back to Saul. "What do you want, sir?"

Saul frowned. "Such a cool reception, and after helping you so much with the book and watching over you this summer ... keeping wolves at bay ... Tsk, tsk, Luke, very rude. However, I will overlook it. I came only to warn you."

"Warn me? About what?"

"About some who would choose to mislead you. You are going to come across some interesting characters soon, Luke. Not all of them have your best interests at heart, and some who do will seem the least likely."

"Who are you talking about?"

Saul shook his head and clicked his tongue. "That would be unfair of me. Allegiances can change. People can come to the realization that what they once thought they knew is no longer true. I would hate to prejudice you against someone who was in fact trying to help." He arched his eyebrows. "But I will tell you this: Betrayal often begets betrayal. You should be careful how much you trust those who have proven themselves disloyal in the past. Letters and a few nice words should not make up for turning you or your family over in the quest for a book, based upon a story you can't confirm."

Luke felt his head spinning like it would after one of Ms. Martha's hour-long "quizzes."

"What do you mea—" A face popped into his head along with a voice.

... has my niece. He captured her last summer shortly before you arrived.

James. Now he understood.

Saul smiled condescendingly. "And I expect your parents would be most displeased to hear of you consorting with this *particular* individual."

"But, but I haven't heard from him ... in a while."

Saul arched his eyebrows. "Hmmm ... good, good. But I imagine that is not the last you will hear of him. Well, I just wanted to warn you." He turned and Luke noticed his friends move again on the porch. "Oh, and one more thing ... Someone is hiding something here in Countryside. If you should hear anything about it, I would very much like to know." His flashing eyes said he would more than like to know. "Good day, Luke. We'll … keep in touch."

Luke swallowed as Saul dissipated into a black mist that faded into the walls and shelves of the room. His heart hammered as he replayed the conversation in his head.

Who's hiding something? And what something? And what about James? I don't think he would lie about his niece, but —

"Luke. Hey, Luke!"

Luke shook his head and looked toward the doors, where Matt stood staring at him. "You all right, man?"

Luke nodded dumbly.

"Do you need help?"

"Help? Help doing what?"

Matt motioned toward the floor. "Help carrying the glasses down the stairs."

Luke looked down. Though he still clutched two glasses in his hands, there were two more glasses on the floor by his feet. Whole and in one piece. The memory of shattering glass filled his head.

How … But …

"Luke?"

Luke shook his head and blinked. "I think I'm gonna need help with more than the glasses."

Matt stepped inside. "Huh? What are you talking about, Rayburn?"

Luke sighed. "Help me get the drinks and we'll talk about it outside with the girls."

Oh, well, here we go again.

The halls of Countryside School filled with laughter, shouts, and children running this way and that. Late-August heat bore down on the valley. People moved slowly, just like the River Algid, not in a hurry to get much of anywhere. Barn swallows still swooped and flitted through the air, capturing their weight in insects, and the sandy shores of Granite Lake still filled with families on the weekends.

It was here on the third day of school that Luke hopped down beside a carriage as rays of morning sunlight reflected off the water. A mat of purple winecups spread across the ground next to some rocks. Wind blew along the edge of the lake, pushing stands of grass back and forth, and Luke shoved his hands into his pockets. A few pairs of teal ducks quacked, paddling away from the children and the horses. Samantha walked up behind him.

Talk to her Rayburn … Just say something. "Hey."

Samantha smiled and pushed her blond hair behind her ear. "Hey."

Say something else! "So, um, are you going to come—"

"If we had to get up in the middle of the night"—Matt yawned—"just to come out to the lake …" Matt stumbled up beside Luke and looked across at Samantha. "This is your time of day, right, Samantha? I mean, you help wake the birds up and all?"

Luke gritted his teeth. *Matt!*

Samantha smirked at him. "It wasn't even that early, Matt. We only had to be there an hour before school starts normally."

Matt arched his back and stretched as Marti and Jennifer walked over. "Hey, if it's before the sun is up, it's the middle of the night!"

Samantha rolled her eyes as Mr. White gathered the students.

"All right, all right, everyone over here. Hurry up, hurry up—Miss Jenkins, sometime today if you don't mind."

Luke walked toward Mr. White, glancing sideways at

Samantha beside him. She wore boots, blue jeans, and a cream-colored shirt and was pulling her hair back into a ponytail. Luke smiled, but when Samantha caught him looking at her, he jerked his head away. Heat rushed to his cheeks.

Idiot, staring at her like she can't see you!

Matt elbowed Luke in the ribs and pointed to where Jon David and his cohorts stood laughing in the back of the half-circle of students, shoving one another back and forth. "Do you think they follow him because he's so pretty?"

Luke snickered as Mr. White's voice rang out.

"All right now, today will be your first discipline class of the year. Your instructor has kindly agreed to live with us this year, moving from her home among the Midway Islands in the Pacific."

Luke looked at Matt. "The Pacific?"

Matt shrugged.

"She has not only studied this discipline for her entire life, she has lived in it." Mr. White stepped to the side.

Oohs and ahhs sounded as, out of the lapping waves, blue water bubbled up and a head emerged, followed by shoulders and a torso.

"Good morning, children. My name is Mayeem."

Her voice was like the whisper of wind racing over the water, and she smiled brightly. She had brilliant green eyes, round as holding coins, long brown hair that glistened in the sun, and pale skin tinged with green and blue that shifted as she moved. A green-purple dress of twisted ribbons like seaweed covered her body as she stepped out of the water and onto the shore. Sunlight reflected off silver around her neck, and Luke's eyes locked onto it, his body still. As Mayeem stood on the shore, the pendant vanished beneath the cloth of her dress. Luke blinked and came back to himself. Whispers and wide eyes stole through the ranks of the children until Mr. White coughed and stepped forward.

"Mayeem, it's so good to see you again. The children will be with you for the morning today and then return to school."

Mayeem tilted her head. "Thank you, Lloyd."

Mr. White nodded. "Children, pay attention, and that includes you, Mr. Prichard." And then, after a tight-lipped glare at the students, he shuffled back to the carriages.

Mayeem looked over the gathering. Her gaze paused on Samantha and then moved on. "Today, children, I will begin teaching you about the discipline of water. Some of you may know the rudiments of this discipline, but for the benefit of all, we will start at the—" She stopped and looked to her right. "Yes, young one?"

Susan Fisher lowered her hand, eyes darting between her friends and the teacher. "Are … are you a mermaid?"

Mayeem smiled. "I will be more than happy to answer your question, child, but first you must let me know who you are."

Susan blushed and dropped her eyes. "Susan Fisher."

"Ah, what a wonderful name. A pleasure to meet you, Miss Fisher. Now, as to your question, yes, I am a mermaid. I am sure this is not a usual sight for you here in Countryside, but—"

"If you're a mermaid, where is your tail?"

Mayeem pursed her lips and looked over at Jon David. "And some do not need an introduction. Jon David Prichard, I believe?"

Jon David grinned. "Yep!"

Mayeem smiled with tight lips and flashing eyes amid the chuckles of Prichard's gang. "Hmmm … I see. In the future, Mr. Prichard, it would be to your benefit if you did not yell things out or interrupt others while they are talking."

Jon David's smile slipped, and the laughter around him died, but Luke felt a smile steal onto his face.

"Good. Now, as to your question, yes, in water mermaids do have tails, but it would be very difficult to get around on land with a tail; would you not agree?"

Jon David hunched his shoulders. "Yes, ma'am."

Mayeem returned her gaze to the rest of the class. "Now, in an effort to alleviate any other unbearable curiosity, I will answer a few questions about being a mermaid before we continue."

Marti raised his hand beside Luke.

"Yes, young man."

"My name is M-M-Marti Stegall. I w-w-wanted to know, if you're from the P-P-Pacific, how do you live here? I m-m-mean, I thought saltwater fis—creatures couldn't l-l-live in freshwater."

Mayeem smiled. "For the most part, you are correct, Marti. But mermaids are not normal fish."

Marti grinned shakily as chuckles sounded behind him.

"We have the ability to change our bodies to be receptive to different kinds of water. Now, some of us do prefer warm water over cold and vice versa, but on the whole we can adapt to almost any type of water found on this planet, unless it is poisoned with darkness."

"Thank you, m-m-ma'am."

"You are quite welcome." She smiled and winked at Marti and then looked around the circle of students. "Any more questions before we get started?"

Heads shook back and forth.

"Very well. This year I will begin your instruction with the discipline water. Some of you will likely progress quickly, others not as quickly, depending on which disciplines you are more naturally adept at."

The students gasped as her hand shifted out over the water. Water bubbled into the air, shifting from the shape of a fish to that of a horse and finally an eagle. Mayeem twisted her hand and the water formed an orb, blue light shimmering from inside. She turned back to the class.

"Water has specific relationships with each of the other disciplines. Some, such as water being used to extinguish fire, seem obvious. Others, such as the ability to produce breathable air from underwater, may seem a bit more abstract. Today"— she moved her hand toward the group of students, and Luke edged back as the orb turned into a stream in the air, weaving among the students—"we will focus on physical control of water that you can see, such as directing a stream to a new course and pulling moisture out of objects." Her green eyes flashed in the morning sun as she stepped toward the students. "Now, pair up and spread out along the bank." A smile flitted across her face. "Make sure each pair has a few feet between them and the others."

Luke nodded to Matt and they stepped to the shore of the lake. Samantha and Jennifer partnered up beside them, and Marti and Trey Andrews stood on their other side.

"One of each pair should stand with their back to the lake, and the other stand a few feet away facing the lake, like so."

Mayeem grabbed Luke by the shoulders but then jerked her hands back. Her eyes narrowed for a heartbeat. She smiled and reached out and held his shoulders again. "I've been looking forward to meeting you, Mr. Rayburn," she whispered in his ear. "It is a pleasure." She straightened up.

What was that about?

She maneuvered Luke down to the soft sand within a few feet of the water's edge. Matt faced him about ten feet away.

"Those closest to the water will begin this exercise."

Luke sighed as Matt grinned.

"This will be much like the egg-tossing competition I have seen at spring festivals in human holdings. I want the student closest to the water to form an orb from the lake. If helpful, you may use the command word 'kadoor' until you master this. When you have control of that, you will *toss* the orb to your partner to catch."

Chuckles sounded throughout the class, and Matt's eyes widened.

"I hear devious thoughts in your laughter," Mayeem said, "but remember your roles will be reversed after a bit." She smiled and arched her eyebrows. "I would strongly suggest you treat your partner as you would like to be treated in return. I will walk among you and assist as needed. Now begin."

Luke turned to the water. "Kadoor."

A few dozen other voices sounded to his sides along the shore of the lake. Near his feet, water bulged up above the surface of the lake and then sloshed back down.

"Kadoor."

This time a ball formed in front of Luke about a foot above the water before splashing back down and soaking his jeans and boots.

"Stupid water … Kadoor!"

Water exploded out of the lake and splashed over him, leaving his clothes dripping. He shivered in the early-morning air as laughter broke out all along the lake. Beside him, Samantha covered her mouth with her hand and looked away, her shoulders shaking. Marti's mouth trembled as he stared intently at the water. Matt's voice shook from behind him.

"Ummm, not sure that's how it's supposed to work there, buddy."

As Luke ground his teeth, the thought of water pouring on top of Matt flashed through his mind. Seconds later, Luke froze as water exploded up out of the lake, arched over his head and dumped onto Matt's head. Matt spluttered and shook, water running down his face in rivulets, his hair plastered to his head. He glared at Luke as laughter echoed across the cove. "Hey, what's the big idea, Luke!"

Samantha giggled.

"Sorry, man, I didn't mean to … really."

"You just wait, Rayburn."

Luke shrugged. "What are you gonna do, man? I'm already soaked to the bone."

Mayeem walked by with narrowed eyes and a low voice. "The centaur Samech mentioned that you had a great deal of power but not much control. Be very careful, young one."

Splashes and shouts sounded up and down the shore as more and more students found themselves getting wet. After thirty minutes, water pooled around Luke's feet and Matt crouched, ready to bound out of the way. Five minutes later, a blue sphere floated in front of Samantha's face. She turned around and the ball zipped through the air and stopped inches from Jennifer.

"Rak-hok," Jennifer's voice rang out, and the water soared back to Samantha and then back into Granite Lake.

Mayeem beamed at the pair, sunlight highlighting her hair and face. "Very good, girls. You seem to have a talent for this. Most of my beginning students are unable to master that skill for many sessions."

Samantha grinned at Luke.

"Show-off," he said.

She grinned even wider and turned back to the lake, where another ball surged into the air.

Practice continued and Luke had managed to consistently send a ball halfway to Matt when Mayeem's voice rang out from the southwest corner of the cove.

"Switch!"

"Let a pro show you how it's done," Matt said.

Luke rolled his eyes and stood in the spot Matt had vacated. A minute later, Matt stood with water dripping from his hair, and Luke's side hurt from laughing. The class continued for two more hours, but besides the initial explosion, Matt never managed to get even a bulge out of the lake. He stood staring at the water with clenched fists and his back toward Luke as Mr. White returned with the first of the carriages from school. Luke stood beside Matt and saw that his eyes glistened and his face was bright red.

"I can't even get ..." Matt swallowed and a tear rolled down his face. "The only reason the water is moving is because of the stupid waves. Even Jon David got a tiny ball to form."

"Matt, that's not true. You ... you got a lot of water to move at the beginning."

Matt looked up, his forehead wrinkled. "Yeah, and soaked myself. A lot of good that did!"

"Not everyone is gifted with every discipline, young one." Mayeem stopped beside them and stared at Matt, holding his gaze. "One cannot be perfect, and as I have heard, the strengths that make you most valuable have nothing at all to do with your abilities with the disciplines and everything to do with your character. Much like your father, from what I remember and from what others have told me." Matt's eyes widened and Mayeem smiled. "Oh yes, I know a good deal about you as well, Mr. Nichols."

Luke turned and watched Mayeem glide away as the last carriage rocked to a halt on the road above. She stopped beside Jennifer and Samantha, and Jennifer stood with her arms crossed, glaring at Mayeem's back, as the mermaid spoke softly to Samantha.

When she stepped back from Samantha, Samantha frowned down at the blue-green water. An orb floated into the air and Luke eased back. Light emanated from the orb as the water swirled faster and faster. After a moment, the orb split in two. Students gathered around Samantha as her face twisted and she watched the balls. "Uhhhhh." Samantha closed her eyes and the balls dropped back to the water with a splash. Her shoulders sagged and her head dropped.

Mayeem stepped up beside her and wrapped her arm around her shoulder. "In all my years, barely a handful of students have been able to control water to that degree so quickly. You have quite a talent, Miss Thompson." She patted Samantha's shoulder and turned around as Mr. White shuffled down the slope from the road. "All right, students, overall very well done today. Many of you have shown considerable talent. For the rest of you, never fear,"—she regarded Luke and Matt with a smile—"we will make up the difference with diligence and hard work."

Luke grinned and winked at Matt, who snorted and smiled grudgingly. Mayeem waved to Mr. White and then looked around the circle of students. Luke felt warmth wrap around him, and a hot wind whipped through the ranks of the students. When he felt his shirt with his hands, it was no longer wet. "It's completely dry!"

"And clean!" Matt said. "Now *that* is worth learning!"

Marti shook his head as Mr. White waved the students back up the hill toward the carriages. "Someday, M-M-Matt, you are gonna h-h-have to tell me your criteria for w-w-what is acceptable to l-l-learn and what is not."

At the end of the gaggle of students, Jon David and his friends shouldered past them up the hill. His normally pale face appeared red in the late-morning sun and was twisted into a snarl. "Don't feel too bad, Nichols. I'm sure there are loads of second-graders who can't figure out how to make a sphere out of water, too!"

Luke felt heat flood his neck and a thought flashed through his head. Jon David stopped laughing and rubbed his throat. He coughed and swallowed and then coughed again.

"Whoa!" Randy exclaimed and jumped back as Jon David spit black water out of his mouth. "JD, you all right, man?"

Jon David shook his head and coughed up more of the black water.

"What's a matter, Jon David, you trying to say something?" Luke said, feeling a cruel grin slither across his face.

Followed by his cohorts, Jon David stumbled up the hill coughing up black fluid.

"Luke!" Matt hissed and jerked Luke around. Luke blinked, coming back to himself, and Jon David's coughing stopped as a few heads turned to look at him. "What are you doing, man?"

"He was ... I just—"

Matt shook his head. "Jon David's an idiot and I can handle him, but you mess with darkness like that and the whole Elder Council's gonna come down on your head, you got it?"

Marti stepped up and nodded. "N-n-not to mention your uncle, and the G-G-Guard."

Samantha and Jennifer appeared beside them. "What's going on?" Samantha said.

Matt shook his head. "Nothing. Just Jon David."

"Yeah, and his b-b-band of weirdoes."

Jennifer and Samantha looked confused.

"He just has trouble making things work in that pea-sized brain of his," Luke said.

Matt and Marti chuckled, but Jennifer glared at him. "Just because Jon David's not rich like you doesn't mean he's stupid, Luke! At least he's not mean." Jennifer shoved past Luke and tromped up the hill.

"What? I'm not mean!"

Samantha stood beside Luke and touched his shoulder. "She didn't mean that, Luke. She ... Just ease up on Jon David for a while, will y'all?" She smiled sadly and followed after her friend.

Luke stood with his mouth open and jumped at the sound of Mayeem's voice beside him. "Mr. Rayburn, if I see you use darkness even one more time, you and I will have a discussion that I assure you, you won't enjoy. Do you understand?"

Luke swallowed. "Yes, ma'am."

"I will not tolerate that from any students, least of all someone from a family like yours." She turned away and then paused. "And Miss Grady is correct, Mr. Rayburn. Mr. Prichard is not stupid. I would suggest you watch him closely. He will not forget your actions."

FOUR

The Stranger in the Forest

Luke watched as a green, chestnut-breasted bird flitted by and lighted on a branch nearby. The bird stared at him, a white ring around its neck. It hopped once, cocked its head, and rattled off a pebbly call. Then the hand-size bird darted off. Beneath the branch, a stream gurgled over smooth rocks. As Luke glanced up at the towering burr oak trees, warmth spread across his chest.

Oh, no … now what?

He looked all around, but all he saw was the stream and trees and grass. The pendant grew warmer. He heard leaves rustle in the shadows beside the trail, and a picture of globs of light formed in his mind as the word "kad<u>ur</u>" formed on his lips.

Steady, Rayburn. Probably just one of those gnomes. He peered into a thicket of elderberry shrubs as a pair of blue eyes appeared at about chest level. *Maybe not!*

"Come on, Luke!" Trent shouted as he came bounding around a couple of live oaks.

The eyes vanished and the pendant went cold. Luke stared for another moment and then took a deep breath. *I wonder if there's such a thing as a* giant *gnome.* His brother waved him on before darting back around the trees. Luke glanced around once more before hefting his backpack and stepping smartly down the trail. A few minutes later, the trees gave way to grass and bushes along the trail, and the path opened onto the western shore of Granite Lake. His parents and siblings as well as Uncle Landon and Matt were already there in the center of a sandy patch of ground near a few oak trees.

"What took you so long, man?"

"Nothing, just looking around." Luke chuckled. "I see you've gotten a lot done."

Matt stood next to a heap of wooden poles and canvas that looked as if it belonged in the back of one of Mr. Acharon's trash wagons. Matt sneered and waved his hand at the jumble. "There's a reason it's called a *four*-man tent, Luke."

Over the next hour as the sun set, they got the tents up and their sleeping bags out. Luke's parents pulled pots and food out of the wagon they'd ridden from the manor and cooked beans and chili and roasted hot dogs and marshmallows over a small fire. Dusk turned to darkness as Luke licked the last of the marshmallow and chocolate off his fingers.

"These snore thingies are pretty good," Matt said.

Luke snorted and Jon giggled beside him. "They're not snores, Matt, they're s'mmmores."

Matt shrugged and reached for another marshmallow. "Well, whatever they are, they taste great. I think next time I'll just skip the hot dogs and go straight to the s'mmmores."

Luke's father nodded. "They definitely taste better out here under the open sky than they did from an oven in the kitchen—what do you say, kids?"

The Rayburn clan nodded as their father scooted forward and tossed another log onto the fire.

"Uncle Landon, can you tell us a ghost story from Countryside?" Trent said.

Uncle Landon's eyebrows rose. "A ghost story, you say?"

Trent nodded and excitement gleamed in his eyes. "Dad always told us some after we'd cook out in the old apartment."

Uncle Landon chuckled and looked at his brother. "*You* tell scary stories to little children? I can't *imagine* that."

Luke's father rolled his eyes.

"I know of a few, Trent, but the one you should really be asking is your father. He was always the best storyteller among us, just like Dad."

Trent turned pleading eyes toward his father.

"Your uncle is being a bit modest, Trent. I remember many a night hanging on the words of his stories and the images that appeared along with them when we were alone in our room. But very well, I'll do the best I can."

He sat up and crossed his legs Indian-style, the light playing off his face and a cool breeze blowing in off the lake. In the distance, a screech owl's mournful cry carried across the cloudless night. With Jodi already asleep, Jon and Amy curled up close to their mother. Uncle Landon slouched down, leaning against an old log, and folded his hands across his chest. Luke, Trent, and Matt looked expectantly toward Luke's father, and then the stories began.

Luke's heart raced with stories about ghosts galloping down the moonlit trails of Old Hargrove Forest as part of some long-forgotten hunting party, or the guardsmen who still stood their posts at the crumbling watchtower in the northwest, and he jumped at the legend of the crippled old bear that used to be a man and would hunt the hills around Countryside for young boys and girls. With each tale, Luke's father would use pale shadows, flames, and wisps of smoke to create shapes that brought the stories even more to life. As he finished the story of the bear, a strand of red flame twisted this way and that with the wind, fading out into the night over the water.

"... and they chased him to the edge of the Sandy Hills, but they never found him, and all that they ever found of the girl was her red hair ribbon."

Luke's heart hammered and he held his breath. He realized his mouth was hanging open and snapped it shut as his father smiled.

Trent looked up with round eyes. "They never found her," he whispered.

Uncle Landon chuckled. "You missed your calling, brother. Spinning stories like that, you should have run for the District Council."

Luke's father smiled without mirth. "Thanks for the vote of character, bro."

Uncle Landon winked at him and tipped his head.

"All right, boys and girls, I think it's time for bed," Luke's mother said, and voices bombarded her from all sides.

"Ahhh, nnoooo."

"Just one more, Mommy."

"Pleeeeease."

She looked at her husband, who coughed and avoided her eyes, and then at her brother, who lifted his hands helplessly. "Bah, you two are like having extra children around. All right, one more story and then bed, no arguments, understand?" Five children and two men bobbed their heads up and down. Luke's mother narrowed her eyes and attempted a scowl, but the corners of her mouth quivered as she snuggled under the blanket with Jon and Amy.

"This last is the legend of the creature of Granite Lake," Luke's father said.

Luke grinned and pulled his knees up to his chest. Beside him he felt Trent scoot closer to him—and farther from the edge of the lake. Sparks danced into the sky, accompanied by the chirping of crickets and the croaking of tree frogs.

"Quite a few years ago, before Landon and I were even born, there was a young man named Peter who lived on the edge of Westcliffe Forest. He lived alone, an outcast from the rest of the holding for reasons no one would talk about. Peter had family in the holding, but they would never come see him, and for his part he would never go to see them."

An image of a log cabin nestled in a grove of trees flitted through the smoke over the fire.

"For years, Peter lived with only his dog and the animals of Westcliffe for his companions. He would hunt and fish in the streams through the forest during the day, and in the evenings he would sit on the front porch of his cabin and watch the sun set over the tops of the Sandy Hills. One day, Peter was out hunting a deer. He had his bow drawn and was about to loose his arrow when a call broke the silence of the morning. The deer bounded away and Peter followed the continued cries for help to a small stream nearby. There at the edge of the stream lay a young girl, motionless except for the ever-weakening cry for help escaping her lips, and with nothing save tattered clothes and a silver locket around her neck. Peter rushed to her side to try and help."

An image of a man crouched over a young girl by the edge of a stream swirled through the smoke.

"The young girl was badly wounded and unconscious. Seeing no one else around and help being too far away, Peter picked the girl up and carried her to his cabin. There he tended to her wounds as best he could. For days he watched over her, never leaving her side for fear she would wake up with no one there, or she would succumb to the wounds while he was gone to get help. Eventually, the young girl improved and even woke up. For days she said nothing, just ate and slept. Finally on the sixth day, she told Peter her name, Anora. Over time, Peter learned her story. Anora's village had been attacked by scores of bane wolves and soulless."

All the young listeners gasped as the face of a snarling bane wolf peered out from the fire.

Slap!

Everyone jumped at the sound of Luke's father clapping his hands together. A small squeak escaped Amy's lips.

"The attack had been swift and caught the village by surprise. Somehow, though, her mother had managed to get her to a traveling tunnel and open it up. Anora made it to the tunnel … but her mother wasn't so lucky. Anora watched as the soulless and wolves fell upon her mother and then came toward her and the tunnel. Crying, she leaped into the tunnel. One of the wolves bit her ankle as she leaped forward and thereby came into Countryside with her, but the rest remained trapped in the village. Anora's mother had used the disciplines in such a way that no one would be able to follow Anora through. The bane wolf was disoriented without his pack, and Anora managed to escape from his jaws and slip into the forest. She ran and ran until she collapsed on the bank of the stream crying for help, where Peter found her."

Luke's father took a deep breath, looking around the campfire. Gray-and-black moths and night bugs flitted around the flames.

"Well, Peter continued to nurse Anora back to health. Soon she was able to go hunting with him and to help him in his

garden. Peter made a second chair for his porch and Anora would sit there in the evenings with him. Months passed and Peter fell in love with Anora. Finally he confessed this to her, and though it almost broke his heart, he asked her if she would like to go back and search for her family. Anora smiled and shook her head 'no.' She told him he was her family now and gently, for the first time, kissed him."

Luke's father smiled as the image of a young man and woman kissing rotated around the smoke column and up into the darkness. Amy sighed and Trent looked up at Luke and stuck his finger in his mouth, pretending to make himself sick. Luke and Matt sniggered.

"*Shhhh!*" Luke's mother glared at the boys and they hunkered down. Luke's father grinned and continued.

"Peter went into town and asked one of the priests to come and marry them. Despite the misgivings of Peter's family and an older priest, the young father gladly obliged. He was a feisty fellow who loved to go against the grain, and for that matter loved Peter. Peter and Anora were married in their little cottage, the only witnesses the priest and the inhabitants of the forest. For years they lived there, happily hunting, tending their garden, and sitting on their porch watching the sun set. Occasionally the priest would come and sit with them, bringing them news of town or just to escape the rigors of shepherding his flock. Peter and Anora even began to talk of having children as they grew closer over the years." He sighed. "But their happiness wouldn't last."

Luke inched closer to the fire.

"One morning Peter went out hunting alone. He traversed up into the hills chasing one of the great black bears that used to live in Countryside. About midmorning he finally found the bear, but what he saw caused a chill to sweep over him and fear to grip his heart. The bear was dead, its body mangled on the forest floor … and its blood drained completely."

Luke shivered.

"Peter knew then that only a creature of darkness could have killed the bear. Afraid not for himself but for Anora, he raced back to their cabin … but he was too late. Bodies of bane wolves and even a soulless were strewn about the forest surrounding the cabin. He found Anora lying on the porch, tears filling his eyes at the sight. He gently picked her up and cradled her head. Anora's eyes flickered open and she smiled up at him. No one knows what she said, if anything, or how long Peter sat there holding her, but at some point she faded from this world, and finally Peter stood up and left. He removed the bodies of the dark forces from the clearing near their cabin and trekked to town to get the priest who had married them. Together they buried Anora next to the cabin under her favorite oak tree. The only token kept was the silver locket Anora had worn. Peter clasped it around his neck and never took it off again."

He stopped and stared into the flames for a time. The image of a grand oak tree grew and twisted up out of the smoke before vanishing. His eyes shone brightly in the orange light.

"Peter thanked the priest, who tried to stay and comfort him as best he could, but Peter had changed. He withdrew and one day he just left, disappeared … At least that's what the priest thought. Peter, though, had begun to hunt. His anger and hate burned strongly in his chest and his vengeance was unforgiving, almost cruel. Within weeks, bodies began turning up throughout the holding, heads of bane wolves on stakes, bodies of soulless ripped to pieces, other darker things. Creatures of the dark became terrified of Westcliffe Forest, and many avoided the holding altogether. As stories began to circulate of Peter terrifying even the people of the holding, concern grew.

Eventually, the bodies of a few darkmen washed up on the shore of Granite Lake and the Elder Council had had enough. They sent the holding Guard out into Westcliffe to search for Peter. They hoped to bring him back to his senses. The Guard hunted for Peter for days, and finally in the late evening of the sixth day, they cornered him on top of a cliff overlooking Granite Lake. The sergeant of the Guard rode forward on his horse and tried to convince Peter to come with them."

A vision of a man standing on a cliff surrounded by a dozen riders blew through the smoke.

"But Peter would not. Half-crazed by loss, he stepped back off the cliff, falling more than a hundred feet into the water below. The Guard searched for Peter for days, but no body ever washed up on shore. The community assumed that Peter had died, and for months it appeared so ... but then one fall evening a young couple was out camping near Granite Lake when they were attacked by a group of darkmen. Just as the darkmen descended on them, though, a strange shape walked up out of the lake. Clothed in mud and water grass, the creature attacked the darkmen, killing several of them and scattering the rest. The creature then turned on the young couple. It had the appearance of a man and glowing eyes the blue-gray color of the lake after the sun has set. And around its neck ... a silver locket."

Amy and Jon gasped.

"Somehow the couple escaped from the creature and made it back into town. As they fled, the creature's piercing scream ripped across the night."

Luke cringed along with Matt and Trent as a wind swirled around them, a bodiless cry splitting the night. Luke's father's eyes widened and he sat forward, his hands sweeping in front of him in an arc toward the children.

"Bodies of dark creatures sometimes mysteriously appear around Granite Lake, and stories have been told of people disappearing, but the Guard has never been able to catch the creature. And even to this day, late in the evenings as sunlight fades to darkness, people often claim to see or even be chased by the Creature of Granite Lake."

Luke's father sat and stared into the eyes of each of the children around the fire. For many moments, Luke held his breath, the only sounds in his ears those of the crackling fire and Trent's breathing. The night sky grew darker and the howl of coyotes carried through the woods.

"Well, I guess it's time for bed!" Luke's father clapped his hands on his knees and grinned as everyone jumped.

"Joe!" his mother exclaimed, pulling her hand to her chest with an exasperated frown.

Uncle Landon chuckled along with his brother. "You'll pay for that later, I'll wager, brother."

Luke felt his heart flutter back down into his chest. "Dad! That's it? What … what happened to Peter? I mean, what if the creature isn't really him? What if the creature is what got him!? Uncle Landon, why hasn't the Guard ever been able to get the creature?"

Jon chimed in. "Yeah, isn't it dangerous to be here, Uncle Landon?"

Uncle Landon rolled his eyes at his brother. "You see what you've gone and done now?"

Luke's father grinned. "Oh, no. I was asked to tell a ghost story and I did. It's just a story, kids. There is no Creature of Granite Lake." He glanced at Uncle Landon. "And for all I know, there never even *was* any Peter or Anora."

"But, Dad—"

"No, now that's enough. It's time for bed. I probably chose the wrong story to tell last, bu—"

"*Nooo*, I can't *imagine* that," Luke's mother said.

Luke's father's face reddened at his wife's tone, a sheepish grin appearing and then vanishing. "*But* regardless, it's time for bed. We've got to be up early in the morning if we want to catch those fish, boys and girls."

Luke complained along with all the others, but after a few minutes he found himself curled up in a sleeping bag under the roof of his tent along with Matt and Trent. For a long time he lay quietly, visions of trees and silver pendants passing in front of his eyes. Finally, though, Trent's steady breathing lulled him to sleep.

Ahooooooooooo.

Luke bolted up off the ground.

What's going on? … Where am I?

He blinked his eyes and shook his head, trying to clear away the last wisps of dreams. Gray light filtered through the canvas roof of the tent. Trent was snoring beside him. He shook Matt's shoulder.

"Hmmm … what is it? I'm not ready to get up yet, Mom."

Ahooooooooooo.

Luke punched Matt in the side.

"*Ommphf.* Hey!"

"Get up, man. Something's not right."

There were voices outside now and shadows moving across the tent. Luke leaned over and yanked the sleeping bag off his brother's head. "Trent, get up. Trent!"

Trent moaned and pushed up onto one elbow, blinking. "Is it time to go fishing?"

Ahoooooooooo.

Trent's eyes shot open. "Luke ..."

The tent flaps snapped back and Luke's father's face appeared, gray light silhouetting him. "Boys ... good, you're up. Get dressed and get outside. Now."

"Yes, sir," all three said, and Luke scrambled for his jeans and boots. A minute later he rolled out of the tent.

Ahoooooooooo.

The howls were louder now. Luke watched his uncle and father hitch the wagon. The horses whinnied as the howls carried across the sand. Jon, Amy, and Jodi stood next to their mother, their faces calm.

Ahoooooooooo.

Luke started, turning toward the trees and expecting a wolf to jump out of the woods at any moment.

"So much for fishing," Luke said.

Matt nodded. "Yeah, how rude."

"Joe," Uncle Landon said, "we don't have time. They're too close."

Luke's father turned to his wife. "Sara, get everyone up here into the wagon."

Uncle Landon walked toward the edge of the grass and trees, his mouth moving silently. Glimmers of light flickered in the air, but Luke couldn't make out what they were. The wind gusted as Uncle Landon walked in a circle about twenty paces from the wagon.

"Boys." Luke's father walked over from the wagon, boots quietly shuffling through the sand. "Boys, I don't know what all's coming, but whatever it is, stay in the wagon no matter what, do you understand?"

Luke, Matt, and Trent nodded.

"Son, if they get past your uncle and me, don't forget about your pendant. It—"

Ahooooooooooo.

"Jooooe!"

Luke's father shoved him toward the wagon and darted toward Uncle Landon. Luke looked over his shoulder and trembled. Two bane wolves lunged out of the trees toward his uncle. They stood almost to his chest. They snarled as their strides ate up the ground.

"Luuuuke!" Luke's mother shrieked and pointed toward the east. Light blossomed on the edge of Luke's vision as he turned his head. Another wolf appeared from out of the forest a hundred feet down shore, running not toward his father and his uncle but directly at him. He bolted toward the wagon ten yards away. The wolf closed the gap.

Light and heat exploded to Luke's right.

Five yards.

He heard the wolf's feet digging into the sand.

Almost ... there.

He lunged toward the wagon, but as he did he felt his shirt and jeans snag and his body jerk away from the wagon. "Mom!" He reached out a hand toward his mother, but she was too far. He heard his mother scream and Matt yell to him, but the wolf raced on, Luke's clothes in its grasp. Luke struggled to turn around, to twist free, but with a few strides the wolf carried them through the grass and into the trees and Luke had to put his arms in front of his face to keep the branches and undergrowth from slicing into his skin. Something jerked and popped against his neck as he spit leaves and dirt out of his mouth. The shouts and noise faded and all Luke could hear was the steady rhythm of the wolf's padded feet on the forest floor and his breath being sucked in and out.

Where are we going?

After what seemed like an hour but Luke was fairly certain was only minutes, the wolf stopped and dropped him. Luke cringed, but the wolf simply snarled at him once and then walked a few paces away and plopped down in a mound of grass, panting. After a minute or so, Luke stood up, wincing as he straightened his legs and rubbed his arms. The wolf followed him with its eyes but didn't move its head.

This is gonna hurt so bad tomor—

He shook his head

Have to make it to tomorrow first, Rayburn.

The clearing was only about twenty feet across. Oak and elm trees lined the edges, their branches blocking most of the sun. Thick blades of oat grass grew up from the floor to Luke's knees. The leaves on the trees hung motionless, and gnats and other small insects were starting to rise with the morning heat. Luke stared at the wolf's unblinking blue eyes.

Blue eyes, like on the trail.

The wolf lifted its head.

"It's almost like you want something."

Light glowed in the wolf's eyes and Luke's pulse slowed, his thoughts fading.

"Hello, boy."

The wolf's head snapped to the left, the light in its eyes gone. Luke jumped and whipped his head around, too, his heart hammering. A few paces away, the man from the Chesterton Station stood staring at him. His golden eyes sucked in what little light shone into the clearing and Luke took a step back. A low growl sounded, and from behind the man stepped out two towering bane wolves. The wolf that had snatched Luke from the shore walked with head lowered toward the man, who patted its head.

"Thought you were gonna keep running for a minute. ... Good girl, Dukta, good girl."

The wolf padded to where the other two stood, one of them snarling and snapping at her, and the man's attention turned back to Luke. "Thought you slipped away from me, did you, lad?" He chuckled. "You can never outrun a hunter, boy, never."

Luke shivered at the ice in the man's voice. "Who ... who are you?"

The man flashed his teeth and a low growl emanated from one of the wolves. "Who am I? ... Nobody, just a man sent to do a job."

Luke stepped back toward the edge of the clearing. "What job?"

"Tsk, tsk." The man shook his head, easing toward Luke. "Now, you see, that's the wrong question, boy. What you should be asking is *who* sent me."

Gotta stall him, give Dad and Uncle Landon time to get here.

"All right, well then *who* sent you?"

The man grinned. "Someone you've met before, lad, someone who wants something you have very much."

The book!

"I don't ... I don't have anything."

The man winced. "Ah, now, we were getting along so well, and then you had to go and lie to me." He took a deep breath and lunged forward.

Luke eyes widened, his shout strangled in his throat. He tried to stumble backward, but the man grasped his shoulders and picked him up in a vise grip. Luke kicked and twisted for a moment, but the man's grip tightened painfully.

"Now, boy, you listen to me." The man's golden eyes narrowed and hot breath blew over Luke's face. "You've hidden it well, but I don't have any patience for games, and neither does he who sent me. Now where is the—" His eyes lost focus.

Luke heard the grass rustling behind the man and whines from the wolves. The man sniffed the air and growled.

Hooooouuuuuuuuuuuu …

Luke frowned. *That's no wolf.* What *is that?*

The long lonesome call blew through the forest and into the clearing. The wolves' whining grew louder, and there were yips and a few growls. The man sniffed the air again and cursed under his breath. He turned back to Luke. "Where is it, boy!?"

Luke felt his body rattle as the man squeezed his shoulders. He gritted his teeth as pain spread from his shoulders toward his spine.

Hooooouuuuuuuuuuuu …

The howl wandered closer and the man snarled and dropped Luke to the forest floor.

"*Umphf.*" Luke coughed, rolling onto his side.

The man knelt close to his face, his eyes gleaming. "I'll be watching you, boy. We'll *all* be watching you."

With that he stood and turned and walked to the edge of the clearing, where he melted into the darkness between the trees along with two other shadows. The wolf that had snagged Luke from beside the beach looked back once, and then she too was gone.

Hooooouuuuuuuuuuuu …

The howl sounded from the opposite direction in which the hunter and wolves had vanished, filling the forest like wind slipping between the trees. Luke moaned, pushing up off the ground. He glanced around and froze. The sound of branches snapping and foliage ripping carried toward him. He staggered forward a few steps and looked over his shoulder.

Sucking in a breath, he watched as a shadow as tall as he was raced by outside the clearing.

Ka-thump, ka-thump, ka-thump.

The pounding of hooves sounded behind him. He closed his eyes. *Hunter and wolves in one direction ... eerie howl and shadow in another ... thundering horses in another ... wonderful.*

He whirled around in confusion and stumbled toward the southwest, the only direction where there was silence. The sound of pounding hooves and ripping undergrowth grew louder. He pushed a few feet into the forest and paused, leaning against an oak tree and looking out from the shadows. Horses exploded into the clearing and Luke's heart leaped.

"Luke! Luke!"

Luke lunged out of the shadows as his uncle called his name.

"Uncle Landon!"

His uncle and half the squad whirled around, pulling weapons seemingly from out of nowhere. Light appeared and then faded around a few of the men. Uncle Landon took a deep breath and jumped down, sweeping Luke up in a bear hug.

"Luke! Thank God. Thank God you're all right."

"Uncle Landon," Luke wheezed—"too tight ... too ..."

"Sorry." Uncle Landon eased his grip but didn't release Luke from his hug.

One of the other riders walked his mount over to Landon. "Sir, tracks are hard to see, just like everywhere else this morning, but they're there. They lead to the southeast, sir, toward the swamp."

Uncle Landon clenched his jaw. "Son of a—" He glanced at Luke. "Sorry."

"It's OK, Uncle Landon."

Uncle Landon smiled. "As long as your mother doesn't find out." He turned back to the guardsman. "Send out a couple of the men to link back up with the rest of the squad and bring them back, Sergeant. We'll meet back near the campsite and move out from there."

The sergeant nodded and turned over his shoulder. "McDonnell, Briggs! Search back toward the lake. Gather the boys and head to the campsite. We'll meet you there."

Two of the guardsmen slammed fist to chest and whirled around in the clearing before dashing down one of the trails.

Uncle Landon stared into the shadows of the forest toward the southeast, muttering under his breath. "I'll be darned if I'm tracking them through that muck without a whole squad … and maybe then some."

Luke rode behind his uncle back toward the shore of Granite Lake and his family. As he shifted in his seat, his chest bumped into the back of Uncle Landon and his heart skipped a beat. He jerked his head down and his hand up to his chest.

Where is it?

He pulled his shirt out and felt around his neck.

Oh, no.

He closed his eyes at the memory of racing through the forest and a tugging around his neck.

It's gone.

He felt a weight settle around his shoulders and groaned, slumping against his uncle.

"You all right, Luke?" Uncle Landon said.

Luke shook his head, but no words came out.

His uncle pulled up and turned in the saddle. "Luke, what's wrong? What is it?"

Luke looked up with stinging eyes. "I lost it, Uncle Landon. It's gone."

Uncle Landon furrowed his brow. "What is, Luke? What's gone?"

"The pendant ... the pendant Dad gave me."

"Dad, I know y'all are going to talk about the hunter, and I should get to come!" Luke glared at his father, who stood a few feet inside the door to the family quarters. Fire danced in his father's eyes, but his voice was a whisper, cold as snow falling in the dead of winter.

"Luke, we've already discussed this. You are not—"

"We haven't discussed anything! You just tell me what to do and then I have to go along with it. *I'm* the one who got dragged through the forest today. *I'm* the one who unlocked the *Book of the Wise,* which you don't even trust me enough to let me know where it is or when it's going to be here at the house. *I'm* the one the hunter was after, and I should be part of the meeting, not sitting here like some helpless kid!"

"Luke ..."

Luke heard the warning in his father's voice, but he ignored it. "It's not fair! I can help, and I can help figure out what's going on and—"

"That's enough!" His father's voice reverberated throughout the family quarters. Luke faltered back a step. "That's enough, Luke. You've made your point. You have done a great deal, more than many, and you are valued by this family and our friends more than you know. But you don't know everything, Luke, and there are many who have given much more than you can even begin to suspect yet. I love you—you are my son—but this is not open for debate. You will stay here. And you will fix your attitude before I return. *Then* we will talk."

With that his father turned and strode through the family

doors. Two of the house servants stood outside the door, and he paused and spoke to them as the door swung closed. "No one comes in, no one leaves ..." The guards looked into the room, faces chiseled like stone as they watched Luke disappear behind the door.

"Agh! Stupid." Luke turned to see Trent standing with round eyes and Matt shaking his head, watching Luke from the north end of the room. "What!?"

"I coulda told you how that was gonna come out, man."

"Whatever."

Luke stamped over and dropped onto the couch. His right arm was bandaged, and pink streaks crisscrossed most of the bare skin.

Matt sat across from him. "Well, at least you got some scars out of the whole deal ... It'll give you something to show off to Samantha."

Trent snickered in a chair beside Luke, but Luke was too angry to respond. They sat alone, Jon, Amy, and Jodi having all gone to bed. Purple-gray dusk crept into the valley outside, the few clouds in the sky outlined in oranges and pinks. Bowls filled with the last meltings of Mr. Robinson's homemade vanilla ice cream sat on the coffee table between the boys; Luke had convinced the estate chef and his parents that the ice cream would make them feel better after the events of the day. Minutes passed in silence. Luke watched flames appear and disappear as Trent practiced with his light globe.

"I wish we knew what they were talking about," Luke said. "It's like they don't trust us, like the way they randomly move around the *Book of the Wise* this year. They tell me when it's here but not when it's gonna leave or come back or where it goes, and nobody tells me anything they find out about it!"

Trent shrugged. "Even if we knew where Dad and Uncle

Landon and the rest were, we couldn't leave, Luke. You heard Dad. Those two lugs on the other side of the door aren't gonna budge."

Luke clenched his jaw. "I know. I just want to—"

Matt sat up with a lopsided grin, light blossoming in his eyes.

Luke frowned wearily. "What ... what are you thinking?"

"That maybe we can figure out what they're talking about."

"How?"

Matt glanced over his shoulder even though the room was empty. "Well, this summer while y'all were gone, I got to spend a lot of time with Captain Rayburn. Sometimes he would talk about when he and your dad were boys and the things they used to do. A couple times he made the comment that they would slip out 'between the cracks.' He would get this sly grin on his face when I asked him what he meant and say, 'You'll have to figure it out on your own, but not everything in this house is exactly as it seems.'"

"So how does that help us figure out what they're talking about now?"

"Secret passageways!"

Trent sat with wide eyes and mouth agape, glass globe forgotten on the couch.

"Really?" Luke said sarcastically. "Secret passageways?"

Matt nodded, ignoring Luke's tone of condescension. "Yes. I think that's what he was getting at, that there were ways to move around the house without everyone knowing about it."

"Even if that was true, how would we find them? I suppose just go up to the bookcase and pull a book down?"

A grin blossomed on Matt's face. "No. We use this." He opened his hand, and resting in the middle of it sat a marble-size ball of orange light.

Recognition dawned on Luke. "A seeker ... Where did you get it?"

Matt winked. "I convinced Mom to make me one the other day to help me look for my old backpack. Turns out I found the backpack without having to use it."

Luke snorted. "And you wonder why everyone eyes you suspiciously. But what do we tell it? How do we get the seeker to look for these *passageways*, much less dad and Uncle Landon and them, without *them* knowing we found them?"

Matt's smile slipped a bit. "I've heard Mom talk about some seekers being able to follow specific commands. It may make it hard to find what you're looking for, but they're supposed to follow your rules. But ... I've also heard her talking about using the disciplines to prevent seekers from finding something, even if you don't give them requirements, or even to confuse them, or to trap or destroy them."

The memory of a seeker exploding as it flew down a dirt road last year popped into Luke's head. "Yeah ... I can vouch for the destroy part."

The boys sat silently staring at the glowing orb. The last colors faded to gray outside. "Madleek," Luke mumbled, and candles on the table and the light rocks along the wall began to glow. He could feel his mood lighten. "It's still cool every time to see those ... what do you call 'em again?"

Matt glanced up at him. "What?" He raised his head. "Oh, the rocks ... Sela'or."

Luke nodded. "Every time those sela'or light up." A cooling breeze swirled into the room and he looked over his shoulder. "Did y'all open the balcony doors?"

Matt and Trent shook their heads, staring at the eastern wall. Luke licked his lips and walked toward the doors swinging slowly in the breeze. He stepped out onto the balcony, the wind ruffling his hair and tugging at his shirt. The pale light of a waning crescent moon struggled to push back the darkness. Banks of clouds pushed in from the east. Glancing down, Luke looked at the horse stables and sucked in his breath. He heard exclamations from Matt and Trent as they appeared beside him. The shadowed silhouette of a man and a wolf the size of a small horse faced the house. Luke stood frozen for a dozen heartbeats.

Ahooooooooooo.

The distant howl sent a shiver down his spine and pulled his eyes toward the North. When he looked back at the stables, the shadows had vanished. He turned to meet Matt's rounded eyes.

"I'll activate the seeker," Matt said.

Luke stepped back in after Matt and Trent and closed and latched the doors to the balcony. He walked over and sat at the coffee table where Matt had laid the glowing seeker. "So, what do we tell it?"

Matt frowned. "We need it to find where Captain Rayburn and your parents are talking about the hunter."

Trent looked up from the orb. "But without them knowing we're watching them."

Luke grimaced. "And getting there without anyone else knowing we're watching them … And what if they aren't all in the same place, or …" His voice trailed off.

"On second thought, maybe we should just go ask the guards to take us to them," Matt said.

Luke sighed. He considered the orb for a minute more and then clamped his jaw shut. "No, we need to know what they're saying. What if we tell the seeker to take us to where Uncle Landon is without going through the main door to the room and without anyone seeing us?"

"Sounds good to me," Trent said.

Matt looked at the orb for a moment and shrugged. "Even if they catch us, how bad can it really be? I mean, we got attacked by bane wolves today, right?"

Luke snorted. "Right. OK, you're up, Matt."

Matt grimaced and focused on the glowing orb. "Take us to Captain Rayburn, without going through the main door to the room and without anyone else seeing us ... and without Captain Rayburn seeing us ..."

The boys sat back as the orb expanded and floated into the air. About a foot above the coffee table, wings appeared, along with a beak and claws. A few seconds later, a red palm-size bird chirped, cocking its head and looking up at Matt. It glanced at the main door and then hopped around to look at the balcony doors.

"Not the balcony! A different way, a different way!" Matt blurted, and the bird squawked and straightened up. Matt breathed a sigh of relief. "Figured we'd save getting caught dangling over the edge of the balcony for another night."

"Good call," Luke said.

Chirping, the bird hopped around until it faced the north wall, and then it flew to the mantel above the fireplace. As it chirped again, the red glow of the seeker intensified. In the wall behind it, one of the stones glowed blue.

Crack!

A section of the wall to the left of the fireplace swung out a few feet and a gust of cool air rushed into the room. Luke rolled his shoulders and shivered as the air swept around him. He looked around the table at two sets of wide eyes and then into the darkness of the hidden corridor.

Trent leaned forward, a grin splitting his face. "Cool."

Voices sounded from the other side of the door, where the guards stood.

Chirp.

The red bird hopped down off the mantel and flew into the shadowed opening in the wall. The voices outside the door to the hallway grew louder.

"Somebody's coming. Time to go." Matt jumped up and darted toward the hidden passage.

Luke looked at the door. *What if they come in and see we aren't here?* He glanced at the slightly ajar door to the bedroom he and Trent shared. *Maybe if I close that they'll think we're asleep and won't look in.*

"Luke, come on!" Matt's voice hissed from the passageway beside the fireplace.

Luke darted over, pulled the door of his room to and scrambled into the darkness of the passageway after Matt and Trent. The section of the wall beside the fireplace swung closed behind them just as the door near the guards began to open.

Click.

The wall shut tightly, and blackness engulfed the three boys except for the red seeker flitting in front of them. Trent looked up hopefully. "Maybe it was just Ms. Lucy … or the servants coming to get the dishes."

"Either way, we can't go back now," Luke said. "Let's just get going."

The boys turned and the seeker flew twenty or so yards down the passage and then stopped. As the light grew farther away, Luke's palms began to sweat. Trent stepped closer to him, bumping against his side. "You don't think it will leave us in here, do you, Luke?"

Luke shook his head and then stopped.

He can't see you in the dark, dumb-dumb. "No, Trent, we'll be all right. I think the bird will lead us and stay close enough so we can see it." *But a light sure would be nice.*

As the thought left his head, a dim blue glow appeared on each side of them. A few lights sputtered to life along the walls, illuminating large tan stones. The walls were dry and curved together above their heads. Below their shoes and boots, the stones were worn smooth, a covering of dust over them.

As the boys stepped toward the bird, new lights flared on in front of them and lights behind them faded out. The bird always stayed twenty to thirty feet ahead of them, allowing them to get closer only when they came to an intersection in the corridors. From time to time, the stone changed from the white and tan limestone of the exterior to a pink granite and then to a rust-brown sandstone and then back again. Every few feet, a small alcove held one of the blue sela'or, and occasionally they would pass a scarred and faded gray door. At one point, they walked into a room with a breeze swirling through it. The walls disappeared into the darkness above. Lining each wall of the room were several openings large enough to drive the coach through.

Matt looked at Luke, his mouth hanging open. "Are we even still in the house? I mean, how could a room this big be hidden behind the walls?"

Luke just shook his head and they moved on.

A few minutes later, the lights beside them faded and the red bird remained motionless on the floor of the passageway. Luke eased toward the bird, and when he was about five yards away from it, voices floated into the passageway. The bird's light dimmed and it hopped forward a few feet and then to the side of the hallway. As Luke knelt beside it, the bird's light extended only a few inches, but it was enough to illuminate a hole in the wall blocked by an iron grate. Dampness and thick air surrounded the grate. Matt's and Trent's heads appeared in the light. His grandfather's voice carried up toward them.

"... and he got in anyway. This isn't the first time."

"Nor will it be the last," Mr. Acharon said, "unless the council will allow for more patrols along the curtain so we can figure out how he's getting in and who's helping him."

A voice Luke didn't recognize cut in. "I agree, but I think the more important question is why he went after Luke. From what Landon and Joe tell us, that wolf tore straight off after Luke, and as soon as she had him, the other two broke off from fighting."

The sound of shuffling boots carried through the grate, covering the next bit of conversation, and then there was silence.

Luke's father sighed. "I don't know, Q. Luke told us he kept asking for something. Luke is sure it's the book, and I understand why, but I'm not so sure I believe that."

"What makes you say that, Joe?" Father Woods said slowly.

"I don't know, I just ... I don't think they're looking for the book. We know they've been searching for something in Countryside all summer, but randomly, never in the same place twice. There's no pattern to it. Sometimes they search places that are associated with Luke and the boys, like the school, and sometimes it's completely off in a corner like down near the falls. You said yourself that the book looked like it had been tampered with already by the time it appeared back on Luke's desk last year. The *Book of the Wise* is hard enough to get into, even for someone experienced like you. It took a great deal of power and no small bit of luck for Luke to unlock the prophecy of the Bloodstar in it. Surely if it appeared to be tampered with, it was something extremely powerful that did it. And if it really was one of the shedon who had the book during the time between when Luke first saw it on the road in Westcliffe and when it appeared back on his desk … well, surely it got whatever out of the book it needed."

Silence emanated from the grate again. Scurrying noises sounded from the darkness farther down the passageway.

"Well, what about the creature—"

"Sergeant," Uncle Landon said.

"*Something* was out there, sir. Even young Luke mentioned it when you talked to him … It wasn't just the boy's imagination." Indignation filled the sergeant's gravelly voice.

"I don't argue that, Sergeant, just whether it was some goopy gloopy mud creature from the depths of the lake." Uncle Landon's calm voice faded into the walls.

"Well, call it what you will, but something was in that forest besides the hunter and us, something that didn't seem too friendly, and in my book that's bad news."

"I tend to agree with Sergeant Chapman," Luke's father said. "We need to know what it is that's running amok through our own forests. We also need to figure out how the hunter is getting in and out. And I don't think it's only the gnomes that are helping him get in. However, speaking of the boys, if y'all will excuse me for tonight, I need to go check on them. I'll talk to Luke again over the next couple days and see if I can figure out anything else from his account."

Luke heard a chair scrape and his father say good night to the other men.

Matt leaned down to the red bird. "Take us back to our room!" he whispered fiercely.

The bird hopped around and took off into the air. The boys jogged after it as its light faded away around them. Luke heard only their huffing as they turned one corner and then another and clambered up some winding stairs. By the time the section of the fireplace wall that opened onto the secret passageway swung shut behind them, Luke could feel drops of sweat on his brow. The boys slipped across the living room and through the door to their room and crawled into bed. Luke doused the lights just as he heard the door to the main family room open. His father's footfalls sounded on the stone floor and Luke held his breath as his heart hammered in his chest. The door cracked open briefly, but only for a moment before closing.

Secret passageways ... brilliant idea.

Luke rolled over and tried to calm his breathing. As his chest slowed and his eyelids grew heavy, images of huge shadows running under the moonlight filled his head. Just before falling asleep, he heard a lonesome howl outside.

Gotta figure out what that hunter is looking for ... and who sent him.

FIVE

The Late-night Letter

Luke rubbed his arm against his pants and a streak of red appeared next to several others on the white cloth.

"Huddle!" Ryan White's voice rang out under the stadium lights.

Luke jogged over from the sidelines to the group of eighth-grade boys forming up on the south end of the field. He tugged on the chinstrap of his leather helmet as warm wind blew over his face and the steady thrum of shouts, laughter, and the band's music filled the evening. The flag on the north end fluttered in the wind, stars and stripes swaying. It was the second quarter, and the mechanical clock read 2:40 as Jeremy Hall ran out toward the group.

"All right, let's get a little breathing room before half. I Left 43 Lead on two, I Left 43 Lead on two, readyyy ... break!"

Luke jogged up to the line and settled in on the left edge of it.

Jeremy's voice rang out from under center. "Down!"

Luke leaned forward on his right hand.

"Set!"

Sweat rolled off Luke's forehead. A corner on the Blueridge defense eased toward him from the outside.

Easy, Luke …

"Hut!"

Luke heard collisions to his right, and the Blueridge defender sprinted forward. Luke wheeled left and slammed his shoulder into the corner, forcing him to the outside.

"Umphf."

The corner shoved against Luke, trying to force him in toward Jeremy. Luke stayed with him.

Tweet!

Luke disengaged from the Blueridge player and turned around. Derrick Hamilton was pushing up from the ground five yards down the field.

"Huddle!"

Luke grinned and jogged over to Ryan's upstretched arms signaling where to huddle, and the process began again. Near the fifty-yard line, Luke caught a midfield pass and a Blueridge linebacker crashed into him. Despite feeling as if his horse, Archer, had slammed him against the wooden fence of his pen, Luke held on to the ball and the first-down marker moved forward. With twenty seconds left in the first half, the Spartans had the ball on the five-yard line with the score 14–7 Spartans. On the next play, Derrick punched his way through the line and into the end zone from the two-yard line, making the score 21–7 with ten seconds left. Blueridge ran the kickoff back thirty yards, but the Spartans left for halftime still up by two touchdowns.

As the game continued, the Spartans' lead grew, and by the start of the fourth quarter, everybody on the team had played, Marti had caught a pass, the first string was standing on the sideline cheering, and Coach Wilson wasn't glaring at everyone.

"Go, Marti!" Matt yelled from beside Luke as they watched Marti go down struggling in a heap near the scrimmage line.

Luke ran his hand over his wet hair and then wiped it off on his now pink, brown, green, and white pants. "He'll be talking about this game for a month!"

"Let's go, beanpole!" Jon David yelled, approaching along the sideline. "The end zone's way down there!"

Luke glowered at the redheaded boy as he and one of his cohorts, Randy, strutted toward him. The thought of black hornets swarming around Jon David's head receded from his mind as Matt punched him in the side and spoke up for both of them. "And here I thought you'd forgotten which end zone we were going for again, Jon David."

Luke choked off a laugh as Jon David stopped and sneered. When Coach Jackson stepped past, he moved on.

The Spartans scored a couple of plays later, and defense rotated with offense after the kickoff. Seconds ticked off the scoreboard, white numbers flicking one after another, until a horn that sounded like it belonged on a ship blared, ending the game. The scoreboard showed the final score of 48–14, Spartans. The team members cheered before lining up in the middle of the field to shake hands with the Ravens.

Thirty minutes later, drier and with fresh clothes on, Luke left the field house with Matt and Marti.

"You ended up with fifteen yards tonight. Well done, Stegall."

Marti grinned and ducked his head at the gruff voice from underneath the green farmer's cap. "Thanks, Coach."

Luke slapped Marti on the shoulder as Coach Jackson walked back to the field house, but he froze when the coach's voice rang out. "Rayburn, you must be lookin' for some extra runnin' next week."

Luke looked down at his duffel bag. "Shoot, my cleats … Coming, Coach!" Luke darted back toward the locker room as Matt and Marti chuckled.

"You need those things tied to you, man!" Matt called behind him.

Luke ran into the locker room and slid to a stop in front of his green locker, where his cleats sat side by side. *I'm gonna end up losing these things and Coach is gonna kill me.*

"… said to watch him and look for it around the school," Luke heard from behind the row of lockers. It was Jon David.

"Why does he want it?" Randy's nasal voice echoed in the locker room.

"I don't know, but he seems pretty excited about it. He wouldn't even tell me what it was, just something about tears."

"Tears … he wants somebody's tears?"

Jon David sighed. "Of course not, you moron. He doesn't want somebody's actual tears. The thing he's looking for is called the Tears. I don't know what they are or even what they look like. But he gave me this."

Randy's voice dropped. "Wow … Uh, what is it?"

Luke tried to look around the lockers, but all he could see was Jon David's red hair a couple of rows over.

"He said it was some kind of modified seeker and that when I found the Tears it would light up."

"Why didn't he just give you a normal seeker?"

"Dunno. He said they wouldn't work on this … Anyway, I'm gonna look around the buildings in the school, maybe Principal Oldham's office, or that hunchback of a janitor's closet full of all those old dusty trophies. You look out in Mr. Brentwood's maintenance shed."

"What about watching Rayburn?"

"Don't worry, I've got that taken care of. If that little punk figures something out, we'll know about it. Now if I can just get Samantha …"

Luke lost the thread of the conversation as lockers were slammed and bags zipped up. *What? Get Samantha to what?* He saw Jon David and Randy walk down the aisle toward the door. *Dang it!* He grabbed his cleats and ran out the door, seeing Jon David and Randy out of the corner of his eye. He ran down the hill toward Matt and Marti and snatched his bag from Matt.

"What took you so long, man?" Matt said. "Was Coach mad?"

"I'll tell you later. Let's just go find where everybody is in the stands."

"You sure you're all right, man?"

"Yeah, come on."

Matt and Marti walked alongside Luke, weaving through the crowd toward the stands. Luke glanced over his shoulder as they walked up the stairs into the stands. Jon David stood next to Randy, his eyes locked on Luke.

Great … Just great, Rayburn.

The carriage rolled along the road and turned in to the Rayburn house as the moon climbed over the eastern hills. Cool air flowed through the windows as torches appeared, lining the drive ahead. The carriage eased to a stop in front of the stairs and Luke hopped down with his father, snagging his duffel bag.

"Thanks, Mr. Brunson."

The man tipped his hat to Luke before giving a flick of the

reins and circling around to the stables. Luke and his father walked inside and across the entrance hall toward the staircase. Luke stifled a yawn as he put his foot up on the first step.

"Long night, son?"

"Yes, sir."

His father smiled and clapped him on the shoulder. "Me, too. Let's try to get some sleep"—he sighed—"before it's time to get up for school all over again."

"Joe."

Luke glanced over his shoulder as Mr. Acharon walked across the polished floor behind them.

"Evening, Q. What in the world is keeping you up at this hour?"

Mr. Acharon dipped his head. "I was actually waiting on young Luke here. I wonder if I might steal him from you for a moment?"

"Sure, Q. Just try not to keep him up too much longer. We have to be up again in a few hours."

"It will only take a few minutes."

"Very well ... Luke, you did a great job tonight ... through the whole game. I'm very proud of you." His father hugged him and continued up the stairs. He paused near the top. "Oh, and Luke, hopefully everyone is asleep. Please try to keep it that way when you come in. It's bad enough talking to your mom before coffee in the morning; I don't even want to *think* about waking her and the kids up in the middle of the night."

Luke chuckled along with Mr. Acharon as his father turned and continued on his way. "Yes, sir."

When his father disappeared through the east door on the third floor, Mr. Acharon reached into his pocket and pulled an object out. As he did, Luke dropped his duffel bag.

"Where ... how ... how did you get it?"

Mr. Acharon smiled. "I had asked a couple of friends to keep an eye out for it. Found it in the forest and brought it to me. I thought you might want it back."

Luke reached out and then paused. "I didn't do a very good job guarding it, sir. I'm sorry."

Mr. Acharon snorted. "I doubt many grown men could have kept it on the ride you were taken on. Don't worry about it, Luke. Just be grateful to have it back." He held up the sphere and chain in the light of the floating chandelier. "I fixed the chain myself. Hopefully it will hold."

Luke grasped the pendant as Mr. Acharon offered it. "I can't even see where it was broken, sir."

Mr. Acharon smiled and put his hand on Luke's shoulder. "I still have a few tricks up my sleeve, son. Now go try to get some sleep, and your father is right—you did a great job ... throughout the whole game. Good night, Luke."

Luke frowned as Mr. Acharon turned and walked back down the stairs. *Why did he and Dad say "through the whole game"?* He picked up his bag and headed toward his room, mumbling. "Too late to think that much anyway."

Luke trudged up to the family quarters. A lion's head appeared and the door clicked open at Luke's mouthed command. The room was dim, with only a couple of lights glowing along the wall. "Ouch!" He bit his lip as his shin met the hard edge of one of the chairs in the darkened corner near his room. He paused to make sure he hadn't woken anyone up; he didn't hear any movement coming from the rooms. He slipped into his room and eased the door closed. Trent's soft snoring sounded behind him, and a lone candle burned on the far side of his desk.

I feel like Trent sounds.

He leaned down to blow the candle out but froze with

puffed-out cheeks. His heart quickened and the images of his bed and pillow fled from his mind. On his desk an envelope had materialized, light sparkling along its edges. As it appeared, so did Luke's name across the front of it. He stared at the letter in the flickering light of the candle and then glanced around him. Trent was still except for the rising and falling of his chest. Luke picked up the letter.

Who …

He turned the envelope over. No markings were on the paper except for his name. Sliding his finger under the flap, he ripped it open along the top edge. A folded sheet of paper was inside. He took a deep breath and pulled the paper out and unfolded it.

It was blank.

He flipped it over and then back again.

I wonder …

He blew across it, and black cursive scrawl appeared line by line as if an invisible hand were writing on the paper:

Luke,

I hope you and your family are doing well. I hope the process of hiding your writing I explained in the last letter has been helpful. I'm sorry it has been so long since I talked to you. I am still searching for my niece and I'm in a position so that communication is … difficult. There are a couple things I felt you needed to know though.

The first is that I came across some information recently that the same forces that captured my niece and coerced me into hunting for the Book of the Wise *last year are searching in Countryside again for*

something. The creatures sent in to search for what-
ever it is aren't kind, Luke. They will do anything to
get what they are after. You can't trust them. That
dark one never intended to give Lilly back to me,
even before I tried to help you escape in the end.

Luke noticed a dark splotch on the paper, almost like a drop of water.

My information doesn't tell me much else except that
the object they are searching for is very powerful and
it seems to have something to do with water. I don't
know if it means the object is made of water or it's
in water ...

The second thing you need to know is that I have
heard your family's name in connection with this
hunt and the darkness searching for it. I am not sure
how the two are connected yet, but I will keep my
ear to the ground to try and figure it out.

Luke, I know this is going to sound laughable com-
ing from me, but you need to be careful who you
trust. This information came through some pretty
dark creatures. Someone in Countryside is feeding
them information, and it's someone who seems to
know a great deal about you, and about people you
and I both care for. Just be careful out there. I will be
in touch however I can, when I can. Oh, and put this
letter down when you are done reading it ... trust me.

Stay safe,

J.

Put it down ...

Luke looked back at the top of the letter.

Crack.

A spark popped and the bottom corner of the letter ignited. The edge of the paper turned to ash, and the flame spread quickly to the top.

"Whoa!" Luke dropped the letter as the last corner dissolved into ash and floated onto his writing desk. "Hmmm."

He glanced over his shoulder as Trent mumbled and rolled over, but his brother didn't wake up. A small pile of ash sat in the light of the candle's flame. Luke grabbed the trash basket from beside the roll-top desk and brushed the ash off with his hand. Setting the trash can back down, he sucked in a breath to blow the candle out, but he paused.

What is that?

He leaned close to the wooden surface of the desk. A few patches of ash clung to it. As he moved the candle closer, he had trouble believing his eyes. There, where he had swept off the desk, were the ashy outlines of two footprints about an inch in length.

I must be dreaming.

He blinked and looked again—the footprints were still there. He stood motionless for a few moments and then shook his head. When he wiped the desk clean, the footprints disappeared.

He stumbled to his bed and, after changing into pajamas, got under the covers. Moonlight fell through the window above him, and he stared out at the stars, part of Andromeda slipping past his view. Thoughts and questions raced through his head.

Why is my family involved? ... Who is feeding information? ...

Why were footprints on the desk? ... What left the footprints? ... Can I trust James?

Finally, only one thought remained.

I have to get up for school soon.

His eyes slowly closed, and even the images of smoldering letters and small footprints faded.

SIX

✦

Redwall Falls

Shadows fell to the west, but sweat already dripped off Luke's forehead. A breeze moved the leaves of a nearby sycamore tree as a wren flitted down and away to the north.

"I swear Mom's weather clock said it was supposed to be cooler today," Matt said.

Luke snickered. "Cooler in Texas just means it takes a little longer to fry your eggs on a rock."

The boys rolled the next cedar post off the back of the buckboard wagon and lugged it to a wooden rack beside one of the sheds. Luke hefted his end up and then helped Matt shove the post into place. A score of the fence posts lay in the racks, with another couple dozen still in the wagon. Shade swept over the boys as a cloud meandered in front of the sun.

"My arms still hurt from Thursday night's game," Matt said. "Each of these things feels like I'm trying to pick Jon David up off the ground."

Luke guffawed as they picked up the next post. "Yeah, oh well."

"Sir."

Luke turned around as Matt finished pushing the post in. "Oh, hey, Jake."

The older boy fidgeted.

"Do you need something?"

Jake's eyes widened. "Oh, no, sir. I just thought … Well, I can help move those posts with y'all."

Matt wiped the sweat off his brow. "I think that's a great—"

"No," Luke said. "Thanks Jake, but Dad told *us* to finish unloading the supplies."

"You sure, sir?"

"Yeah, man—are you sure?" Matt said.

Luke glared at Matt. "Yes, but thanks. We appreciate it."

Jake knitted his brow for a moment before walking away.

"They said we had to finish unloading. They didn't say we couldn't have help, Luke. Besides, I think sometimes Jake just wants to hang out with us. As a friend, you know? He's one of the youngest guys here."

Luke dusted his gloves off on his jeans and slid another post off the back of the wagon for Matt to grab. "Maybe, but you know Dad and Uncle Landon meant for us to finish this by ourselves or they would have sent some of the guys to do it in the first place."

Matt grunted as they shoved another post into place.

"Besides, we need to talk without everyone being able to listen."

"You think someone who works here is actually passing information on to dark creatures?"

"It's happened before, you know."

"Yeah, and the guy that fed them information is the guy feeding you information that someone is feeding them information. Doesn't *that* strike you as a little odd?"

"I'm not even real sure what you just said, but we don't have many options; do we?"

Matt didn't say anything as they picked up another post.

"Either way," Luke said, "I heard Jon David talking myself, so I'm not counting on those details coming from anyone else."

Matt huffed as they walked the post over. "I … still don't … understand" — they shoved the post into place — "what he could possibly have meant by 'Tears.'" He wiped his forehead with the sleeve of his shirt. "I'm pretty sure I've never seen Jon David cry."

"Ha. Well, he made it seem like it was some kind of object, and I bet it's got something to do with the Remnant again, or something they were involved with at least. And maybe it's not the *Book of the Wise* that the hunter was looking for. Maybe it's this."

"And you still think it's Mr. Thompson who's getting Jon David to track it down?"

Luke pulled out another post as a gust of wind dried the sweat on his neck. "Who else would it be, man?"

Matt reached for the post but didn't pick it up. "I don't know man, but even Mr. Thompson wouldn't have anything to do with a hunter." He looked at Luke and sighed. "But if he is the one sending Jon David around looking … you know what that means about who might be watching you then, Luke."

"Samantha's not spying on me, Matt. Just pick up the post."

"I'm not saying she is, Luke, just that it's a possibility. You have to admit that, man. I mean, you said Jon David mentioned her name, right?"

Luke clenched his jaw but then relaxed. "All right, I know. Now can we just drop it? This thing isn't getting any lighter."

Matt nodded and picked his end up off the bed of the wagon. Luke kept his mouth closed for most of the rest of the morning. The sun was creeping past midday as they bolted shut the tailgate of the empty wagon. Matt paused, leaning against the sides.

"Look, Luke, I didn't mean to—"

"It's all right, Matt. You're right, she might be. I just wish I would've heard what else Jon David and Randy said in the locker room. Anyway, I think we ought to go check out the west-wing library and see what we can find."

Matt pulled off his gloves and slapped them against his legs. "Only after I get a shower and—"

"I'm afraid your shower will have to wait, Mr. Nichols."

Luke turned to see Mr. Acharon striding down the road from the house. "Sir?"

Mr. Acharon pulled a stack of clothes from under his arm and tossed half to each boy, along with a pair of boots. "We have more work to do today, gentlemen. Change into these and meet me by the stables in ten minutes." He turned and headed back toward the house.

"What are we going to do, sir?"

"We are going to try and make sure you don't get eaten by a wolf, Mr. Rayburn," Mr. Acharon called over his shoulder.

An hour later, Luke slowed Archer to a walk behind Mr. Acharon. Matt and Trent did the same with their horses behind him. Luke rolled his shoulders, stretching against his stiff deep-tan blouse. Pants of the same color curled around his leather lace-up boots. As they wound around another curve, pecan and oak trees lined the side of the trail. Up ahead rose cliffs that towered over the trees. The cliff tops shone red in the afternoon sun, shadows slipping slowly over their edges as the sun moved west. A single crooked silver streak of water broke

the rock face. As Luke rounded the bend, the sounds of birds, wind, and the occasional chattering squirrel blended in with that of water splattering.

"Whoa." Trent walked his horse up beside Luke and mirrored his wide eyes. "It must be like a thousand feet or something!"

Luke stared at the stream of water that cascaded over the side of the cliff. The water bounced from one rock to another, spreading as it fell. Mist shrouded the bottom of the falls and crept out from the west side to blanket half a pond there.

"*Those* are the Redwall Falls, boys, and yes, Trent, they are a little over one thousand feet tall."

Luke watched the water fall for a few more moments before Mr. Acharon's voice rang out again.

"All right, gentlemen, that's enough gawking. We don't have much sunlight to waste today. We'll be riding back in the dark already."

Luke glanced at Matt, who was wearing a uniform identical to his, and sighed as they rode their horses to the tree line, where Mr. Acharon had already slid down off his horse. "That's code for 'we are going to be dog tired when we leave here.' You know that, right?"

"I don't even know what we're doing yet, but I don't like it already."

The boys dismounted from their horses and hitched them to a couple of low-lying branches.

"What are we doing here, sir?" Luke walked over to where Mr. Acharon sat on an old stump.

The man waited for Trent to finish tying his horse and join them. "Sit down, boys."

For a moment, the estate manager simply sat and stared from one boy to another. Luke felt pressure settle on his shoulders as Mr. Acharon's hazel-gray eyes focused on him, but he held his head straight. His heart slowed, and sounds faded into the distance.

"Mr. Rayburn."

Luke stiffened and felt Matt tense beside him. *Can't be good when he starts off with "Mr. Rayburn."*

"Who was your father with when he was away from home last year?"

Luke darted glances at Matt and Trent. "He was with the Marine Corps, sir."

"And why did he go with them?"

"To fight."

Mr. Acharon nodded. "And, Mr. Nichols, what does Mr. Rayburn—*Captain* Rayburn—do here in Countryside?"

"He's a member of the Guard, sir."

"And what does the Guard do?"

Matt shrugged. "They fight dark creatures and keep them out of the holding."

Mr. Acharon nodded again. "Trent, I assume you would agree with their answers."

Trent bobbed his head.

Mr. Acharon arched his eyebrows. "Ahem."

"Yes … yes, sir."

The estate manager turned back to Luke. "Let me ask you again, Mr. Rayburn. Why did your father go with the Marine Corps last year? Try to think about your answer this time."

Luke frowned and studied the ground beneath him. *Dad went to fight. He told me he …* An image of the front steps of his family's old apartment flashed through his head. Luke's eyes lost focus, and his father's voice sounded in his head.

I promised that I would protect people who could not protect themselves …

"To protect people." Luke turned his face up to Mr. Acharon's. "He went to protect people … to protect us."

A sad smile flitted across the man's sun-worn face as he turned toward Matt. "Mr. Nichols, would you agree that is also the primary goal of Captain Rayburn and the Guard?"

"Yes, sir."

"Good. That is in fact the reason both of these men and many more before them join organizations such as the Marine Corps in the world outside, and the Guard within the holdings. Despite what many who are unfamiliar with the organizations think, these men do not have an insatiable lust for blood and violence, nor are they incapable of functioning in any other role in society. These men choose this path to protect those they care for and love and the ideas they hold dear." A shadow passed across Mr. Acharon's face. "This is not why all men, or creatures, fight, though. Can you boys think of any who fight for different reasons?"

Luke's mind traveled back to a class with Mr. Shepherd. "Mercenaries, sir, like the Hessians."

"Yes, there are some who fight for money."

Trent looked up. "What about the darkmen, sir? Why did they attack us last year?"

A half-smile flitted across Mr. Acharon's face, his words slow as he drew them out. "Excellent question, Trent. Why do you think?"

Trent bit his lip for a moment. "Just to be mean, sir?"

"Some … perhaps. But fighting for the sake of being cruel is rare, generally the role of much darker creatures. Try again."

Trent furrowed his brow and his eyes widened. "To take the *Book of the Wise!*"

Mr. Acharon smiled. "Yes, Trent, to take something, in this case the *Book of the Wise*. There is one more reason in particular that I would like you three to acknowledge. It is a sinister reason, tricky, cruel in its own way and often hard to determine until late in an engagement. Can you think of it?"

Luke's mind rolled through various classes and conversations he'd had with his father and uncle.

Nothing.

Mr. Acharon looked from face to face. "Boys, during football practice, do you run sprints?"

Matt snorted and his voice deepened in imitation of Coach Wilson. "Until I get tired of blowing the whistle or you decide to run—your choice, ladies."

Mr. Acharon chuckled. "I've always liked Coach Wilson. And what would happen if you decided *not* to run?"

Luke exchanged a horrified look with Matt. "Um ... I'm pretty sure he'd kill us, sir."

Mr. Acharon's smile vanished and his voice turned to stone. "Indeed." For what seemed like minutes he was quiet, simply staring at the boys.

What does Coach killing us for not running sprints have to do with whether someone fights or ... ohhhh. "Are ... were some of the darkmen forced to attack Countryside last year, sir?"

Mr. Acharon looked into the distance as a finch landed on the branch of a dead tree nearby. "That is a hard question to answer, Luke. Most likely ... yes, but even if you could ask the darkmen themselves, few could tell whether their answer was truth or deception."

The boys sat for a few moments more. The finch flew off and Mr. Acharon's eyes snapped back onto them. "The point here is that there are many reasons why men and creatures fight. You must keep that in mind as you yourselves learn to fight."

"I wouldn't fight if I didn't want to, no matter what," Trent said, his face hard. "I would fight against whoever was trying to make me."

That's the face he had last year when Dad was telling us we were going to leave Countryside.

Mr. Acharon frowned, his voice soft. "That is a very hard path to follow, young one. Let us hope you do not have to travel it someday."

Trent looked down at the grass beneath him, his lips closed and his face set.

"Is that why we're here, sir," Luke said, "to learn to fight?"

"Yes, and even more importantly, we are here so that you may learn *when* to fight." Mr. Acharon pushed up off the ground and the boys followed suit. "This is not practice for a football game, gentlemen, nor is it for the purpose of making you into modern-day gladiators or prize fighters. These skills are for defending those who cannot defend themselves, for the upholding of ideas when they are threatened and, least of these, for defending yourselves. Your lessons will continue only as long as your integrity and character remain. Do we understand one another?"

All three nodded and said, "Yes, sir."

"Good." He turned to Trent. "Trent, you are here to take part in our conversations, but for now you will only observe the actual fighting skills."

Trent opened his mouth but then snapped it shut at Mr. Acharon's raised eyebrows.

"Generally, as Mr. Nichols is well aware, he and your older brother would not even start training for another year yet, but your father and Captain Rayburn requested I begin their training early … for various reasons, and I agreed. *You* are here at *my* request, Trent, but you *will* do as I say or you will no longer be here, understand?"

Trent's face softened, his voice sullen. "Yes, sir."

Mr. Acharon moved a few yards from the woods and turned to face the boys. "Now, today we will go over a basic fighting stance and some simple punches and kicks. I will explain each stance or move, illustrate it for you, and then ... we will work."

Luke swallowed as a cruel smile crept onto Mr. Acharon's face.

"Gentlemen, you will *not* enjoy this, and it *will* be hard."

Luke felt his stomach tighten as it would right before the start of a football game. *Wonderful ...*

"Now, every move we work on, every skill we learn will have at its core the basic fighting stance. This stance is the foundation for everything else we do. You will learn it well. First, bend your knees ..."

For the next two hours, Luke and Matt went through the movements as Mr. Acharon described them. Corrections were verbal only once. As the sun touched the top of the cliffs, Luke felt bruises in places he didn't know could bruise, and his arms were shaking. Sweat had turned parts of his clothing from tan to a dark brown. Trent watched from yards away, balancing on a fallen tree trunk and mimicking their moves.

"Recover!"

Luke collapsed to one knee, and Matt doubled over panting beside him.

Mr. Acharon grinned and paced in front of them. "Now, gentlemen, part of learning to fight is building mental and physical toughness, being tired but retaining the ability to think and function. In order to accomplish this, at the end of each lesson, when you are most tired, we will work on one or the other. Today, we will focus on the physical aspect."

Luke groaned and Matt dropped his head. Mr. Acharon moved the few paces back to the woods and lifted one foot onto the broken trunk of a fallen tree. It was two feet in diameter and almost four feet long.

Luke closed his eyes. *I wonder if he'll stop if I just pass out here … No, probably just wait until I come to and double what we have to do.*

"As the last part of today's lesson, you boys will move this log from here"—Mr. Acharon looked up and pointed to the pond beneath the waterfall Trent was skipping toward—"to the edge of the pond."

Matt glanced at the log and then over at the pond and then back at the log. "That's, like, a hundred yards!"

Mr. Acharon grinned. "Indeed." He moved away from the log, walking toward Trent and the pond. "You may move it however you like, boys. I'll be over here getting a cool drink of water whenever you care to join me."

Matt glared at the man's back as he sauntered away. "He's got the blood of a soulless in him, you know that?"

Luke snorted. "The soulless don't have any blood in them, Matt."

Matt glared at Luke. "I know."

As Luke chuckled, he winced at the pain in his rib cage. "Come on, let's get this over with." He walked to the log and pushed against it with his foot. It didn't budge. *Not good …*

Matt stepped up beside him and they both shoved against it. The log shifted forward a few inches. They strained for a few seconds and then collapsed on top of the log as it rolled back.

Luke glanced at Matt, who rolled his eyes. "All right, on three … One, twooo, three!" Bark scraped against Luke's hands, and his knees slipped against the ground, rubbing already raw spots. "Come on … almost there." Grunting, the boys pushed the log up and out of the slight depression it was sitting in before they fell to the ground. Luke sucked air into his lungs as the log came to rest a couple of feet in front of them. "I think I'm just gonna lay here and take a little nap."

Matt closed his eyes and mumbled.

"Just thought I'd come back and check on you boys, since you seem to be having some trouble," Mr. Acharon said. "This isn't exactly the tack I would take, but ..."

Luke pushed up off the ground and glared over the top of the log at the crouching form of Mr. Acharon. "You know, sir—"

"Luuuuke!"

The tiredness fled from Luke's arms and legs as Trent's call rang out across the meadow. He surged to his feet. In the distance, Luke saw blue light erupt from the pond and Trent stumble back from its edge.

"Luke!"

Move, Rayburn!

Luke's legs pumped as Matt ran alongside him, but Mr. Acharon was already ten yards in front of them, the distance widening.

How does he move that fast?

Luke felt as if he were in one of those dreams where everyone else moved at a normal speed but he was stuck in slow motion. He reached his brother a few steps ahead of Matt, but by the time he slid to a stop, Mr. Acharon had both hands clasped firmly on Trent's shoulders.

"... sure you're all right? You're not hurt?"

Trent shook his head, but Luke noticed his hands were shaking.

"Luke, you and Matt stay here with Trent."

"Yes ... sir," Luke said, trying to catch his breath. He stepped toward Trent. "You sure ... you're all right ... Trent?"

"Y-y-yeah. I'm sure ... Just surprised me."

Matt frowned. "What … what was it, Trent?"

Luke's brother glanced at the pond a few yards away, where Mr. Acharon walked along the edge scanning the water. "I don't know, really. I was just throwing rocks into the water … and then, then I thought I saw this black shadow underneath the water."

"Like a fish or something?" Luke asked.

Trent shook his head, eyes wide. "No, way bigger than a fish, at least way bigger than any fish I've ever seen here. It was bigger than I am and … well, then there was that burst of blue light and a screeching sound and …"

Luke glanced at Matt, who frowned and gave a slight shake of his head. A cool breeze blew past them from the pond. "Trent, what was the screeching sound like?"

"What do you mean? It was so loud my ears were ringing. How could you not have heard it?"

"I don't know, little brother, but I didn't hear anything. Did you tell Mr. Acharon?"

Trent nodded as the man tromped back over to the boys past patches of waist-high bluestem grass. His face was set and his eyes narrowed. "Time to go, boys. Collect your things and saddle up."

Luke turned and followed Mr. Acharon silently across the meadow as gray shadows darkened around them. As he pulled up into the saddle on the far side of the pasture, Luke looked toward the pond and gasped.

"What is it, Luke?" Mr. Acharon's taut voice growled through the cooling air.

Luke blinked and stared at the south edge of the pond. *It was there.* He blinked again and shook his head. "Nothing, sir. I thought I saw something at the edge of the pond, but … it must have been a shadow."

Wrinkles formed across the man's weathered face. "I wouldn't be so sure … We will ride home quickly, boys. Matt, you lead. Luke, stay close to Trent." He nodded to Matt, who flicked his reins and eased into a trot.

Luke glanced over his shoulder one last time. The pond was shrouded in darkness now, too late for sunlight, too early for stars or moonlight to reflect off the water. He shivered, not sure if the cause was falling temperature or sinking shadows, and urged Archer toward home.

Something was in that pond that shouldn't have been … and I bet it has to do with James's letter about the Tears and water.

SEVEN

The Rat Beneath the Manor

"Luke! Trent! Dinner!"

Luke turned toward the house at the sound of his mother's voice—"Yes, ma'am!"—then turned back around and chucked the football across the front lawn to Trent as his brother jogged toward him through a blanket of red and orange leaves. Glancing up, he saw his mother turn around and run into one of the servants coming out of the entrance-hall doors. The young man stumbled and teetered backward as he untangled himself and gave a deep bow to Luke's mother.

"Excuse me, ma'am. Sorry, ma'am."

Luke bit his cheek as his lips began to quiver.

"It's OK, Brad, I wasn't watching ... Don't worry about—"

A gust whipped away the last of his mother's words as Luke's lace-up work boots crunched across the gravel. He glanced up and waved at Brad, but the man's face colored red and he whirled around and hurried forward to open the door for Luke's mother. Trent jogged up beside Luke and slowed to a walk.

"Why do they always act so strange around Mom?"

Luke smiled and shook his head. "They still don't know quite what to make of Mom, and Mom still doesn't know quite what to do with them."

Luke pulled the sleeves of his fleece pullover down as yellow sycamore leaves swirled below the front steps to Rayburn Manor. A calico housecat lay curled up on top of the concrete banister, soaking up some last rays of sunshine. "Hey, girl." The cat opened one eye as Luke ran his hand over her fur and bounded up the steps with Trent. *It's almost like she thinks she's doing* me *the favor by letting me pet her.*

Just as they reached the top of the steps, Luke heard the steady beat of horses' hooves and the rolling of wheels coming down the driveway. He stopped with Trent and turned to see Father Woods's gig easing around the drive to the steps. The boys smiled and returned the priest's high outstretched wave. "Ho! ... Boys, how are we doing this fine fall evening?"

A groom bounded down the steps toward the gig and took the reins from Father Woods.

"Good, sir. How are you?"

"Thank you, son." Father Woods eased down out of the gig, snagging a brown suede bag from his seat. "Good, good ... Will be even better after some of Mr. Robinson's delightful venison-stuffed pumpkins!"

The gig rolled away as Luke and Trent turned to walk into the house with Father Woods. "You're staying for dinner!?"

Father Woods mimicked Trent's grin and leaned in inches from his face. "Wouldn't miss it for the world. Now! Tell me what you two have been up to. Trent, Mr. Acharon mentioned to me that you were showing particular promise."

Luke's smile faltered as Father Woods's drawstring bag bumped into his leg. *That feels a lot like my backpack full of books when it hits the side of my leg ... except that it only feels like one big book.*

Luke pushed back from the dining table. A low fire crackled in the fireplace behind him. His mother, grandparents, and Mr. Acharon sat in chairs near another fire on the opposite side of the table, while Uncle Landon and Luke's father reclined near the end of the table. Trent, Jon, and Amy sat on a thick rug in front of the fire playing damk'or, the pebbles smoking and glowing across the stone sheet. White plates with the Rayburns' blue brighthawk in their center and a narrow blue line around the rim sat on the table. Luke glanced down at his plate, light sugar sauce still ringing the edge. He ran his finger through it and licked it clean before closing his eyes.

"Luke, you look as if you regret indulging in that last candied pear."

Luke grimaced and nodded as Father Woods sat in the chair beside him. The father set down a stout glass, tapered at the top, with a honey-colored liquid that made Luke's nose wrinkle.

"Um-hmm ... I find myself in that same predicament"—Father Woods arched his eyebrows and sighed—"and always seem to after one of Master Robinson's meals. The man does things with venison I had not thought possible."

Luke gave a half-smile at the priest's perplexed look. The two sat in silence for a few minutes, watching Luke's siblings play. Trent was pitted against the twins and most of the pieces remaining were his, but every time the twins seemed to be lost, they would change colors or structure or make a move that Luke hadn't seen and slip past him. Father Woods took a sip from his glass and smiled, nodding toward the far side of the room. "I think young Jodi is fading quickly."

Jodi sat in Grandma Rayburn's lap, reading. Light would glow from the pages intermittently, but her eyes seemed to grow heavier with each flip of the page. Blue light flared up from the book, and images of the pond beneath Redwall Falls flashed through Luke's mind. His smile faded.

I wonder if Father Woods would know ...

He sat up. "Father Woods, could ... have you had much luck with the" —he glanced around the room and lowered his voice—"the book?"

Father Woods frowned and raised his voice. "You mean the *Book of the Wise*, Luke?"

A few heads turned their way. Luke cringed. "Yes, sir," he whispered.

"Never confuse the power of an object or a word with the source of that power, Luke. Despite what some have said, objects, words, and even a *very* few names *do* have power, but that does not mean you should not use them, only that you should understand *why* they have power and use them with caution." Father Woods leaned in inches away from Luke's face, and Luke could feel his breath on his cheek. "For example, mention of Master Robinson's sugared apple tarts does have a certain power, but that power has less than half to do with their mention than it does with the rumbling of our stomachs and the watering of our mouths that comes along with their mention, eh?" He gave a wink and a conspiratorial nudge, and Luke's shoulders relaxed.

"Yes, sir."

Father Woods nodded and eased back into the blue velvet padding of his dining chair, reaching for his glass. He took a sip, crossed his legs, and rested his elbows on the wooden armrests. "Now, what question would you like to ask me, son?"

How did he know I wanted to ask a question? Feels like his eyes have seen the world ...

"Well, sir"—Luke took a deep breath—"have you heard anything mentioned about Tears?" The words gushed out and Luke sat back in the chair.

Father Woods's eyes arched and a frown settled on his face. "Tears? I assume you are referring to the Tears of Adina, Luke?"

The firelight flickered in Father Woods's narrowed eyes and Luke swallowed. "I-I'm not sure, sir. I just overheard ... heard mention of them recently."

"And you have tried to find information on them on your own, I assume."

"Yes, sir."

Father Woods pursed his lips. "But you have not found anything in your searches?"

"No, sir, not yet."

"Hmmm ... that may be the answer you need, Luke."

"Sir?"

The gray-haired priest glanced behind him at the fire and took a sip from his glass. Laughter sounded from his family on the far side of the room. Servants slipped in and out of the dining hall, removing plates and other dishes. Father Woods remained silent for a few minutes, and Luke glanced over as Grandma Rayburn handed a sleeping Jodi to his mother. He smiled as his mother caught his eye but jumped at the sound of Father Woods's low voice.

"Luke. There is a great deal I still do not understand about the book, and even more about your relationship to it. Even if I understood more, I do not believe I would tell you much more than I am about to."

One of the young girls rolled a wooden cart out of the room carrying a silver coffee pot and white cups and saucers stamped with the brighthawk on them. Out of the corner of his eye, Luke saw his father stand up.

Father Woods turned from the fire and Luke shivered as the old man's eyes locked on him. "The Tears of Adina are almost as mysterious as the *Book of the Wise* itself. They have not been seen in centuries and they are rumored to be a powerful artifact, perhaps even one crafted by the Ancients. But all that most know of them for certain is that they were once protected by the Remnant." Father Woods adjusted his glasses and leaned forward in his chair until his face hovered inches away from Luke's. "Luke, the Remnant was an order formed after the Ancients left this world. They were sworn to defend the helpless, the widow, and the orphan against darkness. The order was born during a time when the power of the Flame was much stronger and had knowledge of much that we have forgotten. If they hid the Tears, I can't imagine anyone finding them after all this time. Although …" He leaned back and crossed one arm over his chest and supported his chin with his opposite hand.

"Wade."

Luke glanced up at his grandfather's voice.

"Ah, yes … very good, Aaron," Father Woods said. "Time already, is it?"

Grandpa Rayburn nodded and the priest stood up. Father Woods took a step forward and then turned. "Be careful," he said, resting slender fingers on Luke's shoulder. "If the Remnant deemed the Tears important, or dangerous enough to protect and to hide, perhaps they are best left alone. Sometimes, Luke, it is not the losing but the finding that is the trouble."

With that he picked his glass up off the table and shuffled away alongside Luke's grandfather.

They're up to something, and they're keeping me out of it ... again!

Luke glanced up at the door of the family quarters and a blue flash illuminated the hallway, followed by a green glow. He stepped past the lion's head as the door swung open. The room was empty, but he heard movement in Jon and Amy's room. Upon returning to Countryside this summer, Luke's parents had moved Jodi out of the room at their end of the quarters and into a small room adjoining the twins'. Luke walked past the room toward the fireplace near his room.

I don't care what they say— I don't remember that room being there last year.

A fire crackled merrily and he stopped and stood in front of it, turning his hands back and forth. Soft light from the sela'or along the wall blanketed the north end of the family room. Luke pulled one of the cushioned chairs closer to the fire and leaned his head against the back and propped his feet up. "I bet they're meeting somewhere right now." He glanced up at a stone just above the mantel and grimaced. *I could help. The hunter is out there searching right now. What if he gets to the Tears first? If I just had one of those seekers ...*

The hair on the back of Luke's neck stood up. He sat forward and looked around the room, his shoulders tensed. The balcony doors were shut tight, as were all the windows.

Something's not right.

He shivered and goose bumps raced up his arms. The light

in the room dimmed and the fire sputtered as his heart rate picked up.

Definitely not good, Rayburn.

Crack.

He jumped at the sound of his bedroom door popping open and turned, firing a ball of light from his hand. The kad<u>u</u>r slammed into the door, causing the door to rock back. He closed his eyes and shook his head. *Nice, Luke, now the whole house is gonna come running because your door creaked.* He slowed his breathing and stood still. The light from his kad<u>u</u>r faded into the wooden door. Nothing else moved. The air sat thick in the room. Luke looked around, but all he saw was the fog of his breath, flames popping in the fireplace and his door swaying.

Now what is that?

As the door to his room bounced off its frame, a red glow seeped out along the crack between the two. Luke stepped forward and then stopped again. Still nothing.

Someone in the house must have heard the explosion.

"Mom?"

He bit his lip and stepped a few paces closer. The light grew stronger. "You're not gonna find anything out standing over here like a little girl, Rayburn." He marched over to the door and shoved it open. "Who's there?" he shouted loud enough to be heard in the hallway.

Empty ... well, almost empty.

On the east side of the room, sitting on his writing desk, was a pulsing red orb about the size of a shooter marble. Luke glanced around again and leaned back outside the room. Thick silence still swathed the room. Even Luke's breathing sounded muted in his ears.

Seekers don't just appear out of thin air.

He stepped over to his desk and peered down at the orb.

"Looks like a seeker … but who put it here? … Probably should go get Mom."

Father Woods's voice sounded in Luke's mind: *Time already, is it?*

"It can't hurt to go take a look." He licked his lips. "Madleek." The word passed swiftly from his mouth. *So much for getting Mom.*

The orb sizzled and popped. Luke stepped back as it stretched and grew. A long rod shot out from one end, followed by four shorter ones. Red light flashed. Luke squinted at his desk as the light faded. On the wooden writing surface, about the size of a softball, crouched a bright … red … rat. It had a long hairless tail, sharp curved claws, and narrow beady eyes that stared unblinking back up at him.

Matt would be shaking his head and rolling his eyes about now.

"Find Father Woods. Don't let him see us, or anyone else … and bring me back when I tell you to."

The rat blinked and squeaked. Luke hunched his shoulders. The sound was more like nails on a chalkboard than an animal sound. The rat scurried off the writing desk and out the door into the living area. Luke hurried after it, watching it scamper to the mantel. A familiar stone began to glow, followed by a loud crack. The door to the secret passageway shifted open. Stillness lifted from the room and Luke heard steps clacking across the stones in Jon's and Amy's room.

"Oh well, nothing else for it."

Luke sucked in a breath and lunged into the hallway. Blue lights flared but then faded to a flicker as red light slithered down the corridor.

"Hello? Luke, are—"

The entrance to the family quarters glided shut, cutting off his mom's voice. Luke set off after the fading red light. The rat twisted and turned down corridors. Cold dry air filled the stone halls at first, but after a few minutes, Luke felt his shirt clinging to him. He gazed at the failing blue lights on the wall next to him.

"Definitely not the same way we went last—"

Splash!

"Ugh ... ah, maannnn." He looked down at his right tennis shoe, now dripping with water. Cold wetness crept in through his socks and the bottom of his blue jeans, too. "Great."

Squeak!

Luke's head popped up. The rat sat a few feet in front of him, beady eyes shifting back and forth around the hallway.

Squeak! Squeak!

Luke frowned at the rat and stepped forward. "I'm coming, I'm coming, jeez," He mumbled as he shuffled down the hall, his right shoe squishing with each step.

Boom!

He stopped dead. *What was that?*

Squeak!

The rat jumped.

Luke felt a tremor in the floor. The rat jumped again.

Squeak! Squeak!

Luke cocked his head. A warm breeze blew across his face from the direction of the noise. His breathing slowed and a smell like cut hay and freshly turned earth filled his nose. His skin tingled and warmth crept up his arms. "Ummm ... that feels good ... Ow!" The smell and the warmth vanished. He jerked his head down and shook his leg, throwing the rat against the wall. He leaned over and pulled up the leg of his pants. Tiny red spots covered his ankle.

"What'd you do *that* for?!"

Squeak! Squeak!

Boom!

Luke squinted through an archway to his left, away from the flickering blue light. The air remained still, but the darkness stirred. The vibration under his feet intensified. "Do ... do you feel that?"

Squeak! Squeak!

Luke bobbed his head up and down. "Yeah, squeak, squeak. Me, too ... Let's go."

The rat darted forward and Luke jogged behind it, his shoe still squishing.

Boom! ... Boom!

Not good.

The rat remained silent but raced furiously forward. Luke picked up his pace. Ahead, the hallway split into a Y. The rat swerved to the left, and they rounded a corner, rushed twenty yards down a hallway and rounded another.

BOOM ... BOOM.

Luke crashed through a couple of puddles. He glanced over his shoulder, but only the receding light of the sela'or chased them.

"Whoa!"

He skidded to a halt, tripping over the rat.

Squeak! Squeak! Squeak!

The creature stood on its hind legs and scratched at a wooden door.

"What, you want to go in there?"

Squeak! Squeak! Squeak!

BOOM! BOOM! BOOM!

Luke glanced over his shoulder. "Sounds good to me." He turned a dented brown doorknob, but it spun freely and the door remained stuck. "Uh-oh." He shook the door.

Nothing.

BOOM! BOOM! BOOM!

He leaped forward and threw his shoulder into the door as if he were trying to stop a pulling guard. The door groaned and crashed inward, and he stumbled to the floor, scraping his elbow. Ahead, the rat bounded up a winding stairwell.

BOOM! BOOM! BOOM! Rawrrrr!!!!

The bellow reverberated down through the doorway.

Crash!

The door exploded in a shower of light, bits of wood and metal flying in all directions and pelting Luke. Ears ringing, he scrambled to his feet and darted up the stairs after the rat.

Rawrrrr!!!!

Reaching the first bend in the stairwell, Luke looked back and froze. His heart skipped a beat. A shadow crammed into the door frame, squeezing toward him. Dark shapes of arms lashed out toward him, but the creature didn't come through. Luke stared, trying to make out the figure, but the light of the rat faded away.

Rawrrrr!!!!

Whosh! Smash!

An object the size of a bundle of firewood whistled past Luke's head and slammed into the stones behind him.

You're gonna get killed standing here, you dope. Move!

He turned and sprinted up the stairwell, taking them two and three at a time.

Rawrrrr!!!!

The scream chased him up the stairs. His legs burned and his breathing became heavy. He turned and turned as he followed the stairwell's spiral path, the sound lessening below him. The red light of the rat vanished and then reappeared as Luke lurched out onto a landing at the top of the stairwell, his head spinning and his heart hammering in his chest. He glanced back down the stairwell, but the rat continued to race away down a new hallway, and Luke stumbled on. Red granite turned to sandstone and moisture receded from the air. After another couple of turns, the rat stopped in the middle of the hallway.

rawrrrr.

boom. boom. boom.

The sounds were muted now, like sound in the forest.

boom … boo … oom … raw … rrrr.

They faded until Luke couldn't hear them or feel any tremors. "What was *that*?"

Squeak … Squeak.

He glanced down at the rat, which was glaring behind them into the hallway as if to say, "Good riddance." It turned around and sniffed the air and then turned around again. It waddled a few paces forward, sniffed the air again, and bobbed its head before scampering back to Luke.

Squeak.

The rat looked over its shoulder down the hall in front of them and back at Luke.

Squeak.

Luke straightened, his hands over his head, still catching his breath. "What?"

The rat squeaked and repeated its gesture.

"You want me …to *go* down the hall?"

Squeak.

Luke looked into the darkness. Blue lights flickered around him a few yards in both directions, illuminating a tattered tapestry on the right and smooth gray granite beneath his feet.

"Alone?"

Squeak! Squeak!

Luke shook his head and stepped forward, mumbling.

"Follow some silly rat … Get chased by howling monsters … Half your clothes are all wet … You must be crazy, Rayburn."

Squish. Step. Squish. Step.

Luke crept past the edge of the light and into the darkness. After a moment, his eyes adjusted and he stepped a few more paces forward.

"… in the north …"

He froze. The voice almost sounded familiar. He shivered as air swirled around his wet legs.

"… most of them …"

He slipped forward to the sound of the voices coming from the left side of the hallway. Uncle Landon's stout voice carried to where Luke stopped.

"… know they've been here since early summer at the latest, but only in small groups until recently. Even the orchard at the end of July … It was one of the worst attacks, but even that seemed clumsy and ill-coordinated."

"I agree," the almost-familiar voice rang out again, "but that is no longer the case. We have seen larger and larger gatherings of the creatures of late … and they seem to be working on something."

Luke heard Father Woods's voice and imagined him tilting his head and narrowing his eyes. "Working on something … Surely you do not mean to say that they are … are building something, Egoz?"

Egoz. Egoz. Who the heck is Egoz?

A confused tone entered Egoz's voice. "We … are not sure. We've been unable to get close enough without alarming them."

"Alarming them! You mean the gnomes … have a guard? They are watching for you?" Disbelief sounded in his uncle's voice.

"Yes, very much so. As I said, they are much more coordinated now. Someone or something is driving them. Their presence is no longer … coincidental."

"But we've never seen—"

"I would like to hear you finish your thought on *what* exactly they are doing, Egoz." Father Woods's voice stilled the room.

"I cannot tell you what they are doing, Been'on, but I can tell you what their *doing* has caused."

Luke wrinkled his forehead. *That doesn't even make sense.*

"The last group that we disrupted up to the north was the largest we have seen yet, somewhere around one hundred of the creatures." Luke heard mumbled exclamations from the listeners. "We were able to drive them off with not much more difficulty than any of the other groups. However, whatever it was that the koder—the gnomes, as you say—were *doing* blackened a half-mile circle of trees and grasses."

"… half-mile…"

"… a blight …"

"… cannot tell …"

For a minute Luke lost the thread of the conversation amid the explosions of anger and protest. He glanced over his shoulder to see that the red light remained about twenty yards behind him. *Make sure the little bugger doesn't run away.*

"… thing we can tell is that they were using earth and trying to combine it with darkness in some way."

The remaining chatter calmed at the sound of Father Woods's question.

"And can you not tell in what manner they were trying to combine the false discipline to earth, or what the goal was?"

"No, Been'on, but it is no simple darkman concoction. Of that we are sure. Whatever they are up to, it is an application of the disciplines that not even our old ones can fathom yet."

Squeak.

Luke looked over his shoulder. The red light was bouncing back and forth. He slipped away from the wall.

"… aware of … search for the Tears …"

Luke stretched back toward the wall.

Squeak! Squeak!

He gritted his teeth and walked over to where the rat was dashing back and forth. He glowered down at the hairy creature. "What?!" he hissed. "You're supposed to leave when I te—"

boom.

His mouth froze in midword. *Oh, no. That doesn't sound close, but I don't want it to* get *close.*

Squeak.

"Maybe just another minute …"

boom.

The rat ducked its head, turned in a circle and dashed off. Luke peered back toward the hidden wall. The voices seemed to have been swallowed by the darkness.

Rats! He jerked his head back over his shoulder and snorted. *Ha! Rats indeed.*

Boom.

Luke's heart rate quickened and he loped after the rat. The sound of the shadowed creature from the passages below vanished as they ran. Twenty minutes later, they came out in a storage room on the first floor of the house.

Hiss! Meoooowwww!

Squeak! Squeak!

The rat scurried down the hallway ahead of a bounding calico housecat.

Ha. Guess she doesn't like the thing either.

Luke slipped from the room and flitted from shadow to

shadow to avoid servants and others roaming the halls. He tiptoed across his family quarters and stole into his bedroom, where he slipped out of his wet clothes and into bed. As he lay there shivering, his mind raced along with the deer chasing sparks across the fireplace screen.

What were the gnomes trying to do? And who or what is Egoz? And what was that thing under the house?

The weight of Luke's eyelids finally overcame the questions darting around his mind, but as he faded toward sleep, an image of him flying down dark hallways trying to escape from a huge lumbering rat filled his head.

EIGHT

A Poem & Professor Lewis

Ahandful of brown and yellow leaves whispered in the wind above Luke's head. Laughter rang out across the courtyard between the wings of the school as seventh and eighth graders sauntered out for lunch. Groups of various sizes clustered around wooden or concrete tables or on the mix of pine needles, leaves, and browning grass. Matt, Marti, Samantha, and Jennifer sat with Luke around a stone table under a towering sycamore tree. Matt shook his head, holding a sandwich in one hand.

"I swear, Marti, I've never seen someone eat as much and weigh as little as you do."

Marti smiled and licked the last crumbs of his ham-and-cheese sandwich off his fingers. As the girls laughed, Luke noticed a strained tone in their voices. *Something's not right with those two.* His gaze shifted with the sunlight filtering through branches and leaves overhead and the thought left his mind. Samantha's hair changed from brown to gold and back again. She leaned toward Jennifer and, after whispering something, brushed her hair behind her ear.

I wonder if she—

Green eyes turned Luke's way and he jerked his head and mind away.

A few minutes later, a bell chimed across the courtyard. Samantha and Jennifer sighed and stood up, collecting paper bags and backpacks.

"Ugh," Jennifer said. "Forty-minute workouts right after lunch are worse than any three-hour afternoon practice."

"Yeah," Matt said. "Coach Wilson seems to lose the concept of time and the fact that we *can't* do twenty reps of two different stations at the same time."

Marti groaned. "That an-an-and the concept of a human actually n-n-needing to *breathe* during that forty-minute torture s-s-session."

Luke chuckled and then winced as a spasm passed through his right arm.

Matt stood up and executed a mock squat, his voice deepening. "All the way, Mr. Nichols, all the way. Faster, that's not a—ow, ow, ow ... cramp, cramp." He grabbed his hamstring and eased back onto the bench as Luke and Marti guffawed.

"See, that's what h-h-happens when you go 'all the w-w-way' down."

Samantha and Jennifer shook their heads and headed back across the courtyard toward the gym on the northeast side of the school. About half the students filed out of the courtyard, and Luke stretched his legs out along the bench he was sitting on and took a drink of water. A flash of blue flitted among the remaining leaves, branches, and brown balls overhead.

Jaay-jaay ... jaay-jaay.

Luke listened to the blue jay as its head twitched.

"S-s-so I f-f-found a poem that mentions t-t-tears."

Luke bolted upright. "What?"

"Waf?" Matt swallowed his bite whole. "As in the tears like what Jon David is looking for tears!?"

Marti nodded and looked around the courtyard. "Shhhh."

"No one is within thirty yards of us, man, and even if they were, who would care besides Jon David and his goons? Anyway, where did you find it?"

"Who cares?" Luke said. "What does it say?"

Marti looked around again and then leaned over and pulled a book out of his backpack. Luke scooted closer as Marti opened the book and pulled out a folded piece of paper. "I was r-r-reading an old book on p-p-poetry that my mom had and I f-f-found it."

"How do you find this stuff?" Matt said. "I mean, you just randomly pick up the right book."

Marti smirked. "I go through a l-l-lot of books. I have that disease c-c-called reading, r-r-remember?" Matt's face colored as Marti smoothed the paper and ran his finger down a few lines. "The p-p-poem is called 'The G-G-Guardians.' It's pretty long, so I j-j-just copied the few lines that mentioned the tears." Marti's finger came to a stop. He focused on the page for a few moments and then slid the paper toward Luke, turning his head away. "Here, Luke, you r-r-read it. I w-w-will just make a m-m-mess of it."

Matt clapped Marti on the shoulder with a sad smile.

"OK," Luke said. He took the paper and held it down against the breeze. After scanning it, he started to read:

Over the foam and moonlight passing

of the Guardians, the lone and last.

Behind him darkness always grasping

its breath like fog that shrouds the past.

Upon the secluded shore a shadow lingers

and greets his call with light of hope.

The precious package falls from his fingers

securing a promise of greatest scope.

The man to leave, his heart relieved

his duty done, the shore recedes.

Tears fade away by the mist received

and no soul alive is aware his deeds.

But on the sea darkness sneers

and rushes in with rage and fright.

The messenger, though, fails not to fear

Death's sting has lost this knight.

Death wails and screeches pushed back with the dawn

and the last of the Guardians finds sleep.

He and his Tears are gone.

Luke read through the lines again and then sat still. The wind and laughter swirled around the boys and a squirrel chittered overhead. The blue jay called out and flitted away.

"You really think this is about the Tears, Marti?"

Marti leaned forward. "You s-s-see how the w-w-word *tears* is capitalized?"

"Yeah, but that is the beginning of a senten—"

Marti pointed to the last line and Luke's mouth formed an O.

"I kn-kn-know it's not much, but ..." Marti shrugged.

Luke looked up and smiled. "It's more than we had before. You have any other ideas about the poem? Like who are the Guardians?"

"Just th-th-that the tears w-w-were left on an island."

Matt frowned at the page. "How do you figure that?"

Marti pointed to the word *secluded* on the page. "I'm n-n-not positive, but in the book it looked like two w-w-words were written differently than all the rest: *mist* and *s-s-secluded*. A synonym for *s-s-secluded* is *islanded*. I don't know why the w-w-word *mist* was written differently, but I think *s-s-secluded* was written differently to indicate that the shore w-w-was the shore of an island."

Matt leaned back and peered skeptically at Marti, but Marti's face turned hard and he jabbed a finger at the paper.

"Look, I'm not a g-g-great athlete and I don't h-h-have a knack with the disciplines like you two, but I have read a t-t-ton. Authors don't just italicize two w-w-words in a poem randomly. It m-m-means something. I may be wrong about w-w-what it means, but I know it means s-s-something."

Matt's eyes widened at the tone in Marti's voice and turned back to the paper. Luke winked at Marti and looked back down at the paper, too. The boys sat quietly for some minutes. Luke stared up at the hills east of the school and Old Hargrove Forest, which crawled up into them. Wisps of clouds floated past, and fewer students remained in the courtyard.

How do we find out what island? And who are the Guardians?

Another minute and a bell rang out across the grounds. Luke came back to himself and gathered up his books and what was left of his lunch. As the boys shuffled across the courtyard, a grin spread across Matt's face and he wrapped his arm around Marti's shoulders.

"Marti, it's awesome you found this. Luke and I sure couldn't have … but we really need to get you out more often. They have these things called horses, you know … and girls."

Marti rolled his eyes. "W-w-whatever," he said and gave Matt a shove, but he couldn't help laughing.

Matt peered down the corridor and then back at Luke and Marti. "You sure Mrs. Hughes said room 7H was at the end of the hall?"

"Yeah, man, I'm sure," Luke said.

Marti shook his head. "This doesn't m-m-make any sense. Nothing is d-d-down here except that ja-ja-janitor's closet. B-b-besides, all the other room n-n-numbers are three d-d-digits."

Luke shrugged as some of their classmates wandered down the hall toward them. "Well, at least we'll all be late together."

"Hey, Nichols," Jeremy Hall called out, "this where Intro to Cartography is?"

"Supposed to be."

A low rumble of voices filled the hall as more eighth-graders arrived. Jeremy glanced around and frowned. "Well, where is it?"

"No idea, man. Mrs. Hughes told Luke the room was down here, but the only thing down here is this janitor's closet and there isn't even a handle on it."

Jeremy squinted at the smooth wooden door. "I thought this was supposed to be a class about mapping, not mopping." A few chuckles sounded in the group. Marti rolled his eyes and turned back to the door. "At least mopping might be fun."

Blue light glowed in the center of the door. Luke stepped back and shielded his eyes as it was flung outward, the smell of smoke filling his nose.

"Mopping can be arranged for a select few, Mr. Hall, but I promise … it won't be fun."

Luke's eyes widened. In front of him stood a man only a few inches taller than he was, with a bald head, a white mustache, and a bit of a potbelly. He wore leather lace-up boots, khaki pants bloused around them, and a canvas field jacket open to the waist. He clutched a curved pipe between his teeth, and his bright brown eyes swept over the faces of the now-silent children. He narrowed his eyes at Luke before blowing a puff of smoke and looking away. "Now, since you all seem to have enough time to stand in the hallway and gab, perhaps we'll start the day with a quiz."

"But, s-s-sir, there wasn't any r-r-room number to m-m-mark the door," Marti squeaked as the man glared down at him.

Luke stepped up beside him. "And there wasn't any handle either, sir."

"Poppycock." The man closed the door partway so everyone could see the outside of it. "The number's right there."

There was nothing there.

"Sir, I s-s-still don't see a number."

The man scowled at Marti and reached out a fat sausage-like finger. "That's because you aren't"—Marti winced as the man tapped him on the head with each word—"using … your … head, Mr. Stegall." He turned around and rapped on the door three times with his knuckles. Luke's mouth hung open as whispered oohs and ahhs sounded behind him. The alphanumeric room number emerged in the center of the door and grew larger until a *7H* about the size of a small book rested there as if burned into the wood.

"And as for a piddling thing like a handle"—the man cocked his head and eyed Luke, Matt, and Marti in turn with a devious smile—"I doubt you boys let little obstacles such as *that* get in your way. Now, come along, lads … and gals. We've already wasted enough time for the day." With that, he disappeared into a cloud of smoke and shadows on the other side of the door.

Luke grabbed his backpack and jumped forward with the rest of the students. The shadows soon gave way to a yellow light like that of old gas lamps, but there were no gas lamps and, as far as Luke could tell, no lights in the room at all.

"I've never seen a classroom like this before," Matt whispered.

With the exception of a few long granite-topped tables in the center, every surface in the room was covered. There were piles of plain brown sandstone rocks, light-gray limestone with strange fossils imprinted into them, bright crystals of greens and purples and blues, and jars filled with murky fluids and floating objects barely seen. The bones of a winged creature with a tail and tooth-filled jaws floated overhead, rotating; Luke didn't see any strings holding it up. In another corner, what looked like a saber-toothed tiger skull peered at him, but with a small horn in the center of its forehead. And mixed in across the room were stacks and piles and rolls of yellowed parchment, all of it permeated by the sweet smell of tobacco.

The man stomped to the podium at the front of the room. He grimaced and mumbled something, searching the top of his desk, and the light in the room brightened. Lifting a pinch of dry tobacco leaves, he tapped his finger on the side of his pipe, and flames danced in the bowl. He puffed a few times and then turned to face the students. "I ... am Professor Lewis." The last of the students scrambled into the room and found seats as he spoke. "The goal of this class will be to introduce you to the profession of reading and making maps. Some of you may think you already know how to read maps." He scowled around the room. "You don't."

"Can we still take the learning-to-mop option?" Matt whispered to Luke, forcing him to stifle a laugh.

"A few, like you, Mr. Rayburn, will learn that maps from a holding, while similar in appearance, are often vastly different than maps from the outside." Luke felt heat rise to his cheeks as heads around the room turned to look at him. "Some of you"—Professor Lewis sighed—"hopefully, will gain at least a *meager* level of skill with the tools of the trade and how to create maps. But all of you will learn that maps"—he raised a finger—"especially certain kinds of maps, contain great power ... and by default, great danger." Snickers sounded around the room. "You will learn this"—he placed a hand behind his back and stepped toward the students, his face like a steam engine and his voice dropping to a whisper—"or you will not survive my class."

The snickers were cut short and dense silence descended on the room. Across the aisle, even Jamie Martin and Karlie Barnett were still, their bottoms fixed in their seats. The only noise came from the clicking gears of a beaten bronze-and-glass weather clock in the corner of the room. Clouds, light, and metal hands shifted inside the globe.

"Now"—Luke let out a breath as Professor Lewis turned back to the chalkboard—"I want you to pair up and go to the west side of the room and pull out the maps labeled 'CS Westcliffe Quad.'"

Luke nodded at Matt's nudge as Marti paired up with the tall skinny boy to his left, Jonathan Simmons. Luke glanced around the room and saw that one wall was lined with wooden racks filled with rolled parchments. He scrambled over with half the class, scanning the labels beneath each box in the rack.

"The title of each map is determined by the holding or area they are in and then the specific quadrant or section they cover. This can be deceptive at times, because many maps contain information and partial sections from areas not part of the quadrant that the map primarily covers."

Luke snagged a map from the rack and slipped back through the cluster of bodies to his wooden barstool seat next to Matt as Professor Lewis wheeled about to face them.

"In addition to this, often two maps that cover the same area in part will have unique information. The quality of the information is dependent upon the quality of the mapmaker. Notice I did not say the quality was dependent upon the quantity. You can have a great deal of information and it can be a great deal of rubbish. Mapmaking is a painstaking process if done correctly." He sneered. "And quite often there is an inverse correlation between the quality of a mapmaker and the quantity of the information that mapmaker puts into his maps." He harrumphed and puffed out a cloud of smoke. "Now, use the map weights to keep your map flat. Once you all have them rolled out, we will continue."

Luke helped Matt roll out the map and place four egg-size leather bags weighted with pebbles on each corner. After a few minutes of snarls and puffs of smoke from Professor Lewis and maps flapping in students' faces, the rustling died down.

"Today we are going to focus on …"

For the next thirty minutes, Professor Lewis took the students through the process of reading a map legend and the various indicators there. He talked about reading scale, the difference between the markings of a depression and those of a hill, and half a dozen other items. By five minutes before the bell, Luke felt beads of sweat forming on his forehead and information leaking out of his head at about the same rate as water from an overfull sponge.

"Lastly for today, just to make sure that Mr. Hall is not bored, we will walk through mapping tunnels." Professor Lewis pointed to a row of symbols drawn on the chalkboard. "Here you will see the seven symbols required to travel from Countryside to Stonewall Creek. Now, looking at your map, I want you to touch the traveling tunnel on the far southeast corner near Old Market Road. Using the light discipline, illuminate the image of that tunnel."

Luke looked at Matt.

"Just do it," Matt said.

Exclamations of surprise and whispers broke out around the room. Luke shrugged and touched the image of the traveling tunnel on the map.

Madleek.

He eased his hand away. Below the tunnel, the image of a stone appeared on the map, about the size of a silver holding coin. The stone glowed blue around the edges.

"Now, just as you would with an actual traveling tunnel, activate the symbols one at a time. You may either say them or draw them with a map pencil onto the image of the stone. However, if you draw them, make sure they are drawn correctly or you may find something other than what you were looking for."

Luke glanced up at the symbols and sketched in the first one, a horizontal line crossed by three others of varying lengths. The blue light intensified and faded. The symbol appeared just below the tunnel, and the stone looked blank again. Luke drew the next symbol. The light flared and faded, and the second symbol appeared next to the first. All around the room in tiny fountains, blue light burst up from maps.

As Luke got to the sixth symbol, he heard Marti's hushed voice. "Awesome."

Luke peered over at Marti and Jonathan's map, on which black lines, symbols, and letters shifted on the paper. After a few moments, the images settled and the last strokes of the title *Stonewall Creek Holding, Waters Quad* appeared. Luke blinked, but the map remained the same. "Wow."

He turned back to the chalkboard and then to the map in front of him. He sketched a straight line and two more at an angle and then set his map pencil down.

"Um, Luke," Matt said, "I don't think that—"

The arch glowed blue.

"Whoa!" Matt leaned away as the symbols turned to orange embers and smoke curled up from the map.

"Professor Lewis!" Luke called out across the room.

The professor turned from looking at a student's map on the other side of the room. Luke and Matt jumped back from the table as flames flared up from the parchment. Their stools crashed to the floor.

"*Lakhok!*"

The flames lowered and flickered out at the word from Professor Lewis, the roar of his voice echoing in Luke's ears. He stared at the table, his mouth hanging open. Bits of blackened paper drifted off the tabletop.

"Back away if you will, Mr. Rayburn."

Luke obeyed, slipping backward at the professor's hushed tone. Professor Lewis warily eyed the smoking map as he sidled across the room. His eyes narrowed, he whispered something and the ash on the table swirled. He ran his hand across the surface, collecting a pile of the ash. He raised it to his face and sniffed. Wrinkling his nose, he allowed the powder to sift through his fingers.

"Which of the two of you input the symbols?"

Luke hunched his shoulders. "I did, sir."

Professor Lewis nodded but never moved his eyes from the remnants of the map. He reached out to a larger piece of the map that remained mostly unburned and turned it over. "Please tell me *exactly* what you did, Mr. Rayburn, starting with illuminating the tunnel."

Luke swallowed. "Yes, sir. Well, I used the discipline ..."

He explained the illuminating of the map and the entering of each symbol and even how he watched Marti and Jonathan as they placed their last symbol. The professor said not a word. "And then I drew the curved part."

Luke started as Professor Lewis's head snapped up, his eyes bright. "What curved part, Mr. Rayburn?"

Luke felt sweat on his palms. "The bottom part of the ..." His throat went dry as he pointed toward the symbols written on the chalkboard. His eyes locked on the last symbol. *Oh, no ... I drew the wrong one.*

"Hmmm." Professor Lewis rubbed a hand over his mustache as whispers were heard across the room. Luke saw Matt wince out of the corner of his eye.

Tingggg ... Tinggggg ...

The bell chimed in the background and papers and backpacks were shuffled.

"Mr. Rayburn, you and Mr. Nichols will stay."

Luke sighed and closed his eyes. *Wonderful.*

Samantha gave a quick wave and mouthed "sorry" as she walked out with Jennifer. Marti remained standing by his stool, his face downcast. Professor Lewis turned and arched his eyebrows. "I don't recall asking you to stay, Mr. Stegall."

"No s-s-sir, but—"

"But as you will most likely find out whatever I say to these two in short order, you might as well." Marti snapped his mouth shut and the professor turned back to Luke. "Gentlemen, I assume you have no idea what happened just now?"

The boys shook their heads. "No, sir."

The professor gave a curt nod. "Well, let me tell you, the map was not booby-trapped, as you may suppose. I would most likely have discovered that when I inspected the maps prior to class, and if not, we most likely would not be having this conversation."

Luke shuddered as the professor glanced down at the burned parts of the map.

"What happened today is that you tried to look into an area not covered by the map." He hefted up his pants and stuck his thumbs in his belt loops. "That in and of itself is not that unusual. The result, however, is extremely rare. Normally, when you input a sequence of symbols for an area that the map does not cover, nothing happens. The map simply remains the same and you have to reenter the symbols." His face darkened and he leaned forward. "However, in very rare cases, the set of symbols you enter attempt to show you an area that has been concealed."

"Concealed, sir? You mean like hidden?"

"Yes, Mr. Rayburn, but even more than that. A place that has been *concealed* in the sense of the disciplines is far more … complete. There are probably less than a dozen places in all of history that have been concealed, though, of course, it's hard to be sure …"

As Luke listened, Matt and Marti and the clicking of the weather clock receded from his consciousness.

"*Concealing* a place takes an enormous effort, in part because of the massive power it takes to accomplish the feat, and in part because so few people have the ability to carry out the task. The more people you have involved, the harder it is to conceal a place, you understand?"

Luke nodded. *Not really.*

The professor snorted. "I doubt it. And you probably shouldn't. The point is that when a place — a building, a forest or mountain, a person or even a whole city — is concealed, for all practical purposes it ceases to exist."

Luke's heart beat faster.

"Oh, you can still find mention of it perhaps, but only cursory mention, and you can't actually find it … and therefore you can't find your way to whatever it is … not in history books or travel guides, and *not* on a map. And even more than that, when you try to find such a place, there are" — a gleam lighted the professor's eyes — "shall we say, consequences. In this case, the disciplines reacted by burning the map when you tried, albeit accidentally, to see that area."

"Is that what would happen with any map, sir?"

Professor Lewis put a finger to his lips and peered at the ceiling. "Hmmm, no, not necessarily." He looked back at the boys. "That would depend on who set up the concealment and how they set it up, as well as the mapmaker of the other map. I have only come across a reaction to concealment on two other occasions, each in a different way and with a different result."

Luke stood there staring off into the distance. *I wonder where those symbols lead.*

Tingggg … Tinggggg.

Luke came back to himself. He heard the clicking of the

weather clock again as wind rustled the leaves of a tree in the globe.

"The point, gentlemen, is that you need to be careful, and in your case, Mr. Rayburn, perhaps an extra dose would serve, hmmm?"

"Yes, sir."

"Now, off with you. And as much as any eighth-grade boy is able to keep this information to himself, please do. I won't take kindly to hearing talk of it in the halls, you understand?"

"Yes, sir."

Professor Lewis jerked his thumb toward the door and walked back toward the podium, mumbling. Luke crammed his papers into his backpack and scrambled toward the door. Just as he stepped across the threshold, Professor Lewis's voice halted him.

"Oh, and Mr. Rayburn ..."

Luke looked over his shoulder. "Yes, sir?"

"I suggest you do everything you can to try and forget that sequence of symbols you wrote today. Do you take my meaning?"

Luke shivered under the professor's scrutiny. "Yes ... yes, sir." He stood still for a moment, and his mind began to cloud. The professor's gaze never wavered.

What symbols?

"Luke."

Luke jumped at Matt's sharp whisper and leaped through the doorway. Matt let out a whistle as they walked down the corridor. After a few steps, he elbowed Luke in the side. "I told you to just say the words."

"No you didn't."

"Well, I thought it."

Marti guffawed, and Luke let out a long breath.

NINE

District Championship

Luke hopped down out of the back of the wagon and turned to grab one of the whiskey-barrel halves full of white corn. Matt snagged another beside him that was full of okra they'd picked early that morning.

"I think the third shower finally got the itch off my arms," Matt said.

Luke snorted and glanced at the short green pods. They lumbered over and lowered the containers to the ground at the direction of Luke's mother. After a few trips back and forth, the bed of the wagon sat bare.

"Mom, can we have—"

Luke grinned as his mother pulled out a few silver coins and tossed them to the boys with a wink. "Have fun. And try to stay away from dark alleys this year, hmmm?"

The boys ducked their heads, chagrined, as memories surfaced of stumbling into a pair of soulless the previous year. "Yes, ma'am."

As they turned toward the courthouse square, Luke stood still and stared for a moment. Pumpkins floated all around the square, their orange skin aglow. They swayed in the wind, with no visible strings attaching them to tree branches or storefronts.

"Come on, man," Matt said.

As torches flared to life along the streets, the boys dashed from one corner of the square to the other, although they kept their distance from the southwest corner, near the *Countryside Courier* office. From pumpkin tarts and pecan-caramel tassies at Cornelia's to howling geodes and staurolite warming sticks at Norm's, the boys passed treat after treat as they raced around the town square until joining up with Samantha, Jennifer, and Marti. Trent ran by with Parker Stegall, Marti Stegall's younger brother, calling over his shoulder, "Luke, look at this, look at this!"

Across Adams Avenue near the Stone—a square stone monument on the east side of the courthouse—a large crowd of kids stood in a semicircle. Luke crossed the street with his friends and saw a man facing the children. Luke stopped beside Trent and Parker and watched for a moment. The man wore brown leather shoes, the edges worn, too-short pants, a ratty wool coat and a flat cap. He alternated between standing and squatting, weaving his arm through the air and tracing with his finger.

Luke leaned down to Trent. "What's he doin—"

"Shhh." Trent put his finger to his lips, never taking his eyes off of the man. "Watch."

Luke frowned but buttoned his lip. As time passed and the sun dipped lower behind the roof of the courthouse, a quiet descended on the crowd. After several more minutes, the man stopped and dropped his arm to his side. He glanced around the audience with a wry grin. Luke cocked his head, and even the chittering of the birds and the squirrels receded. Luke felt himself holding his breath along with the rest of the crowd.

What's he waiting on?

The man's grin spread to the audience, and his hand inched up from his side until it pointed to a spot in the air near his waist. He gave a twitch of his finger and the crowd erupted. "Ohh!"

The air in Luke's lungs rushed out and his mouth dropped open. "Wow."

Spreading from the man's finger, lines of light raced in every direction, curving and twisting through the air. Strands of brown light thickened and coiled shooting up and then plummeting back down before burrowing into the ground. Green light popped up in places and faded to a yellow gold, flattening, spreading out, curling, and drooping back down. The form took shape and Luke shook his head as the last arch of light sparkled and swayed into place. "Amazing."

Matt smiled. "Every time." He glanced at Luke. "Not something you see *outside*, I take it?"

Luke shook his head. In front of the crowd now stood a weeping willow that reached to the second story of the courthouse. Gold light sparkled along its spiral leaves much like after Mr. Jacobs, the city gardener, finished with the rose bushes along the sides of the courthouse. Luke stole a look at Samantha's face under the glow of the light. Some of the adults stepped forward, and flashes of silver and copper dropped into a basket beside the man, each accompanied by a "my thanks" and a tip of his cap. After a few more minutes, the man waved his hand back and forth in the air, and the willow drifted away in a fog, carried across the courthouse lawn by the wind. Smiles faded and oohs and aahs sounded until the man winked and began weaving his finger through the air again.

"Let's go get some cider and then come back," Matt said. "This will take him a few minutes anyway."

Luke nodded and looked to his side as Matt and Marti walked across the street. *Where'd she go?* He scanned the crowd until he spotted Samantha. *Now, what's she doing talking to* him?

Toward the north side of the courthouse lawn, Samantha stood with her arms crossed talking with Jon David. Jennifer stood between them with her back to Luke.

Sam doesn't look very happy. And Jon David doesn't either, but then, he hardly ever does.

Samantha shook her head at something Jon David said. She pointed back toward Luke and froze when her eyes met his.

Uh-oh ... busted.

Luke jerked his head away as Jon David and Jennifer turned toward him. He stepped away from the crowd and crossed back to the other side of the street, where Mr. Volf's bear-paw-size hand was waving him over. The man grinned and poured Luke a cup of steaming amber liquid. Mr. Volf's mother stood nearby scowling and stirring one of the other pots.

"I see you are enjoying the t'sabeem's work across the way," Mr. Volf said.

Luke frowned. "T'sabeem, sir?"

"Ah, yes, that is what we call those who do that for a living in a holding." He paused in his stirring and then, coming back to himself, peered down at Luke. "I believe on the outside you call them street artists, or perhaps painters."

"Ohh ... yes, sir." Luke took a sip of the cider and felt warmth run down his throat.

"Well, what a pleasant surprise. Mayeem, it is good to see you."

Luke turned to see his water-elements teacher strolling toward them in a green gown.

"William, so very good to see you. I wish you a good evening."

Mr. Volf's deep voice danced as he handed her some cider. "And you as well, my lady."

Mayeem smiled, her eyes brightening, and glanced down at Luke and his friends. "And how are we tonight, young ones?"

"Good, ma'am … Good, thank you … Good," five voices replied, and Luke looked to his left at the sound of Samantha's. She smiled, quickly brushing back her hair over her ear, but Jennifer stood beside her with a sullen look on her face.

Luke whispered out the side of his mouth as Mr. Volf introduced Mayeem to his mother. "You OK?"

Samantha nodded. "Yeah, it's nothing."

Sure didn't look like nothing.

Mayeem smiled and looked around the square. "It has been too many years since I have attended one of the human holding festivals."

"I hope this one has not disappointed?" Mr. Volf said.

Mayeem smiled and laughed, the sound sending goose bumps up Luke's arms. "No, William, it is very much to my liking."

Luke listened to them talk for a few minutes until he felt pressure on his arm. He turned to see Samantha half-smiling. "You wanna go back over and watch the t'sabeem?"

He looked around, but Matt and Marti were talking to Mr. Volf and peering into one of the cider vats, and Jennifer was asking Mayeem about her necklace. Luke turned back to Samantha.

She's not gonna hurt you, Rayburn, jeez.

He felt his head bobbing up and down, his thoughts of Samantha and Jon David's conversation fading like the morning mist. "Sure. Yeah." He sucked in a deep breath and stepped off the sidewalk beside her. He moved across the street as if he were lining up for the first kickoff of a football game, with hippos dancing to the tunes of a mariachi band in his stomach. Samantha smiled at him.

Just relax! No one's here to interrupt this time ... Luke took a deep breath. *OK, Rayburn, now is when you say something. Just tell her you like her!*

"Sam, um, I ... I wanted to ..."

"What!?"

Luke froze with one foot up on the sidewalk as Samantha turned in the direction of the shout. *You've got to be kidding!* He turned around to see Uncle Landon and one of the holding guardsmen standing near Mr. Volf and Mayeem. As Uncle Landon spoke, a cold storm passed across Mr. Volf's face, and Mayeem's shoulders sagged. Samantha looked questioningly at Luke with arched eyebrows. Luke sighed and nodded and they walked back over to where Matt, Marti, and Jennifer stood in a huddle.

"Matt, what happened?"

Matt looked at Luke with round eyes as more heads in the surrounding crowd turned toward the front of Volf's pharmacy. "Captain Rayburn just got a report from one of the Guard patrols that Mayeem's house was destroyed."

Marti's head bobbed up and down. "S-s-said it was b-b-burned to the ground."

"Burned! Was it an accident?" Four faces turned to stare at Luke. "What? What'd I say?"

"Mermaids don't exactly get along with fire, Luke," Matt said.

"They hardly ever use it or are around it on their own if they can avoid it," Samantha said. "It's ... I doubt it was started by accident."

Luke saw his mother rest her arm on Mayeem's shoulders. "Why ... why would someone burn her house down?"

Marti snorted. "The s-s-same reason the school receives so m-m-many complaints about Samech."

"I didn't know people complained about Samech," Luke said. "Don't people like him?"

Matt sighed. "Marti means because they aren't completely human, a lot of people don't like them, and they especially don't like them teaching their kids."

"There's a reason they're called half-creatures, you know," Jennifer said.

At the sound of her voice, Luke recalled walking into Countryside School for the first time. "Oh, yeah, half-creatures. I remember that from when I signed—"

"Shhh!" Matt, Marti, and Samantha all hissed.

Luke started. "What? Jeez."

Matt glared at Jennifer. "*Half-creatures* is a term lots of people use to degrade folks like Mayeem and Samech. It's as if you're saying they're just like ... well, it would be like saying Samech is like ... well ... like he's only part-human."

"Which is true!" Jennifer scoffed.

"But that doesn't mean he's only *worth* half a human, and that's what people mean." Samantha's voice sounded like the wings of a butterfly, but her face was carved of ice.

Luke frowned. "But I didn't mean—I mean, how could someone even think that?"

Matt shook his head. "A lot of people don't, but the point is *some* do."

"Why's it on the school sign-up sheets I had to fill out last year, then?"

"Because a few years ago some people convinced the Elder Council to do it. They said it was important to know if kids or their families that moved into the holding had contact with any half-creatures, in case they were dangerous." Disbelief filled Matt's voice. "The vote barely passed, and a lot of other holdings in the district were upset about it."

Jennifer crossed her arms and sulked. "Not all of them."

Matt glowered at her. "But most of them ... and the council has never had the votes to take it back off, or they just don't care enough. Mom says we're really lucky that Samech, and Mayeem and others like them, are willing to still come and teach here at all."

"Not everyone thinks we're lucky to have them here, you know!" Jennifer said and stomped away.

Samantha cocked her head and sighed, her face softening. "Nice ... I'd better go after her." She looked at Luke and opened her mouth but then shut it and turned and jogged into the crowd.

"Luke. Matt."

Luke's father was standing behind them on the sidewalk, his face like stone.

I've seen that look before ... Not good. "Yes, sir."

"We need to get home."

"Yes, sir," The boys waved good-bye to Marti and trudged behind Luke's father back to the wagon in the dirt lot across Hanover Avenue. They helped load in a few crates of squash and some jars of clover honey before jumping in with the rest of Luke's family. The trip back home was quiet except for the sucking sound of the traveling tunnel, the crunching of gravel beneath the wheels, and the occasional giggles of Jon or Amy.

Forty minutes later, as they rode under the emptying sycamore and pecan branches along Rayburn Road, Matt leaned over to Luke. "I don't think it was someone who just didn't like Mayeem who burned her house down," he whispered.

"What? Why?"

Pale moonlight and shadows crossed Matt's face. "I heard Captain Rayburn say something to your father as we were loading up the crates." Luke winced as the wagon rolled over a bump. "I didn't hear everything, but I heard enough … He said they found bane wolf tracks all around the place … bane wolf tracks and the boot prints of one man."

A gruff voice filled Luke's head, along with the memory of flashing yellow eyes. In the distance he heard the searching cry of a barred owl.

Hoo, hoo, too-HOO. Hoo, hoo, too-HOO.

As Matt leaned back on his seat, cold filled Luke's chest.

The hunter.

Noise roared in Luke's ears. His heart hammered, his eyes darting back and forth. The smell of cut grass, sweat, and sizzling meat filled his nose. Beside him girls in green skirts and tights jumped and screamed, and across the field boys in padded uniforms stood in a cluster and yelled.

So many people.

Groups of four to eight beige-uniformed guardsmen in jackets clustered around the field, and both sides of the stadium were filled with people pressing against the fences. Matt shoved him a few paces down the sideline, grinning and shouting. "It's always a little crazy when San Leon comes here to play," he said, "even more now for the district championship."

"Why are there so many guardsman this time?"

"Wha—" Matt frowned and then his mouth formed an O. He pointed across the field to the north end of the stands. "That's why."

Luke looked where Matt pointed and stared for a minute.

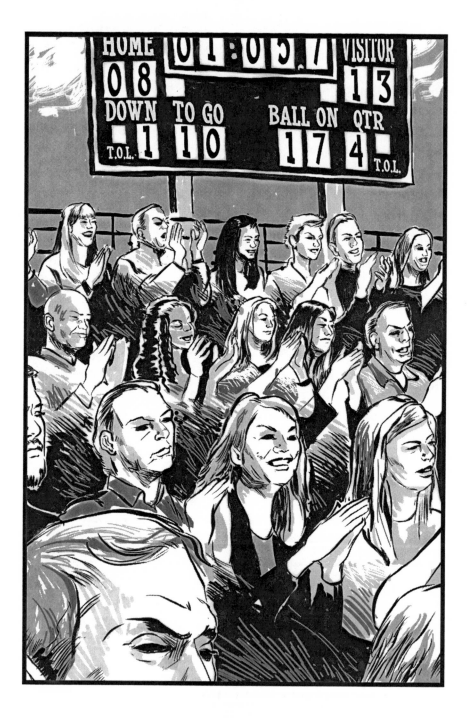

Then he scanned the stands, where purple-black haze popped out at him and then vanished.

How did I not see them before?

Darkmen. Interspersed throughout the visitors' side were men and women who practiced with darkness.

"Normally when we play San Leon, the Elder Council doesn't let darkmen in, but we haven't played for the district championship, even if it's junior high, in a long time either," Matt said. "I guess since it's for the championship they decided to let them."

"Rayburn, Davis!" Coach Wilson bellowed down the sideline.

Matt thumped him on the shoulder. "Try to get the coin toss right this time!"

Luke smirked. "I'll see what I can do." He jogged over to Coach Wilson and listened to his instructions before loping out onto the field.

The head official stepped up to the boys, his face grim. "Boys, this is my field now." He glowered at Luke and Johnny and then across at the San Leon boys. "No matter what happens off the field, we're gonna have a clean game tonight."

Ha. Tell that to "Too Tall" and the "troll" over there. Luke scowled back at the San Leon boys. *I'm pretty sure they've never even heard the word* sportsmanship.

"Are we clear, gentlemen?"

"Yes, sir." Luke and Johnny answered. The San Leon players nodded.

"Good. San Leon, call it in the air."

Luke watched the silver arc toward the sky.

Two hours later the scoreboard read 1:05 in the fourth, Spartans 8, Blackhawks 13.

Wham!

Luke crashed to the ground beneath a defender.

Tweet! Tweeeeeeeet!

He shoved the San Leon player off him. Get *off me, you big oaf.* He struggled to his feet and tossed the ball to the referee. The seconds were ticking off the scoreboard clock.

Not enough time.

Jogging back to the huddle, Luke wiped blood off his arm onto his pants and sweat off his brow.

"Nice catch, Luke." Luke nodded as voices greeted him between gasps of breath. Jeremy Hall ran over to the sidelines and then back out. A long cut crossed the right side of his face, and more cuts zigzagged across his hands. Luke nodded to him and Jeremy winked in return as he stepped into the huddle. "All right, let's go," he said. "Thirty more yards and we win. Easy day, right? Here we go: I Right 42 Lead on two, I Right 42 Lead on two."

"Break!"

Luke jogged to the line of scrimmage.

"Dowwwn ... seeet ... hut ... hut!"

Smack!

Luke collided with the Blackhawk defender, wedging his head between him and the play.

Tweet! Tweeeeeeeet!

Red-faced and blowing their whistles, officials dashed in and pulled players apart and shoved them back to their respective huddles. Luke jerked away from the defender and snorted.

So much for a clean game.

Three more plays found the Spartans on the five-yard line with three seconds left on the clock. Luke stood in the huddle with his hands behind his head, sucking in air. Between the yelling from the stands and the thundering in his ears, his head was about to explode. Jeremy stepped into the huddle and his eyes met Luke's. "One more time, Rayburn."

Luke closed his eyes and nodded.

"Easy slant out ... nothing fancy ... Twins right."

Luke sucked in one last breath and jogged to the line.

"Dowwwn ..."

His heart tried to hammer its way out of his chest.

"Seeet ..."

Five steps and out ... don't slip, don't slip.

"Hut ..."

Luke's muscles tightened.

"Hut!"

Luke surged forward, his feet slamming down. *Three, four, five, left!* He looked over his shoulder. *There it is.* His eyes tracked the ball as it arced down. *Got it!* He turned around and —*wham!*—darkness filled his vision.

Pain exploded in his head and neck. He felt his feet lift off the ground, and then nothing. Lights flashed up and down. Noise. Shouts.

Slam!

Luke's body collided with the field. "Uhhh ..." He blinked and rolled his head around. Bodies jostled him on both sides. Cleats pressed down on his arm, drawing a shout from his throat. "Ah!"

Tweet! Tweet! Tweet! Tweeeeeeeet!

"Luke! Luke, you all right?" Jeremy knelt beside him and shook him. "Luke!"

Luke shrugged him off. "Yeah! If you would quit ... making my teeth ... rattle." All around them officials darted this way and that. Green and black jerseys jostled back and forth.

"Spartans! Back on the sideline!" Luke winced as Coach Wilson's voice crashed down on him. The wave of players split and receded. Coach Jackson knelt beside Luke. "You all right, son?"

"Yes, sir. I think so."

"Hall, get him back to the sidelines."

"Yes, sir. Come on, lug." Luke blinked again and swallowed as he struggled to his feet. He leaned on Jeremy and half-walked, half-stumbled back to the sidelines.

My face ...

"What happened? It feels like someone hit me in the face with a hammer."

Jeremy snorted. "Someone did. The Blackhawk linebacker clotheslined you and dang near took your head off. You flipped around like a rag doll, man."

Great. Everybody saw that ... Samantha saw. "What about the ball? What happened? I know I had it. Did I get across ..."

Jeremy frowned and shook his head as he lowered Luke down on the bench and Matt and several others rushed over. "Nah, man, they got it."

Luke's heart dropped.

"Hey, man, you OK?" Matt asked.

Tweet!

Luke turned to see the head official in the middle of the field. His voice boomed throughout the stadium. "Personal foul, number 25. There's no fumble on the play. Half the distance to the goal, first down. Please reset the clock to three seconds."

Boos thundered from the San Leon stands and Matt's face darkened. "Yeah, of course, no penalty *there.* Idiots."

Coach Wilson turned away from the sideline official, quivering. "Offense!"

Luke was shaking as he pushed up off the bench. Coach Jackson appeared and pushed him back down. "You're done tonight, son. Just sit."

"But, Coach—"

"Sit."

Luke sighed but eased back down, blinking. *Can't see straight anyway.*

Derrick Hamilton ran the ball on the last play but missed the goal line by inches. The San Leon sidelines erupted. Guardsmen spilled onto the field from both end zones, eyes darting back and forth.

"Your uncle looks l-l-like he's been chewing on a m-m-mouthful of sand."

Luke squinted in the direction that Marti was looking. Uncle Landon stomped up and down the field, his face dark. Luke sighed. "This is gonna be a long night for him, I bet."

A couple of hours later, Luke toted his bag over his shoulder and shuffled toward his father, who stood grinning beside the carriage. He nodded a greeting toward Mr. Brunson sitting in the driver's seat as his father took his bag and tossed it inside. "Been an interesting evening, son," his father said as they climbed in.

Luke guffawed. "That's one word for it, Dad."

"Grandma says she thinks you're fine, although she had a few choice words to say about the whole thing."

"Yeah, she wouldn't even wait on me to come out of the locker room. She came in along with Dr. Rush. Half the team wasn't even dressed yet."

Luke's father chuckled as the carriage rolled forward. "Hmmm … yes, she's a bit defensive when it comes to family. Luckily, Dr. Rush has a pretty high opinion of her skills … and her temper."

Luke smiled. He talked with his father about the game and rehashed the last few seconds as they wheeled their way home.

"And Derrick swears he felt like all his energy just vanished right before the snap."

Luke's father frowned. "Hmmm … that sounds like something I've heard of with a combination of darkness and life, but I would think the Guard or someone would have noticed darkness or even any of the true disciplines being used … I'll mention it to Uncle Landon, though."

They rode in silence, winding their way toward Westcliffe Forest and home. After a few minutes, Luke looked over at his father. "Dad, why did the Elder Council decide to let darkmen into the holding tonight?"

His father grunted. "Because half of them are a bunch of cowards and blind old fools that allowed themselves to be misled." He took a deep breath. "Forgive me, Luke, that's not fair; I'm just a bit sensitive when it comes to decisions that put our family, or any others for that matter, at risk … especially unnecessarily. They had their hearts in the right spot, Luke. At least some of them did, I hope, but they … just made the wrong decision. They wanted to reach out to any darkmen who might listen, but in my experience there are very few darkmen who ever do. You see, it's not the darkmen themselves that cause Countryside and other holdings to refuse them entrance. It's their refusal to abide by the laws and their continuing to go their own direction"—he sighed—"despite obvious damage to the communities they live in … and themselves."

Luke sat back, staring at the opposite side of the carriage. The white light of the moon darkened outside as a cloud passed in front of it. "Is that why there were so many guardsmen out tonight, because the Elder Council didn't think the darkmen would follow the laws?"

Luke's father chuckled. "Yes, Luke, that's why, but it still didn't stop them from trying, possibly on more than one occasion."

Luke sat forward. "What do you mean, Dad?"

His father rubbed the sides of his head. "Well, I'm sure you'll find out about it soon enough … One of the patrols of guardsmen found two darkmen using darkness tonight. They were along the Algid, and the guardsmen managed to stop them, but …" He shook his head.

"What were they doing?"

His father stared across the carriage. "We're not sure … They didn't get anything done. It looked like they were trying to combine water or earth and darkness somehow, but to what end …" He seemed to come back to himself. "It's nothing for you to worry about, Luke. They didn't get anything accomplished, and I think the Elder Council will be a bit more reluctant to let darkmen in any time soon." He reached over and ruffled Luke's hair and pulled him into a crushing embrace. "All that aside, I'm very proud of you, son. You did a great job tonight … and you got up even when you were knocked down pretty hard … Very proud of you."

Luke smiled and felt a warmth in his chest that had nothing to do with his pendant. He sat quietly beside his father for the last couple of miles of the ride. At the house, he stumbled up to his room, snuffed out the candle on his writing desk next to his journal and fell into bed. As he stared at the embers in the fireplace and listened to Trent's breathing, his thoughts became more and more disjointed. Two very clear questions managed to flit into his head before sleep overtook him, though.

What are they trying to do combining darkness with the other disciplines? And what does that have to do with what the hunter is looking for?

TEN

Mr. Roberts's Warning

Luke crouched behind the McCartney rose hedge. He filled his lungs and exhaled and then repeated the process, but his hands still quivered as they held the limbs of his bow. Out of the corner of his eye, he saw Uncle Landon standing at the edge of a cedar tree, stock still.

Just a few more yards …

Fifteen yards away, the turkey turned its head from side to side. Black breast feathers covered the tom's chest.

Gobble, gobble gobble.

Luke saw Uncle Landon move the turkey call in his hand.

Cluck, cluck, purr.

The turkey glanced toward the cedar tree. Luke felt the wind on the side of his face and heard chirping in the background. Sweat formed on his forehead as the sun rose higher.

He's not buying it.

Luke eased his hand over the fletching, feeling for the nock of the arrow. The bird stepped toward the cedar tree and froze.

Cluck, purr, cluck, purr.

Gobble, gobble gobble.

Luke held his breath as the turkey looked straight at him.

A little closer …

The tom turned and walked a few paces away from Luke and Uncle Landon. Luke's legs throbbed. The turkey kept walking.

Now or never, Luke.

He raised his bow, clipping a branch on the way up, and pulled back on the string.

Gobble, gobble gobble.

The turkey ran as Luke loosed his arrow, which flew high and to the right. At the same time, a shaft of light whizzed across the meadow from where Uncle Landon stood.

Gobble, gobble, gob—

Luke shook his head as the bird went down beneath the top of the grass.

Weeks of practice and I miss twice this morning!

Uncle Landon waded through the knee-high blades. He walked up to Luke and patted him on the shoulder. "Considering how little time you've spent practicing, that was pretty good, Luke."

"I missed twice this morning, Uncle Landon. How is that good?"

His uncle grinned and tightened his grip. "Because you tried. We'll practice some more and next time you'll get one, you'll see."

"I still wish you would teach me how to make my bow and arrows out of the disciplines like you do."

Uncle Landon sighed. "There is a time for everything, Luke. This is just not the time for that. Right now you need to focus on your lessons with Q. He tells me you and Matt are progressing."

Th-thump, th-thump, th-thump.

They turned toward the sound.

"Samech!" Luke said.

The centaur returned his greeting with a smile. He bent down and then straightened up again, and as he approached from the edge of the meadow, Luke saw that he was carrying Uncle Landon's turkey by its feet. "A good morning to you, young one. And how is your first hunt going?"

"Terrible. I missed two turkeys this morning and scared off another one. If Uncle Landon wouldn't have been here, we wouldn't have much of anything for Thanksgiving tonight."

A wry smile crept onto Samech's face as he dropped the turkey into the canvas bag Uncle Landon held open. "Hmmm … I remember my first hunt. We were hunting lions in the mountains and—"

"Lions?!"

Samech chuckled. "Yes, yes, but not very big ones, and a good thing, too. I slipped and fell, dropping my spear. Had my father not been there, I would most likely not be here talking to you. You seem to have managed to stay on your feet and keep hold of your weapon … Altogether not a bad outing, I would say, hmm?" Samech raised his eyebrows.

"I guess, sir. I'm just glad *we* weren't hunting lions, big or small."

Uncle Landon and Samech chuckled, and the three turned to the south, away from the junipers, hickories, and scattered mesquite trees on the edge of Westcliffe Forest.

"So, you will be joining us tonight then, Samech?"

"Yes, most of my brethren have returned to the clan for the winter months. There are some … troubling rumors."

Uncle Landon's face darkened. "Mmm … those seem to be everywhere … but"—a smile appeared as he looked up at Samech—"we will certainly be glad for your presence. Perhaps Katherine will have better luck than I did last time convincing you to play for us tonight. She's been very eager to hear you, and you'll find she can be quite persuasive when she wants something."

Samech dipped his head but said nothing. They walked back across an open meadow covered in oats as cattle grazed to the east. Archer looked up and trotted over to Luke, who was whistling to him. Luke grinned and patted him on the side as he pulled up into the saddle. Uncle Landon mounted beside him and tied the last turkey to his saddle horn along with a couple of others from earlier that morning. Luke glanced at Samech and then back down at Archer as they continued toward Rayburn Manor.

That's so strange … How could anyone think they're only worth half?

They rode along for a few more minutes, talking about the hunt and the cooler-than-normal temperatures. The manor rooftop rose into view along with a red-tailed hawk winging its way across their path, and then both disappeared again as the trail descended to cross a small creek. Luke splashed across, grinning and laughing alongside his uncle. Suddenly, a thought passed through Luke's mind and a large ball of water shot up at his uncle, who only barely raised his arm in time.

"I think perhaps you're learning a little too much from Mayeem, Luke," he said, shaking water out of the sleeve of his coat.

"Sorry, Uncle." Luke straightened his face, but a chuckle escaped.

Uncle Landon cocked his head with a mischievous grin.

"Wha … whoa, ah-ha, ah-ha, ah-ha," Luke spluttered as water cascaded down over him and Archer.

"Laugh at me, will you? You don't have the upper hand yet, nephew."

Samech snorted and laughed as they continued along. "And will Mayeem be present tonight, Landon?"

"No, I'm afraid not. She seems to have been called away on some errand or other. I think she's still recovering her items and moving them to the new house on the shore of Granite Lake." He barked a laugh, his mouth twisted. "I would've loved to see the surprise on those bast—" He coughed. "On their faces as they watched all her possessions sink into the lake."

Luke frowned. "What sunk into the lake, Uncle Landon?"

Uncle Landon grinned. "Mayeem set her house up so that when the dark creatures attacked it, all of her most important belongings were sealed and transported to the bottom of Granite Lake. Pretty hard to get them there"—his smile faded—"but I'm not sure it will work twice. I plan on talking to her again about posting a guard when she returns … She's as stubborn as … well, as a woman."

Samech chuckled and pursed his lips. "Nothing too serious called her away, I hope. No trouble from … home?"

Uncle Landon exchanged a glance with Samech. "No, not that I'm aware of, just … a previous engagement."

Luke smirked behind them. *Yeah, right. You expect me to believe that?*

For a few moments, there was only the clopping of horses' hooves and the dashing of a couple of scissortails across their path, twisting and turning in the air.

"Uncle Landon, where is Mayeem from? Mr. White said she lived in the Midway Islands."

"Hmmm ..." His uncle turned from looking at the red winter wheat in the field beyond and arched his eyebrows. "Oh, yes, but her clan is from the Misty Isles. She was born and raised there."

"The Misty Isles? Where are those?"

"Off the coast of the Carolinas, I believe. Isn't that correct, Samech?"

Samech nodded as they rounded a bend in their path and the Rayburn house filled their view. "Yes, it's a cluster of a half-dozen or so islands." The centaur furrowed his brow. "Though I think the mermaids only inhabit a few of them."

"And why are they called the Misty Isles? That sounds spooky."

Samech chortled. "Because, young one, mist covers at least a part of them each day. I think the mermaids would be glad to hear your opinion of their name, though. They have worked hard for many centuries to keep the interest of the outside world at bay, almost to the point of secluding themselves from even other holdings."

Secluded ... Why does that—

Luke's mind flashed back to the stone table at school, and Marti's voice echoed through his head. His body quivered as they walked the horses into the stables. After dumping the tack into a wooden chest and running a brush over Archer's coat a couple of times, he sprinted out of the stables and up to the family quarters. Trent's head popped up from a book as Luke flung open the door to his room, sucking air into his lungs.

"Luke! Did y'all get anything?"

Luke leaped toward his writing desk and riffled through the papers on top.

Trent frowned and closed the book. "You OK, Luke?"

"Yeah ... Know I put it somewhere here."

Trent sat up on his bed, scratching his head. "Put what where?"

Luke pulled open the top drawer. "You know the poem that Marti found that I showed you a while back?"

"Yeahhh ... you've looked at it, like, a thousand times."

Luke shoved the drawer shut and pulled open another. "Well, I need to look at it again ... to check someth—ah-ha!" He pulled out a piece of paper folded into a square. Moving papers, books, and a map aside, he smoothed the paper on the desk and sat in the chair. Trent walked across the room and stood looking over Luke's shoulder.

"Here"—Luke pointed to the paper—"you see these two words, *secluded* and *mist*?"

"Yeah, so? I know they're supposed to mean something or whatever."

Luke shook his head. "You and Matt really need to learn to trust Marti more ... There's something different about them, like the author was trying to tell us something, and I think I know what now."

Trent's body stilled and his eyes focused on Luke.

"You know how Marti said he thought the word *secluded* was italicized to mean the boat went to an island?"

Trent nodded.

"And you know how he never figured out why the word *mist* was italicized?"

Trent nodded again, but slowly.

"Well, this morning as we were finishing hunting, Samech showed up, and on the way home he and Uncle Landon got to talking about Mayeem and where her home was."

Trent's head stopped moving.

"Samech described the place she lived as *secluded*."

"Where did she live?"

"The Misty Isles." Luke grinned as Trent's eyes widened. "I think the Tears were taken to the Misty Isles and given to the mermaids, and I bet *that*"—he jabbed his finger into the desktop—"is why the hunter destroyed her house. He thinks Mayeem knows where the Tears are."

Luke and Matt glanced down at the first floor as the library doors swung open. Trent rushed across the stone and wood floors and up the main stairs to where they were. "Mom said about ten more minutes and we have to be down in the dining hall, Luke."

Luke turned back to the leather-bound book in front of him. He stood in front of the south wall facing towering columns of books. Amid the books hung a painting of two wooden-hull ships engaged in battle, with cannonballs flying under thick clouds.

"Have y'all found anything?"

"No."

"Well, not about the Misty Isles anyway," Matt said, "but I found a pretty cool book—*Gladiators: The Last Players to Use the Disciplines*. It's about how they used to play football with the disciplines"—he pointed to one of the illustrations—"and why they stopped."

Trent recoiled. "Ouch."

"I know, right?"

"Matt!"

Matt snapped the book shut and put it back. "Sorry."

Luke sighed. "Just check out the next couple books on the list and then we're gonna have to go."

Matt and Trent scanned the piece of paper lying on the

library table. Luke turned around and replaced the book. "Now ... 6009b, 6009b ..." He ran his finger along the books' spines.

"I'm pretty sure this library is why Mom likes to spend so much time over here," Matt said.

Luke snorted. "Right. Nothing to do with Uncle Landon."

"I mean, it must have taken a lifetime to collect all the *junk* in here!"

Luke laughed. "Grandpa says the collection has grown in the family for generations, and I'll make sure to tell your mom what you think of all this 'junk.'" After a moment, his finger stopped at 6009b. "All right, let's see." He pulled out the book. "*The Extraordinary Mines of the Betoolat.*" He shook his head. "How could this have anything to do with mermaids?" He flipped it open and scanned the list of chapters in the table of contents. "'Techniques for Mining Underwater' ... 'Mining Matekhet' ... 'Resources for Mining' ..." His finger froze toward the bottom of the page. "'The Lost Island' ... hmm. Page 253." He thumbed through the book until he came to that page. He flipped the page over and then back again. "Only one paragraph ... weird. Oh well." He lifted the book up and read silently:

The Lost Island of the Betoolat is a legend to most, but according to some it contained the greatest of the Matekhet mines. The island was supposedly part of the Misty Isles holding and vanished some time ago, although even the date of its disappearance ranges from a thousand years ago to within the last century. The location of the island and the size of her mines vary equally. Many suggest the tale of the Lost Island is based upon Plato's Atlantis *or some other tale from outside the holdings, others that it is one of the handful of locations truly* concealed.

Either way, the subject is one to be covered by another book, and for those curious, much information can be found in Rudbeck's The Lost Island of the Betoolat. *At least as far as this author is concerned, however, the Lost Island does not exist, and its mention is merely used to spur on treasure seekers or to entertain one's imagination.*

Luke's heart hammered as he reread the paragraph. He jerked his head up. "Matt! Trent! I think I found something." The boys scooted close together as Luke showed them the paragraph. His leg twitched as they read.

"I don't know, Luke, just because—"

"Come on, man. Think about it. The poem talks about an island shore and mist. This is an island covered in mist that probably was concealed."

Matt shook his head. "No, the poem says secluded or whatever, not anything about an island, and this author says some people think this lost island, *if* it even existed, *might* have been concealed. We're going a lot on what Marti said, Luke."

"Well, do you trust him or not?"

"Well, yeah, but—"

"We don't have anything else to go on right now."

Matt stared at Luke for a moment and then sighed. "You're right, but for the record, I don't think we're gonna find the Tears, whatever they are, on some lost island."

Luke grinned. "Duly noted."

Trent tapped him on the shoulder. "Uh, Luke, time's up."

Luke looked at the clock on the wall. "All right." They shelved the few books stacked on the library table and dashed down to the first floor and out of the library. Down stairs and across hallways they ran before bursting through the doors to the dining hall and sliding to a stop. Servants scurried to and fro. Light from candles, fires, and a few sela'or reflected off the long dining table in the middle of the room. Samech stood talking with Uncle Landon and Luke's father, and Jon and Amy stood near a wall fidgeting and stealing glances between the adults and the table. It was there that Luke's gaze fixed.

"Whew, made it. Look at all the food, and—"

"Not quite." Luke's mother was striding toward them from across the room.

"Uh-oh."

She stopped in front of the three boys, green eyes flashing.

"Mom, I'm sorry, we were in the library looking for a book and …" Luke swallowed the last of his words as his mother cocked her head. *She looks like a chicken or something eyeing a big bug.*

"Your grandfather isn't back yet and we'll wait on him to eat, but when I tell you to be somewhere at a certain time, particularly when we have guests, I expect that you will be there"—she looked the boys up and down—"and be present-able. Understand?"

Luke looked down at the wrinkles covering his clothes.

All three boys nodded. "Yes, ma'am."

She gave a curt nod and swept them with a glare before gliding past them. A few paces away, though, she stopped and turned with a roguish smile. "Oh, and boys, don't even *think* about touching the food."

They all dropped their heads.

She whirled around and walked away. Luke's stomach grumbled and he groaned. "That's got to be illegal to make us just stand here and smell everything but not be able to eat it."

They trudged over to stand beside Jon and Amy and the crackling fire. A few minutes later the doors leading toward the entrance hall opened and Grandpa Rayburn walked in.

"All right! Now we can eat!" Luke said.

"I see you couldn't convince Jeremiah to come in tonight, Dad."

Grandpa Rayburn shook his head. "No, the story is always the same ... other places still to go tonight."

Luke's father looked at his brother. "His reasons are still his own."

Uncle Landon stared back unblinking. "And not for us to decide."

The room quieted.

What does that mean?

At the sound of the opening of the door on the east side of the room, all heads swiveled in that direction. Clearly not expecting all the attention, the young servant girl squeaked and froze.

Ms. Lucy's voice broke the hold on the room. "What is it, Joanna?" The housekeeper glided over to the young girl and Luke turned back to the fire. Trent and Matt started a conversation about the most recent high school football game. Luke listened for a moment, but his mind strayed and his feet moved back and forth. He looked over at his mother, now conferring with Ms. Lucy.

Doesn't seem like everything is quite ready. I'll just walk down the hallway and back ... so I don't have to sit here and be tortured.

Luke slipped away from the fire and out the south doors. As he meandered down the hallway, his thoughts turned to Mr. Roberts, wondering about his father's and uncle's comments. *He seems so strange ... almost like he's not human.* He snorted. *And I guess here that's a distinct possibility.*

Green eyes filled Luke's head as he shuffled through an open door and into the entrance hall. Luke watched his feet move forward step by step.

Sometimes it seems like Dad and everybody else have known him forever ... and sometimes like they've never met him before and don't even know who he is.

A breeze blew across Luke's face and he raised his head.

"Whoa!"

He started as luminous green eyes stared down at him.

"Mr. Roberts. I th-th-thought you left already." *Jeez, where did he come from. Give me heart failure.* He squirmed under Mr. Roberts's gaze. His eyes burned through Luke so that he wondered how they'd ever looked kind or comforting. Luke opened his mouth and then closed it.

Probably one of those times that Dad talks about when it's good just to keep my mouth shut.

"There are some things in this world, Luke Rayburn, that are worth searching for. Some things, whether object or idea, need to be found."

"Y-y-yes, sir."

Mr. Roberts's gaze never moved. "And then there are some things which need to remain hidden, some things which are no longer part of this world or never should have been, objects or thoughts that need to be left alone."

"Yes, sir."

"The Tears you search for are one such object. They are a power that should not have been. You will not touch them and remain unscathed."

Luke quivered at the doom in the man's voice. Quiet. Final. Time froze as Luke stood there, lost in Mr. Roberts's eyes. Leaves swirled by the wind along the concrete patio slowed until motionless. Luke's mind fled, but with nowhere to hide. When he came back to himself, Mr. Roberts's hand rested on his shoulder and warmth poured from his eyes. His smile made Luke smile, and then he felt a silent laugh roll through his shoulders. Mr. Roberts nodded.

"You will do well, Luke. Focus on what is most important."

"Yes, sir."

Scarred hands patted Luke on the shoulder and thick arms embraced him before Mr. Roberts turned his green eyes toward the door. He slipped silently through the archway over the entrance and then stopped. Luke returned his smile questioningly.

"You would do well, young one, to heed me, but"—he chuckled—"on the offhand chance you choose otherwise, there is something you should know. Those who seek will always find."

Luke frowned. "Sir?"

"Seek me, Luke, when you most need to, and you will find me … you will find me. And you would do well to get inside by a fire soon."

Mr. Roberts settled his hat on his head and eased into his seat in the wagon. He tipped his hat and flicked the reins, and the wagon pulled away from the house, gravel crunching under the wheels. Blue moonlight twinkled over the white rocks and the fountains, and as the wagon neared the end of the drive, Luke's breath fogged in front of him. He closed his eyes and a laugh escaped. Opening them, he shook his head as tiny white flakes floated onto the lawn in front of him.

Snow!

Filled with warmth, he whirled around, darted back into the house, and shouted all the way down the hallway. "Mom! Dad! Everybody, come look!"

ELEVEN

✦

Winter Ball

Luke's eyes popped open and his heart hammered. Gray dawn crept in through the window above his bed. A smile grew on his face as he sat up. "Trent!" Luke hissed at the still lump on his brother's bed. "Trent!" He leaned down to pick up a slipper and chucked it across the room.

"Mmmm ... Wha ..."

The blankets exploded and Trent's head popped up, eyes blinking and hair shooting off in different directions. He squinted around the room and then at Luke, grinning. "Christmas!"

Luke shoved the blankets back and slipped off the bed. Gray ashes were piled in the fireplace and the air stirred, causing goose bumps to race up Luke's arms as he struggled into a tan sweater. They burst out of the room, Trent still wrestling with clothes and sheets halfway out the door. Fires crackled in both the north and the south fireplaces. Their parents, grandparents, and uncle looked up from the table in the middle of the room and smiled. Steaming mugs, plates teetering with biscuits and butter, scones filled with ham and cheese, and pastries stuffed with apples and apricots lined the table. Luke's mouth watered but his eyes were drawn to the south end of the room. Garland and ribbons decorated the mantel, light twinkling down their length. Stockings hung below, filled with the shapes of hidden treasures. Sparks popped and toy soldiers and ballerinas whirled around the fireplace screen to catch them. To the left, surrounded by chairs, stood a Christmas tree soaring to the ceiling. Candles and baubles of all shapes covered its branches. Crystal bells and glass balls mingled with wooden horses and candy canes, all of them suspended by nothing but air. Two tiny red birds flitted out of the tree and onto the branches. Made of light, the birds danced from one branch to the next, leaving a trail of sparkling dust behind them.

It was toward the bottom of the tree, though, that Luke's eyes fixed on a cluster of glittering boxes. A squirrel poked its head out from behind a sparkling blue package, blinking at the boys. Luke and Trent grinned at each other and then raced to the tree. The squirrel vanished up the trunk, chittering away at them as they slid to a stop in front of the green-and-red skirt around it. Luke scanned the boxes and bags as Jon and Amy exploded out of their room behind him.

"Mommy! Daddy!"

Trent pulled out three of the presents and sat in one of the chairs next to the fire. Luke looked and looked and finally found some packages for him. He bit his lip for a moment and then ripped into the largest of the boxes. Inside, neatly stacked, were three leather-bound books. He opened one to the title page.

"*The Fall of the Ancients.*"

He looked up at his father, who shook his head and nodded toward Grandpa Rayburn.

Luke's grandfather smiled. "It's a history of sorts, though I'm afraid to use that word for fear of scaring you off. It's more a collection of stories about the last days before the Ancients left. It was one of my favorites when I was a young boy. Your grandmother and I thought it would give you a feel for some of the history of the people and creatures who live in holdings."

Luke ran his hand over the covers of the three volumes. "Thanks, Grandpa and Grandma."

Voices grew around him as Jon and Amy found their presents and Jodi came tottering out of her room. Trent had a football in hand and was attempting to coax Uncle Landon into throwing it across the room.

"Please, Uncle Landon, please."

Luke looked back down at his other presents. He opened the smallest of the boxes and grinned as an orange glow emanated from it. He looked back up just in time to see Uncle Landon snag the football inches from one of the candlesticks on the table.

"Thanks, Uncle Landon," Luke said.

Uncle Landon nodded and winced at Luke's mother's scowl. "You're welcome, Luke. Have fun with it. Come on, Trent." He sheepishly ushered Trent to the other end of the room.

Luke picked up the last of the packages and looked up to see his father lean forward, resting his elbows on his knees.

"From Mom and Dad," the label read. "What is it, Dad?"

Luke's father just arched his eyebrows and smiled. Luke laughed and tore into the box. Seconds later, he was holding a glass sphere filled with water and about the size of an orange. The water swirled, twisting first one way and then the other, and he felt a tingle in his hands.

"What is this, Dad?"

His father's face lighted up and a mischievous grin appeared. "Let's go find out."

Minutes later, bundled up in beanie, jacket, and boots, Luke carried the sphere in the palms of his hands, following his father down through the house and out to the front lawn. Snow sifted through the air and dusted the grass, though there were piles in some places. Luke's breath fogged the air in front of him as his father stopped and turned around.

"All right, here we go. Luke, what you are holding is a mandreekah. I want you to set it down here."

Luke placed the sphere on the ground. "What's a mandreekah, Dad?"

His father grinned. "It's a trainer of sorts. There are many different kinds, but they all serve the same function: to train you in the use of disciplines, and particularly in using the disciplines to fight."

Luke's heartbeat picked up a notch.

"Now, just like with other tools, such as a seeker, the trainer has certain limitations. This kind of mandreekah is used to train you in the discipline of water, how to attack with it and how to defend with it. You may use any disciplines you wish, but it will only use water." He smiled. "This is not a weakness. Also, in the case of trainers, they only respond to three commands, regardless of whether you give them verbally or just by thought. You can do either, of course, Luke, but I suggest you use verbal commands in the Ancient language. In my opinion, that helps to focus you." He chuckled. "And you seem to have a knack for the language."

Luke snorted. "Yes, sir."

"The words are *leeftoakh*, *lehatkheel*, and *sof*. *Leeftoakh* will cause the trainer to activate, *lehatkheel* will begin training, and *sof* will end it. You understand?"

"Yes, sir."

"Repeat the words to me, Luke."

A tingle ran through Luke's body as he said the words.

"Good. Now, every time you win, the mandreekah will return to its sphere form until you activate it again." His eyes narrowed. "Luke, this is not like training with a partner in the outside world. The mandreekah is meant to train you, but it will learn from you and use what you teach it, and each time you use it, it will improve."

Luke frowned. "I don't understand."

His father's face hardened. "You will. Your mother and I wouldn't have given you this if it weren't needed. This world is a fantastic place, Luke, but it is a hard place, too. Now repeat the words again."

Luke obeyed.

His father stepped to the side. "Now activate the mandreekah."

Luke looked down at the sphere and then back at his father. "Dad, what will happen if I lose?"

His father chuckled. "Scratches, bumps on the head, unconsciousness, maybe a broken bone or two … It's not pleasant, Luke, but the mandreekah won't harm you past a certain point, unlike in the real world. In order for you to stop it, though, you must either command it or you must make it so that the mandreekah can no longer fight, until there is no life left in it. In that sense it very much represents the real world, and how a fight ends when it is about something more than injured pride or careless words. Do you comprehend what I'm saying, Luke?"

Luke's mind flashed back to Thanksgiving morning and a poof of feathers and roasted turkey on the table. "Yes sir."

His father stared for a moment and then a half-smile appeared. "I'm here, though, Luke, right beside you."

Warmth filled Luke's chest and he glanced down at the still sphere. Wind gusted and swirled around him.

"Leeftoakh."

The sphere glowed blue and swirled and expanded, shooting upward. Arms and a head formed from a trunk, and ice-blue eyes blinked open. As tall as a basketball goal, the trainer stared down at him, its body of water twisting and turning.

What is this thing?

Luke's father crouched with his hands on his knees. "Now, Luke, as soon as you activate the mandreekah, you must be ready. Think of it like Coach Wilson's whistle blowing during hitting practice in football."

"Yes, sir." *I have* no *idea what I'm doing.* Cold air filled his lungs. "Lehatkheel."

He dived to the side as a ball of snow shot through the air where he'd been standing.

Smack!

Another ball hit him in the side.

Think, Rayburn!

Snow thickened, twisting around the trainer and hiding it from view. Luke pushed up from the ground and jumped away as balls fired at the spot where he'd been.

His father clapped his knee. "Well done, Luke, well done."

Luke grinned, but the smile faded along with the snow swirling around the trainer. Ice-blue eyes snapped toward Luke's new position and Luke stumbled backward as a snowball the size of his head shot toward him. He raised his arms and the snowball split in two, showering him with powder.

Nasty thing.

Luke fired his own back. It slammed into the trainer and

knocked it backward, but then it surged up and shrugged them off.

Jeez, they hardly even seem to phase it.

Now the trainer was moving and firing.

No cover here. He dodged two more balls and fired his own, circling toward the northernmost of the now-dormant fountains. *I need something more than snowballs.*

Snow exploded around him, filling his eyes and nose. He coughed and sputtered.

Slam!

One of the snowballs knocked him off his feet. Pain blossomed on the left side of his face as he spit snow and grass out of his mouth.

Mmm … that didn't feel good.

He crawled toward the fountain and around the side, keeping his head below the concrete ring.

Smack! Smack! Smack!

Three balls slammed into the concrete above his head.

How do you stop this thing? Just tell it to stop. He shook his head at himself. *No, I won't take the easy way out.*

Smack! Smack!

He cringed as bits of ice showered down on him from the edge of the fountain. He blinked and his mind stilled. His father's voice sounded in his head.

… can no longer fight.

Luke stood up and the trainer's head snapped toward him. A ball formed in front of the trainer.

Now.

Luke thought and a plank of ice a foot across swung around and slammed into the head of the mandreekah. Another band hit its body, and another. The trainer moved to the left and two more bands of ice sliced through its body. The trainer blocked some of the blows, but Luke hit it with more and more. Chunks of ice that were arms or pieces of torso broke off the mandreekah.

Whoosh!

What was left of the trainer's body erupted into the air, leaving only a mist of ice carried on the wind. The ball of snow near where the trainer had stood dissolved. Luke stood huffing, cold air burning his lungs. Twenty feet in front of him, water coalesced and trickled back into the clear sphere on the ground.

His father nodded. "Well done, Luke. You understand now?"

Luke gulped air into his lungs. "No life ... fantastic but hard ... Yes, sir."

His father picked up the sphere and handed it to Luke and, with a chuckle, put his arm around his shoulders and turned him toward the house. "Let's go see if we can steal some early hot chocolate from Mr. Robinson, hmm?"

A few weeks later, lights and shadows danced along the drive as Luke stared out the window. A white blanket spread over grass, stones, and tree branches alike. Only the drive was clear. Luke looked down at his hands, which were blistered because of all the shoveling he'd done in the driveway. *Not quite as bad as last year.*

"Dad never did have much of a sense of humor when it came to work."

Luke looked over his shoulder and gave a half-smile as his father peered down at his hands.

"You fared pretty well, though, son." He turned and stared out into the graying evening. Carriages rolled past beneath them, and men in blue house dress ran from stairs to doors and back again. Women's laughter bubbled up to them, mingling with children's shrieks and the boom of men's voices. Blue orbs of light floated along the drive, interspersed with torches. Luke tugged at his collar and rolled his shoulders. His father snickered.

"Never did like these things as a kid either ... Come to think of it, I'm not sure I like these things as an adult—except that I get to see your mother all dressed up."

Luke looked up at his father and grimaced.

His father laughed and clapped him on the shoulder. "Come now, son, Miss Thompson doesn't seem to make you have that face."

Luke felt heat rush to his face and his father laughed all the harder. Luke turned toward the window, and after a moment his father's laughter died down. He wiped his eyes and pulled Luke to his side. "Fair enough, fair enough. Well, better get movin'. Your mother will have my hide if I'm late, and yours, too, so don't wait too long."

"Yes, sir."

"At least you won't have to dance the first dance this year ... unless your mother has finagled something, that is."

Luke's head snapped up and his father chuckled and winked before turning to leave. "You worked hard today, Luke," he said over his shoulder. "Enjoy the rewards."

Luke watched his father disappear down the hallway and turned back to the window. A face flashed through his mind.

Where is—

He felt a smile settle in as the coach pulled up to the drive behind four midnight-black horses.

There.

Luke watched as Ricardo jogged to the door.

Pants with one crease above the shoes ... brighthawk emblem on the left side perpendicular to the second button ...

Ms. Lucy's voice rang in Luke's head, detailing the dress requirements of the male members of the house staff. A man's top hat appeared above the door on the far side of the coach. Ricardo opened the door, and Luke felt his heartbeat in his ears. A gloved hand appeared, followed by blond hair that was pulled up and a bright smile. Ricardo handed Samantha down with a nod. She pulled a brown fur coat tight around her and turned to look over her shoulder. Her father walked up, giving Ricardo a brief nod, and then Mr. Jefferson, in too-long dress pants, walked up behind father and daughter. As they ascended the stairs, Mr. Jefferson glanced up at the window where Luke stood, and Luke felt the hair on the back of his neck stand up. Behind him Mr. Thompson stared as well, not moving. The pendant on his chest warmed.

Something's not right.

The men moved again but as if through molasses, and the muted flames of the torches moved as if a potter's hand were forming them into different shapes. Luke's breath fogged in front of him, and the sela'or in the hallway dimmed.

It's here.

He whirled around, kad<u>u</u>r resting on his raised palm. He lowered his hand, but the ball of light remained in place.

"Saul, what do *you* want?"

The man in the black suit cocked his head and looked down at Luke's hand with raised eyebrows. "I come bearing gifts and this is how you greet me? You father would not approve."

Luke frowned and the kad<u>u</u>r winked out of existence.

Saul smiled. "Thank you."

Luke's stomach tightened. "What have you done ... outside?"

The man's smile vanished. "Just bought us a little time together, Luke, nothing more. You accuse me without even saying anything, but have I ever hurt anyone?"

Luke's mind raced.

"Have I not tried to help you every time? Who got the book back for you, hmmm?"

After a moment, Luke shook his head.

"No. Nor will I hurt anyone tonight. I am here to help you, Luke."

"How, sir?"

"Right to business. Well, I have come to understand you are looking for a piece of information, yes?"

The Lost Island. "Maybe."

Saul's face hardened and his eyes brightened. Luke faltered back a step. "Don't play coy with me, little one."

"But we've looked everywhere, sir, and besides, the island is probably concealed. Even if we knew how to get there" —he glanced down at his feet and then back up—"we wouldn't be able to remember how to get there!"

The man chuckled, making a sound like deer horns scratching against bark. "You have known this world existed for less than two years and yet you think you know all the answers." Saul leaned forward and his voice dropped to a whisper. "You know *nothing*."

Luke trembled. He felt his mind moving away from his body. He yelled and scrambled for purchase in his head. Saul's eyes bored into his mind and soul.

Luke.

He snapped back to himself at the sound of the voice in his head, blinking and shaking.

Saul stood back, frowning. "Hmm."

Luke's breathing was labored. "What's … the information?"

Saul peered at him for a moment and then started. "The information … yes … You have a mermaid for a teacher this year, correct? A Mayeem?"

"Yes, sir."

"She is here tonight and she wears a pendant. That is the key that you need."

What pendant? "But how is that the key? Do I need the pendant to get to the Lost Island?"

Saul shook his head. "You will have to figure that out. If you can't, you aren't who I thought you were, and you don't deserve to find what you are looking for."

Luke felt heat flood his cheeks. "What exactly *am* I looking for? You haven't told me anything and you disappear for months on end. What are the Tears? Why does everybody want them so bad?"

Saul glanced out the window behind Luke and frowned. He stepped back into the shadows of the hallway, eyes still glued to the window. "You will have to find that out for yourself, Luke. And I am not the one you need to be concerned with."

Blackness spread around Saul and he turned his gaze to Luke. "Remember, the halfling's pendant is the key." Saul's body began to dissolve into the shadow. "And one warning, Luke: The enemy known is the one you can trust; it is the one who hides from you that you must beware of."

"What!? What enemy? Who?"

The red of Saul's eyes faded and light increased in the hallway again.

Luke glanced around and then jogged back to the window. Below, servants darted this way and that. Flames flickered and danced along the drive. He watched Mr. Thompson slip from his view and into the house. *Time to go, Luke.* He turned and walked down the hallway toward the marble-floored ballroom. His thoughts raced as he passed a few of the maids in the hall.

"Good evening, ma'am." He nodded at the woman's reply without hearing it. *Gotta find Matt and Samantha and go look at that map in the library ... Gotta figure out the pendant first, though ... What pendant is he talking about?*

He strode through the door on the south side of the ballroom and scanned the crowd as the quartet's music died down. Women in evening dresses and men in suits of black or midnight-blue were scattered throughout the room. Fires roared on the north, south, and west sides of the room, and tables filled with food lined the windowed east wall. Familiar faces nodded to Luke as he slipped through the crowd.

Samech ... Coach Wilson and ... Who is that?

Father Woods winked at Luke as he stuffed the last bit of a cheese pastry into his mouth. The quartet began again and voices quieted throughout the room. Luke stopped and looked up to the top of the stairs. Mr. Acharon stepped out onto the landing and moved to the side as Luke's grandparents stepped out, followed by his parents and then Uncle Landon. Luke watched as his mother glided along next to his father, a smile etched into his face. The music continued until they reached the floor and then altered course and faded into the background. As people walked forward to greet them, Luke's eyes searched the crowd. A tall man in the mess dress of the holding guard dipped his head to Luke, a smile flitting across his face.

Luke nodded back. *Lieutenant ... ah ... too many people to remember!* "Hello, sir." He shook the man's hand and moved on. *Where are they?* As he neared the north end of the ballroom and the last table filled with coffee, teas, ciders, and water, a sparkle of light caught his eye. He turned and stopped. His mouth dried.

Samantha stood alone with her back to him, silver dress twinkling in the firelight and hands clasped behind her. Luke glanced around.

What are you waiting for, Rayburn? Gnomes?

Luke walked over and stopped beside her. "Hey, Sam."

She turned dancing eyes toward him, and a smile bloomed on her face. "Luke!"

"You ..." *Just say it.* "Your dress looks really great tonight." *Your dress looks really great! Ugh. Idiot.*

Samantha wrinkled her nose, smiling and laughing. "Thank you. Your suit looks really great, too."

Luke laughed and took a deep breath. He looked from one side of the room to the other as the music stopped and then started again. "Do you like the party?"

Samantha nodded, looking around the ballroom. "It's wonderful. Your grandparents always have the best parties."

Luke smiled and stood quietly. He greeted Professor Lewis as he stopped with his plump, smiling, rosy-cheeked wife on his arm.

"Good evening, Mr. Rayburn, fantastic night. Miss Thompson you look l—" Mrs. Lewis's attention was drawn to a couple a few tables away, and she pulled her husband in that direction. Professor Lewis sighed with a pained expression before winking at them and trudging along with his wife. Luke grinned and a giggle escaped from Samantha before she covered her mouth. Luke opened his mouth and then closed it as the quartet began again and another tune whirled toward the ceiling. Couples twirled around the dance floor like pinecone seeds spinning toward the ground.

Ask her to dance, Luke. It's not that hard ... Yes it is!

"Sam, do you ... would you want ..."

Samantha smiled hesitantly. "Yes?"

You big sissy!

"Would you like—"

"Luke. Samantha, how does this evening find you?" Mayeem's voice broke into Luke's head and his thoughts crashed in a tangled wreck.

"Mayeem!" Samantha smiled and gave their teacher a hug.

I was doing great until you showed up. Luke bit his tongue and forced a smile as Mr. Acharon's lecture about politeness sounded in his head. "Very well, ma'am. And you?"

The mermaid smiled and turned to look across the room to where Luke's family stood laughing and talking with guests. "Very well, very well indeed. Your grandparents host quite a wonderful ball, young Master Rayburn." As she turned back to him, a flash of silver caught the light of the room and an image of Mayeem stepping up out of the water of Granite Lake filled his mind. *The Pendant.*

"Will you be dancing tonight? I have heard you do quite well."

Luke frowned in confusion. Samantha's face colored and she looked away. "Uh, thank you, ma'am, but, um ... I ... Not as well as most."

"I am sure, but that does not preclude many from trying, and we must all start somewhere, hmm?" Mayeem arched her eyebrows and Luke's mind snapped back to the hallway upstairs. He glanced at her neck, where a silver chain dangled and disappeared into her dress.

"At any rate, you have a perfect partner standing not a foot away."

Luke coughed and glanced at Samantha. She smiled and

then looked at her slippers, her cheeks glowing red under the light.

Her laughter like tinkling bells, Mayeem put her hand on Luke's shoulder and leaned close to him. "Timidity does not suit you, Mr. Rayburn," she whispered, "and I'm afraid it will not do in this situation. Do not fear—there are others nearby besides I who are fond of you." The tightness around Luke's chest loosened at Mayeem's words.

"Darling, you did very well today," she said to Samantha. "Truly, you have surpassed expectations. I am so proud of you. I wish Miss Brady had kept up the lessons as well, but … If you have time, perhaps we might speak more a little later?"

Samantha nodded and grinned. "Thank you, ma'am. Yes, ma'am."

"Very good. Now, I have bothered you two enough. Besides that, I see charming William Volf across the floor and would very much like to speak with him. He mentioned something about me having another student perhaps. Good evening to you both." She smiled and returned Samantha's hug before dipping a shallow curtsy to Luke's bow and departing.

Cold air and flaming red eyes flashed back into Luke's head. *Maybe Sam knows what the pendant looks like.* "Sam have you … have you noticed the pendant that Mayeem wears around her neck?"

"The pendant?"

"Yeah, do you know what it is, what it looks like?"

"Yes … I think … it is …" Her eyes had lost focus but now they were clear again. "It's one of the symbols in the Ancients' language."

"Can you draw it for me?"

Samantha leaned back. "Well, I don't have anything to write with, but sure, I think so."

Luke nodded and glanced around. His eyes latched onto the table a few feet away. "Here, come over here."

Samantha picked up her dress and hurried behind Luke as he half-jogged to the table.

"Luke, slow down … Why do you want to know?"

He took a sugar dish and a saucer and dumped a pile of the white grains onto a plate. "I have an idea. Here, use this. Can you draw it in the sugar?"

Samantha glanced around the room and a couple walked by staring at the plate in Luke's hand.

"Sure, I guess so." Samantha took the plate of sugar and with her finger traced out a line crossed by two other lines at angles to each other. "That's pretty close, I think, but I still don't understand, Luke … Luke?"

Luke's body went rigid. A picture of a map bursting into flames flashed in front of his eyes. Pain seared the back of his head as a rasping voice echoed through his mind. Images of sand and a silver trail leading to dark shapes crossed his vision and a tremor ran through his body. Music and voices faded into the background as if heard through someone else's ears.

When fingers brushed his arm, he gasped air into his lungs. To his left, Samantha's wide blue eyes and small round nose filled his vision. "Luke? What happened? Are you OK!?"

Luke smiled shakily. "Yes. I think so … but we need to find Matt and the others."

Samantha's eyes narrowed. "OK … but—"

"There you two are! Why are y'all way over here by yourselves?"

Matt was approaching with Marti and Jennifer. Matt's eyes darted from Luke's face to Samantha's and back again and the color drained from his face. "Oh. Sorry, man, I didn't mean—"

Luke shook his head. "We were just coming to look for y'all. We need to get to the library."

Panic passed over Matt's face. "The library? What? Why? We don't have something for school, do we?"

Luke smirked. "Come on, I'll tell you when we get there."

"But they're just about to let us eat!"

"Come on. We'll just be a few minutes. It's not like there won't be any left."

Matt grumbled but walked with Luke across the smooth stone floor. "Nothing with you *ever* takes just a few minutes."

They weaved among the attendees, through the open double wood doors on the west side and past gloved men of the house staff. A few minutes later, Luke pushed open one of the doors to the west library. A gust of cool air and darkness greeted them. Luke looked up at the ceiling. "Madleek."

Light spread throughout the room.

"You all right, man?"

"Yeah." Luke rushed over to one of the map tables while the others exchanged shrugs. Rummaging through the rolled parchment in the shelves beneath, he spied one and pulled it out. "I was almost ready to give up on it …" The others gathered around as he rolled out the map. Marti and Matt placed stones on it to weight it down. "You remember the map in our cartography class?"

"I d-d-don't think anyone has f-f-forgotten that, Luke."

The others chuckled.

"Whatever. And you remember I couldn't remember the last symbol after we left Professor Lewis's class that day?"

The boys nodded.

"Well, I think I know what that last symbol was now."

Wide eyes and open mouths looked back at him. "How?" Matt said. "I mean, how all of a sudden? Why—"

"I just ..." Luke sighed. "I think the symbol is the same one as the one on Mayeem's necklace."

"The mermaid teacher's?" Jennifer said. "What makes you think that?"

Matt and Samantha frowned at him with narrowed eyes and crossed arms.

They know there's more ... Oh well, I'll have to tell them later. "It's just a hunch, OK? We'll see if it works. Marti, this is the map that you found a few weeks ago of the Misty Isles, you remember?"

"Y-y-yeah. It's still w-w-weird that there isn't any n-n-name on the map, not even who the m-m-mapmaker was. Usually there are at l-l-least initials or s-s-something."

Luke wrinkled his brow and glanced at Samantha and Jennifer. "We think the Lost Island is here." He pointed to the map and the girls leaned forward, Samantha holding her hand over the top of her dress. "See how all the other islands are closer together and pretty much evenly spaced?" The girls nodded. "And then there's this larger opening right here, almost like something should go there ... but there's nothing there." He watched light dawn in Samantha's eyes and then turned back to look at the yellowed parchment. "I think I still remember, but ... Marti, you remember all the other symbols still, right? All we need to do is write them under one of the tunnels."

"But, Luke, e-e-even if you get the symbols right, w-w-won't the m-m-map just burn up like the l-l-last one? And who knows if the m-m-mapmaker even p-p-put the Lost Island *on* this one?"

Luke took a deep breath and stared at the map. "I don't know, but I think it's at least worth a shot." He looked from one face to another. Wind pushed against the windowpanes behind them, and a smattering of snow appeared in the air.

Matt sighed. "All right, I'm game. Let's give it a go. You have some plan about putting the fire out once it starts, right?"

Luke snorted. "Thanks for the confidence, man."

Matt raised his hands. "Hey, I said I was game. That doesn't mean I don't think you're gonna catch yourself on fire."

Luke smirked and turned to Samantha. "Could you douse the fire with water based on what you know now if it starts?"

She closed her eyes for a moment. Her nose wrinkled and she tipped her head to the side before her eyes flashed open again. "Yes, I think there's enough moisture in the air. But, Luke—"

Luke winked at her. "It'll be all right. As long as all y'all are here, it'll be just fine."

Samantha sighed and shook her head, but her mouth turned up slightly at the corners.

Luke turned to Marti, who was rummaging through a drawer on the table. "All right, man, you ready?"

Marti pulled out a map pen. "R-r-ready." A smile crept onto his face. "But Matt's p-p-probably right, you know."

"Just draw the symbols," Luke said.

Marti leaned over and scratched out one symbol after another. Luke's mouth moved along with the pen until Marti stopped. "That's it, L-L-Luke."

His mouth dry, Luke swallowed and took the pen. *What are you so worried about? Worst case, you singe your eyebrows and your friends laugh at you. Come on.* He bent over and drew the first line of the symbol that Mayeem wore around her neck.

Luke …

He paused at the sound of the voice and then shook his head and drew the next dash.

There are some things that need to remain hidden.

Wind howled against the window. Luke's breath slowed and he shivered.

Cold?

Luke gritted his teeth. *I can do this! We have to find the Tears before the hunter does.* He pushed the voice and the temperature from his head and drew the last line. His eyes widened—black lines moved and shifted and other lines appeared, as if drawn by an invisible hand. Voices filled his ears, assailing him from both sides.

… should not have meddled …

… left alone …

Darkness will follow with you …

Hooooouuuuuuuuuuuu …

He jumped back as the howl rose above the wind. His heart thundered in his chest. "Did any of you … did you hear—"

"That howl?" Matt said. "Yeah, man, pretty sure everyone in the holding heard that, and pretty sure whatever we just did, we probably shouldn't have done it."

"Did … did you hear anything else?"

The others shook their heads. Luke looked around the library. Wind battered the windows from outside, but inside all was books, steady light, and the breathing of his friends.

Weird.

He looked back at the map. His heart, still thudding, skipped a beat. Where the open water had been on the map, an island now sat. Four other heads leaned in around his.

"It w-w-worked!"

Gray clouds surrounded the island, and a few birds were winging their way away from it. At the lower right, several words were written. Luke leaned closer, trying to make them out. "The Lost Island ... concealed at the hand of the Guardians in the Year of our Lord ... Reachable only by light of a full moon, verified, P. M. Randell, Cartologist, '57."

A full moon? I wonder why?

Luke moved his gaze back to the island.

Squawk!

Luke's head popped up at the sound and light glowing on the map. The birds on the page soared away from the rock, and moonlight-pale clouds floated over and around the island. A streak of blue light twisted from the edge of the island inward before fading, and the map resumed its original form.

Luke smiled. "Awesome." He looked up to see four faces staring at him, eyes unblinking. *Uh-oh.* "What?"

Matt snorted. "Do you actually practice doing that at the freakiest times, man?"

"What do you mean? The words are right here, in English!"

"Luke, even the writing is in the Ancient language," Samantha said. "I can't read it, except for the name at the end, P. M. Randell."

Luke stared at the letters. A hazy halo surrounded them and his vision blurred. He blinked, and when he looked again, he saw that the letters were Ancient symbols. "Oh boy."

Marti patted him on the shoulder and Matt stepped up beside him with his hands clasped behind him. "It's all right, man. Kinda gettin' used to it now. So, what's the bottom line? How do we get there?"

Three sets of eyes studied Matt.

He shrugged. "Come on. You all *know* we're going."

A smile flitted across Luke's face. "Next full moon."

Matt nodded and looked at Marti. "So, master of all knowledge useless, when is that?"

Marti grinned mischievously. "Two w-w-weeks from tomorrow."

As servants called names and raced back and forth down the hallways, guests filed out of the ballroom in small groups or by ones or twos.

Where are they?

Luke's head darted left and right, his eyes scanning the faces around him. The crowd dwindled.

"See ya, man," Matt said. "I think Mom said we'd be coming back tomorrow."

"All right, man. Talk to you then," Luke said.

Matt walked out with his mother, Uncle Landon escorting them.

Samech dipped his head as he walked by, and Luke waved or greeted people good night as they left. Out of the corner of his eye, he saw a short man in a crumpled suit scamper into the room. Luke's eyes followed him to the doors.

Bingo.

Samantha stood a few feet from her father, talking to Mayeem. Mr. Thompson nodded toward his assistant and reached back and touched Samantha's arm. She nodded, said something to Mayeem, and then turned with her father. Luke started forward as Father Woods walked up.

"Luke." The priest smiled, his eyes dancing.

Luke forced a smile but groaned inwardly and glanced at the door. Samantha looked over her shoulder and then disappeared through the doorway.

"And a very good night to you. What a wonderful ball."

"Yes, sir."

"I didn't see much of you tonight. How are you doing?"

Luke fidgeted. "Very good, sir."

Father Woods frowned as Luke darted glances toward the doors. "Don't let me keep you from your friends, Luke. I will talk with you later."

"Sorry, sir. Thank you, sir. Good night, sir."

Father Woods chuckled as Luke dashed toward the door, around guests claiming hats and coats, and down the hallway. He ran into the entrance hall just as Samantha and her father stepped to the door. He slid to a halt.

"Samantha."

Heads turned toward Luke and he winced.

Too loud.

Heat rushed to his cheeks as Mr. Thompson and Mr. Jefferson turned as well. A smile bloomed on Samantha's face, though, and Luke's heart warmed. He approached her and bowed. A sprinkling of snow dusted the rug they stood on.

"Mr. Thompson, Mr. Jefferson."

Mr. Thompson frowned but dipped his head in return. Mr. Jefferson sneered at Luke.

"Sir, I … I wondered if I might have a word with Sama—with Miss Thompson."

Samantha looked up at her father with arched eyebrows and a tight-lipped smile. Her father glanced out the windows next to the doors as their black carriage rolled up. "Just for a moment," he said. "I don't want us out in this longer than we have to be." He peered at Luke, his face carved of stone, then whirled around and stepped through the doors with Mr. Jefferson in tow. Samantha turned bright eyes toward Luke.

Feeling his tongue swell, he looked down at his feet.

"Luke?"

You will look the person in the eye when you speak to them, Mr. Rayburn.

Ms. Lucy's voice rang in his head and he felt the pull of her hand on his chin. He looked up with a shaky smile. "I just wanted to tell you … I'm sorry … I'm sorry we didn't get to dance. I should have asked, I wanted to, and if you're still willing next time, I would like very much to dance the first dance with you."

There. That was almost not as bad as being eaten by wolves.

Samantha looked at him for a moment, and the room grew brighter. "I would like that a lot, Luke."

"Miss, I believe your father's ready."

Samantha glanced over her shoulder at the man in the midnight-blue suit and heavy coat. "Thank you."

Luke jumped to the door. "I'll get it, David." The man stepped back, his grin only half-hidden.

Luke waited for Samantha to pull her coat tight and then opened the door to a draft and flakes of snow. He walked out the door and toward the carriage, the wind slipping under his dress jacket. One of Mr. Thompson's servants opened the door and reached out his hand, but Samantha stopped and glanced at Luke.

Oh! Luke stepped forward.

Her fingers wrapped around his and the wind seemed to stop. He lifted his hand up, and with one more smile she let go and the door shut.

Luke stood there, frozen.

"Oye, boy. Move back!" the driver said.

Luke leaped back as a whip snapped and the wheels churned forward. The coach rolled down the drive until trees and darkness hid it from view, and he turned back to the manor, grinning as widely as he'd ever grinned. As he reached the top step, though, he looked over his shoulder and a chill blanketed his heart. Under the bare branches of a sycamore tree on the west side of the drive, light flickered on the face of a man. A sad smile and brilliant green eyes stared at Luke until a tremble ran through his body that had nothing to do with cold.

I can do this!

The man's gaze held Luke until a gust of wind swirled around Luke and over toward the man. Then, as if made of snow himself, the man blew away, from his boots to his cowboy hat.

Luke stood silently. People walked behind him and horses whinnied. Nothing remained under the tree but shadows and light swaying back and forth.

"Master Rayburn." Ricardo stood frowning down at him. "Es cold. You need to go inside, señorito."

Luke nodded and trudged back inside, where he walked over to the windows edged with frost and peered out into the night. Words echoed through his mind and his heart hardened.

Someone has to find the Tears before the hunter and whatever darkness he's serving ... I have to.

TWELVE

✦

The Lost Island

A low rumble sounded as the Algid pressed southward. Moonlight twinkled off the water fifty yards away and illuminated the forest floor below. Pecans, oaks, and a smattering of cedar trees stood thick around the edge of Westcliffe Forest. Buds struggled forth on a few of the deciduous branches.

Swish, swish ...

A dark shadow flapped twice and then glided its way through the forest overhead. Luke shivered, hunching his shoulders under his wool sweater. Marti stood in front of the stone arch a few feet away, wiping off dust and dirt and ripping vines away. An orb floated a few inches from his head, swathing the stones in blue light.

"You sure this one will even work, man?" Matt asked.

Marti leaned forward and the ball moved with him. "Y-y-yes. There are a few of the t-t-tunnels around the holding that aren't u-u-used anymore, but they still w-w-work ... I th-th-think. This was the b-b-best one I could find that w-w-was out of the way but still c-c-close enough for us to get to quickly."

Matt rubbed his hands together and glanced at Luke. "Hope your dad and Captain Rayburn don't come out to *visit* us tonight like they did last time we went camping. I don't think they'd like being the ones surprised."

"I still say this is a bad idea and we should go back," Jennifer said, frowning at Samantha. "Your dad is gonna freak if he finds out we're gone ... and it's cold."

"It's not *that* cold, and he already told us good night," Samantha said. "He's not gonna come check on us in the middle of the night ... I hope."

Luke watched her as she blew the hair out of her face. *Hope you don't get everybody in trouble tonight ... Actually, "in trouble" is the least of your worries, Rayburn.*

He turned to Jennifer, who stood hugging herself and occasionally stamping her feet. "We already went through this earlier, Jenn. We have to go tonight or we miss the chance for another month. You said you wanted to go, but if you don't—"

"I know, all right? I just ... We should at least tell your uncle and the Guard or ... *somebody*."

"They'd never let us go then, and the Guard is already stretched too thin, Uncle Landon says. He doesn't have the people to let go on some wild ..." He paused and sighed as Jennifer raised her eyebrows. "On some wild goose chase, if it is one!"

All was silent except for a rustling of leaves on the ground as a creature scurried over them.

"And if you haven't noticed, Jenn," Matt said, "Luke here kinda seems to be the only one able to figure this stuff out."

Luke felt warmth rush to his face and ducked his head. "Anyway, you didn't seem so concerned a couple days ago."

Jennifer shrugged. "I … I just hadn't had time to think it all through, that's all."

Samantha nudged her with her shoulder. "Don't worry, Jenn. As long as we're all together, it'll be all right. The boys'll take care of us."

Jennifer barked a laugh and gave Samantha a skeptical grin. The girls' laughter filled the air of the hollow as a gust of wind washed over the group.

Crazy girls …

"Ah-ha!" Marti smiled triumphantly, his face bathed in blue light. "Found it! That's th-th-the last one … except for the o-o-one you have to find, Luke."

Luke stepped forward. He pictured an orb floating next to his head, and one appeared. It sailed over to the arch and up toward the keystone.

"Teth … nun … shin," Luke mumbled. "There!"

The light paused over a stone to the left of the keystone. He glanced around at the others and was greeted by blank stares. The smile slid from his face. "There, you see it, right?"

Matt shook his head. "Sorry, man, all I see is a plain old stone with a bit of dirt on it."

The others nodded and Luke sighed. "Oh well. Marti, just get the rest of them going and I'll watch this one, make sure nothing … funny happens."

Marti nodded and peered back up at the arch, his tongue peeking out the side of his mouth. Blue light glowed in the first stone, and Luke's breath caught in his throat. Light erupted from another stone and then another until six stones glowed around the arch. "All y-y-yours, man," Marti said.

Luke took a deep breath. *Here goes nothin' … Aleph!*

Blue light glowed in the stone overhead.

Crack!

Exclamations sounded as everyone jumped back. A flash of fire-orange light forked through the arch before the normal white-blue of an open tunnel. Luke's heart settled back into his chest.

"Just for the record, I'd like to change my vote to Jenn's side that this is a horrible idea," Matt said. "Oh, I still say we go, I just want to make sure everybody heard me say it was a bad idea so when someone finally finds us I can at least pretend to my mom that I tried to convince you it was a dumb idea."

Luke looked around the forest at the circle of faces. *Hope you know what you're getting them into, Rayburn.* His eyes paused on Samantha and she smiled and nodded. *Good enough.* "All right, here we gooooo." Without another word, he stepped into the tunnel, where white light surrounded him. His breath rushed out.

Pop!

He stepped out from underneath the arch and sucked air into his lungs. He took a few steps forward and blinked, his eyes watering as the white shapes branded into his vision faded.

Pop! Pop!... Pop!... Pop!

Gray surrounded him on every side. He turned in a circle, but even the arch had vanished. He heard feet shuffle around him. "Hey! Matt! Marti!" He winced at the high-pitched squeak in his voice.

"Yeah, man, I'm here, but I can't see anything. You sound like you're a million miles away. Where are you?"

"I'm right here."

"Uh ... where's here?"

Dumb-dumb, they can't see you. "Just hold on, don't move any more. I can't tell where your voice is even coming from and we might be moving away from each other. Is everybody here?"

"Yeah."

"Yes."

"I'm h-h-here."

"All right, good. Now—" A ball of light appeared beside Luke's head. "Ah, jeez." Blue light flashed and seared his eyes, reflected off thousands of droplets.

"What?"

"What happened?"

"Luke?"

The light winked out and Luke blinked. "I'm fine, I'm fine."

"Ow, sheesh!" Matt said.

Luke chuckled. "Tried to use light to cut through it?"

"Yeah … bad idea."

"Yeah, so light won't help us much. It just gets reflected off this … muck or fog or whatever. Anybody got any ideas about how to see through this stuff?"

Samantha's voice sounded in the mist. "I think so. Give me a second."

Whoosh.

Luke felt a tug on his coat and the gray swirled around him. "Uh, Matt, that you?"

"Was what me? I'm just standing here, man."

"Would you two be quiet," Samantha said. "OK. I think this will work."

The mist swirled around Luke and then stopped and moved past him all in one direction, like the tide going out. A shadow appeared to his left and he crouched until he saw three other shadows appear. The mist continued to flow past, and in a few moments the gray pillars transformed into his friends, the arch towering over them. Samantha approached with a grin.

"It's just mist, so I moved the water around like Mayeem

taught us and kinda made a bubble around us that will turn the water back."

Luke watched the edges of the area Samantha had cleared. The mist flowed toward them, but at some point it seemed to bend upward and turn and flow back, almost like a wave crashing upside down. "Awesome."

"Most definitely," Matt said.

Samantha blushed.

"But h-h-how do we get anywhere f-f-from here? I mean, h-h-how do we even see where to g-g-go?"

They could see only for a few yards in each direction. There were no trees or bushes in their bubble; the ground was covered in sand and grasses.

"We can't go on now," Jennifer said. "We have to go back, right?"

Luke detected relief in her voice. *There has to be some way to—*

"I thought from the map that—"

"Hey, look!" Matt said.

All around them the fog thinned. Shapes appeared and materialized into scrub brush and small bent and twisted dogwood trees. As the mist faded, sound filled their ears.

"The ocean," Luke said.

The gray of the mist vanished and was replaced with the glow of moonlight, and so too appeared the whitecaps of breaking waves about fifty yards away over the dunes.

"That c-c-cloud must have been w-w-why we couldn't see at first. It was b-b-blocking the moonlight."

A cloud drifted away from the moon above, allowing light to pour down. "And that must be part of the concealment," Luke said, "why you have to come on a full moon—to clear away the mist."

"Whew, good thing there aren't too many other clouds in the sky here ... wherever here is," Matt said.

Luke's eyes swept the dunes, brush, and grass between the tunnel and the sea and a smile crossed his face. "I'm pretty sure, Matt, that *this* is the Lost Island"—he pointed away from the ocean—"and that *that* is the way we need to go."

"What makes you say th—" Matt's mouth suddenly formed an *O* as Marti, Samantha and Jennifer gaped.

In the direction Luke pointed, a silver line glowed under the moonlight and expanded, highlighting a trail that weaved its way inland.

Marti smiled, his eyes never moving from the trail. "Well, w-w-what are we waiting for?"

"Let's try not to use any light unless we have to," Luke said. "The path ought to give us a good bit, but we need to stick close together. If any clouds cover the moonlight, just stay where you are until they pass. It doesn't look like there will be many. I figure we've got about two hours and then we're gonna have to get back. Everybody ready?"

Heads bobbed up and down.

They headed in the direction of the gleaming silver line. The path climbed inland, and grasses and shrubs were replaced by live oaks, palm trees, and even the sporadic cedar tree. They heard the occasional cry of a bird or scurry of another small creature. After about five minutes, they walked over the squeaking planks of a wooden marsh bridge past a towering cypress tree. A gasp escaped Jennifer's lips and Luke picked up the pace as a large splash sounded underfoot.

Twenty yards on the far side of the bridge, Matt pulled on Luke's arm. "Hey, man, wait a sec." He stepped a couple of yards in front of Luke and knelt. A silver disk of light about the size of a holding coin appeared near his head, further illuminating the path. "Hmmm."

Luke squatted as Matt traced something with his finger.

"I don't think we're the first ones here tonight, man."

Luke squinted at the spot where Matt's finger hovered.

"I thought I noticed some broken branches a bit farther back and some flattened grass," Matt said, "but I wasn't sure if you were doing it and I just missed it, and it's hard to see even with the path all lit up."

Three other heads appeared in the sphere of light cast by the disk.

"W-w-what's up?"

Matt pointed to the ground again. "Somebody's in front of us. See the boot prints in the mud?"

Three sets of eyes widened.

"*Now* do we go back?" Jennifer said. "I mean, who knows who or what's in front of us?"

Luke sighed and looked around the circle.

"It doesn't seem like a big group, man, but who knows?" Matt said. "Captain Rayburn has taught me some, though I'm not exactly an *expert* tracker."

Luke nodded. "Marti, what about you?"

Marti shrugged. "W-w-we're already here."

"Samantha?"

She darted a glance at Jennifer. "I say go ahead, too. Just be careful, and if we see anything at all bad, we go back."

Jennifer sighed and rolled her eyes.

Luke started down the path under the moonlight. A few hundred yards ahead, the path curved around a bend and past a break in the trees. Luke glanced to his right and saw the glimmer of moonlight on the sea.

What's that? He stared into the distance and nudged Marti. "Did you see anything down there just then?"

"Like w-w-what?"

"I don't know … It was almost like it got darker down there somewhere or something, like there was light and it … went out."

"All I s-s-see is the moonlight."

"Whatever. Must just be my imagination working overtime. Let's keep going."

As they walked on, the path steepened. Luke felt his face flush and his breathing speed up. His legs began to burn just as the path flattened out and a large cleared area opened up. He stopped and looked up ahead.

"Whew, that's as b-b-bad as … running l-l-ladders for Coach—"

"Shhhh!" Luke held his arms out, stopping Marti and the others from passing him. Ahead, about half a mile down the path, lights bobbed back and forth. Luke crouched and moved behind a bush on the side of the path. Figures stalked this way and that around a cluster of more than a dozen figures illuminated by firelight and the hovering orbs. They stood in a circle around a collection of shapes Luke couldn't identify.

"Man, what happened here?" Matt said.

Thanks to the moonlight and the floating orbs, the outline of jagged shapes and heaps of rubble spreading out across the cleared flatland came into focus. Luke peered at the closest of the shapes, about twenty yards away.

"It's been destroyed." Samantha's voice trembled. "It was … The whole village was destroyed."

Luke's eyes widened as he took in the broken and charred remains. Half-walls and piles of crumbling debris lay strewn across the area where the village had been. Like scattered giant's teeth, tree trunks dotted the landscape. Dark soil and destruction covered a rough circle about a mile in diameter. "This didn't happen tonight?"

"I don't s-s-smell any smoke," Marti said. "And s-s-some of the buildings look like they h-h-have vines or stuff growing on them. It was probably a l-l-long time ago, Luke."

Luke frowned as a voice floated out to them.

"… said n-no!"

That sounds familiar.

"There's something in the middle of that group of men near the center of the village, man," Matt said. "If we're gonna find something out on this island, I bet it's there."

About two hundred yards ahead stood a building taller than those around it, with three walls remaining. Sentries walked back and forth among the rubble, pausing at every turn to listen and scan the landscape.

There's only a dozen or so. I bet if we …

"That big building on the side of the path would get us pretty close. I think we can get to it if we just move a little bit at a time when the sentries are walking the other direction."

"I don't know, man." Matt regarded the sentries quietly for a minute. "It looks like every time one of them turns their back on this side, one of the ones on the other side is looking this way."

"What if we move to those shrubs first and then to that building over there and then the next one where the chimney still is," Jennifer said. "That would get us most of the way there without them seeing us, right?"

Matt snorted. "*Now* you want to keep going?"

Jennifer shrugged. "I … I just figured … I mean … well …"

Luke grinned. "I think Jennifer's right. If we move in two small groups, every time they turn on this side it might work."

Three heads snapped toward Luke.

"Whoa."

"And what if it doesn't work?" Samantha said, glaring at Jennifer. "We don't even know who those people are." Now she glared at Luke. "They could be darkmen or soulless or … or worse."

Luke eased backward.

"She's right, Luke." Matt said. "We don't know anything about them, but"—now it was his turn to draw Samantha's glare—"I think Luke's right, too. If we stay pretty low, we ought to make it. Besides, we came here to learn something, right?"

Marti nodded. "I'm in."

Samantha rolled her eyes. "If we get caught—"

"We won't," Luke said. "I won't let us."

Samantha narrowed her eyes at him. "You better not." There was a hint of a smile in the corners of her mouth, though, as she turned away from him to say something to Jennifer.

Luke felt his chest swell until Matt scooted closer and elbowed him. "Now you have to keep your word, you know, for the rest of us, too—not just for the pretty girls."

Marti snickered and Luke sneered at them both.

Twenty minutes later, after hopping from building to bush to building, holding their breath and praying all the while, Luke and Marti darted toward a grove of burned tree trunks about thirty yards from the building with three walls. Luke slid to a stop, huffing, and looked around the corner.

No shouts—so far so good.

When Matt, Jennifer, and Samantha caught up, Luke kept his eye on the guards. "One more time. When that guard turns there, we have a few seconds when that building is between us and him and that guard over there still can't see us. All right?"

Bobbing heads and quick breathing answered him. "Almost there ... Ready, Marti?"

"Y-y-yes."

Luke's voice dropped to a harsh whisper. "Wait ... waaait." The guard turned. "Now!"

Luke dashed forward with Marti right behind him. They ran huddled over, dodging shrubs as they went. Seconds later they were inside the building with the three walls. Luke tip-toed to an old window and looked through it. The first guard was still walking away from them. Luke strained to see farther around the corner and then pulled his head back in. *Where's the other one?*

They sat quietly in the dark for several minutes. The guard Luke had lost came back into view and then disappeared again. *This is taking too long.*

He eased over to the window again, stepping over stones and dirt, and raised his head to the windowsill. The guard was just outside, and Luke quickly ducked again.

Marti stared at him from the shadows across the room. Luke held his breath until his lungs hurt. No noise sounded on the other side of the wall. A few seconds later, Marti waved him over and Luke crept back across the room. He glanced out the side of the building. Under the moonlight, he saw three figures race toward them. Halfway to the building, Jennifer slipped.

"*Umpfh.*"

Luke winced at the sound. To his ears, it sounded like an explosion in the night. Matt jerked her to her feet and half carried, half shoved her the rest of the way, but the damage was done. Shouts sounded outside the building. Luke's heart sank.

Nowhere to hide.

Jennifer whimpered as she and Matt reached the building.

Samantha's voice called out as she reached the building too, but Luke couldn't make out what she said.

Great job, Rayburn.

He turned his head, scanning each corner in the building. As his gaze swept the corner farthest away, a shadow caught his eye.

What is that?

A chill raced up his arms and he pulled them close. The shouts outside grew louder. He stepped toward the shadow.

It's darkness, and it's almost like it's … moving … like it's alive.

And then he heard a voice that wasn't his own.

Get inside, Luke.

His eyes widened and his skin crawled. Red eyes flashed in his head.

You'll be safe inside. The shadow will hide you. Trust me.

Then, like a counterpoint, he heard his father's voice. *Darkness only hurts, it never helps, son.*

He shook his head. *No, no, I won't.*

The shouts grew louder. "Luke, if you've got a plan, now would be a great time to use it," Matt called over to him.

It's the only way, Luke. Those men won't be kind to your friends.

Luke gritted his teeth, glanced at the shadow in the corner and then looked over his shoulder. "Everybody get over in that corner, hurry," he said.

"Wha—" Samantha said.

"Just do it."

Matt frowned at his tone but picked up Jennifer and walked her over behind Marti and Samantha. They walked into the corner, and as they entered the shadow, they vanished.

Impossible.

"Hey!" a deep voice shouted on the other side of the wall.

"Over here!" another shouted.

Luke looked out the window in time to see two of the guards running past.

Shoot!

He leaped forward as footsteps sounded behind him. The shadow swallowed his body, enveloping him in cold. His vision darkened and his lungs burned with the stale, thick air. As he turned around, using his arms as if swimming in one of the tanks back in Countryside, his breathing became shallow. He looked around as three guards rushed into the crumbling building, glowing weapons in their hands.

Where is everybody?

He was alone in the shadow. His friends were gone.

THIRTEEN

The Last Five Yards

Luke trembled. Darkness pressed down all around him. It crept into his mind, reaching out tendrils and rifling through his thoughts. He shuddered and his knees shook.

"Something was here! I heard it!" one of the guards shouted, staring around the room with eyes ablaze.

Luke snapped back to himself, shaking the darkness out of his head.

Surely they would help me find my friends ... But what if they wouldn't? What if they serve darkness? ... It's safe in here.

Darkness crept back into his mind. Light exploded in the room and he shielded his eyes as orbs materialized above the guards' heads. After a few moments, the light dimmed a little but still hurt his eyes when he lowered his hand.

Why does it hurt so much?

He shivered in the cold.

"Madleek," the guard commanded. He waved his hand through the air and silver moonlight was pulled into the room from outside. The moonlight slid along the walls and across the floors, moving in sync with the guard's hand. Outside the windows, the night darkened as moonlight was sucked into the building. Luke pushed back into the corner until pain registered in his back.

"Dageem, you and Ladoog go, search the other buildings. There is darkness here. I feel it!"

Luke watched as two of the three guards bowed and jogged out of the room in leather sandals. The guard giving orders remained, standing ten feet away.

Luke's mind seesawed. *Maybe he would help ... What if my friends are in trouble? ... Maybe they're not. Maybe they'll come back in a minute.*

The man was bare-chested and wore skirts made of a cloth that shifted colors between chocolate and sea green as he moved. Black hair hung behind him in a braid. Round eyes the size of coins blinked above sharp cheekbones. Luke peered at his eyes, and the face of Mayeem floated into his head.

A merman!

The man carried a long spear with a shaft of black wood, edges gleaming in the moonlight. As he moved, the silver light moved with him. Glaring from wall to wall, his gaze paused in the corner where Luke stood and he stepped closer, cocking his head. Luke squirmed as the man's eyes blinked and his mouth turned down. He raised the spear and the head glowed red.

He definitely won't help ... I'll just get myself locked up or hurt by jumping out of this shadow.

The merman eased the tip of the spear into the corner, moving it from side to side. Luke ducked as it swept over his head. The shadow Luke hid in moved around the spear, never touching it. Sweat formed on Luke's head and chilled his body. He huddled in the corner as the merman continued his search and lowered the spear toward him.

Just reach out and touch it—it'll pull you out of the shadow! Get out and get help for your friends, Luke! ... No! I need to stay here ... where it's safe.

The merman's eyes narrowed, and the spear weaved along faster. Luke's heart hammered in his chest.

"Ketseen."

The Ancients' name for a captain!

The spear froze a few inches above Luke's head. The merman stared for a second and then snorted and whirled around. A second merman stood at the edge of the light, where the fallen wall once stood. The captain bowed and then raised his arm to his chest.

"Aloof."

Aloof ... Aloof ... Major or Colonel or something. What was it? Aloof, aloof on the roof. Ha ha ha. Hearing the laughter in his head, Luke shook himself. *Not the time to go crazy, Rayburn.*

The other merman returned the salute, clasping fist to chest. "Gather your men. We leave."

"Have the children provided information?"

"No."

"Why do we leave then, sir?"

"I fear the concealment is failing."

"Failing, but surely the darkness cannot know yet."

"I do not know, Enias, but ... I feel the presence of great darkness. One of the shedon was here tonight."

Captain Enias sucked in his breath. "One of the dark ones? That ... is not *possible!*"

The other merman chuckled and a sad smile played across his face. "No? And just today, would you have thought it possible for a group of human younglings to venture upon the Isle of Lost Souls?"

The room remained silent and the captain's shoulders sagged.

Now, Luke, just step out and ask them for help. If they don't like darkness, they're probably on your side. Your friends need help!

He began to stand. *But what will they think of your coming out of a shadow built of darkness?* He sank back down and wrapped his arms around his knees.

"Oh, it is quite possible, Enias."

"But, but what of the search, sir? What of—"

The merman in command shook his head, his face hardening. "Nothing. She has not found them, and she sends word that darkness is growing bolder, sneaking in hordes of koder and probing the wards almost daily." Silence enveloped the room.

"What of the one that escaped?"

"We will come back and look, but I am afraid one powerful enough to get into the heart of the village and then back out will not be easily captured."

"And what of the secret?" Captain Enias said. "What of our task?"

The elder merman laughed harshly. "There is no task. The secret is no more." He turned and stepped out under the night sky, glancing over his shoulder. "We must go and help search and pray to the Fisher that we find them before the dark ones do … We can no longer pretend to guard the Tears of Adina."

Luke sat in the shadow as the mermen walked back out into the night. His breathing sounded in his ears, and his eyes stared off into nothing. A cloud rolled across the sky near the horizon, and shadows swung across the floor of the building as the moon moved through the sky.

Coward.

A trace of a cruel chuckle rang in the shadow. Luke's mind jumped from the words of the mermen to the faces of his friends to Countryside and his family.

Some friend you are. Now how will you help them?

His heart felt like a stone in his chest.

I can't leave without them ... but how do I find them? ... And even if I do, how can I help them? Matt! ... Marti! ...

Luke's voice echoed in his head. He opened his mouth to scream, but silence filled his ears.

Samantha! ... Jennifer! ... Anybody!

His head dropped between his knees. His eyes burned, and doubt and cold enveloped him.

Thump, thump, thump, thump, thump, thump ...

Luke.

The darkness in his mind shivered. Luke lifted his head, blinking away the moisture in his eyes.

Who ... who is it?

Thump, thump, thump, thump, thump, thump ...

As the pounding grew louder, Luke slid up the wall, his knees aching. When he looked out the window, heads bobbed by.

"Stop. Hey, wait up," someone said.

"Not so fast!"

Jon David! Randy! That's why the voice sounded so familiar.

A squad of mermen jogged by with Jon David, Randy, Joel, and a couple of other boys clustered in the middle. The mermen were herding the boys along like cattle, prodding them with the butts of spears.

I should help them … but how? … I can't even find my own friends!

Cold crept back into Luke's bones and his voice wailed in his head. He felt pressure on his shoulders and trembled, retreating deeper into the shadow.

Besides, I'm safe here … I'm …

Trust me, Luke.

Warmth fought into his chest with the sound of the voice. He looked down at his arms and the shadow surrounding him, and his stomach roiled.

Never should have come here. Never should have jumped into this stupid shadow … I should have listened to Dad … How am I going to get out?

Luke!

He started at the shout in his head. *I know that voice.*

Thump, thump, thump, thump, thump, thump …

"Slow dowwwn."

The sound of feet pounding along the dirt trail faded along with Jon David's whining.

Luke. It is time to leave.

Warmth streamed into him. The shadow began to fade, and he clenched his jaw. *Move, Rayburn.* He slid his foot forward. The darkness quivered. He took a step forward, and then another. The shadow stretched around him. *Just…get…out!* Luke growled and leaped forward.

Smash!

The shadow shattered and shards of darkness exploded into the room, slamming into walls and slicing through vines before evaporating. Moonlight swept back around Luke and he sucked air into his lungs. The room expanded around him, the sounds of the night and his breathing his only companions.

The faces of his friends flashed through his head. Bent over, he shivered and squeezed his eyes closed.

"*Huuuuuhhhhh.*"

His eyes shot open and he whirled around at the sound and saw them on the ground.

Thank you ... wherever you are ... whoever you are ... thank you ...

Matt groaned again as he pushed up off the ground. Samantha, Jennifer, and Marti coughed and hacked.

"I'd like to vote ... No more jumping into shadows," Matt said shakily.

"M-m-me, too. I felt like a c-c-clam trapped in m-m-my own shell."

Jennifer sat up and shuddered. "Ugh!"

Luke leaped over to his friends. "Ha! You're all right! You're OK!"

Samantha eyed him warily as Luke pulled her to her feet. "That depends ... on your definition of 'all right.'"

"What happened anyway?" Matt said. "I mean, how did we get out?"

"I'm not real sure," Luke said. "I just ... I heard this voice calling to me and ... and it gave me the energy—that and thinking about y'all—to jump out of the shadow."

"You heard a ... voice?" Jennifer said.

"Yeah, I mean I heard the mermen talking when they were in the room, you know, and I heard Jon David and Randy when they marched them by, but—"

"Jon David?!"

"Mermen?!"

"What do you mean 'marched them by'? Who?!"

"You ... you mean you couldn't see them?" Luke said.

"Man, I couldn't see anything in there, and I sure didn't

hear them talking," Matt said. "You better start from when we jumped into the shadow."

Luke sighed. "OK."

"What about Jon David ... and Randy and the others?" Samantha said. She looked quickly over at Jennifer. "I mean, we should help them, right?"

Marti chuckled. "S-s-seems like we need to h-h-help ourselves right now. Besides, why sh-sh-should we help those two m-m-misfits?"

"Yeah, I mean, what are they even doing here anyway?" Matt said.

"She's right." Heads whipped toward Luke.

"Say what?" Matt said. "You remember who we're talking about, right?"

"Yes," Luke said.

Marti's face scrunched up. "You know he w-w-would *never* help *us*, Luke."

"That doesn't mean we can do the same thing, Marti, and you know it." Luke stared around the room at his friends. Marti glared back, but Samantha's gaze dropped to the floor and Jennifer remained silent.

"I really don't like it when you're right sometimes, you know that?" Matt said.

A smile crept onto Luke's face. "I know. They left in the direction of the beach, and I think—"

Ahooooooooooo!

Matt stared at Luke with round eyes. A half-dozen howls answered the first call.

"You don't think ..." Luke said.

Matt arched his eyebrows. "That bane wolves just happened to find their way here tonight? No."

"What are y'all talking about? Why are they here?" Jennifer asked.

Luke and Matt turned toward her and answered in unison. "Hunter."

Ahooooooooooo!

"It sounds far, but it won't be for long." Luke looked out the window, past piles of stones and half-broken walls. "We can't stay here. They'll find us for sure. We've got to try to get to the tunnel."

"Maybe they aren't looking for us," Jennifer said.

Luke frowned. "You wanna stay here and find out?"

"We'll never m-m-make it, Luke. They'll catch us in a s-s-second."

"Better than being cornered here, or jumping back into that shadow, even if we could."

Four faces stared back at Luke. No one spoke.

So what now, Rayburn?

"Marti, you lead. Just follow the path back, fast. Samantha, you and Jenn next, then Matt, and I'll come last." Matt opened his mouth but Luke shook his head. "Marti is the best with the gate, you're the best fighter, and I'm the one they've been looking for. Just do it. Marti, as soon as you get there, start activating the symbols. Just get us back to Countryside some-where, *anywhere*."

Marti stepped over the rubble and out under the night sky. Luke smiled at Samantha but got a frown in return.

Ahooooooooooo!

Jennifer pulled on her arm. "Come on, Samantha."

Samantha sighed and dashed off after Marti down the path.

"You get caught and you can hang it if you think I'm not coming back," Matt growled and then wheeled around and darted off after the others.

Luke loped off after the four shadows in front of him. With the moon hanging low in the west, they sped down the path toward the tree line and the beach. As Luke reached the corner where the descent began, he glanced over his shoulder. Movement caught his eye on the far side of the village.

So close already?

He leaped forward and the trees cut off his line of sight.

Won't take them long to figure out we aren't there and where we went.

He watched the shadow that was Matt bound along in front of him. The trail twisted and turned, dropping toward the sea. A few minutes passed, and howls sounded in the distance behind and above them. With silver light illuminating the path, Luke dodged rocks and holes as they appeared. Cedar and oak trees crowded in around them, but after another hundred yards, the tree line broke. Luke could see the white crests of waves below them.

Still no cry. Maybe someone … something stopped them or —

Ahooooooooooo!

Maybe not.

Everyone picked up the pace. Luke jumped over a rock in the path. *What are you gonna do if … when they catch up?* He wiped sweat off his forehead. His sweater pulled down on his shoulders, stretching with the moisture, as he jogged on, the ground passing beneath his feet. *Maybe if they catch you it will at least slow them down enough for the others to get through.* He slowed his pace.

They turned again in the path and the marsh opened up before them. Four shadows raced along under the moonlight in front of him.

Ahooooooooooo!

He glanced over his shoulder. *Closer … They're on to us.*

Another minute and Luke heard Marti's footfalls smack across the wooden bridge. Luke saw a cypress tree to the right as his foot hit the bridge. *Almost there.*

Ahooooooooooo!

A tingle ran down his spine as he raced across. On the other side, dunes spread out in front of them, and a few hundred yards ahead the gray stone arch rose toward the sky.

Luke's legs pumped along the path as the dirt and grass gave way to sand. Brisk air dried the sweat on his skin, and the taste of salt filled his mouth. As the sound of waves hit his ears again, he bounded over a dune and half-slid, half-dropped down the other side. The stone arch stood outlined against stars and black sky.

Ahooooooooooo!

Luke slid to a halt, and when he looked over his shoulder his heart dropped. Near the tree line on the far side of the marsh, three large shadows bounded toward him. He turned and ran again, faster this time. "Here they come!" A pinprick of blue light flashed ahead and his heart leaped. *Marti's there. They'll make it!*

Glancing back again, he heard the yips and snarls of the wolves across the calm night air. Their stride ate up the distance. One pulled ahead and a flash of sea-green light was all the warning Luke and the wolf had.

Whoosh!

As the wolf's paws hit the wooden planks, a wall of water exploded thirty yards up into the air. Luke caught a glimpse of a dryad with water rushing around her as he tripped and fell back away from the marsh, wind rushing past his face.

"Umpfh!"

He slammed into the sand and slid for a few feet. Coughing, he staggered back up. Water shot into the air and plummeted back down in waves, and whines replaced the snarls. Luke stared as the dryad girl in a green dress of moss turned and waved him on. Her voice sounded in his head.

Go. Quickly. I cannot hold them for long.

He waved back and then turned and ran.

Just another hundred yards.

The shadow in front of him slowed down and turned back.

"Go!" Luke shouted.

Matt paused but finally turned and ran again.

Seventy-five yards.

Raouwlll!

The glowing form of a gray wolf burst through the water with a snarl and raced past the dryad.

Not good!

Luke sprinted on.

Fifty yards.

Blue light swept across the tunnel's opening.

He's got it.

"Come on, Luke!" Matt waved him forward.

Grrrrrr …

The wolf was right behind him.

Twenty yards.

He glanced over his shoulder.

"Luke!"

"Luke, hurry!"

He saw that Samantha and Jennifer were gone. Marti jumped through.

Ten yards.

"Come on, man!"

The wolf's galloping grew louder.

Five yards.

Matt stared behind Luke with wide eyes and stretched his

hand out. He jumped into the tunnel, grabbing Luke's hand. Luke felt a tug on his leg and stumbled. His foot jerked back and his world swung forward. Matt clamped down on his hand and pulled.

Not gonna make it.

Blue light swept toward Luke. Pain shot up his leg as he fell forward. As air rushed out of his lungs, he looked back.

The blue-eyed bane wolf from Granite Lake was coming through the tunnel with him.

FOURTEEN

The Algid

Luke's shoulder smacked into the ground.

"Owww!"

Blue-white light winked out and his eyes burned.

Grrrrrr.

He felt pressure on his leg. Darkness mixed with flashing white.

"Get away from him!"

He blinked in the blinding light until tears rolled down his cheeks. He looked up.

Uh-oh.

A couple of feet above him hung the snarling head of the bane wolf. Behind him, he heard the crunching of twigs and leaves as his friends slipped closer.

The wolf watched them for a few seconds. *Grrrrrrrr.* The growl deepened and her lip curled back.

Something's wrong … If she wanted to kill me—

"Get away from him, you, or I swear I'll make a throw rug out of you … you … you overgrown fur ball!" Matt yelled and the wolf crouched.

Feeling her breath warm his face, Luke cringed. "Matt, just ... just back off for a second, OK?"

"W-w-what!?" Marti said.

"Uh ... Luke, maybe you aren't seeing the same thing I am here, but there's a really big wolf standing over your head and I'm pretty sure it's not interested in talking to you," Matt said.

Luke lifted his hand from the ground. "Just ... just back up for a minute, all of you. You don't have to let her take me, but just give her a few feet."

Matt growled. "Of all the harebrained ideas, Rayburn, this one takes the cake."

The wolf stared at Luke.

Just hope it doesn't take my head.

Round blue eyes watched him unblinking.

Are ... are you trying to tell me something?

A gust of wind brought the smell of young grass, water, and something else that prompted Luke to gag and breathe out of his mouth. *What is that?*

The wolf's nose wrinkled and her lips quivered.

"Uh, Luke ..."

Raouwlll!

"Luke!"

The wolf's body coiled. She snarled and snapped her jaws and Luke closed his eyes. He felt her nose brush against his cheek and then air stir over his body. The sound of feet rushing forward filled his ears and he felt hands pulling on him and sitting him up.

"Luke!"

"Luke, you OK?"

He opened his eyes in time to see a shadow bound into a grove of trees and vanish. Samantha was sitting next to him staring at him as he elbowed up into a sitting position. She leaned forward and wrapped her arms around him but then shoved him over and stood up. "You're an idiot, you know that?!"

Marti and Matt pulled him to his feet. "Yeah, but he's a lucky idiot," Matt said, "and as my grandpa says, 'I'd rather be lucky than good.'"

Luke stared in the direction in which the wolf had vanished. *She was trying to tell me something. And what is that smell!?*

He heard the sounds of cracking branches and thundering hooves to the south. A blue orb of light shot into the clearing like a rocket and exploded around Luke and his friends. Two shadows twice as tall as Luke burst from the forest and slid to a halt, illuminated by the sphere of blue light. Two men sat astride horses ten yards away, neither one smiling.

Luke swallowed. "Hi, Dad. Hi, Uncle Landon."

For the next hour, Luke and the others sat under an umbrella of gathered moonlight and answered questions. The expressions of the men darkened throughout, but there was no rebuke. Luke's friends never took their eyes off him as he talked about the conversation the mermen had while he was in the shadow. He told his father and uncle everything that had happened, with the exception of the fact that a voice had helped him to break out of the shadow. As Marti finished telling about coming through the tunnel, Luke's father crouched and rolled up Luke's torn pant leg. He peered at the scratches where the wolf had bit him.

"Are you sure it was a bane wolf?"

"I think so, Dad. I mean, she was huge, and ..."

Uncle Landon pulled a pouch out of his saddlebag and

handed it to Luke's father. He glanced at the wound. "Hmmm … no darkness."

Luke's father dipped his finger into the pouch and spread a white cream over the wounds. The smell wiped out all others in Luke's nose, and he winced as the cream seeped into the wounds, stinging. His father looked up at Uncle Landon. "No reaction. What else were you going to say, Luke?"

Luke took a deep breath. "Well … it was the same one that snatched me up and carried me into the forest when we were camping last summer."

Both men's faces tightened. "You're sure, Luke?"

"Yes, sir, pretty sure."

"She was with the hunter both times, yet her bite leaves no trace of rot, no infection of darkness. Strange."

Luke frowned. "Why is that strange?"

His father cinched the pouch and handed it to Uncle Landon. "Because most bane wolves serve darkness, certainly any who consort with a hunter, and that darkness becomes part of them, just like with darkmen. Because of that, the wounds they give are doubly bad. They injure not only by the initial damage but also by the resulting infection as darkness spreads through the body."

"Much like my wound you saw Grandma treat last year when I was injured," Uncle Landon said. "You remember, Luke?"

"Yes, sir."

His father wrapped Luke's leg with a bandage and then tore the end and secured it before rolling the tattered pant leg back down. He sighed and got to his feet, glancing at his brother. "We need to get Samantha and Jennifer back home."

"Yes, I can only imagine that Phillip's reaction to this is going to be … less than pleasant. And make no mistake, boys" — Uncle

Landon's eyes narrowed and his face hardened—"*you* will be the ones explaining to Mr. Thompson why you dragged his daughter and her friend out in the middle of the night to a *lost island thousands* of miles away."

"But, sir," Samantha said, "we—"

"No, Miss Thompson, this is something they must deal with. You and Miss Brady will have your own repercussions to shoulder if I know your father, as will you, Mr. Stegall, but I know where the idea started, and if it wasn't with one of these two boys, it was with the other one."

Matt and Luke hung their heads, and Marti patted Luke on the shoulder. "R-r-rough night."

The clopping of hooves echoed through the forest, and Luke felt movement pass by him and saw a shimmering under the moonlight as two shadows appeared between the trees. His father tensed beside him.

"Captain Rayburn!"

Luke heard his father let out a sigh as his uncle stepped toward the shadows.

"Sergeant Tibbs ..."

A pale red light bloomed around the two guardsmen.

Luke's father spoke quickly toward a floating ball of moonlight about an inch in diameter. "Q, we're coming from the old North Algid Gate tunnel. We'll be walking southwest along the edge of Westcliffe toward the hay meadow. Send out a couple men with mounts for five. Holekh."

"Whoa." Luke started back as the orb flashed over his head and raced away through the trees before vanishing into the forest. "What was *that*, Dad?"

"A messenger of sorts. It's like a seeker but it delivers a message instead. It's often the fastest means of communication, though not always the most trustworthy or secure, and you have to know where it's going or someone on the other end has to be waiting for it."

"Joe." Uncle Landon's face was flat, his eyes stormy. He looked back over his shoulder. "You're sure, Sergeant?"

"Yes, sir. Just step over and look. I'm pretty sure it's even worse this far north. The smell is certainly stronger here, even in the wind."

Uncle Landon sighed and he and Luke's father headed toward the sound of water shifting along the river path. The guardsmen dismounted and led their horses toward the river. Matt nodded at Luke, and the five friends followed Luke's father. The hemisphere of moonlight surrounding the party and centered on Luke's father moved with them away from the tunnel. Oak and sycamore trees thinned as they neared the river, replaced by a half-dozen sprawling pecan trees. Thick grass carpeted the ground beneath their feet as it sloped toward the water. A stench filled Luke's nose, pushing out the stink of the cream on his leg.

"That's the s-s-same stink I smelled when we got b-b-back through the t-t-tunnel."

"I caught a whiff of it, too," Luke said. "What is it?"

Sergeant Tibbs glanced over as they walked the last few feet to the edge of the Algid. "It's the river."

Samantha and Jennifer gasped. Uncle Landon growled under his breath. In front of them, the Algid flowed by, the water dark and thick.

"That's disgusting," Matt said.

Jennifer covered her nose. "It reeks. What happened to it?"

The guardsman frowned, still watching the water crawl by. "Gnomes. Little beasties finally showed their hand. This is what they've been workin' on since last summer."

"How—" Uncle Landon stopped himself. "What do we know so far, Sergeant?"

"Started late in the afternoon, up north around the lake, from what we can tell so far, sir. Reports didn't get to us in town until a few hours ago, about the time the darkness did." The sergeant spit into the water and glanced at Samantha and Jennifer. "Excuse me, girls." The girls nodded and the sergeant turned back to the river. "The Elder Council's been out and at it, as has the women's circle, but no luck so far."

Luke frowned at Matt. "Women's circle?" he whispered.

"Like the Elder Council but unofficial, and made up only of women. Not real sure what they do."

"The women's circle is the counterpart to the Elder Council, Luke," his father said. "And although they don't make any of the laws and have no say in the actual voting of the council, many in the community would argue they have more influence on the council's decision than the council itself."

A wry grin split Uncle Landon's face. "After watching your mother and grandmother, surely you can appreciate that?"

Luke paused for a moment. "Yes, sir."

"Grandma is one of the leading members of the circle, Luke." His father chuckled. "Although as with much else in life, we men are never allowed to know the actual inner workings, so I can't tell you exactly how she fits into it."

"At any rate, you say they haven't had any luck cleaning the river, Sergeant?" Uncle Landon said.

"No, sir. Maybe they've had more luck by now, but they'd tried a good bit by the time me and Corporal Stevens left to come look for you, sir. They tried putting light into it, or separating the darkness out. Whatever those little devils did, they made it stick awful good."

Luke's father crouched and looked at the bank of the river

a few feet in front of him. Tendrils of blackness stretched from the water into the dirt and curled and blackened the grass in the river itself. "And what damage is it doing?"

Sergeant Tibbs sighed and arched his eyebrows. "Pretty good bit, sir. The water's not safe to drink, makes anybody who does sick. They retch up whatever they drink and then some."

Luke's father reached his hand toward the water.

"I wouldn't recommend doing that either, sir. Seems just touching it irritates the skin almost as bad as poison ivy. Private Lejeune got it all the way up his arms and his back after just splashing his hands in it."

He pulled his hand back and stood. Luke and the others eased away from the water.

"Joe, we need to get them back," Uncle Landon said. "I'm gonna have to get into town and talk with Colonel Henderson."

Luke's father nodded. "Nothin' else to do here anyway." After one last look, he turned to Luke and the others. "Head back up to the tunnel. We're going to have to hoof it until Q gets out here with some more mounts."

He took a few steps and then stopped. A smile lighted his face and he shook his head as he turned to Uncle Landon. "Bane wolves, lost islands, gnomes—I can't believe you and I caused *half* this much excitement for Mom and Dad, brother."

Uncle Landon chuckled and walked up from the river and patted his brother on the back. "Don't worry. Somehow this will still end up being our fault."

FIFTEEN

Shields & Stars

Luke puffed air out and struggled forward again. He pulled and tugged, the muscles in his back straining and the soles of his boots slipping on the grass. The pressure around his chest increased, and he squirmed from side to side within Uncle Landon's grasp. He inhaled and felt warm breath on his shoulder.

"You're not trying, Luke."

Luke gritted his teeth at the sound of his uncle's voice in his ear. "I *am* trying!"

"No, you're not, Luke, and you will not survive giving only a half-effort."

He surged again, pushing against the ground with his feet. The pressure remained. Out of the corner of his eye, he saw Matt sitting cross-legged watching him. *How did he do it so easily?*

About fifty yards away, on the other side of the meadow, Luke caught a glimpse of trees and grass, red cliffs and the shimmering surface of Redwater Pond, along with a team of four brown-clad holding guardsmen. *Great. They must think this is hilarious … Weak little boy who can't do anything.*

Uncle Landon squeezed and Luke's mind jerked back to the thick, tanned arms around his chest that were pinning his own trembling arms to his side. He felt his cheeks flush. "I survived … bane wolves."

"Ha! Luck. And help. And they weren't trying to kill you, nephew." He leaned close to Luke's ear and his voice dropped to a whisper. "And what will you do next time when your family is in trouble, or your friends? … Trent, Matt, Samantha … Jodi … Is this the effort you'll give?"

Faces flashed through Luke's mind as his uncle spoke. His throat tightened and he closed his eyes. *Come on, Rayburn …* He replayed his uncle's instructions from that morning.

Distract. Give your enemy something else to think about. Somehow you must loosen the grip.

Luke smiled.

Distract.

He lifted his knees to his chest. Uncle Landon's body shifted forward with his weight and Luke slammed his feet down.

"*Ehhh!*" his uncle grunted as the heel of Luke's boot found the toe of his. When his uncle's grip slipped for a second, it was all Luke needed. He slipped down through his arms, grabbed his leg and pulled up.

"*Uhhh!*" Uncle Landon stumbled backward but kept his footing.

Luke jumped forward a few paces and whirled around. He crouched, fists raised and staring at his uncle.

A smile crept onto his uncle's face. "Well done, nephew." The smile faded, though, as he stepped over the grass toward Luke. "But don't make me bait you again. Your enemy will give you no such advantage nor show any restraint. Do you understand?"

Luke took a deep breath, dropping his fists and his head. "Yes, sir."

His uncle's brown boots stopped on the ground in front of him and rough fingers pulled his chin up. "Don't look down. You made progress today. You've no reason or right to look down."

"But Matt did it," Luke said, still struggling to catch his breath.

His uncle's face hardened. "You are not Matt … and he is not you. You must use what strengths you have, Luke." He walked a few paces toward the saddles and the gear sitting under the shade of a gnarled oak tree and then stopped and turned back to Luke. "As a Rayburn, and even more as a boy growing into a young man, you must traverse a line between pride and arrogance on the one hand and doubt and self-pity on the other. It's a fine line and no easy task. Ask for help on the way … That's why we're here."

Matt's feet rustled toward him through the bluestem grass behind Luke as his uncle turned back to the tack.

"You did good, man. And he's right, you know."

Luke snorted. "Yeah, I know. Between him and Q and Grandma, you'd wonder if any of them were ever wrong."

As grass waved in the wind and sweat dried on Luke's face, a wagon rolled around the bend from the east. Honks sounded overhead as two great *V* formations of Canada geese flew north. The creak of wheels sounded and Luke looked back toward the wagon as Ricardo pulled up next to them. He dipped his head, touching his fingers to the brim of his hat.

"Hey, sir."

"Muchachos. You survived, el capitán?"

Luke chortled. "Barely, and not for lack of trying on Uncle Landon's part."

A wry grin slipped across Ricardo's sun-darkened face. "Hmmm."

"Ricardo." Uncle Landon tromped back over to the wagon. "You comin' to fill up at Redwater Pond?"

"Yes, señor."

Uncle Landon nodded. "Good, we'll help fill 'em. Boys, hop on up. We've got a bit of time to spare anyway."

The young man next to Ricardo stood and started to step to the back. Uncle Landon waved him back down and hopped into the bed of the wagon as Luke and Matt clambered over the side. Ricardo waited until the boys settled in around the wooden barrels and then flicked the reins. Luke braced himself against the side and one of the barrels as the wagon jolted forward.

"Any news from town this morning?"

Ricardo shook his head and spit tobacco over the side of the wagon. "Nothing good, señor. Another of the mermaids come to help has the sickness, from el río, and the blackness has spread. Another chunk of the Joneses' peach orchard es gone."

Uncle Landon pursed his lips and mumbled under his breath.

"Señor Rayburn, su hermano come back this morning. He es going back this evening … to talk with los mayores." Ricardo glanced over his shoulder and arched his eyebrows. "They no seem to listen so good, though."

"Fools." Uncle Landon went on to mutter some more, and Luke and Matt exchanged a shocked glance at the stream of words. Uncle Landon sighed. "Have they at least agreed to adding another company for the Guard?"

Ricardo nodded and spit again as the wagon pulled up

to Redwater Pond, the surface of the cliffs coloring the water rock-red. The four guardsmen posted around the water nearby stood, and mist spread through the air behind them as the sound of the falling water rose in Luke's ears. "Yes, señor. They have ... but they are *slow* about it."

Uncle Landon hopped over the side and saluted the men before turning back to Ricardo. "Well, at least there's that. We couldn't have stretched much thinner with increased patrols and having to man the various tanks and ponds where there's still clean water in the holding."

Luke and Matt crawled to the back of the wagon and helped unlock it so that the tailboard swung down freely. They handed down the buckets to the men and then turned back to unlatching the barrels' lids. A wild turkey glanced up from the reeds on the far side of the pond before racing behind a pecan tree. The men walked over and filled buckets with the water and then walked them back over. After Luke and Matt dumped the water in, the process began again. Thirty minutes later, as the boys replaced the lid on one of the last three barrels, Luke glanced up.

"Matt, look ... Samech!"

The centaur galloped down the dirt trail toward them. "Ho, boys! And how do we do this afternoon?"

"Good, sir."

Samech stomped his feet and dipped his head toward the guardsmen. "I apologize for my lateness." A frown settled on his face. "The work in town goes poorly."

"Late ... for what?" Luke asked.

"Samech is here today to begin your lessons in defense with the disciplines."

The boys turned at the sound of Uncle Landon's voice.

"Good morning, Samech."

Samech grinned. "Good morning, Landon. And do you approve, young ones?"

Luke and Matt nodded enthusiastically. "Yes, sir."

"Good, good. Well, finish up and we shall begin."

Luke and Matt sealed the last of the barrels and helped secure the tailboard of the wagon. While Ricardo tied a rope around the barrels, Luke put a leg over the side of the wagon to climb up, but Samech stepped in front of him. Luke paused and eased back. "Landon, you have no further need for them this day?"

"No, Samech, all we have planned for the rest of the afternoon is training with you."

"You can manage with the horses and the help you have here?"

Uncle Landon frowned and then his eyes rose and a half-smile formed on his face. "Ha. Yes, yes indeed."

Samech turned to Luke and Matt. "You boys will ride with me today … if you are willing."

Luke exchanged an open-mouthed stare with Matt and then looked back at Uncle Landon, who smiled. "To ride with a centaur is a rare privilege, boys. And to be *asked* to ride with one is an even greater honor. You will remember who you are."

Luke swallowed. "Yes, sir." He motioned with his head toward Samech. "You first, Matt, you're the better … rider."

Matt hesitated and then turned toward Samech. He stepped over the side and eased onto Samech's back. Settled in, he nodded to Luke. After taking a deep breath, Luke lifted his leg and swung it over Samech's back. He settled in, and just as he opened his mouth, Samech surged forward.

"Whoa!"

Luke grabbed on to Matt, who leaned forward and wrapped his arms around Samech. Samech's hooves thundered forward and the trees rushed at them. Luke heard shouts from behind as muscles tensed beneath them, and Samech lunged into the southern edge of Westcliffe Forest.

This isn't even close to riding a horse!

The wind whipped their faces and still Samech increased his speed. He leaped over fallen trees and brush and sped across meadows. Fifteen minutes later, he slowed to a trot and then a walk, his chest heaving. Oak and pecan trees ringed a meadow of calf-high wild rye grass, and limestone and sand lined the bottom of the stream where Samech stopped at the meadow's edge. He swung the boys down off his back, smiles plastered to their faces.

"That was awe—" Uncle Landon's admonition sounded in Luke's head. *What do you say to a centaur about the chance to ride?* "Thank you, Samech. I am … very honored."

Matt bobbed his head up and down. "Me, too, Samech. Thank you for letting us ride."

"You are most welcome, young ones." His eyes lost focus. "I had forgotten what it felt like to have a rider."

"Did … did you used to let people ride more often?"

Samech came back to himself and grinned. "I forget how much has changed, how little you know."

Luke frowned. "Know about what?"

"Years ago, when *halflings* were more … common in the human holdings, there were units of the holding guard composed of men and our races. Of these there was often a section of centaurs and humans. The humans were known as Riders."

"And you were one of them? One of the centaurs in these units?"

"Yes, for many years, young one. It was a great privilege."

"I've heard of the Riders before"—Matt counted on his

fingers—"but the last one was gone almost a hundred years ago, I mean … you must be … like, over a hundred!"

Samech chuckled. "Yes, young one, you are correct, but surely you knew many of the ta'arovet lived much longer lives."

"I didn't realize it was *so* much longer."

"What was it like, sir?" Luke said.

Samech smiled. "A story for another time, Luke." He glanced up at the sun as it dropped toward the Redwall cliffs. "Daylight is fading and our chore will be easiest with the help of the sun. Now, let us get a drink and then we will begin."

Samech and the boys knelt next to the stream and, after drinking a few handfuls of the cold water, stood back up. Luke pushed off the ground and groaned as his legs tightened.

The next two days are going to be long.

"Today we will begin your training in use of the disciplines for defense. I assume you have both seen many weapons formed from the disciplines?"

Matt nodded, but Luke shook his head.

Samech frowned. "No?"

"Well, maybe, sir, but I didn't know that's what it was, except for a sword or two and Uncle Landon making a bow out of light to hunt turkeys with."

"Well, I will show you both then, but we will focus on the defense today." Samech tromped a few feet away from the boys. "During individual combat, one of the advantages to the use of the disciplines is that you do not have to carry tradition- al weapons. There are some weaknesses as well. For example, whatever you make your weapons or armor out of has to come from the area around you, generally. That means that if you make something out of air, that air is taken from around you.

This can get to be a bit of a problem in huge groups and battles where air is needed desperately to breathe, you see?"

The boys nodded.

"Most of these obstacles can be overcome with training, and we will talk of them another time. There are also some differences between weapons made of the disciplines and defensive items such as a shield or armor, but they are in most respects similar. I will instruct you in the making of human weapons and items, but your knowledge must also stretch beyond to include those of other races. A traditional centaur weapon, for example, is a claymore, or long sword."

Luke sucked in his breath and started back as a silver-blue sword glowed in front of Samech, stretching five feet from his hands. Samech twisted and the sword whistled in an arc in front of him, slicing a cluster of yaupon trees in half. The sword vanished and Samech continued.

"Our defenses are more limited as far as shields go, but often in combat we wear some form of breastplate."

A silver plate depicting two gray centaurs rearing and facing each other appeared in front of Samech's torso. Luke stared with mouth agape until the silver light vanished.

"You'll catch flies like that, you know," Matt said.

Luke snapped his mouth shut and sneered at him.

Samech chuckled. "Now, as with all things with the disciplines, your ability to use them is controlled by what you can think of and what you think can be done. Are either of you familiar with bucklers?"

Both boys shook their heads. "No, sir."

"Very well. Let us try with that today. I will form a simple one for you to see. What I want you to do is look at it, see how it is made."

Brown light appeared in front of them, forming a round shield a bit less than two feet across.

"For most objects, especially as you begin, they will have to be touching you to exist, but as you progress in ability, you will be able to have them remain even when they are not in contact with you, although you do not always want this."

He held out the buckler and Matt took it. He turned it over in his hands for a few minutes and then handed it to Luke. The light was cold and hard to the touch.

Just like metal ... "Is it real metal?"

"No, it is a combination of light and earth. It is similar to metal and contains some metal, but it is not the same as a shield wrought solely out of bronze or steel. You must focus on the attributes more than what the shield is made of, though you will have to adjust the object by adding or taking away disciplines until you get the correct temperament."

Luke flipped the shield over and ran his fingers along the surface and the straps attached to it.

Neeeever gonna happen.

He sighed and passed it back to Matt, but the shield vanished as Matt's hands touched it.

"There is little to do that will be as helpful as practice. Let us see how each of you fares. I want each of you to try to re-create the buckler. Focus on what you want the disciplines to do and believe you can create that."

Sure ... sounds easy enough ... no big deal ... riiiight!

For the next hour, as the sun touched the top of the Redwall cliffs and then sank below them, Luke and Matt stared at their hands. Sometimes light would pop and explode; sometimes it would appear, shimmer, and fade. At one point, Luke ended up forming a rock out of earth and light that was so heavy it slipped from his grasp and fell to the ground an inch from his toe. Another time, Matt ended up with a face full of mud as the ball in his hands erupted. Finally, toward the end of the session, Luke was able to hold a round object that glowed brown and was at least not easy to bend. His satisfied smile morphed into an *O*, though, as his "shield" vanished.

Matt held a copy of the buckler in his hands. Sweat poured off his forehead and his jaw was clenched.

"How are you doing that?" Luke said.

The shield remained for a few seconds and then wavered like air on a hot summer day and vanished. Air rushed in and out of Matt's lungs and his shoulders sagged.

"Very well done, boys," Samech said. "You have just achieved in one lesson what takes most a month. In your case, Matt, almost two."

Matt grinned shakily.

"That was awesome, man!" Luke said.

"You, too, man. I couldn't figure it out until I saw your last one and how the earth seemed to mix with the light."

Luke recalled his uncle's words: *a line between pride and arrogance on the one hand and doubt and self-pity on the other.* He smiled. "Good."

"An outstanding first day, young ones, but we must get moving home now."

Samech knelt beside the boys and they climbed on. He walked out of the meadow and trotted along the path to the northeast, rolling along over knolls and hills and winding among trees. Dusk settled in as they rode, and a gray and brown scissortail swooped into the air, twisted, and dived back down chasing a dragonfly. Luke followed the flight of the bird, turning his head to the north. A red light twinkled in the sky and he shivered in the breeze.

"Are you cold, Luke?"

Luke swallowed. "No, sir."

"Ah, yes ... ever present even though we wish it were not." He was looking at the red light, too. "Let us not think upon such a star and focus on what is good and right, perhaps your schooling or another light in the sky."

Luke sighed and looked away.

"Perhaps I should see how much you have improved since last year with your skill with light. Do you think you could illuminate the road before us as I taught you at the Pavilion last year, Luke? Though perhaps not in quite such *dramatic* fashion."

Luke grinned. "Yes, sir." He glanced ahead at the gray path and then into the sky as lights twinkled to life. *How do I get the path to light up but keep it moving with us?* Thoughts of a bird hopping down dark passageways of Rayburn Manor and a silver trail winding across a marsh flat flitted into his head. He closed his eyes and pictured Samech plodding along with Matt and him on his back, the gray dirt beneath them and the trees and clumps of grass to either side.

"Wow," Matt said

Luke opened his eyes.

"How did you do *that*?"

Reaching out twenty yards before and behind them, blue-silver light sparkled along the ground, extending a few feet past the sides of the trail. Fireflies and other flying insects added to the show, glowing when they flew over the light. Tendrils of light climbed up Samech's legs as he walked on, and the halo of light moved with them along the trail.

"*Very* well done, young one."

Luke felt heat rush to his face and ducked his head. "Thank you, sir."

"That is *way* cooler than my shield!"

"I still think the shield was pretty cool, man."

Samech increased his pace again. "Now, what do you remember of the stars, hmm? Virgo, Cassiopeia?"

Luke peered into the sky and a star sparkled low on the horizon to the east. As he stared at it, the face of a woman with blond hair and blue eyes flashed through his head and he gasped.

"You OK, man?" Matt asked.

A shudder coursed through his body. "Yeah, man … fine." He stared at the star for a moment more. *Who is she?*

"Samech, sir, can you tell us about that star hanging low over the trees there, just to the south of Knob Hill?"

"Ah … yes, there is quite an intriguing tale to that star, one of the tragedies of legend. That light is called the Star of Adina."

Luke's ears perked up.

Samech looked over his shoulder, blue-white light illuminating his questioning expression. "You are familiar with that name?"

"Only a little bit, sir. We heard the name recently."

Samech frowned and narrowed his eyes. "Hmm … Well, the tale is not a short one or a simple one in whole, but I will tell you briefly about it. The Star of Adina was named after a woman who lived during the Breaking of the world, when the Ancients left this earth for their new home. She was a beautiful woman, noble, tall of stature and powerful with the disciplines, yet humble and kind. There were also three brothers at this time, the greatest leaders, save their father, among the men who stayed and did not leave with the Ancients … and one of these she fell in love with. This man loved her, too, and soon they were married.

"The years passed and thoughts of children came, and the couple's love grew deeper. Darkness also was pushed back then and the servants of the Evil One forced to flee and hide or be destroyed. It was at this point of greatest happiness, near the end of the War of Breaking, that the Dark One struck back one final time. He struck the servants of the Flame with a great illness and Adina fell to this. The brothers tried everything they could, but Adina's body weakened and faded. Distraught and frustrated, her husband turned to the Dark One himself. He traded his soul for the power to heal her body. Using one of the few remaining objects of pure Flame and knowledge of the Dark One, he healed his wife."

Trees crowded the trail, blocking out the stars until Samech eased up a rise. "Adina was distraught upon recovering and learning of her husband's compact, but she loved her husband still and they told no one. As time passed, though, her husband became darker and darker, violent and strange and brooding. At one point, Adina could no longer hide the truth from his brothers and they came to him to try to help. The darkness, however, had corrupted the mind of her husband and warped his understanding. He viewed his own brothers as his enemies, convinced they had turned Adina against him. War erupted again, between the brother tainted by darkness and the other two, ending only when he was slain by them. Brokenhearted, with her husband dying in her arms, tears poured out of Adina, and with them, the great power that had healed her. Her husband died, and she, overcome with sorrow, faded away, her body dissolving into the various disciplines. It was then that the Star of Adina was born, for the light of her body fled into the night sky, lost forever in the darkness and her loneliness."

Luke and Matt sat quietly, their bodies shifting up and down with Samech's rhythmic plodding. They heard the sound of wind whispering through pine needles, the calls of night birds and even the howls of coyotes hunting through the fields. Samech remained quiet as well, walking along and watching the sky or the pastures as often as the glow of the road before them. One question prevailed over all the thoughts teeming in Luke's mind: *Do the Tears have the power of the Flame? Maybe that's why they're so special. Maybe that's why darkness wants them, something so powerful that it can heal even a dying person. Surely that would be worth having, even to darkness.*

At some point, the slate roof of the Rayburn House peeked above the treetops and lights reached out to greet them. As they neared the stone steps, the front doors opened and Luke's father stepped out. Luke and Matt slid off of Samech's back.

"Thank you, sir," Matt said.

"For the lesson and the ride," Luke added.

Samech chuckled. "You are most welcome, young ones."

The boys trudged up the stairs, yawning and with their heads drooping as Luke's father walked down to meet them.

"That bad, huh?" Luke's father smiled and wrapped his arms around the boys' shoulders.

"They did very well this evening, Joseph. Better than I would have expected."

"Indeed? Well, that combined with Uncle Landon's praise of you two makes for an outstanding day. I'm very proud of you … both." Matt smiled at the recognition. "Now, off to bed with you. You look like you've been run over one of Ms. Lucy's washboards with the dirt scrubbed in instead of out."

Luke looked down at his scraped hands, torn pants, and mud-caked boots and snorted. "Yes, sir."

Grrrrr …

Luke's father chortled at Luke's rumbling stomach. "Mom had Mr. Robinson leave some food laid out in the family room upstairs."

Luke smiled and headed toward the door but looked back over his shoulder. "Night, Dad. Love you."

Luke's father winked. "Love you, too, son." He turned back to Samech. "Samech, do you have time to come in to talk?"

The door closed, cutting off his father's words. Luke and Matt shuffled up staircases and down hallways. Sitting in front of a low fire, his mother smiled as they walked into the room. The boys fell on the food and, after showers, stumbled into the bedroom. Gray darkness and a light chill filled the room, pushed back only by a handful of embers in the fireplace.

"Man, long ... day," Matt said before breaking into a yawn.

Luke caught the yawn and stumbled toward his bed. Trent's snoring rose and fell, whispering across the room. As Luke stepped past his writing desk, he froze. A line of ivory-colored light bloomed to life, sparkling and racing around to form a rectangle on his desk. He glanced at Matt, who stared back with wide eyes, no longer yawning. Luke leaned forward and saw the outline of a letter. As he drew closer, cursive script flowed across the front, spelling out his name.

"James," Luke said.

"Whaddya think he wants?"

Luke smirked. "Does it look like I've opened it yet?"

"Well, open it already."

Luke picked up the letter and broke the wax seal stamped with a *J* on the back of it. As he unfolded the paper and blew across it, handwriting again appeared on the page, as if an invisible hand were doing the writing. He shook his head. "Not sure I'll ever get used to that, even when I do it."

Matt nodded. "Cool, but kinda freaky."

They started to read:

Luke,

Hope you're doing well. I'm pretty good, just having to keep on the move more than usual. I have one promising lead on my niece, so I'm hopeful. I've managed to keep tabs on you by a few channels. One in particular has opened up recently … shockingly, and you seem to be doing great, learning well and having a great year between football and … other training. I know it's been a few months and I'm sorry, but as I said, safe communication is difficult. I'm working on a way to solve that, but for now … some more information has come to my attention that I think you should know.

I've figured out what the people who are searching in Countryside are looking for, something called the Tears of Adina. You may already know this, and I don't know much more than that. Another thing is that the person feeding information to the darkness is someone working for Mr. Thompson. I won't scare you with how I managed to come across that information, but I can vouch that it's good intelligence.

Luke exchanged a wide-eyed glance with Matt.

That rather rotund Prichard boy was mentioned, I don't think it's him based on the intelligence, but I can't be sure of that. At any rate, watch your back and don't trust anyone unless you are sure of them. Someone close to you isn't who you think.

The last thing I have for you is a bit of knowledge of the old Rayburn Manor. I caught wind of your little

*camping adventure a few weeks ago. I'm assuming
your parents and Mr. Acharon have a pretty close
eye on y'all, but I think I can help you get out of the
house and around on your own without those in
the manor finding out, certainly without raising as
much suspicion as any future camping-trip requests
might. The original parts of the Manor were built a
few centuries ago on top of some ancient ruins in the
holding. If you don't already know, and I feel pretty
sure you do by now considering the level of curiosity
and ability to get into things I've known in other
boys your age, there are a set of secret passageways
running throughout the house. There is always a "le-
ver" at each opening, though the levers are different.
Sometimes you just lift or push an object, sometimes
you have to use one of the disciplines. You'll have
to figure each one out. At any rate, getting into them
should be fairly easy. It's the using them and getting
out of the house that is the tricky part. If you have a
seeker they are immensely helpful; if you don't, well
… I made a rough map of the place over the years
that I worked there. It doesn't even begin to cover
all the tunnels, but it will get you around the house
quickly, and it will help get you to the one way that
leads out of the house. Go to the second floor of the
library and look behind a book labeled Treasures of
the Ancient World, 5503a.*

*The way out of the manor is in the lowest part of
the ruins in an old great hall of some kind. The room
is huge, probably the size of the whole house above
ground and filled with columns too big for even three*

*people to wrap their arms around. In that room, if
you go due north from the center of the room, there
is a small crack in the wall. The tunnel through this
crack will lead you up and out about a mile north of
the house in a small grove of Westcliffe Forest. This
is where the tricky part comes in. Others must have
known about the passage over the years, because
there are sentinels there to keep things out. Trouble
is they don't distinguish much from things trying to
get in ... and people trying to get out. The only way
to get past them is to touch a stone obelisk on the
far side of the room and fill it with light, earth, and
water, and then run like the Dark One himself was
after you. The sentinels apparently have to turn the
obelisk off before they can come chase you. Don't ask
me why, maybe whoever set it up still wanted there
to be a way to get out of the house. Whatever the
reason, they come. Also, try to stay a bit out of the
middle of the room as you run across, the sentinels
seem to head that way at first. Once you're past the
door you're good ... until you have to come back in.
That is pretty much impossible ...*

Matt sighed. "If it's *impossible,* why is he *telling* us to do it?"
he whispered.

Luke snickered and kept reading.

*I've only found one way to do it ... you have to have
a decoy, a living breathing decoy that can draw them
away while you make a run for it. The decoy has to
get the sentinels far enough away that you have time
to get to the other side, and it has to convince all
the sentinels to follow it. You don't want to make*

the mistake of running before all the sentinels have given chase; it's not fun. Once you reach the other side, you can touch the obelisk and that will allow your decoy to get back out while the sentinels come toward your side of the room. I always thought there must be a simpler way, but I couldn't figure it out—maybe you can. For now, this is the only way I know. It's not fun, and it's not easy, so don't use it unless you have to.

Matt snorted. "I'll say. Who's gonna volunteer for *that* job?"

As far as the sentinels themselves go, I don't know what they are or what they look like and I would strongly suggest you don't get close enough to them to figure either one out yourself. They make an awful howling/wailing sort of noise. Believe me, you'll know it when you hear it. Oh … and they will leave the room and come up into the higher passageways if they sense darkness there. They have a smell about them too if you ever get that close. It's kinda like fresh-cut grass and this clean earthy smell. Unless you're a dark creature—then it smells horrible, almost debilitating, but you shouldn't have to worry about that.

Luke's thoughts flashed back to a rat racing down the halls and splashing through puddles in the dark. *Well, that explains that. Would have been nice to know before I went traipsing down there following a creepy rat.*

That's all I have for now. Hope it helps some. Keep this letter at least until you have the map. I'll work on better comm. Use the map and add to it as you can. I'll be watching and will be in touch as soon as I can.

Your Confidant,

J.

Matt frowned. "'Your confidant'—hardly."

Luke shrugged. "Maybe he's trying to be."

"Hmm. Doubtful."

"Well, whatever, it's still good to know. I just wish we knew who he was talking about. Jon David seems like a good candidate."

"But he said it was someone close to you. Jon David doesn't exactly fit the bill. *If* James is even telling the truth, man."

Luke sighed. "I know. I don't know. I'm tired—let's just go to bed. We can try to get the map tomorrow. If it's still there, it won't go anywhere tonight."

Matt nodded, covering his mouth as his yawns returned. "… eeeee, tooo."

Luke shuffled to his bed and tucked the letter into his pillowcase and collapsed onto the mattress. Stars twinkled in the sky outside his window. As his breathing slowed, Luke pictured two sets of glowing eyes.

We have to find the Tears before the hunter … and whoever else is looking for them.

His eyes fluttered and a green glow slipped past the edge of his vision.

That's a strange star …

He let out a long breath and his mind moved on to glowing roads, ancient stars, and sandy-blond hair.

SIXTEEN

The Abandoned House

Luke watched Mr. Jacobs shuffle up the stone steps. His hair speckled with gray, he paused at the top step and waved a hand over the last of the pink-and-white apple blossoms on a nearby branch. He glanced down at Luke and winked before turning and walking through the polished-wood doors into St. Barbara's. Curious, Luke walked up the steps to where Mr. Jacobs had stood. A cool breeze wrapped around him and stirred the nearby leaves and blooms. Two of the blooms broke loose, and pink-and-white light twinkled as the blooms twirled to the ground like spinning sparklers on the Fourth of July. Another breeze slipped in among the trees and Luke heard Jodi squeal and Jon and Amy whisper. Other people stopped and stared as dozens of the blooms fell from the tree and swirled in the wind, leaving trails of glittering dust.

"You should have seen what Mrs. Jacobs could do with snapdragons in the summer."

Luke turned and looked at his father, who stared after the blossoms. "Mrs. Jacobs?"

His father smiled sadly. "Yes. Grandma told me she passed away just a few years ago. When I was a little boy she would plant white snapdragons all around the courthouse in containers. Sometimes she would cut a few of them for us and when we threw them in the air, they would turn into little dragons and flitter over grass and shrubs. We'll have to ask Mr. Jacobs if she ever taught him how to do that."

As they walked into the cathedral, Luke watched the last of the blooms fall to the ground. Inside, a low rumble of voices filled the sanctuary. Luke scanned the crowd and spotted Matt and his mom on the family's bench about halfway from the front. Luke's family filed into the row with them, with Uncle Landon sitting on the far side of Ms. Nichols and Luke and Trent sitting next to Matt on the end. Luke nodded to Tommy Caskey in the row behind them.

Shafts of colored sunlight shone through the stained glass windows on the east side of the sanctuary. Members of the choir filtered in at the front, and more people filed in from outside, dresses mixing with suits and hats of all kinds. Tapestries hung from the cedar pillars throughout the room. There was a murmur among the attendees until Father Woods entered near the front.

"… to pass on to us tonight."

Luke's ears perked as he heard Randy's voice whispering in the aisle behind them.

"Where does he want to meet?"

He glanced sideways at Matt, who was sitting perfectly still to listen.

"The abandoned house … Market Road."

When Randy walked past them to the front, Luke kept his face turned straight ahead. When Father Woods's voice boomed out into the cathedral, Luke leaned forward to reach for a book in the back of the pew in front of them and Matt eased forward as well. "If Randy is involved, you know who else is," Luke whispered out of the side of his mouth.

"They're up to something."

"We haven't learned anything new the last couple weeks. Might have to try James's tunnel sooner than we thought."

"Can't tell you how thrilled I am about *that*."

When Father Woods finished speaking and stepped away from the lectern, the sound of rustling clothes filled the room. The choir stood and a young woman moved forward from the group.

Maybe he's learned something about the Tears, or the —

A hum rose from the choir, interrupting Luke's thoughts.

Maybe... maybe it's about the Algid ...

"O Lord my God ..."

Luke paused as the woman's soft voice spread through the sanctuary:

> When I in awesome wonder,
> Consider all the worlds Thy Hands have made;
> I see the stars, I hear the mighty thunder,
> Thy power throughout the universe displayed
> Then sings my soul, My Savior God, to Thee,
> How great Thou art, How great Thou art.

Luke shivered and his thoughts fled.

Dusk settled in behind Rayburn Manor. Jodi danced around the patio, and Jon and Amy bounced up and down, tugging on their parents' arms and pointing toward the garden. Trent twitched, peering into the lavender shadows of evening with narrowed eyes.

"They've hidden them, Trent," Matt said. "You won't be able to see them until they light them up."

Trent frowned. "Hmmm … I bet I can."

"Ha!" Matt shook his head as two shadows walked out of the falling darkness.

"You did actually make it so that they can find them, boys?" Luke's grandmother said.

Luke's father and Uncle Landon feigned hurt expressions. "They have no faith in us at all, brother," Luke's father said.

Uncle Landon shook his head, face somber. "It's sad, really. Trustworthy boys like us …"

Grandma Rayburn snorted. "Trustworthy *indeed*. I lived with you for twenty years. Lucy still can't get the stench out of the Farmer Room."

Luke saw color rise in his father's and uncle's cheeks.

"Uh-hum, well, yes, time to get started, I think," his father said.

Laughter sounded around the patio, and Mr. Acharon and Grandpa Rayburn shook their heads.

"Now, Luke, you and Matt will wait for a moment before you start. Everyone else, when we say the word, you can go, all right?"

Heads bobbed and bodies bounced up and down. "Yes, sir."

"You sure you're ready?"

"Yes!"

"Daaaaddy!"

Luke's father laughed and winked at Jon and Amy. He turned toward the lawn and Luke saw his mouth move silently.

"Wow." Luke stood with his mouth agape. His brothers and sisters stood still, too, their goal forgotten. Sweeping across the lawn to the north, ovals of light blossomed to life. Reds, pinks, blues, oranges, and a dozen other colors appeared. Some lay in the open, some hidden in tufts of grass or the crook of a tree branch or behind a stone, the only evidence of them their glow. The croaking of frogs and the hoot of an owl carried to Luke's ears.

"Well?" His father's voice brought them all back to themselves, and with shrieks and shouts, Jodi, Jon, Amy, and Trent dashed out into the night. Luke laughed as Grandma Rayburn raced after Jodi.

"Nana, Nana, there's one, there's one!"

"Yes, yes."

"And 'nother one! Nana, the yeggs *gyow!*"

Uncle Landon turned to Luke and Matt. "All right, boys, now it's your turn."

Luke's father grinned mischievously. "And it won't be *nearly* as easy."

Luke frowned. "We're not hunting eggs here?"

"Ha. And where would the fun be in that?" Uncle Landon pulled two leather pouches about the size of his fist out of his pants pocket and tossed one to each boy. "You boys will be hunting in the North Garden, and in order to find your 'eggs'…" He pulled a smaller pouch out of his shirt pocket and dumped gray-and-silver sand into his hand. He stepped over and tossed the dust into the air so that it sifted onto a wrought-iron table and some chairs. "You will have to truly 'find' them first." Light sparkled wherever the sand landed, and splotches of silver, blue, and green light bloomed on the surface of four eggs lying on the table.

"Awesome," Luke said.

"The hidden eggs will only appear if the sand lands on

them, and you only have the sand in the pouch. Once it's gone, the hunt is over."

Luke's uncle nodded toward his father. "And *we* get to keep the rest of what's out there."

Luke narrowed his eyes. "What's out there, Dad?"

His father chuckled. "Eggs ... and a few other surprises. You'll have to find out. Now, when I say—"

Luke nodded at Matt and the boys darted toward the arched entrance to the garden.

"Go! Ha!"

Luke heard laughter and shouts behind him as he and Matt raced through the gate and then slowed down. For the next hour, they took turns tossing pinches of dust into the air along the paths in the garden. Laughter and exclamations echoed throughout the garden, interspersed with the sigh of the wind and the sound of shoes shuffling over the stones. By the time they returned to the patio, their pockets were full and Luke's siblings were racing under the glow of moonlight and floating orbs. Jodi grinned and waved, chocolate smeared across her face. Trent and the twins chased a ball of clay that morphed into a cat darting around a chair and then a toad that hopped into the fountain with a splash.

"Aw, it turned to mud! Get another one, Trent, get another one!"

Trent pulled out another bit of clay the size of a bird's egg and dropped it to the ground, and the chase was on again as a rabbit bounded away.

As Luke and Matt pulled objects out of pockets and bags, Luke's father walked over. "Let's see what you left us?"

Candy, silver coins, a couple of glowing seeker orbs and even two mandreekahs plopped onto the table. Luke's father sighed and glanced at his mother as she walked up and wrapped her arms around him. "So much for them not finding everything."

Luke grinned, his thoughts filled with light and laughing faces, as Mr. Acharon plucked the stings of a guitar.

Boom. Boom. Boom. Rawrrrr.

"Uh, Luke, I'm pretty sure that sound getting louder is *not* a good thing."

Glowing light illuminated the air around them as Luke squinted, leaning closer to the parchment. "Just give me a second, all right? The map's confusing and I'm trying to make sure we don't go running in the wrong direction. You don't want us to go running into the sentinels, do you?"

Boom. Boom. Boom. Rawrrrr.

Matt glanced down the tunnel and shook his head. "No, but if you don't hurry up, we're not gonna have time to go running in *any* direction! Honestly, we should just have told your dad and Captain Rayburn."

Luke looked up at the stone arch in front of him and the circled symbol in the keystone and then back down at the map. "You know they'd never let us go, Matt. Besides, what are they gonna do anyway? Meeting in an old abandoned house after dark might be crazy, but it's not a crime. It's not like the Guard is gonna stake out the house to listen to Jon David and his goons."

Matt shrugged. "Well, we could have at least tried sneaking out of the house some other way."

Luke snorted. "Right, like climbing down from the fourth-floor window? There are too many people still up in the house. Someone would see us for sure if we tried to just waltz out. Dad and Uncle Landon are still suspicious of us after our little 'camping trip' anyway. We wouldn't even make it out of the family quarters, man. ... Got it." He rolled up the map and looked through the doorway.

Boom. Boom. Boom. Rawrrrr.

"All right, once we touch the obelisk, we need to go to the right past two pillars. Hopefully that will keep us far enough from the center of the room to keep from running into the sentinels as they come running in toward the obelisk. Then there should be seven pillars across to the north wall. As long as we see a pillar every twenty yards or so, it looks like we should be good."

"Riiiiight, we just won't talk about the giant nightmares roaring in the dark. Do you think the sentinels will at least stop making that gosh-awful racket if they catch us?"

Luke turned and stepped through the doorway. A cold wind slammed into them as soon as their feet hit the stone floor of the room, and Luke staggered backward. He shivered and gasped, clutching the map in his hand and bracing against the wall.

BOOM. BOOM. BOOM. RAWRRRR.

Not exactly a welcoming party. Luke regained his footing and glanced around until his eyes latched on to a stone obelisk a few yards in front of him. *That's got to be what James was talking about.* The gray pillar was a few feet across at the base and almost ten feet tall with Ancient symbols carved into each side.

Sure hope this works, Rayburn.

He staggered forward, reaching toward the obelisk with Matt pushing him from behind. "Madleek ... Leezrom ... Lehav." He spoke the Ancient words for lighting an object, condensing water and forming stone as his fingers brushed the pocked stone surface. Yellow light flared outward, water flowed from the top of the obelisk, curling down its length in streams, and a dozen of the pockmarks filled in. The wind died and he heard his breath rushing in and out. Beside him, Matt bent over to catch his breath. The rest of the hall was silent.

"What … what was that?" Matt said. "James … didn't say anything … about the wind!"

Luke huffed and looked over his shoulder. "Maybe—"

BOOM. BOOM. BOOM. BOOM. BOOM. BOOM. BOOM. BOOM. BOOM.

The sound of feet slamming into stone echoed across the hall.

Matt jerked upright. "Time to run."

Luke sprinted to the right. *First pillar.*

The light from the stone obelisk faded behind the boys and Luke grimaced. *We need some light.*

Two blue orbs appeared in the air near the boys' shoulders, Matt's thoughts obviously tracking Luke's.

There's the second pillar … Luke dodged around the pillar, with Matt a step behind. *Time to turn. Now, seven pillars to get to the other side and the tunnel.*

As they raced across the cavernous hall, the sound of the sentinels' crashing footfalls began to fade. They passed six of the pillars, one only a pile of crumbling rocks, before the stone wall rose in front of them. After skirting around the seventh pillar, they slid to a halt in front of a solid wall of sandstone.

"Where … where's the tunnel!?" Matt said.

Luke took in the smooth surface of the wall, blood pumping through his ears. The pounding of the sentinels stopped. He looked back and his heart dropped. The yellow light winked out.

BOOM. BOOM. BOOM. BOOM. BOOM. BOOM. BOOM. BOOM. BOOM.

"Luke, where's the tunnel?"

"I don't know! It should be here. We ran two pillars to the right and then seven … agh, *idiot!* Come on, we gotta go back to the left two pillars. The tunnel's in the center of the wall!"

BOOM. BOOM. BOOM. RAWRRRR. RAWRRRR. RAWRRRR.

Wind howled through the room, and the frequency of the pounding increased. Luke took off sprinting again, his lungs still burning. Matt growled and leaped after him.

Whoosh!

The wind found them, swirling, pulling, and pushing against them.

Oooone … Luke passed the first pillar leaning forward, his speed dropping. *Come on!*

The wind increased.

Twoooo … The second pillar passed to his left and he wheeled to the right. *Almost … there.*

BOOM. BOOM. BOOM. RAWRRRR. RAWRRRR. RAWRRRR.

His legs churned.

Where's the tunnel?!

Smash!

A chunk of stone slammed into the wall above their heads, raining dust and rock fragments on them. Fire swept through Luke's chest and legs. He scanned the wall.

Come … on …

Smash!

Another block of stone crashed into the wall of the room a few feet to Luke's left.

There!

Near the edge of the light offered by Luke's glowing orb, a jagged several-foot crack appeared, filled with darkness. Strength swept through Luke and he surged forward.

BOOM. BOOM. BOOM. RAWRRRR. RAWRRRR. RAWRRRR.

He lunged the last couple of feet into the crevice. Matt

bowled him over from behind and they collapsed to the floor. As the wind died, the pounding footfalls and howls ceased as well. Luke sat up and leaned against the rock wall.

Breathing heavily, Matt looked up at Luke. "I'd just … like to—"

"Don't," Luke said. "Just don't."

Matt grinned and dropped his head onto his arms.

The moon climbed into the sky as Luke stared through a bare spot in the hedge. The plants stood skewed, some parts overgrown and some bare and dead. On the other side of the shrubs, clumps of grass and knee-high thistles quivered in the breeze. Hackberry trees with broken limbs dangling in the air stood guard in front of a house with a sagging roof. Bricks were missing in places along the wall, windows and screens were broken and torn, and the door leading to the screen porch hung by one hinge.

Matt sighed. "Had to be this place, didn't it? They couldn't have made the meeting at, like, the school library or the burger bar. Not even *darkmen* would be seen here."

Luke stifled a laugh and pointed to a yellow glow from a window in the rear. Two shadows stole across the lawn, slinking around trees and fallen branches. Luke dropped down as he neared the wall and crouched under the windowsill. Shadows moved back and forth in the room, and Jon David's voice floated out to them. "… know that the mermaids don't have the Tears anymore. They weren't on that stupid island."

Then Randy's dull voice filled the air. "But whadda we do about Luke and them?"

"You mean crazy who hears voices in his head? He won't bother us. He doesn't even know what's really going on."

How does he know about the voices? I've only told a few—

"Uh, J.D., what *is* going on?" Randy said. "Why are they looking for these tears or stones or whatever?"

"I don't know," Jon David answered nonchalantly. "He wants it to open some stupid gate or something. I don't really care. I just want to show up Rayburn and his band of goodie-goodies."

Jon David's voice sharpened. "He did say, though, that there would be a *huge* reward for whoever helped him open the gate."

Luke's skin crawled.

Randy's voice brightened. "Reward? Like what?"

"I don't know, but he said they still need three other things."

"What three things?" This was a new voice.

Is that Tommy? ... No.

"I don't know," Jon David snapped. "He hasn't told me yet, you dodo!"

For the next few minutes, there was joking and teasing on the other side of the window. The sliver of moon moved higher in the sky and the milky glow of the galaxy shone above. Luke shifted his legs, stretching one and then the other. Matt opened his mouth and his breath fogged. Luke felt warmth on his chest.

Uh-oh.

Red light flashed through the windows and the voices inside the house cut off. "Ah, good to see you all made it," another new voice said from inside.

Luke squirmed. *That voice sounds familiar ... but strange, too. Twisted or muffled or something.*

"S-sir." Jon David's voice trembled.

"I'm sorry our little trip to the islands was ... unfruitful. But we have new information."

"How ... how come you left us there, sir?"

Silence filled the room. "*You* ... question me?"

Luke trembled at the icy voice. *It's almost enough to make you feel sorry for Jon David ... almost.*

"N-no, sir."

The house was silent for another moment. "It would not have done for me to be caught, and you provided the necessary distraction to look for the Tears."

Luke drew air into his lungs and winced. To his ear, it sounded deafening.

"Do not question me again, *Prichard*."

"Yes, sir."

"Now, I understand that it was a hard thing for you, though, and that the Elder Council was not pleased. We will deal with that. We watch over those who help us." There was the sound of rummaging in a bag and objects being caught on the other side of the window. "You did as you were told and these are for your troubles."

"A light rod!"

"A seeker!"

"Money!"

"What's this?"

"And what about this?"

The questions stopped short at the sound of a half-growl, half-snarl. "I am not here for lessons tonight, and I do not have time to explain everything to you. I have information and a task for you."

Luke strained to hear.

"We now believe the Tears are here, in Countryside. We also believe that the mermaid Mayeem knows about them."

Luke and Matt stared at each other.

"She is the key to finding the Tears. She will lead us to them. You must find out what she knows."

"What does she want them for?"

"She and those with her think the Tears will cleanse the Algid, among other things"—Luke shivered as the speaker chuckled—"but they are fools."

"But ... but how do we find out what she knows, sir?" Jon David said.

"Search her house at the edge of Granite Lake, and if that doesn't work, well, perhaps a visit from some other ... helpers ... will deliver the information."

We've got to warn Mayeem. Luke heard a sniffing in the room.

"What? What is it?" Jon David said.

"Shhhh, boy. Something's out there ... almost ... hidden, but not quite."

Luke felt warmth seep into his chest, pushing the chill away, and grabbed at his shirt. The pendant underneath burned. *Time to go, Rayburn.* He motioned to Matt with his head, and they dashed away from the window. As they crossed through the hedge, Luke looked back to see a shadow staring out the window. Darkness outlined the figure and Luke shivered.

Who is that?

Matt yawned as they walked back toward the entrance to the tunnel. "Maaaan ... this late-night stuuuff is gonna kill me." He shivered and dropped his hand from his mouth. "And how are we gonna get back in anyway? You figured that out yet? I mean, we might as well go through the front door and get caught. Be better than facing those sentinels again."

Luke scanned the trees. Shadows and gnarled branches turned into hands in Luke's mind, and shrubs became crouching darkmen and wolves. Leaves hung motionless, and the crunching of the boys' boots and the snapping of twigs filled his ears. "It feels like something is following us, or watching us."

Matt glanced around. "Might be dryads" — he narrowed his eyes — "but you'd think they'd show themselves."

A hillock appeared in front of them, with granite stones scattered around it and a willow tree with drooping arms near the top.

"Here we are," Luke said.

As the boys approached, what had looked like a shadow near the base of the rise was revealed to be a hole covered by vines — the entrance to the tunnel leading back into the manor. Luke leaned down and ran his hand over the first of the lichen-covered steps dropping down into the darkness. "I don't know, man. Maybe if I run ... but then how would I get back in? Maybe we could use a seeke — no, he said it had to be living." He felt a tap on his shoulder.

"Uh ... Luke."

He looked up and then jerked to his feet. Ten feet behind them, stepping out of a grove of oak trees, the bane wolf that had followed them back from the Lost Island had materialized. Blue eyes shone in the darkness of the forest and the wolf eased forward. Luke took a step back and the wolf snarled.

"OK, not that direction, got it."

The wolf turned and circled around the boys toward the hillock, keeping her eyes locked on them. Her fur shifted from gray to black and back as she slipped in and out of the light. When she reached the hill, she faced the boys and walked toward them. Luke and Matt backed away. The wolf made no noise and stopped at the entrance to the tunnel.

"Well, we definitely aren't going that way now," Matt said.

The wolf stepped into the shadow, placing her paw on the first step, and then turned and stared at the boys.

Matt leaned toward Luke. "What's she doing?"

The wolf stared at them, unmoving. The chirp of crickets and the buzz of June bugs rose around them.

"I don't ... think she's going to hurt us."

Matt shook his head. "Me neither, but I'd just as soon not test that theory."

"Yeah."

Yip!

They started. The wolf watched them, blinked, and turned and leaped into the tunnel.

Luke watched her tail vanish. "You don't think—"

"That going into the tunnel to face scary growling shadow giants and following a bane wolf is a bad idea? Yeah, I think it's a bad idea. I think it's one of the worst ideas you've had today, and that's saying something. But I'm pretty sure that's what you're thinkin' we should do."

Luke regarded the entrance to the passageway, gritted his teeth and stepped forward. "Come on."

Matt sighed. "Yep, that's what I thought you were thinkin'."

Light floated along around them, and they scrambled down stairs and around corners. The wolf bounded in front of them, always just at the edge of the light.

"Have you stopped to wonder how she knows where she's going, Luke?"

"Yeah, I still don't think she's going to hurt us. She could have done that already." He hurried forward, stepping over a rock in the path and balancing against the wall. "But there is something strange going on for sure."

The tunnel narrowed for the rest of the way until, ten

minutes later, Luke skidded to a halt as the wolf's curled nose and teeth appeared in the light.

Matt bumped into him from behind. "What … Oh."

The wolf stared at them for a few seconds and then turned and padded forward. A few feet in front of her, light brought the stone floor of the sentinels' great hall into view.

"Wonder why the yelling and stomping hasn't started yet," Matt said.

After one last glance over her shoulder, the wolf lunged forward, and as her paws hit the stone floor, noise exploded across the room.

BOOM. BOOM. BOOM. RAWRRRR. RAWRRRR. RAWRRRR.

Wind howled into the room and swept down the passage behind them.

"Guess that's why!" Matt said.

Luke leaped forward, but Matt's hand clamped down on his arm and jerked him back.

"Gotta wait, remember?"

Luke swallowed. "Right, thanks!"

BOOM. BOOM. BOOM. RAWRRRR. RAWRRRR. RAWRRRR. Ahoooooooooo.

BOOM. BOOM. BOOM. RAWRRRR. RAWRRRR. RAWRRRR. Ahoooooooooo.

Luke quivered as the howling of the wolf mingled with the roaring and stomping of the sentinels. Soon, though, the sounds began to drift farther away.

Boom. Boom. Boom. Rawrrrr. Rawrrrr. Rawrrrr.

The boys nodded at each other.

"Straight ahead this time," Matt said.

They raced across the room. Stone pillars flashed by and the balls near their shoulders floated along with them.

boom. boom. boom. rawrrrr. rawrrrr. rawrrrr.
ahooooooooooo.

The noises changed direction as the boys leaped over stones and the rubble of metal, wood, and rocks, wind buffeting them as they went.

Five ... Two more ...

Seconds later, the towering wall rose above them. Luke slid to a halt beside the stone obelisk with the symbols etched into it.

boom. boom. boom. rawrrrr. rawrrrr. rawrrrr.
ahoooooooooo ... ahoooooooooo.
boom. boom. boom. rawrrrr. rawrrrr. rawrrrr.

The sounds echoed through the hall. Luke stood still.

"What are you waiting on, man? Touch it."

Luke stared out into the darkness and goose bumps raced up his arms. "I could stop them."

Matt frowned at him. "What? Stop the sentinels. How?"

boom. boom. boom. rawrrrr. rawrrrr. rawrrrr.

"I could use water and earth ... and darkness. I could freeze them, bury them in darkness ..."

ahoooooooooo ... ahoooooooooo.

Matt shook his head. "No, Luke. You can't use darkness. It ... it just never works out. Come on man, you've seen it. Darkmen, soulless, that shadow on the island—it just doesn't work, man. Now touch the stone!"

boom. boom. boom. rawrrrr. rawrrrr. rawrrrr.

Frustration welled up in Luke's chest. "But we're gonna have to do this again sometime. If I just stopped them ..."

ahoooooooooo ... ahoooooooooo.

"Luke, you can't use darkness, and I can't do this. I would if I could, but the water ... I still can't work with it at all. You have to do this or the sentinels are going to catch the wolf, man."

"Fine. You're right," Luke growled and reached out and brushed his fingers along the stone. Water rolled down the side as yellow light flared to life. The wind faded and silence filled the room. As he held his breath, he heard the sounds of galloping and claws scraping against stone.

BOOM. BOOM. BOOM. BOOM. BOOM. BOOM. BOOM. BOOM. BOOM.

The boys turned and jogged under the arch and away from the sound of feet pounding on the stone.

Thirty minutes later, after climbing staircases, backtracking for locked doors and winding down two hallways that dead-ended in stone walls guarded by empty suits of armor, the boys slipped out of the hidden passages in the west library. A wall of bookshelves slid closed behind them.

"I still don't understand why we came here, man. We're just asking to get caught."

Luke glanced around the room. Books, tables, and chairs surrounded them. "It's the middle of the night. If they haven't caught us yet, they won't now. I need to check on something."

Ah, there's the west stairs ... and the globe. The map room should be just over there.

Luke jogged down the stairs. Across the west library, two wooden doors stood closed. Matt caught up to him just as he reached for the handle.

"Ha-peteekhah ha-sodot."

Pop.

Red light flashed at the edges of the doors.

"And here we go with the gibberish again," Matt said.

Luke pulled the doors open and gave him a questioning look.

"You're speaking Ancient … again."

"Oh … sorry."

"'S'ok. I just like messing with you now, but what are we doing here still, man?"

Luke walked in and strode to the back of the room. Glowing lights appeared, and he stopped in front of a painting of a man sitting at a desk holding a pen and others standing in line in front of him. Luke stretched his hand out and the painting shimmered and vanished. He reached into a nook behind where the image had been.

"You know how I told you the *Book of the Wise* is being passed around this year?" he said.

Matt nodded and Luke pulled the book out and stepped over to a sloped wooden map desk.

"Well, one of the places is here. They won't tell me the schedule, if there even is one, but every time we have it, my dad lets me know. Father Woods thought I should have access to it when it was here. Don't ask me how he convinced my parents."

When he flipped the book open, green light bloomed and then faded away and black ink swirled on the page.

"But what are you looking for in there?" Matt said.

"You remember tonight when Jon David was talking about why whoever he is working for was looking for the Tears?"

Matt nodded.

"Well, it reminded me of something, but I couldn't think why until we got back." Letters lined up on the page. "There was something in the Prophecy of the Blood Star." He ran his finger along the lines that had appeared on the page. "There … And to mark the last days—" He looked up. "Am I speaking in English?"

"Yep, for now. I'll let you know."

Luke looked back at the book. "And to mark the beginning of the last days, the Star of War will rise in the north and the Lost Gate will appear." He scratched his head. "Well, I thought maybe there was more, but whatever. Maybe that's the gate Jon David was talking about ... even though he didn't know it. Maybe they're trying to open this lost gate."

"Man, lost islands and now a lost gate. I'm beginning to think that if it is lost, maybe it should stay that way."

Luke heard Mr. Roberts's comments in his mind. "Me, too."

Matt put his hand on Luke's shoulder. "Man, I know this isn't exactly our M.O., but we have to tell somebody. We can't just go charging off. We need to at least tell someone about Mayeem."

Luke's shoulders dropped. "I know. I agree."

Matt leaned back and eyed Luke. "You do?"

"Yeah. We can't tell Marti and the others anyway."

"Why?"

"Because one of them is passing on information to Jon David."

"Luke, that's ... Are you sure, man?"

"Yeah. I'm sure. Tonight when Jon David talked about me hearing voices in my head, the only people I ever told about that were you, Marti, Samantha, and Jennifer. *Nobody* else knows, man, not even my parents."

Matt let out a low whistle. "Man ... you think that's who James was trying to warn you about?"

"I don't know, but probably. I'm pretty sure it's not Marti, but he might let something slip even if it's not on purpose. I think it might be Samantha. I mean we know Jon David is involved and we've seen Samantha talking to Jon David. And on the island she was the one who thought we should help him."

Matt sighed. "I know I suggested that earlier in the year,

man, but … I just don't see it. I mean, she thinks you're awesome. She like"—he shook his head and looked down at his shoes and then back up again.—"likes you!"

Luke chuckled, but his voice was cold. "Maybe it's just an act."

"You know it's not me right?"

Luke chuckled again but with a bit of mirth this time. "Yeah, I know. Besides the fact that you loathe Jon David about as much as anyone, if you were feeding him information and then still running around with me being chased by wolves and hunters and who knows what else, then you're even dumber than you pretend to be."

Matt feigned hurt and Luke smirked. They stood quietly, lost in their thoughts, for a few moments. Finally, Luke sighed and closed the book. He picked it up and walked to the niche in the wall and put it back.

"Anyway, we do need to tell someone. I'm sure my dad and Uncle Landon will want to know."

Luke touched the wall again and the painting shimmered into view. Then he turned around and froze.

His father stood at the entrance to the room in jeans and a white undershirt staring at the boys with his arms crossed.

"I think you're quite right, Luke. Your uncle and I would like very much to know what *exactly* is going on."

SEVENTEEN

P. M. R.

Pinks and oranges spilled into the sky, outlining a cluster of clouds far to the east. A pair of painted buntings, having arrived early for the season, sat on a wooden fence chirping and watching, their heads twitching. Cool air blew across the pastures, and dew was heavy on the grass. Luke tugged at the sleeves of his work shirt, riding silently as Archer plodded along. Beside him, Matt sat on a brown mare from the stables, and Luke's father and Uncle Landon rode up ahead. Luke yawned.

"I wonder if we'll get to sleep again," Matt said, "like, ever."

Luke snorted. "I think the concern is if they ever let us leave the house alone again." His thoughts flashed back to the last few hours. His father had roused half the household, and Luke and Matt found themselves standing in the middle of the library surrounded by Luke's parents and grandparents, Uncle Landon, Mr. Acharon, and even Ms. Lucy. There were haggard looks, tousled hair, and no smiles in the crowd. By the time the boys finished their tale a second time, there were bright eyes and numerous scowls. Word was sent to the Guard via the dryads, and after quite a few minutes of what his parents called "discussing," the decision was made that Luke's father and uncle would visit Mayeem as well. Just as they were leaving, one of the guardsmen thundered up to relay the message that Mayeem was fine and that a team had been posted outside her home. Luke's father and uncle decided they'd go anyway and Luke and Matt needed to come, in case Mayeem had questions or other information from their previous adventures became relevant. That's how they'd come to find themselves in the saddle on the north end of the valley, trotting away from the hamlet of Lakeshore and its handful of sleeping homes toward Mayeem's house.

A hundred yards ahead, a wooden house built on piers appeared over the waves lapping the shore of Granite Lake. Steps led down from a porch and straight into the water, disappearing beneath its surface. Luke's father pulled up.

Luke straightened in his saddle. "Something wrong, Dad?" He noticed dark mounds in the sand surrounding the house. "Matt, what are those—" His eyes widened and the muscles in his shoulders tightened.

"Yah!"

"Sssss!"

Luke's father and uncle spurred their mounts forward, kicking sand into the air.

Suddenly, Luke was wide awake as he and Matt spurred their own horses. When they reached the house seconds later, his father and uncle leaped off their horses beside the dark mounds that turned out to be four guardsmen. His uncle raced to the men while his father scanned the area and then bounded into the house. Luke glanced around at the torn earth and ripped grasses. A rust-brown paw print covered the chest of one of the men his uncle was kneeling beside. Light and water flared from his uncle's fingers into scars across the man's chest. Blackness oozed out of the wounds and the guardsman's eyes fluttered. Uncle Landon slung the blackness to the side as if flinging grease or tar off his hands. The glob of darkness sizzled on the sand and evaporated into the air as Luke's uncle dashed to the next guardsman.

Luke's father leaped back down the stairs. "House seems clear, Landon."

Uncle Landon motioned toward the guardsmen. "These two are fine, a little bruised and battered but all right. Private Knutson will need some attention, but he can wait on it. Corporal Bolton over there needs to get back now. A bane wolf sliced into his chest pretty good. I managed to pull some of the darkness out, but it's spreading rapidly."

Luke's father looked around and grimaced. He uttered an oath under his breath.

"Pretty sure he never says *that* around Mom," Luke said quietly.

Matt chuckled. "He must be tired."

"Just take my horse," Luke's father said. "I'll stay here with the boys and the other three. Get Corporal Bolton back to town."

Uncle Landon hesitated for a moment but then grabbed the corporal by the wrist and braced his foot against the man's legs. The muscles in his arms straining, he flipped the corporal up over his shoulder, quickly carried him to his brother's horse, and laid him across the saddle. A dark stain marked Uncle Landon's shoulder as Luke's father helped tie the corporal into place before handing over the reins.

"I'll be back as soon as I can," Uncle Landon said.

"Be careful, brother. I don't think they're here anymore, but they might still be somewhere near."

Uncle Landon whirled around and galloped to the west toward Lakeshore. Luke's father helped one of the lance corporals sit up. "Luke, I've got to tend to these men. You and Matt check inside and see if you find anything of note … or if you find Mayeem. I think the hunter and his wolves are gone, but be careful." He looked up and Luke shivered under the stare of his gray-blue eyes. "That whoreson must've been in a hurry or these men wouldn't still be alive … but go in expecting to find something."

"Yes, sir."

The boys headed up the stairs, but a few steps below the landing they paused and peered over the top step.

"See anything?"

Matt shook his head.

Luke swallowed and stepped up to the porch. Shattered windows lined the front of the house, and the door lay in splinters across the planks of the porch. Black ash lined the edge of the doorway.

"Pretty sure they weren't invited in," Matt said.

They stood in front of the doorframe and stared in at the chaos. Overturned wicker chairs and a couch lay broken and torn. Papers fluttered around the room, blown by the breeze off the lake. Scratches were etched into the walls and broken glass carpeted the floor.

Matt motioned with his head. "You see that?"

Luke took a deep breath. "Blood."

"Not a little, but not so much you'd think someone—"

"I don't see any reason not to go in. You?"

Matt shook his head and the boys stepped in. They went from room to room scanning floors and looking into nooks and crannies. Luke looked on the back porch and down at the stairs that sank into the water. "That's weird, it's like they just fall into the water."

"Yeah, never seen a mermaid's house before. Maybe it makes getting in and out easier. Who knows?"

"You think she made it in?"

"I don't know, man. Looks like there was a battle royale in there. Doesn't seem like she's much for running away."

Luke's face twisted, half his mouth turning up. "Yeah."

"Boys! Y'all OK?"

"Better go back."

Luke went back into the house. "Yeah, Dad, coming!" He stepped around thrown furniture and over broken glass and wood.

"Hey, Luke, what were the initials of that guy who made the map to the Lost Island?"

Luke stopped a few paces from the door and looked over his shoulder. "Huh? What?"

Matt was leaning over a table and pushing papers around. "The guy that made that map of the Lost Island. What were his initials?"

"I don't know. P. A. or J. K. or something. Why? What does *that* have to do with anything?"

Matt looked up, light dancing in his eyes. "P. M. Randell—P. M. R., right?"

"Yeaaaahhh, I think sooo."

Matt riffled through the papers in front of him, mumbling as he inspected them. "P. M. R. ... P. M. R. ... P. M. R. ..."

"Luke! Matt!"

"Be there in just a sec, Dad!"

Matt shuffled from paper to paper faster and faster. When he got to the last one, he jerked his head up. "P. M. R.! Look, his initials are on everything here on this table. It's written or circled on everything from letters to maps to books!" He shoved papers in front of Luke's face. "Maybe," he said breathlessly, "maybe the hunter wasn't here to get Mayeem. Maybe he was here looking for information. Maybe ... maybe whoever or whatever from the house last night sent him, like he told Jon David he might send someone."

Luke stared at the papers. "But he just said that last night, man. And he seemed like he wanted Jon David to look first. Besides, why would—"

"Luke. Whatever's going on, whatever Mayeem knew about the Tears"—Matt jabbed his finger at the initials scribbled on the dog-eared page of a book—"whoever this guy is or was has something to do with it."

Two days later, Luke sat on the concrete bench next to a table in the shade of the sycamore tree in the schoolyard. A squirrel chattered down at him before whirling around and racing along its chosen branch. Marti and Samantha sat on the other side of the table, and kids around the yard darted glances at the three of them.

Word does travel fast in a small town.

Matt came walking across the grass lawn carrying a tray piled high with rolls, cheese, sausage, beans, and an apple.

"Th-th-that for all of us, m-m-man?"

"I'm hungry," Matt said before shoving in a bite of sausage. "Luke keeps me out tromping across the valley half the night."

Marti frowned. "I th-th-thought you said you went to see Mayeem in the m-m-morning?"

Luke cringed inside.

Matt chewed slowly and then swallowed his bite. "Well, we

did, but I mean … you know me and early morning—it's just like night. I still can't even think straight."

Marti's frown softened, but Luke could tell he didn't quite buy it.

Samantha shook her head. "I still can't believe that you two and your father and uncle just happened to be making a trip up there to see Mayeem. Maybe if y'all just would have been a little earlier … but then the hunter might have attacked y'all, too." She looked at Luke with a sad smile.

Luke shifted his gaze from her stare. He and Matt had decided not to include the parts about sneaking out through the tunnels, Jon David's meeting at the old abandoned house or even the bane wolf's leading them back into the manor. Guilt over not telling Marti churned his stomach a bit, but it was a pretty easy decision considering that they still weren't absolutely sure *who* was passing information on to Jon David—that and the fact that his parents had basically threatened them with death if they told anyone.

Samantha's face brightened. "At least y'all found all those papers with the initials of that mapmaker on them."

Luke looked back over at her, frowning. *Hmm … wish that little bit of information hadn't slipped out.* He studied Samantha for a moment. *Can you really not know anything? Are you really not passing information on to Jon David?* He glanced past her as a couple of sixth-graders walked by whispering and pointing in their direction. "Yeah, well, just *try* to keep it to yourselves. We don't need the whole world knowing everything we learn."

Samantha and Marti started. Matt frowned and gave a slight shake of his head that the other two didn't see.

"Luke, we w-w-wouldn't tell a-a-anybody."

Samantha nodded. "Besides, it seems like y'all are the only friends I have now."

Luke opened his mouth to speak but paused as Jennifer walked by.

"Hey, Jenn," Samantha called out, but Jennifer kept walking, looking straight ahead, her face smooth as stone. Samantha's shoulders sagged.

"What gives?" Matt said. "Isn't she going to sit with us?"

Samantha's voice came out in a whisper. "No. She got all weird yesterday and told me she can't hang out with y'all anymore, and she told me I shouldn't either. She's been trying to pull me away all year ... and I guess she finally figured out I wasn't going to abandon my friends."

Luke's mind flashed from the Fall Festival to traveling tunnels in a moonlit forest to the map room at his grandparents' house to an abandoned house on Old Market Road, voices mixing with the images.

Oh, no.

Samantha lifted her face, her eyes wet. "I told her I wasn't going to not hang out with my friends for some boy, especially not ..." She dropped her eyes again and Matt and Marti leaned forward.

"W-w-what boy, Samantha?"

She looked up and lightning flashed in her eyes.

"Jon David." Luke murmured.

Three heads turned to Luke, Matt's eyes widening in understanding.

Marti winced, lifting his shoulders and squirming. "J-J-Jon David—no way, yuck!"

Samantha cocked her head. "How ... how did you know it was Jon David?"

Luke stared past them all, his eyes losing focus. *I'm an idiot. How could I not have seen it?*

The image of Jennifer shoving past him and stomping up a

hill flashed through his head along with her voice. *Just because Jon David's not rich like you doesn't mean he's stupid, Luke! At least he's not mean!*

Thoughts spiraled around him. *And what do I tell Marti and Samantha now?* The screech of a hawk sounded overhead as it glided away on the thermals, and Luke's heart felt like lead. *Sam really does like me ... or she did.* He closed his eyes. *I can't believe this. I totally blew it.* "Because someone's been passing information on to Jon David this year." He came back to himself and saw Marti and Samantha raise their eyebrows. "I knew that someone was either you two or Jennifer, but I didn't know who until just now."

"What?" Marti and Samantha exclaimed together.

Luke sighed, and then with a nod from Matt—and ignoring his parents' warning—he told them everything. He told them about the sentinels beneath his family's home, the meeting at the old abandoned house and how the bane wolf helped them get back into the manor. He finished by repeating Jon David's comment about hearing voices and James's warnings about someone close to him who was leaking information. As he talked, his heart sank even further, like a pebble falling toward the bottom of a lake. Marti's face fell and Samantha drew her arms in tight.

"And I'm sorry. I should've known, but ... I'm sorry."

The leaves overhead hung limp, and laughter and shrieks sounded across the yard. After a moment, Marti looked up with a shaky smile. "It's OK, man. How w-w-would you have known?"

Samantha sniffed, and Matt put his hand on Luke's shoulder.

Luke hung his head. *Stupid boy ... you should've known.* Heat filled his face, and his chest tightened. "Except for Trent, you three are the best friends I've ever had." He forced his head up and looked at Marti and Samantha in turn. "You were my *only* friends when I first got here last year. You help ... you're the only reason ... I can't do any of this without y'all." As he looked at Samantha, his breath came in shallow and quick. "Please. I didn't mean to hurt you." Feeling that the corners of his eyes were wet, he closed them and dropped his head again. A lump formed in his throat and a deep ache settled into his chest. He didn't know how long he sat there like that, alone in his dark world.

He heard Samantha shift on her seat. *She's leaving.* And then he felt something graze his side. Another rustle of clothing and a hand came to rest on his shoulder. He opened his eyes and saw through his blurred vision that Samantha was sitting beside him and Marti was standing to his other side. When Samantha rested her head on his shoulder, the ache shifted in his chest and his heart floated back up out of the cold darkness.

"I won't make the same mistake again," he whispered. "I promise."

Samantha nodded against his shoulder, and Marti squeezed his other shoulder.

Matt winked at Luke and gave him a straight-faced nod as if to say that everything would be all right. Wind dried Luke's eyes and kids began filtering back into the school building.

"If everybody is up to it, I have a suggestion," Matt said. Three faces turned to look at him as sunlight and shadows shifted over his face. "I think we need to go back and have a look around Mayeem's house."

"W-w-what?"

"Are you kidding?" Luke said.

"You can't be serious." Samantha stared at Matt incredulously.

Life jolted back into the group of friends and Matt raised his hands. "Easy, jeez. What, Luke's the only one that can come up with harebrained ideas?"

"Y-y-yeah, but Luke actually th-th-thinks his will work at first."

Luke snorted.

Marti shrugged. "They do … m-m-most of the time."

Luke turned to Matt. "Why do you want to go back there?"

Matt leaned forward. "There's some connection between the Tears and that cartographer's initials. Somewhere in that stack of papers, Mayeem was looking for a clue or had already found it, and we need to know what it is."

"Matt, the p-p-place is crawling with g-g-guardsmen. And the whole t-t-town knows about it. There's no w-w-way we'll get in without th-th-them seeing us."

"We'll have to find the information some other way," Samantha said. "We can check the library or … or somewhere else."

Matt shook his head. "There might be other ways in. Ways people might not expect, like stairs leading out of the water."

Luke stared at Matt's imploring eyes. He took a deep breath and closed his own eyes. *Matt always supports you, Rayburn, always.* His eyes snapped open. "I'm in."

Luke popped out of the tunnel into Lakeshore. Matt, Marti, and Samantha turned as he stepped out, and the few people walking along the main street turned grim faces to stare at them.

"Town looks pretty tense, man," Luke said.

"Probably best to walk out away from the lake and then make our way back," Matt said.

They headed south, and an hour later they were walking

along the northwest edge of the Greenwood Hills. A cluster of houses and stores marked Lakeshore a couple of miles back to the west, while Granite Lake stretched to the north, sparkling and silver in the distance near the headwaters of the Algid.

"You can s-s-still smell it, e-e-even up here."

A hint of garbage and stagnant water was on the breeze. Luke pointed down the slope of the hill to the edge of the lake. "Marti was right, man. They're everywhere."

Below them, figures walked back and forth in front of Mayeem's house. One horse rode up from Lakeshore and another headed off.

"Looks like a t-t-team out front, but I can't tell how m-m-many are in the house."

Samantha stood staring down the hill and shading her eyes. "The corporal that just rode up makes five out front, and I think I see two more inside the house."

The boys turned and stared at her.

"What?" she said.

Luke snorted. "You're kidding, right? Samantha, we can hardly tell how many men are there and you can tell one of them is a corporal."

Samantha blushed, looking down at her feet. "Oh."

"I'm not sure what's more interesting," Matt said, "the fact that Luke can speak Ancient or that you can see forever."

The boys turned their attention back to the house. After a few moments, Matt shook his head. "I still want to get closer. Maybe we can see something."

"N-n-no way, man."

Samantha sighed. "Matt, I want to know what happened to Mayeem, too. She's been really great to me this year, especially when … Jennifer started to pull away, but us going down there and getting caught isn't going to tell us where she is or ... it's just gonna get us caught."

Luke watched the guardsmen walk around the house. *Maybe if we waited until it got dark.*

"I think I'd be stickin' with the gentleman's and the young lady's opinion, if I were you boys."

All four whirled around at the sound of the voice. Twenty feet above them on the hillside stood a man with tanned face and arms and gray hair pulled back in a ponytail. He wore a blue shirt, loose gray trousers, and black leather boots. Ocean-blue eyes stared down at them, but Luke's gaze was drawn to something else. The man's hand was resting on the head of a dog crouched beside him. With mist-gray fur, black eyes and a red lolling tongue, it appeared to be a normal dog except for the fact that, even crouching, it came up to the man's waist.

"Oh, boy," Matt said.

"S-s-sir?" Luke said.

"I said, I'd be listenin' to the gentleman th're and the young lady if I were ya, lad."

"Yes, sir. Uh, sir, who are you, sir?"

The man narrowed his eyes.

Wrong question, Luke.

"Seein' as how yer the ones sneakin' 'round, figure ya might be the ones tellin' me who *you* are."

Luke swallowed. "I'm Luke Rayburn, sir. This is Matt Nichols, Samantha Thompson, and Marti Stegall."

The man nodded at each of them in turn as Luke motioned toward them. "Pleasure to meet ya. Well, best be gettin' ya lads and ya lass back to your homes. Some things crawlin' around these parts ya don't want anythin' to do with."

With that the man patted the dog on the head and started

back up the hill. The dog straightened, rising to the man's shoulder, and stared at Luke and his friends.

"Uh, sir," Luke said.

The man turned around and his eyes widened. "Oh, beggin' yer pardon. This here's Kaleva, and my name is Peter, Peter M. Randell."

EIGHTEEN

✦

The Key

P.M. R.

Luke and Matt stared at each other.

"Maybe he knows what happened to Mayeem," Luke whispered.

"Yeah, and maybe *he's* what happened to Mayeem."

"Y'all come along now. Kaleva'll follow behind," Mr. Randell called.

"Should we r-r-really be going with h-h-him?" Marti whispered.

Luke jerked his thumb toward the hound. "Does it look like we have a choice?"

"We could sh-sh-shout for the guardsmen."

"Unless you figured out how to use air to carry your voice as far as Samantha can see, that dog would eat us in four bites before they ever heard us, much less saw us."

When the man started climbing west back toward Lakeshore and the Algid, the children followed him. Kaleva stared at them as they walked by, and Matt leaned away when it was his turn.

"Is it just me, or does he seem like he's thinking about whether we might make a good snack?" he said.

Just then, Samantha reached her hand toward Kaleva.

"Samantha, wait!" Luke said.

She patted the dog on the head. "First of all, if you paid attention, you'd notice that *he* is a she. And secondly, Matt, everyone knows rock hounds prefer eating bane wolves to people. You boys really ought to pay more attention in Mr. White's Higher Animals Feeds and Feeding class."

The boys stared with open mouths as the dog closed its eyes and wagged.

"I figured *you* at least would know, Marti." Samantha smirked and skipped past the boys.

"Mam ma mamma ma ma maaaa." Matt stuck his tongue out at Samantha.

"Kn-kn-knowing in a book doesn't m-m-mean believing in real l-l-life," Marti said, edging around the rock hound.

Ahead, Mr. Randell was descending the far side of the slope, weaving among cedar and oak trees. As the children trod through the rocks and trees behind him, Luke noticed Lakeshore in the distance to the north. He jogged a couple of steps forward. "Uh, Mr. Randell, sir, where are we going?"

The man kept his gaze straight ahead. "Takin' ya young'uns home, back to Rayburn Manor," he said over his shoulder.

How does he know where I live?

"And 'Peter' will suit just fine, lad," the man continued.

"But, sir," Matt said, "there's a tunnel in Lakeshore—"

"Mmm-hmm." The man kept walking.

"Guess we'll be walking home today," Matt said quietly to Luke.

As they followed Peter down out of the Greenwood Hills and across pastureland and wooded areas, Kaleva nipped at cottontail rabbits and squirrels as they bounded across the trail. An hour into the journey, Luke plucked up the courage to voice his question. "Sir, how … how did you know where to take us? I mean, how did you know I live at Rayburn Manor?"

"Well, yer a Rayburn aren't ya? Not many of those in these parts." Peter chuckled as Luke felt his face flush. "And I been 'round Countryside a long time, lad. I may live out in the boonies, but I still know a thing or two o' what goes on in the holding." Peter looked down at Luke with a lopsided grin. "Yer great-great-grandpa and I used to go fishin' in that pond up north o' the manor when he was a young lad." Peter's smile vanished and his gaze stretched out into the distance. "O' course, that was a long time ago … before I lost my …" He shook himself and continued on, and Luke could tell the conversation was over.

Twenty minutes later, Peter held his hand up near the edge of an oak grove. A road crossed the path in front of them.

What's he waiting on? Luke opened his mouth, but Kaleva growled and nudged him in the side with her head and he clamped it shut.

A moment later, the rumbling of wheels over gravel could be heard, and another moment later a farmer with a wagon-load of lettuce rolled past them going south. Peter waited until the wagon disappeared and then motioned the children across the road.

"Ask him about Mayeem," Matt whispered.

"How? What do you want me to say?" Luke made a face and deepened his voice. "Hey, sir, you know anything about our mermaid teacher that disappeared or this really old powerful thing called the Tears of Adina? We think she was searching for them."

"Yes, lad, I know a good bit about both."

Luke stopped in his tracks, and Marti bumped into his back, sending Luke stumbling forward a few paces. Peter stopped and grinned at Luke.

"Th're's quite a few things the Creature o' Granite Lake knows."

In his mind, Luke heard his father's voice and saw the flames of a campfire. "The C-C-C-Creature of Granite Lake?"

Peter chuckled. "Yessir. But don't worry, young'un, th're's a good bit o' that story they didn't get right." He winked and resumed walking.

"D-d-definitely shouldn't have c-c-come with him," Marti said.

"Maybe we could sneak off?" Matt said.

Kaleva trotted by, grinning at them.

"Before getting eaten by Toothy?" Luke said. "Doubtful."

"Well, we should at least keep our mouths shut," Matt said.

"Maybe we c-c-can yell for help when s-s-someone passes by again?"

"I hope none of you are serious," Samantha said, hands on hips. "We need to help Mayeem. And find the Tears. Remember?" She stared at each boy in turn.

Marti nodded first, and then Matt.

"You're right, Samantha," Luke said. "Come on, let's go." He leaped forward, dodging a fallen tree covered with tangles of berry vines.

"Sir, can you tell us? About Mayeem and the Tears, I mean."

The man looked down at Luke. "Depends, boy. Why do you-uns want t' know?"

Don't lie now, Rayburn. Just tell him. You're in way over your head anyway.

He took a deep breath. "Because we think Mayeem is in trouble. We think she was looking for the Tears of Adina and so was darkness. We think a hunter got her, and we ..." *What do you want to do, Rayburn?* He sighed and his shoulders slumped. "I just want to help, sir. I want to help Mayeem and keep the Tears from darkness if we can. Maybe I shouldn't be looking, but them having the Tears seems like a pretty bad idea."

The man snorted. "Jeremiah's right about ya."

Luke frowned. "Mr. Roberts?"

Peter just smiled at Luke and looked away. "Fair enough, ya gave me an honest answer, and I'll return the same. Well, first things first. I 'magine I'll need to correct a few things ya 'know' about the Creature o' Granite Lake."

Matt, Samantha, and Marti moved closer to Luke and Peter.

"A time ago, I did live alone in Westcliffe Forest. And my Anora, my wife, she was chased 'ere through a tunnel trying to escape darkness. But what ya most likely don't know is she was carryin' the Tears of Adina with her."

Luke's mouth dropped open.

"That's right. She was the daughter of the last of the Guardians, an order of the Remnant sworn to protect the Tears, and some other things, from darkness. Her mother had taken the Tears when she was younger, just before they concealed the island of Eeyeem, the Lost Island. Yer familiar with the Lost Island?"

Luke and the others looked at each other and nodded.

"Figured as far along as ya were in yer search ya would be. Anyway, by some vile trickery, darkness finally found out where the Tears were kept, and they managed t' attack the island. The village where my wife lived was destroyed. Darkness tainted everything ... Far as I know it still sits that way, unnaturally preserved by the darkness that defiled it."

Luke thought back to the charred buildings, deformed trees, and the shadow he'd jumped into and shivered.

"Well, Anora made it t' Countryside, just barely. I found her and nursed her back to health … and fell in love with her in the process." His eyes glistened and he cleared his throat. "Uh-hum. Anyway, we took the Tears and hid 'em 'ere in Countryside. Only the Remnant and a few of the merpeople and darkmen knew the Tears had disappeared, but nobody knew what had happened to 'em. We didn't tell a soul either, not even her family, though they pressed pretty hard for a bit when they discovered she was alive. The Tears woulda given darkness a power unseen since the Breaking, and we couldn't let that happen. So … 'ere the Tears have stayed and 'ere they've been safe, until of late. That hunter you-uns run into has been on the trail for a while, and I don't know how he's gotten this close or who sent him, but"—his face hardened—"he and his pack are involved in yer teacher's goin' missin' … and it's my fault to boot."

"Your fault, sir? Why?"

Peter gritted his teeth. "That mermaid was 'ere searchin' for me. She is part of the family of my wife, part of the nobility of the merpeople. Anora only made a couple trips back to the Misty Isles in all her years 'ere. She missed it terribly, but she was afraid to lead darkness back to the Tears. She let what bit o' 'er family remained know she was well and even introduced me to 'em on one o' the trips." His head fell and his cheeks colored. "'Er family must have thought me a waste, but she loved me so much they never …" He closed his eyes and then opened them again, snapping his head up. "Doesn't matter. This young maid was looking for me and I knew it … but I hid from 'er. Partly because I didn't want to risk the Tears, but mostly because I didn't want to see 'er, to be reminded of my Anora. I didn't realize how close darkness was behind 'er, how much they knew already or how much trouble she was in … If

I woulda just gone and met 'er, sent 'er home … but now I've gone and lost 'er, just the same as my Anora." He stumbled and came to a stop, leaning down with his hands on his knees. His dog padded forward and nudged him, whining.

Luke looked away, into the crown of a cottonwood tree. The wind was rustling the leaves and sending white puffs of seeds whirling to the ground like snow. After a few minutes, Peter straightened and turned to Luke. Pain welled in Luke's chest as the man's eyes bore into him. "You see, the last part of the story that never was passed down is when I got back that day after the wolves and soulless had been at the cabin … my Anora was gone. I never found 'er … never have."

Silence blanketed the group for the next several minutes as they plodded across the fields. As the sun dropped toward the horizon, a breeze filled Luke's nose with the stench of stagnant water.

Brown grass and shrubs with curled leaves dotted the landscape. After another quarter-mile, a lone red bird flitted past. The group topped a rise out of a peach orchard full of leafless and blackened trees, and there below them sat the choked brown waters of the Algid. Dirt covered its banks, and all the plants were withered and wasted.

"It looks worse," Matt said.

"It'll continue to get worse, too, lad, until they find a way to stop the spread of darkness," Peter said.

"Sir, there's no bridge here," Luke said. "How will we get across?"

Peter winked. "The water in the river 'ere may be polluted, but I learned a trick or two bein' married to a mermaid, and th're's still clean water in the ground." He turned back to the river, his eyes narrowed. He moved his hands up and down as if he were pulling on something.

Slup.

Luke looked to see mud suddenly stuck to the sides of his boots. Moisture was spreading through the ground in a circle around Peter. "Whoa."

"Hey!" Matt said.

Then tendrils of water rose from the ground. The children lurched back as the water spun and twisted, stretching across the water of the Algid. Steps and rails formed out of water, rising up and reaching toward the west bank, and more water poured out of the ground.

"Look!" Samantha said, pointing across the river.

Water rose out of the far bank and stretched toward them. As it met the water extending from the near bank, white light flared and raced toward each bank. A few seconds later, Peter dropped his hands. Luke leaned toward the newly formed bridge until his face was a few inches away. *That's not water.* A breeze swirled around the bridge and carried cool air toward Luke. "It's ice!"

Peter grinned. "Won't last long in this heat, so let's be gettin' across." He turned and whistled and Kaleva bounded forward with a bark. She slipped and slid across the bridge, kicking up poofs of snow with each paw. Luke and the others raced up the stairs and scrambled and skidded across the arch of the bridge, too, before dropping down on the west side of the Algid. Peter crossed last and stood staring at the river. As the bridge melted, drops of water splashed into the river. Then the drops turned to trickles and the trickles to streams. Where the streams of water entered the river, rings of clear water formed. As more and more of the bridge melted, the clearer the river became.

"You did it!" Luke said.

Peter gave a wry grin. "No, lad, 'tis only for a moment; then the darkness takes over again." He pointed downstream and Luke's heart sank. As the clear water flowed away, darkness crept back in until, fifty yards away, no trace remained. "She needs more 'an just clean water dumped in to fix 'er, I'm afraid." Peter shook his head and walked toward the west.

Crack!

Chunks of the bridge broke off and fell into the river, and small islands of clear water drifted downstream. As Matt, Samantha, and Marti walked away, Luke watched pieces of the railing splash into the river. *There has to be something they're missing.* He spun around and jogged to catch up with Peter. "Why doesn't that work, sir? Putting clean water into the river, I mean."

Peter walked silently for a moment and then peered down at him. "Have ya ever seen a bane-wolf bite, lad?"

"Yes, sir, my uncle got bit last year." Luke shivered, thinking of Uncle Landon lying on the couch in the family room. "It was pretty bad."

"Then you've seen the bite ain't the worst of it. It's the darkness spreadin' afterward that's the real problem."

"Yes, sir."

"Well, just like with the bite, the healin' is helped by drink or poultice of some kind, but the real fight is on the inside. If the body won' fight, won' clean it from inside you"—he jabbed a finger at Luke's chest and then stuck his chin out and shook his head.—"won' do any good. Th're has to be somethin' on the inside."

"But how do you clean it from the inside, sir?"

Peter tapped his finger to the side of his head. "That's the question, lad … That's the question."

Luke sighed and trudged on. Clusters of oaks and dog-woods grew thicker as they moved away from the river, and thirty minutes later they splashed across Rayburn Stream and angled to the southwest.

"Sir, have you ever heard of a bane-wolf bite that darkness didn't spread from?"

"That's a might strange question."

Luke ducked his head. "It's just that I ... I got bit by one earlier this year and the bite never got infected. No darkness spread from it."

Peter stopped in his tracks next to a barbed-wire fence. On the far side of the meadow inside the fence, horses galloped along a tree line. A breeze pushed his ponytail over his shoulder and Samantha's into her face. Matt and Marti stopped alongside them, forming a semicircle around Luke. "Th're's a few times I've heard o' that happ'nin', but they're rare indeed. Tell me what happened to ya."

Luke told him about the return from their trip to the Lost Island and how the wolf had come through the gate with him. Kaleva padded back to the group and, with a sigh, plopped down on the ground. A tree could be heard falling in the forest, and Peter's wrinkled face stretched thin at the mention of the island, but he remained silent.

"My uncle thought it was strange, too, but ..." Luke shrugged

Peter let out a long whistle. "The Lost Island ... Ya four have seen a good deal more than many a man ... and risked more than many, too." Three heads turned toward Luke, and Peter chuckled. "I reckon I see who the ringleader is 'ere. Well, as to the wolf bite, th're's a couple things might explain it. The first is the wolf mighta been forced to serve the hunter. Most people think bane wolves are born dark, but that's just foolishness. They 'et to choose just like any other creature." He sighed and arched his eyebrows. "Just most choose darkness is all. Anyway, the second thing mighta happened is the wolf changed her mind and chose to serve light instead. Same thing happens th're that happens with a darkman. The internal effects of darkness dissipate with time, but the scars are left. Only difference is if the wolf entered into the service of a hunter voluntarily … well, it's a might bit harder to get out of than it is to get into."

Luke mulled Peter's words. "I guess … I don't know. It seemed … it seemed like she was trying to tell me something, like she wanted me to know something, and her eyes … I could almost understand her, just not quite."

Peter's eyes lost focus for a second and then fire seemed to flare inside them. "Th're is *one* other way, but it's rare. And it's evil, an old kind of evil, spawned from back when the Ancients were 'ere."

Samantha, Matt, and Marti leaned forward, and the galloping of hooves and the chirping of birds vanished.

"Th're's the chance th're's the soul of a person in that wolf, guiding its actions. Th're aren't many who can do it, and even fewer who are dark enough t' try, but a few can willingly part with th'er soul, or even worse"—Peter turned smoldering eyes toward Luke—"trap another's. Doesn't matter whether it's objects like stones, wood, or metal or whether it's in an animal or other creature. It's like a dryad, I s'pose, but not. Because the dryad is, o' course, the soul o' the tree itself, not another soul trapped th're." A rumble formed in Peter's throat. "It's a twisted use of the disciplines, trappin' a person's soul, and in the end it'll destroy 'em, both 'em and the thing they're put in, cause it's not natural, it's not right."

Luke swallowed, his breathing loud in his ears. "Can … can you get the soul out?"

Peter pursed his lips. "Ya can, but it takes a great power, and a desire of the soul to come out ... Course, ya would think any poor soul trapped like that would want to, but not all do."

Surely somebody isn't trapped in that wolf ...

"And one more thing, lad. If it's an animal that the soul was trapped in ... Once the soul leaves, it's an animal that's left, *just* an animal, and if it's a bane wolf, most likely a dark one at that. Don't ever forget that, ya lot." He scanned their faces. "No matter what ya think or how much you care for 'em"—he nodded down at Kaleva—"at the en' o' the day, an animal is just that ... an animal."

Grrrrr ...

Luke started at Kaleva's growl. She was looking to the north across the fields. The horses seen galloping across the field a few minutes ago lined the fence next to them now, whinnying and stomping the ground.

"Whaddya see, girl?" Peter said. "What's out th're?"

Kaleva sniffed the air and her nose quivered. She got to her feet, her body level with Luke's head, and growled again. When Luke turned to Peter, his eyes were closed.

"Sir ..."

Peter's eyes snapped open and he looked at the children. "Can ya ride bareback?"

"Sir?"

Peter stalked over to one of the horses. "Ya know these animals, lad. They're yer family's, are they not?"

"Well, yes, sir. I mean, they belong to my family, and I've seen a few of them, but ..."—Luke looked around at his friends—"... we don't even have any bridles, sir."

Peter stared at the horses lined up there. He glanced at his feet and knelt to the ground. Luke craned his neck, peering over Peter's shoulder and into the grass. Strands of yellow and green light wove together, Peter twisting and turning them with his fingers. Metal rings formed and the strands looped through them. Brown light flashed and Luke and the others gasped as four leather bridles hung coiled and twisted in Peter's hands. As he stood up cradling them, a call sounded to the north in Westcliffe Forest and Luke's blood ran cold.

"Oh, no …"

Ahooooooooooo.

Matt groaned. "Wonderful."

"Ya lot stop gabbin' and get over the fence."

Luke scrambled over to where Peter stood whispering and slipping the first bridle onto a gray horse.

"Come 'ere, lass."

Peter lifted Samantha onto the back of the horse and moved on to the next horse. Whispering again, he placed a bridle on her, too. The horses whinnied and danced a step or two, but none ran from him.

"How's he doing that?" Luke said. "I can't even get Archer to stay that calm sometimes."

"Maybe it's because Archer isn't more concerned about the dog that's the same size he is," Matt said.

Kaleva stood growling and looking toward the forest, the fur on her neck raised. Samantha guided her horse, turning the mare in a circle, and shook her head. "It's not because of the dog. It's because he's talking to them."

Luke smirked. "Talking to them. I talk to Archer all the time—"

"Boy! Learn to hold yer tongue 'n' listen. Lassie's got the right of it. Th'er animals and th'er animals, but some animals are smarter than others, and some ya can convince to do what ya want talkin' to 'em with the disciplines."

Luke watched as the man helped Marti to mount and moved on to the next one, still whispering.

Ahooooooooooo.

Peter paused and looked north, grumbling. "… don't have time … know we're here, girl."

Kaleva trembled and raised her head. *HOOOOOUUUUUUUUUUUUUU!*

Luke quaked at the sound, covering his ears. All but the four horses Peter spoke to bolted and thundered down the fenceline away from the hound. She bounded over the fence and out into the pasture, where she raised her head again.

HOOOOOUUUUUUUUUUUUUU!

Chills swept through Luke with each howl, and Matt crouched next to one of the horses. But after a couple of lifts up from Peter, they were sitting astride their horses as well. Peter stepped back and looked at them. "I don't dare leave ya to fend for yerselves here. Ya'll have to go and get the key and the Tears now on yer own."

Ahooooooooooo.

"Once you have the Tears, ya'll have a chance against that hunter and his lot." He glanced over his shoulder. "Ride for the Redwall and the pond, stand near the edge of the pond and say the words *otee lavo Anora*. The box has the key. Take it and ride for Clearwater falls."

Ahooooooooooo.

Peter stepped back. "The Tears are hidden th're at the falls, where the moonlight mixes with water … Hurry!"

Ahooooooooooo.

"I'll send word to the dryads … They'll help as they can on the way!"

Ahooooooooooo. Ahooooooooooo.

Peter jogged toward his dog. "I'll meet ya at the falls. Just hold on 'til I get th're," he called over his shoulder. "Now go! Ride!" With a bound, he mounted Kaleva's back.

HOOOOOUUUUUUUUUUUUUU!

The hound dropped her head, crouched, and exploded toward the forest. Taking great strides and keeping her body low to the ground, she reached the first of the trees within seconds and vanished.

Luke's heart hammered as three faces stared at him.

Here we go again.

"Ride fast … Stay together."

Luke urged his mount on, racing across fields of summer corn just poking through and scattering herds of cattle as they lumbered toward water for the evening. Howls followed them until they reached the Old Market Road, where a few startled shouts and shaken fists greeted them as they dashed between wagons and crossed the gravel road south of Rayburn Manor heading west. Luke angled a little south of west, and twenty minutes later they slipped into the grasping shadow of the cliffs as the sun dropped toward the horizon.

Tha-thump, tha-thump, tha-thump—the horses galloped along the trail from Luke's grandparents' house and wound through trees and grass-covered knolls. His breathing deepened and the air chilled as the sound of splashing water reached his ears.

Rounding the last bend in the road and emerging from behind a thicket of yaupon shrubs, Luke saw Redwall Falls come into view and his eyes darted back and forth around the edge of the pond.

Where are the guards?

He pulled up on the reins and his horse slowed. Her sides heaved as she sucked in air.

Matt eased up beside him. "Somebody's been here already," he said.

"You see anything?"

Matt snorted. "No, but that doesn't really mean much."

Luke twisted around. "What about you, Marti? Samantha, your eyes see anything?"

Marti shook his head. Samantha peered around the meadow to the falls and at the trees to the south. "I don't see anything, but … something feels wrong here."

"I s-s-second that."

"I agree," Luke said. "Keep looking around. We'll get to the edge and see if we can get the key to … float to the surface or something." The others nodded and Luke eased his horse forward.

As they neared the edge of the pond, the sound of falling water filled the air and mist concealed the bottom of the cliffs. *Sure would be easy for someone to hide here.* Luke slid off his horse and dropped to the ground, feeling a twinge on the insides of his thighs. *Wonder if bareback bothers the horse as much as it does me.* He handed Matt his reins and motioned for the others to stay mounted.

He slipped over to the edge of the pond and peered into the clear green waters, but nothing moved under the surface. Peter's words sounded in his head.

Otee lavo Anora.

Luke stared at the water as it lapped onto the grass and mud at the edge. He looked back at his friends and shrugged, and Samantha motioned toward the pond and said something that the water swallowed up. When Luke turned back to the water, green light was glowing beneath the surface, bubbles racing to the top. Water gurgled and splashed onto the shore and stirred the grass and reeds that lined it. Then Luke noticed that it was lapping against a rust-brown chest. He watched the chest shift in the shallow water for a moment.

It's not gonna bite you, Rayburn ... probably.

He reached down and picked up the half-foot-long box, which had metal straps across it. He carried it back to where the others were waiting with wide eyes. *Here goes nothin'.* He popped the latch and lifted the lid.

His heart sank.

After he turned the box around and inspected it from every angle, there was no doubt.

"The key's gone!"

NINETEEN

The Tears of Adina

Luke handed the box to Matt and took the reins back. After he half-scrambled, half-pulled himself onto his horse, Matt returned the box and the four of them trotted away from the pond until the sound of falling water could barely be heard. Luke opened the box again. It was still empty.

"Maybe you h-h-have to say s-s-something else."

"Or maybe the box is the key?" Matt said.

"I don't think so. He would have told us if there was something else we had to do. Somebody just got to it before we did. It might have even been gone for months, maybe longer. Who knows? You remember that light we saw the first time Mr. Acharon brought us out here last fall? Maybe somebody got it then."

Matt sighed. "Yeah, I guess, man."

Luke closed the box and his eyes along with it, grinding his teeth.

"Well, now what do we do?" Samantha said, sitting tall in her saddle and glaring at Luke. "I hope your plan isn't to just sit here."

Luke stared for a moment and then a smile played at the corners of his mouth. *Kinda looks like Grandma Rayburn when she's mad.* His smile spread to Matt and then Marti.

Samantha scowled at them. "What is so *funny* about this?"

Luke chuckled, and then his chuckle turned into an all-out laugh. His laughter proved contagious as well, and red seeped into Samantha's cheeks as all three boys laughed giddily.

When her scowl finally cracked, Luke regained his composure. "No, no, we won't sit here. I doubt Peter and Kaleva will keep the wolves busy forever. We'll head down to Clearwater Falls … though who knows how long that will take or what we'll do when we get there?"

"Uh, Luke, there's a t-t-tunnel on the south e-e-end of the holding, p-p-pretty close to the falls."

"And do you just *happen* to know the symbols to get us there, Marti?"

Marti grinned. "M-m-maybe."

"Well, let's get going. I assume the closest one to us now is the one at the fork on Old Market Road?"

"Yep."

"Lead the way," Luke said as he looked at the sky to the west. "I'd say we've got about thirty minutes of sunlight left … maybe an hour more at most."

The four trotted, walked, and galloped back the way they'd traveled earlier. The pastures were empty by now, as was the road. Oranges, purples, and reds faded from the sky and gray dusk settled in as they neared the tunnel. Samantha moved up beside Luke.

"Something's going on," she said. "We should have seen someone by now. And Peter said he would send word to the dryads. I know not all of them are active still, but we should have seen one by now."

"Yeah, something's way, way not right," Luke said as the tunnel appeared ahead.

Marti cantered up to the tunnel and blue light glowed within one stone after another. A few seconds later, light flashed in the middle of the arch.

"Let me go first," Luke said. "I wish there was some way to warn you if they were waiting on us, but if there is someone ... or *something* waiting, I'll try to lead them away. Just—"

"Just shut up and go, Rayburn," Matt growled.

Samantha shook her head. "We're not just going to run away if you're in trouble, Luke."

"Y-y-yeah, man."

Luke smiled. "All right then." He turned to the arch and, taking a deep breath, urged his horse through.

Click, click. Pop.

He blinked flashes of white away and stepped his horse forward a few paces.

Pop. Pop. Pop.

Blue-white light winked out and darkness covered them. After a few moments, the darkness formed into shapes. A handful of lightning bugs blinked across the field and brought back images of suitcases, a carriage, and his family.

Quite a bit different from two years ago.

The smell of garbage and rotting fish overpowered the scents of grass and trees, and the horses whinnied and shook their heads. A sliver of moon floated above, the stars winking awake. There was a red glare far to the north.

"I'd like to use some light, but if they're waiting on us, I'd just as soon give as little warning as possible," Luke said. "Samantha, can you see well enough to get us to the bridge?"

She looked down the road that led from the tunnel. "I think so ... yes."

"You lead. The road is wide enough, if I remember. We can walk almost side by side. Once we get to the bridge and the falls, we'll have to use light to look around, I'm sure."

Before they reached the first bend, their bridles began to glow. The horses shook their heads for a moment and then became still. A circle of green light seemed to expand from the bridles, and the glow crept outward about ten yards in all directions until a sphere of light surrounded them.

Luke grinned at the illuminated faces of his friends. "Well, I woulda liked not to look like a beacon as we left the hills, but it *is* nice."

"If they're waiting on us, they'd see us anyway, man," Matt said. "Without knowing the land better, there's no way to sneak up to Clearwater Bridge."

They passed a grove of trees, and then the road sloped downward. Luke recalled a meeting with Mr. Acharon and James and racing through the darkness without lights. *I wonder how they saw that night … Sure would be a handy bit of knowledge right now.* When the bridge and the falls came into view, his mind snapped back to the present. "So … anybody have *any* idea what Peter meant by 'where the moonlight mixes with water'?"

"No clue," Matt said.

"Maybe Peter w-w-will be there already."

As the wind covered the sounds of hunting swallows, Luke turned to Samantha. "You're awful quiet, Samantha. Do you know something?"

She bit her lower lip. "I've been thinking about it … I think he means something Mayeem told me about. When water is broken down really fine, like into a mist, from water smashing into something—you know, like waves or *falls*—then the disciplines of water and light or even air can mix. There are only a few places I know of in Countryside where that happens on its own. I'm not sure, but I think Peter meant that the Tears are at the very bottom of the falls."

"Of course they are." Matt rolled his eyes. "Why would they be anywhere else? It's *obviously* too much to ask for them to be at the top—you know, like, sitting on the bridge in a box wrapped up with a pretty pink bow or something."

The edge of the light glided along the ground and pulled Luke's gaze forward. A few yards away, the first wooden planks of Clearwater Bridge were visible in the green light cast by their bridles. Luke and the others pulled up on their reins. Beyond the green glow, the bridge disappeared into a gray shadow stretching across the chasm. Wind gusted down the road, hitting their backs.

"Well, guess we'd better find some way down to the bottom," Luke said. "Matt, you and Samantha search that side and Marti and I will search this side. See if you can find a path or … anything. And use whatever light you need. We might as well let the world know we're down here. Maybe it will bring some help our way. I still don't like that we haven't seen anyone."

Luke dismounted and patted his horse before walking to the south side of the bridge with Marti. Four orbs of blue-white light winked into existence, bobbing in the air and illuminating shrubs of Mexican heather and grass lining the road.

"Hey, I th-th-think I found something," Marti called out.

The others walked toward where Marti was pointing. Flattened grass and a freshly turned rock beside the road led to a rabbit trail that zigzagged away from them and down into the darkness.

"Well, it looks promising," Luke said, "but it also looks like we aren't the first ones here."

He led the way as they descended the cliff side single file. The trail wound back and forth, sometimes packed dirt, sometimes little more than a space between rocks, and sometimes running through a tunnel of blackberry vines. Matt grumbled as they crunched through a patch of the vines.

"If the light didn't give us away, the noise sure as heck would."

The sound of water crashing onto rocks and into some kind of pool below crept up to meet them. Halfway down, droplets of water splashed onto Luke's arm.

"Ow, jeez, what is that?"

"It's the darkness in the water," Samantha said. "It stings and burns your skin as the water touches it."

"Wonderful. First the smell and now this. Not real sure which is worse."

Marti sniggered. "The s-s-smell won't hurt you, s-s-so I'd vote for the w-w-water."

"Good point," Luke said.

"Must be what those nasty little gnomes feel like when they get hit with clean water," Matt said. "Wonder what a bath would do to them."

Luke guffawed as he continued down the path. The sound and the sting of the water intensified as they neared the bottom. When they got there, they found a lone cypress tree, its bare branches brown in some spots and blackened in others, and huddled behind the trunk. When Luke peered around it, a splash of water hit the tree, causing a hissing sound, and he pulled his head back.

"Now what!" he yelled over the roaring water.

Suddenly, the sound of the falls diminished, and brown-green light bloomed from the tree trunk. Luke recoiled as a dryad stepped out. Its boyish face was covered in burns, patches of his green hair were yellowed and curled, and the vines of his clothes were brown in places.

The dryad smiled at the expressions greeting him and shrugged, his voice broken. "I've had better days. Name's Bros. Heard you lot might be coming."

Samantha stepped forward and reached her hand out. As she touched the dryad's arm, she smiled sadly.

His lips trembling, Bros closed his eyes, obviously comforted by her touch. "Thank you."

"Sir, we … we think we can help, but we need to know—"

His eyes snapped open. "You must go into the cave behind the falls. That is where the mermaid went"—his head fell—"though she has not returned."

Luke looked at the murky water coursing down the side of the cliff and slamming into the pond at the bottom. "How? I mean, the water would crush us."

"Not to m-m-mention the darkness b-b-burning us alive."

"I can do it," Samantha said.

"What?" Luke said. "You're not going through that!"

A smile played on Samantha's lips and she shook her head. "I'm not going to walk through the water." Her eyes lighted up. "I'm going to move the water."

His face contorting, Bros put his finger to his lips. "Yes, yes, that is what the mermaid did."

Marti stared at the falls and cocked his head. "It m-m-might work."

"Can we all fit through the opening?" Matt said. "Is the cave big enough?"

"Yes, if you can hold the water for long enough," Bros said.

"I'm glad all of you seem so confident in your plan," Luke said, "but would someone please tell me what the heck the plan *is*?"

Samantha smiled. "I'm going to open a gap in the falls, kinda like pulling back a curtain, and then we're going to walk through."

"Just walk right in, huh? And you can do that with something this big?"

"I ... I think. Mayeem showed me something like it earlier this spring. You just get the water to flow a different way."

"What about the darkness?"

Bros shook his head. "The darkness is inside the water. For the most part, it will move with it." He turned his intense brown eyes to Samantha. "And I will help shield you as much as I can, young one. I'm weak but not wholly disabled." He winked.

"Thank you, sir."

Marti smiled and gave her a thumbs-up. "We're right behind you, Samantha."

She turned to Luke and his chest tightened.

"Samantha, you—"

She shook her head and took a deep breath. "It'll be fine, all right?"

He clenched his jaw. "All right."

"Here we go." She turned to the waterfall and stepped out from behind the trunk of the cypress tree.

Bros followed her with his eyes. His muscles tightened, strain showing on his face. Drops of water splashed and steamed in midair, most hitting an invisible wall a few inches in front of Samantha. She flinched as a couple of drops hit her arms and pink spots appeared.

It's not working ... It's too big.

Luke raised his arm, but Matt grabbed it. "Wait!"

The torrent of water bulged away from the cliff and then fell back again. Samantha stood with her fists at her sides, her eyes unblinking.

"Come on, Samantha!" Matt yelled, and Marti bounced on his toes.

The water bulged out from the rock face again. It moved a foot, and then two.

Luke shook his head. *She can't hold that. It's not gonna work.*

"Another foot and you will have to go!" Bros called to them over his shoulder. "Stay close to the cliff! I will protect you as much as I can without endangering your friend, but she will have to stay here with me!"

"What?" Samantha looked away from the water and the falls sank back toward the cliff. She jerked her focus back to the falls and grimaced. The water rose from the rock again.

Bros's chest rose and fell rapidly as he watched her. "When you get in," he said to Luke, "give us some kind of signal and we will let the water drop. Do the same when you are ready to return!"

Luke nodded and stepped toward Matt and Marti. "Y'all ready?"

They nodded.

Luke watched the water. *Almost … wait …* "Now!"

He leaped forward and slipped on the first rock but grabbed on to the cliff wall. "Ow!" He straightened and jerked his hand away. The palm was red. Continuing on, he moved forward under a hail of droplets. The wall curved toward the falls, forcing him closer to the water. Some drops hit his skin and clothes, some hissed in the air beside him. Nearing the edge of the stream of water, he turned sideways and glanced back. Matt and Marti slid along behind him, the wet blackened rock to their left and the crashing water to their right.

A few seconds later Luke slipped under the falls and

blackness swallowed him. His thoughts shifted to sand dunes and a burned-out village. The memory of cold clamping down on him and the sound of voices inside an unnatural shadow flashed through his head and he shivered.

It's just dark, Rayburn, nothing more.

An orb of light popped into the air above his head, and light spread along the cliff wall. Scanning the wall, his eyes locked on to a fissure in the rock a few feet ahead. As he moved forward, darkness sucked up the light of the sphere.

No idea what's in there, but you know who's coming behind you.

He took a deep breath and plunged in. Silence engulfed him, and his light orb illuminated the first few feet of smooth limestone walls. Seconds later, Matt jumped in, and then Marti. Their light joined his and he blinked. "Marti, can you send them some kind of signal?"

Marti nodded and turned around. A ray of green light shot out away from him, exploding through the falls. In less time than it took Luke to exhale, the water crashed down against the opening to the cave. Marti jumped back as water sloshed in, splashing the rock and sizzling in the spot where he'd just stood.

"That w-w-was close."

Matt smiled. "Maybe next time you step away from the burn-you-alive-water before you get them to let it drop."

"All right," Luke said, "let's figure out where this thing is and get out. Who knows how long until someone—or something—comes and finds Samantha and Bros out there alone."

"Not l-l-long, I bet."

Luke sighed and peered into the darkness. "Am I going blind or is this cave sucking the light right out of my orb?"

"You're not blind," Matt said. "I can't see anything past a few feet either."

"Me n-n-neither."

Luke stepped slowly away from the entrance. "Hmmm … let's push forward a little bit more. Maybe it's just the darkness in the water that—" He stopped. Sela'or glowed on the walls, a pair of them at a time, stretching to the back of the cave.

"Why do I get the feeling that lights coming on right now *isn't* a good thing?" Matt said.

"Keep your eyes—" Luke's heart jumped in his chest as light illuminated the back of the cave. "Look!" In the far corner of the cave, Mayeem stood perfectly still, as if she were frozen in place. Her body faced away from them, her hand reaching out to the back wall of the cave.

Luke jumped forward. Two spouts of water exploded into the air, and he scrambled backward as the water formed torsos and then arms and heads of creatures made out of water. Within a few seconds, ice-blue eyes blinked at him. Water swirled inside the creatures' bodies and they surged up and down as if bouncing on the balls of the feet they didn't have.

"They look kinda like mandreekah," Luke said.

"I'm p-p-pretty sure those are actual w-w-water elementals, Luke."

Matt moaned. "Of course, the one discipline I've got less than zero skill with."

"What do you think the chances are that they're here to help us?" Luke said. The creatures' heads snapped toward him and he cringed.

"Not g-g-good."

A burst of water blasted toward Luke, and when he dodged it, another slammed into the wall by his head and broke off a chunk of the stone. He swallowed and darted off again, jets of water crashing all around him.

"Hey! Over here!" Matt yelled.

One of the creatures turned to him.

"N-n-no! Over here!"

The creature jerked its head toward Marti. Luke dodged another stream, and pebbles slid under his boots and he slipped to the floor. When he stretched his hand out to catch himself, pain shot up his arm. As he shoved up off the cave floor, he saw that a red line of blood had welled up across his palm, and then he noticed the sound of rushing water above his head.

"Who … huuuuuu!"

He gasped as a wave crashed down on him, and when he opened his eyes, water surrounded him.

I'm in a big bubble … of water!

He was floating suspended in the middle of a ten-foot sphere of water. He swam to his left and the bubble moved with him. He swam to the right and the bubble moved that way. When he twisted and turned, the bubble twisted and turned, the edge of the water and the fresh air outside always inches from his fingertips.

I can't hold my breath much longer.

He became still, floating in the center. Outside the bubble, Marti danced back and forth, evading rock-shattering bursts of water, while Matt leaned into a stream of water behind a glowing shield. Luke's lungs began to burn.

Not gonna win on defense, Rayburn.

He glared at the creature that had enveloped him in the water bubble. The creature stared back at him unblinking.

Is that thing gloating?!

Luke felt heat rise in his chest, but then he had a thought and he smiled. The creature's eyes narrowed and then grew round as Luke restructured parts of the water bubble around him into ice. Daggers of ice flew out of the bubble around Luke and slammed into the creature, splashing water in all directions and separating gallons' worth from the main body of the elemental. The bubble shrank and Luke sank back to the ground. As he bent over and gulped in air, the last of the water bubble around him changed into ice and flew across the room. Part of the elemental's body pooled on the ground.

It's not enough, I have to destroy its entire body!

Luke straightened up. Parts of the creature regrouped, the body reforming. Luke sent more ice slicing into the elemental and smashing its body apart, but it was forming faster than he could break it apart. Meanwhile, the other, still-whole elemental had Marti and Matt pinned. Shots of water kept Marti dodging behind boulders and stone pillars, and a steady stream pushed Matt back behind his shield, slamming him toward the wall. "Marti, distract that one! Get all of its attention and keep it busy!"

Marti jumped and rolled behind a boulder as water swept over him. "Oh, r-r-right, no p-p-problem!"

Light exploded near the elemental's head. The creature winced and then turned its full attention toward Marti. The stream blasting Matt stopped and he dropped to his knees.

"Matt, I need ya, man. Come on!" Luke yelled.

"Luke, I can't do anything with water!"

"Yes, you can!"

Eyes appeared again in the creature in front of Luke as it reformed. *Not much longer and this thing's gonna be back in action.* He sent more ice flying its way. "When I tell you ... I need you to make this thing explode."

"What?!" Matt's voice rang out to his right. "Luke, I can't ... I can't even make a drop of water do what I want and you want me to make a lot of water go in a million different directions!?"

Luke stopped and grinned at Matt. "Matt, I can't do both

things. I need your help. You can do it, I know you can. You always come through in the end."

"Luke!"

At least I sure hope he can. Luke faced the elemental again. The creature's body was whole now. It lifted an arm toward Luke.

Luke heard his father's voice. *You must make it so that the mandreekah can no longer fight.*

The creature's arm jerked, and then its whole body shuddered. It looked down with wide eyes and Luke grinned. *Too late.* "Now, Matt! Do it now!"

Crystals of ice formed all along the creature's body, expanding and working their way through it. With only its head and one arm still in liquid form, the elemental used its available hand to sling water and hailstones of ice. Luke saw Matt thunder by, sprinting toward the pillar of ice with his shield in front of him and ice and water glancing off of it.

What's he doing? It's not completely frozen!

"Arghhhh!" Matt lunged forward, and the last segment of the elemental froze as he slammed into it.

Crack!

Ice shattered and slid across the floor of the cave. Matt flew through the frozen body and smashed into the wall before crumpling to the floor.

Luke darted forward, slipping on shards of ice. "Matt! Matt, are you all right?" He slid the last few feet as Matt rolled over groaning.

"Ohhhh, that didn't feel so good."

Luke shook his head as the sound of water slamming into rock carried to his ears. "Of course it didn't. You just ran full tilt into solid rock! What'd you go and do that for?"

"You said make it explode," Matt said as Luke hauled him to his feet.

"I didn't mean for you to use your body, you idiot! I hadn't planned on freezing the whole thing. I almost couldn't get it to freeze all the way!"

Matt shrugged his arm around Luke's shoulders. "I couldn't make the thing come apart using the water discipline, and then when I saw what you were doing, I just figured smashing into it would do the trick. Besides, I 'always come through in the end.'"

Luke growled and shook his head. "And I'm the one with the harebrained ideas." Flashes of light appeared in the corner of Luke's eye and he turned to the far side of the cave. "Come on, we've got to go help—"

Yellow light and heat exploded in front of them, knocking them to the ground. A weight like a load of feed sacks fell on Luke and forced the air out of his lungs.

"*Oooommmffffhhhh!*"

Luke shoved Matt off of him and rolled to his side, gasping for air. The heat and the light faded, and dead silence filled the cave.

"Marti!" Luke rubbed his eyes. "Marti! Are you OK?!"

Luke blinked as the blue-white light of the sela'or replaced his blindness and he could make out shapes and forms around him.

"I th-th-think so."

Luke sat up and leaned around the side of a now-blackened boulder.

"It w-w-worked!"

Luke sighed, his shoulders relaxing. "What worked? You did the heat and the light?"

Marti nodded. "I was running out of p-p-places to hide and

that thing was getting pretty nasty. I saw w-w-what you did out of the corner of my eye, shattering the other o-o-one and, well ... my dad started w-w-working at a foundry this year and I f-f-figured if ice could shatter, then—"

Luke snorted. "Water could evaporate. Awesome."

Marti pushed up to his feet, his arms quivering. "I just wasn't s-s-sure it would work."

"It worked, all right, a little too good," said Matt, sitting on the floor of the cave. "You singed all the hair on my arms."

Luke snickered. "Well, don't look at your head then."

Matt's eyes widened and his hand shot up to the top of his head. His fingers brushed across a singed spot near the front.

"Aw maaan! Next time warn me before you decide to give me a haircut by fire, huh?"

Marti smirked. "So s-s-sorry."

Matt glared at Luke. "And you! Next time, just leave me on the ground if you're just gonna drop me again!"

Luke chortled. "Me?! You're the one who landed on me, you big oaf!"

"Whatever." Matt struggled to his feet. "Come on, we still gotta find the Tears."

Marti shuffled across the room as Luke staggered to his feet. Luke's hand throbbed as he regained his bearings and staggered toward Mayeem near the rear wall of the room. The boys walked to within a few feet of her.

"I wonder what happened to her," Luke said.

The mermaid was standing stock-still. A gust of air blew past the boys, and her hair and clothes shifted, but her body remained motionless.

Luke leaned closer. "Her skin's ... wrong ... It's like it's almost gray."

"I don't know what's wrong," Matt said, "but whatever it is, if she managed to get past those thugs by herself, I'm not sure I want to find out what stopped her."

"Maybe she … activated s-s-some trap or something."

Luke looked at her eyes again and then followed their gaze along her arm to her hand. He started back. "Whoa, look at that."

Matt stepped around Luke and peered at Mayeem's hand. "Half of it's in the rock!"

The boys stared at the fingers that disappeared into the limestone wall.

"Now, how d-d-did that happen? How do you s-s-stick your fingers through s-s-solid rock?"

Luke's mind flashed back to the map room at his grandparents' house. "You don't."

Matt and Marti turned frowning faces toward him. "What?"

Luke dug his hand into his jeans pocket. "You don't stick your fingers through solid rock. You stick them through light."

Matt's frown faded into a smile. "Like the map room!"

"Exactly."

"Huh?" Marti looked bewildered.

"That rock's not really there," Luke said. "It's just an … illusion, sort of. I mean, something is there, but it's just made up of light, maybe air or something else, but it's meant to hide something behind it."

Marti's eyes lighted with understanding. "Ohhh!" Then his face fell. "But d-d-don't you think whatever it's h-h-hiding is what froze Mayeem? Won't it d-d-do the same to us?"

Luke pulled something out of his pocket. "That's why we're not going to stick our hands in there." He held out a small leather pouch. "We're just going to take a peek."

Marti peered at the pouch. "What's in th-th-there?"

"Seeing sand," Matt said with a grin.

"Ahhhh … I s-s-seeee."

Luke uncinched the pouch and took out a pinch of the silver-and-white sand. "Carried just a little bit around after Easter. Figured it might come in handy at some point." He tossed the dust onto the wall of the cave where Mayeem's hand vanished into the rock. Light sparkled as the dust hit the rock. A two-foot section of the wall shimmered and vanished.

"Aw-aw-awesome."

"Too cool."

The niche in the wall was about as deep as it was wide. In the center, with Mayeem's hand resting on it, sat a wooden chest about the size of a lunch box. The polished surface of the dark wood gleamed.

"Either someone has been d-d-down here polishing that or s-s-somehow the disciplines are keeping the d-d-dust off."

Matt snorted. "Man, I need to learn that trick for when Mom makes me clean."

"What is …" Luke peered at the top of the box, and recognition set in. "That's the same symbol that's on the *Book of the Wise*, the symbol for the Remnant!" The teardrop shape of the open flame was carved into the top of the chest. He reached toward the box.

"Luke, wait!"

He jerked his hand back and shuddered. "Sorry, right."

"How do we open the chest? It looks like we can't even touch the thing without being—"

"P-p-petrified."

Matt nodded. "Yeah."

Luke stared at the mermaid's hand resting on the edge of the chest. *Something's not right … Something's missing.* His head popped up. "The key! We need the key!" He smacked his hand against his forehead. "And we left the box outside with Samantha!"

"But it w-w-was empty anyway. Maybe Mayeem's the o-o-one who got it."

Luke shrugged. "Maybe. Seems like she would have used it, though. But let's look arou—"

"Hey!" Matt said. "Lookie there."

Clenched in Mayeem's fist was a leather cord, and dangling from the cord was a bronze key with a cylindrical shaft and tooth at the end. The boys huddled around.

"That's a skeleton key," Matt said.

"A *what*?" Luke said.

"I've h-h-heard of those, but h-h-how would *you* know that?"

"I know *some* things, you know," Matt said. "Besides, my mom has a few of them in our store to lock up the rare books. See, it's only got a couple teeth at the end." He leaned forward and squinted at the round end of the key. "But the bow looks like it's in the shape of a traveling tunnel except with the Remnant's symbol in the middle … There's something else, but I can't make it out."

"I w-w-wonder why sh-sh-she didn't use it."

Luke sighed and shrugged. "Probably thought she could pick the box up first and then unlock it."

"Yeah, and then—bam—frozen," Matt said.

"Well, either of you got a knife or something so we can cut this cord? I left my pocket knife at home."

Matt fished his knife out of his pocket.

"But w-w-what if you …"

Luke grabbed the key and sliced across the cord. As his hand wrapped around the key, orange light twisted around the shaft. "Ow!" He dropped the key and wrung his hand, blowing on it. "Jeez, that thing got really hot." He crouched and watched as the key's orange light faded. "Hmmm." He wiped his hand on his pants. "Still got blood all over." He blew on the key and tapped it with his finger. "It's ... *cool* now." He picked it up and examined it under the light in the room. "Well, *that's* interesting." All along the shaft, a series of lines swirled and twisted, some etched into the metal of the shaft, some raised. He moved closer to the box. "Maybe you have to touch the key to the box first."

Marti stepped back. "And m-m-maybe you still turn p-p-petrified, Rayburn."

"Yeah, man, I'm not sure that's—"

Luke's hand darted out.

"Luke!"

As cold raced up Luke's arm to his chest, his fingers stiffened and his jaw clenched shut. His body quaking, the chill and stiffness spread. *B-b-b-brilliant, Rayburn.*

Blue light flashed around the chest.

Sizzzzz.

Smoke wafted from the box and the chill seeped out of Luke.

"Whew!" He exhaled, flexing his hand as his muscles relaxed.

"You wanna maybe talk about it before you reach out and touch something that turns people into living stone, man!" Matt said.

Luke could feel his face flush. "Sorry, but we really didn't have time, and it worked, right?"

Marti sniggered. "That's s-s-something you would say, M-M-Matt."

Luke turned back to the niche in the wall and lifted the box out. He stepped a few paces away and placed the box on the floor.

"Wonder why Mayeem didn't unfreeze when you got the box," Matt said.

"Don't know, but maybe she will when we open it, or maybe someone can use the Tears to … fix her." Luke paused, holding the key a couple of inches from the keyhole.

"We're right here, man," Matt said.

The boys sat in a tight semicircle and stared down at the front of the chest. After taking a deep breath, Luke plunged the key into the lock and all three boys shrank back away from the box.

Nothing.

Luke leaned back in and twisted the key.

Pop!

The boys flinched as the lid sprang open, but then Luke chuckled. "Ha. We're a bunch of scaredy girls. It's just a simple lock now, I guess."

Marti smirked. "S-s-simple. Right."

Luke eased the lid open.

"Whoa." Matt let out a low whistle.

Marti's mouth dropped open.

Luke stared into the interior of the chest. "Well, that's not what I expected."

"I'll say," Matt said.

Inside the chest lay a purple-black pouch with a leather drawstring, and beside it a necklace, its clasp locked. A dozen silver strands the thickness of hair twined together to make the chain of the necklace, but it was what was attached to the chain that was cause for admiration.

Matt spoke out of the side of his mouth. "You don't think those are …"

Marti shook his head, his mouth still hanging open. "C-c-can't be."

Luke pinched his arm. "They sure look it."

Every inch along the chain, shining in the light, were clear-cut teardrop-shaped stones. Light reflected and refracted off their surfaces and the room brightened.

Matt whistled again. "The smallest one has to be, like, the size of my thumb, man."

"I don't know w-w-what your thumb size is in carats, but I b-b-bet it's a lot."

"Whaddya think the pouch is for?" Matt asked.

"You've gotta have s-s-something pretty to carry those th-th-things around in."

"We've got to get out of here," Luke said, "but maybe if we touch the Tears to Mayeem"—he hesitated, glancing at Matt and Marti—"we can at least try it real quick."

Matt scowled. "I guess."

Marti nodded and Luke reached out. When his fingers brushed the stones, his eyes shot open. Light and heat exploded up from the stones. A scream sounded beside him, and the face of a woman appeared in his mind. Blond hair, blue eyes, her face confused. And then her eyes widened in shock and … her face vanished.

Luke dropped to his knees, gasping for breath.

TWENTY

◆

Ambush

"Luke!"

Luke winced, grabbing his head with his hands.

That face …

"Luke!"

He blinked away the searing image of the woman's face, but the herd of elephants thundering through his head continued its stampede. Hands tugged at his shoulders and arms and he looked up.

"Luke, are you OK?"

Matt's voice …

Luke moved his head up and down. "Yeah … I think so."

"What h-h-happened?"

Marti …

"I … I don't know. I touched the Tears and … I saw the same face I saw two years ago when I first crossed the bridge into Countryside."

Matt and Marti exchanged a worried look.

"We were just rolling over Clearwater Bridge and seeing Countryside for the first time and … I saw this lady's face."

"Do you know wh-wh-who it w-w-was, Luke?"

"No. No idea. She had blond, almost white hair, and she was older—or at least it seemed that way—but it was hard to tell, really. She had these blue eyes, almost painfully bright. The first time, that's about all I noticed, but this time ..."

"What man, what is it?"

"This time it seemed like she recognized me, like she was actually seeing me."

Quiet filled the cave for only a moment and then a tremor shook the walls. Dust showered down from the ceiling, and Matt locked onto Luke's arm with a vise grip. "We'll have to discuss that later. We need to get out of here *now* ... and we have a problem."

Luke slammed the lid shut on the chest. "*What* problem?" he said as he struggled to his feet.

"Her."

Mayeem lay crumpled on the floor of the cave. A flush had replaced the gray tone of her skin.

"How are w-w-we going to get her outta here w-w-without getting burned?"

Rumble ...

"We're *gonna* get burned," Matt said. "It's not about getting burned, it's about not *slipping* and falling headfirst into the torrent of water."

"Well, we're not gonna leave her," Luke said, strength trickling back into his arms. "Marti, signal Samantha and Bros. Let's see if they're even still all right and out there. Matt and I will wrangle Mayeem over near the entrance and then you and I will carry one end while Matt carries the other."

Marti opened his mouth, incredulity on his face. "Luke, I can carry half of Mayeem by myself. You j-j-just collapsed to the floor and—"

"No, Marti," Luke said. "Matt is the strongest of us and so he's on his own. I feel kinda wobbly, but I can still help some, and we'll need all the help we can to get out of here in one piece."

Marti sighed and ran to the entrance of the cave. Luke put the box under his arm. *Not gonna work. They'll slip out from under my arm. We can't go losing the Tears now that we just got them.* He shoved it under his shirt. The box poked out and then slipped back down. *Not gonna work either. I'm gonna have to take them out of the box and carry them.*

Light flashed near the entrance to the cave, where Marti was sending a signal to Samantha and Bros. Luke knelt and opened the box again. He stared at the Tears and then at the pouch next to them. *I wonder ... maybe it won't feel so bad this time.* He closed his eyes and grabbed the pouch and the Tears.

"What are you doing?" Matt said, jerking his head away from the light that exploded from the Tears as Luke touched them.

The woman's face flashed in Luke's head and his muscles tensed. Energy surged up his arm and throughout his body. He pulled out the Tears and, fumbling with the opening of the pouch, shoved them inside, releasing them. The light winked out and the energy drained from his body. Purple light sizzled over the pouch and then faded. Luke ran his fingers over it. *Feels like velvet, but cold, and it tingles.* "Wasn't as bad that time ... I might even feel less wobbly ..."

Matt glowered at him. "What happened to talking about it first?"

"Come on, you girl." Luke pushed himself to his feet and grabbed Mayeem's arms. "Since when do boys 'talk.'"

Matt muttered under his breath and put his arms under the

mermaid's shoulders. When he nodded, the boys lifted her and shuffled toward the falls.

"They're out th-th-there!" Marti said as he rejoined them. "The w-w-water's moving." He took one of Mayeem's legs. "What h-h-happened with the Tears? I felt the h-h-heat and light all over again."

Matt growled, still blinking. "Genius touched them again and put them in his pocket. Half-blinded me again."

Marti looked at Luke. "You've g-g-got issues, y-y-you know that?"

"Just move!" Luke huffed and puffed as they maneuvered Mayeem toward the falls. *Maybe I'm more wobbly than I thought.* Droplets of water splashed onto their arms as they lumbered through the crevice at the cave entrance and turned to the right. Luke winced as water landed on his arms and sizzled. He saw steam rise from Matt's arms and Marti's neck. *It's hitting them, too, Rayburn. Keep moving.*

Luke and Marti slipped and squeezed their way along the path behind the waterfall, bumping, dragging and dropping Mayeem's body as they went, despite their best efforts to do it gently. They reached the edge of the water and emerged from behind the falls. A few steps more and Matt slid past the edge of the water, which came crashing down near his heel. The boys continued to lurch forward, avoiding most of the splashing water.

Jeez, that was close ... Must have taken all Samantha and Bros had.

After the boys reached the end of the stone path, darkness blanketed the bottom of the falls and three orbs popped up around them. As they crunched across brown grasses, Luke could see, in the green light emanating from the tree, that Samantha was standing still next to Bros, staring at Luke with round eyes. They walked past the trunk of the tree, the sound of roaring water fading, and they half lowered, half dropped Mayeem to the ground.

"Whew." Luke wiped his brow and rubbed his arms where burns had appeared. "So, have you—" He looked up and froze.

Samantha was shaking, her eyes wide and her arms straight down at her sides.

Bros looked at the boys, his mouth turned down. "I am sorry, young ones, truly, but I had no choice."

Luke's heart thumped faster. "Sorry for *what*? What do you mean you had no choice? What's he talking about, Samantha?"

Samantha squirmed and scrunched up her face, her mouth closed. "Mmmm … mmmmmm …. MMMMMMM!!!" Her shoulders heaved and her eyes darted toward Bros, but her arms stayed pinned to her side.

She's tied up. He used air to tie her up!

Bros shook his head. "He came weeks ago … and"—tears streamed down the dryad's face—"he said to watch for you children, for *you* in particular."

The hair on the back of Luke's neck stood up as Bros's eyes bored into him. "Who … who came weeks ago?"

Sobs shook the dryad. "He … he said I had to keep you here when you came … If I didn't, he said … he would … come back and kill me. He knew you were coming tonight. They cleared everyone out of your way so you would get here and *I* would be the only one you saw!"

Rumble …

"We've got to get out of—"

Ahooooooooooo.

Luke jerked his head toward the top of the falls and shivered as the howl split the night.

Matt nodded. "Get out of here—couldn't agree more, man."

Blackness moved above them, crawling and slithering over the rocks, as Mayeem lay motionless on the wet ground, her chest rising and falling. Samantha went from shaking and squirming to muttering and staring daggers at Bros.

"Maybe we can make it along the path to the other side of the falls," Matt said. "But how do we get you out, Samantha? Bros, you have to let us go."

We'll never make it. They're too close already, and we can't carry Mayeem and Samantha.

Bros shook his head and wailed. "I ... I ... I can't."

"I've never tried it, b-b-but I bet if you knock a dryad out, his h-h-hold on the disciplines will go, too." Marti glared at Bros and the dryad faltered back a step.

There still isn't time. Luke ground his teeth. *Think, Rayburn.* Thoughts flashed through his head. *Matt ... Samantha ... Marti ... Mayeem ... the Tears ... Bros ... Darkness ... Matt ... Samantha ... Marti ...*

Ahoooooooooo.

RUMBLE ...

The tremor sent dust clouds ballooning from behind the falls and for moments even the roar of the falls was silenced.

"G-g-guess we're not going that w-w-way."

Cold air seeped around Luke, fogging his breath, and the pendant on his chest warmed.

"Luke, engage, man. Come on!" Matt said.

And what will you do next time when your family is in trouble, or your friends?

Luke's eyes locked on to Bros. The dryad was shaking his head and sobbing. Luke thought of darkness, and a cloud surrounded Bros's face. The dryad coughed and sputtered, waving his arms blindly. Luke intensified the darkness and the dryad stumbled backward. "Let her go."

A muffled scream escaped Bros's lips. Luke added air to the mixture and the darkness swirled around the dryad. "I said let her go!"

A ball of water and light smacked into Luke's face and a hand clamped down on his arm and jerked him around.

Aha, aha, aha ... Luke coughed, shaking his head and glaring. Darkness receded from around Bros, the dryad whimpering from the ground.

Matt held Luke's arm firmly in his grasp. Marti stood beside him, an orb of water and light hovering near his hand, poised to be thrown at Luke.

"Not that way, Luke. Never that way," Matt said, his voice flat but his eyes on fire.

Marti stared at Luke, unblinking. "Darkness will always c-c-come back to haunt you."

Listen to your friends, Luke.

He shivered at the voice. *They're right. It's not worth it. Now what?* Thoughts clicked into place. *They're after the Tears.*

Bros clambered to his feet, coughing and spluttering. He looked at Luke and cowered. "I'm so—"

"Hush!"

Luke looked up the cliff again. Shadows zigzagged and hopped down the trail.

Almost here. Hurry, Luke.

"Do you want them to leave you alone?" he asked Bros. "You want the water clean again?"

Bros whimpered and nodded slowly.

Luke narrowed his eyes. "I've seen dryads, I've seen them fight and I've seen them help when no one else would or could. Are you truly sorry? Do you have any of the decency and courage of your kind left in you?"

"Yes." A whisper passed the dryad's lips.

"Then use whatever honor you have left and *help*! Protect my friends here, fight for them—you understand?"

A spark flickered in Bros's eyes. "Yes."

Matt shook his head. "Rayburn, what are you up to?"

Marti glared at Luke. "I don't think we're g-g-going to like it."

Luke eased away from the falls.

"What are you doing?" Matt said, stepping toward him.

"You two were right … about the darkness. I can't use it to fight against darkness. But you're wrong about carrying Mayeem, and the falls are probably blocked now anyway."

"Luke …" Marti edged toward him.

Ignoring Samantha's muttering and her stare, Luke looked at Bros. "No matter what, you find a way to protect them."

The dryad nodded, his face stoic.

Ahooooooooooo.

The branches of nearby shrubs rattled. Matt looked at Luke, confusion in his eyes.

"Fight," Luke said. "Fight hard. Once they're gone, get everybody out of here."

"Rayburn, don't you do anything crazy," Matt said.

Hope this works … Hope you can still manage to run, Rayburn. Luke gave a half-grin. "Never."

Grunts, snarls, and pants sounded in the darkness a few yards behind him.

They're here.

Luke glanced at Marti, looked at the fire in Samantha's eyes, and squeezed his eyes shut tight. He slipped his hand into his pocket and inside the pouch. He wrapped his fingers around the Tears and yanked them out.

"Hey!"

"Luke!"

Heat exploded from his fist and light bombarded his eyelids. The hollow was filled with shrieks and squeals, shouts and curses.

One, two, three …

He fumbled blindly for the pouch and pulled it out of his pocket. Taking a deep breath he jammed the Tears back into it. When he released them, the heat and the light died. Opening his eyes, he saw his friends blinking and reaching out blindly.

"Luke! Luke!"

Good luck.

He wheeled around and ran behind a small orb floating a yard or so in front of his feet. Shadows formed into vague shapes, which then revealed themselves to be creatures of darkness bumping into trees, stumbling over rocks and colliding with each other. A bane wolf snarled and snapped at Luke as he bounded past. Two darkmen shouted and grasped for him as he ran beneath flailing arms. The sound of his friends' shouts carried behind him.

Luke raced ahead another ten yards and jumped over a bush. A soulless writhed to Luke's side, its hands covering its sizzling face and its shriek making Luke quake.

Several gnomes squealed, running blindly and slamming into each other. Other shadows twisted and turned at the far edge of Luke's vision. He ran twenty yards more, dodged around a couple of trees and came to a stop. Turning back toward the falls, he raised the orb from near his feet to thirty yards into the air above his head, and poured more light into it. *Like the flares Dad talked about in the Marines. That ought to get their attention.* He waited, counting in his head.

And what will you do…

He took a deep breath. "Hey!" Shadows turned toward him

and voices quieted. "I've got the Tears. If you want them ... Come and get them!"

He grasped the Tears in his pocket and felt their heat. Light and heat exploded around him, turning the landscape as bright as noon. He winced and looked away over his shoulder. Out of narrowed eyes, Luke saw trees and shrubs poked up along the banks of the river, and limestone rocks the size of dinner tables jutting into the water. The cool night air was whisked away, and howls and cries lifted into the sky.

Turning away from his friends, Luke doused the light of the Tears and stumbled into the night.

Luke's feet pounded south away from the falls and the holding. Branches and the wind tugged at his shirt. Screeches and calls of all kinds pursued him. Several minutes later he stopped. As the shrieks and calls grew louder, he pulled the Tears out of the pouch again, holding his eyes closed. Cries and screeches erupted behind him as the creatures fell back from the light. *I want you to follow me, just not that close.* When he dropped the Tears back into the pouch, the light went out and he raced on. And so the pattern went: racing up hills, lighting up the night and forcing the creatures back with the Tears, wheeling around bends in the river, touching the Tears, splashing across streams, touching the Tears. He paused in a small oak grove and leaned his hands on his knees, trying to catch his breath.

Ahooooooooooo. Aeeeiiiiiii ... Eeeeekkkeeeeeee ...

The calls and shouts grew louder, and glancing over his shoulder, he saw dark shapes bounding ever forward under the weak glow of moonlight. His pendant warmed and he shuddered and ran on, but trees passed by him more slowly now.

Can't run forever. Think of something, Luke.

He snatched the Tears out of the pouch. Shrieks and calls of retreating bane wolves, gnomes, soulless, and some creatures he couldn't identify bombarded his ears. Opening his eyes to slits and shielding them with his hand, he glanced around and then stopped dead in his tracks.

Can't be.

He squinted to his left. Pools of darkness remained in the river, but streaks of silver twisted and turned, winding their way downstream and sparkling in the light of the Tears.

Maybe ...

As he stumbled toward the water, heat and light poured from the Tears. In their glow, the darkness in the water sizzled and evaporated, leaving the water clear.

I can swim across! ... But how can I hold the Tears and keep my head above water?

He put the Tears back in their pouch. *Gotta find something to hold on to.* Green light blossomed near the shore and he rubbed his eyes. A tree branch floated a few yards away.

How ... Never mind.

He lunged down the slope and into the river toward the branch. When he reached it, he pulled it under his arms and floated with the current. Behind him, bane wolves lunged into the water, and he jerked the Tears out, forcing the wolves to retreat to the shore.

Darkness sizzled on the river's surface. All along the water's edge, gnomes and other dark creatures appeared. Snarls and howls echoed across the water as the current swept Luke to the center of the river and downstream. On the shore, a man lurched into the water, and through narrowed eyes, Luke could make out the silhouette of the hunter.

"No!!!" the hunter roared into the night.

Water erupted all around Luke, jostling him this way and that. Pellets of darkness flew through the air from where the hunter stood and glommed on to Luke's arms, face and neck, causing his skin to sizzle. A wave lifted him and slammed him down, causing him to smack his chin into the branch. *Don't drop them—they're your only chance!* He squeezed the Tears in his hand until the stones cut into his skin.

"Awww … ehhhh …" Luke coughed water out of his throat and felt the sting of fresh cuts. He felt the current change and start to tug him. *He's pulling me back to the shore!* His thoughts flashed back to the orchard beside his grandparents' house and the kadur the dryads used. Instantly, drops of orange light rained down on the hunter and the other dark creatures. The rain of light intensified until sheets of it were pouring down. Shouts and curses sounded as the creatures ran for cover or used the disciplines to stop the pounding on their heads. The tug on Luke's body went slack.

Need to douse the homing beacon, Rayburn, while they're still distracted.

Luke struggled with the branch, clamping it under his arms and kicking to keep it from rolling over. Darkness, water, and cool night air blanketed him as he wrestled the Tears back into the pouch. He floated along in the river until his eyes adjusted and then kicked for the far shore. Huge spouts of water and bursts of light exploded in and over the river behind him. As the current quickened, creatures splashed along the west bank and shouts and curses competed with yips and whines.

The sliver of moon traversed the sky and clouds glided overhead. Luke kicked through the water, fumbling his way around pools of darkness as best he could. As howls and splashing faded behind him, energy seeped from his arms. Shadows appeared, outlining the east shore, and he brought his leg up to kick, but his knee struck the rocks on the bottom of the river. Though pain shot up his leg, exhaustion dulled it.

He clawed forward and shoved the branch downstream. Half-crawling on hands and knees and half-stumbling, he lurched out of the water before collapsing onto the shore, his chest heaving.

Pad, pad, pad …

He shuddered and lay sprawled out on the sand and grass. *Whatever it is, I'm too tired to run anymore.*

He felt a pull on his pants and shirt and then felt his body being lifted off the ground.

Pad, pad, pad …

Grass and branches whipped over his face and he felt hair rub along his arm. As a breeze blew over him, goose bumps raced over his body.

Thump.

"Ooof."

He fell to the ground and something nudged his side. He mumbled and lay still. The nudge came again. He sighed and grumbled but didn't move.

"Do whatever you're going to … or leave me alone."

Energy dripping back into his arms and legs, he heard something whine. And then he felt something nip him.

"Ow!"

As he jerked upright, the muscles in his legs cramped. He rolled onto his stomach and looked to his side. Pale moonlight outlined trees, shrubs, and …

His heart jumped and he clawed backward on the ground, unable to force his cramped legs to function. After a few feet he stopped, huffing and puffing.

She would have killed you already if she was going to, Rayburn … But what if she wants the Tears?

He lay still, his head on the damp grass.

Can't run anymore anyway.

He stared across the few feet of grass and scrub at the gray shape of the bane wolf. She sat on her haunches, tongue lolling to the side, eyes gleaming at him in the moonlight. After a few minutes, his legs relaxed, the cramps fading to spasms and then nothing. He pushed up on an elbow, rolled over, and sat hunched over in front of the wolf.

"You've let me live three times now, although not without leaving me a couple of reminders. What do you want?"

The wolf closed her jaws and Luke sat up straighter. Sea-blue light shone from her eyes, creeping out into the woods, and Luke felt a chill run up his spine. Crickets and frogs could be heard again, and he watched the eyes of the wolf. He stood up and hobbled toward her.

"What are you trying to tell me?"

The wolf whined.

Luke reached out his hand and paused. "Don't bite my hand off, OK?"

The wolf stared at him and he rested his hand on top of her head. He stood listening to the symphony around him and his own heartbeat as he peered into the glowing blue of the wolf's eyes. After a moment, he took his hand back, chuckling. *Stupid, like I could just touch her and figure it out.*

Ahooooooooooo.

He jerked his head to the west and closed his eyes. *They're this close already!?* "Come on … just give me a break. At least let me catch my breath."

Images of his friends flashed through his head.

Better me than them —

Ahooooooooooo.

Ahuh, ahuh …

Whining, the wolf leaned her head down and nudged Luke's pocket with her nose.

Luke stepped back frowning. "What do you want with th—"

Hoooooouuuuuuuuuuuuu!

The wolf's head snapped to the north, her ears perking up.

That's Kaleva's howl!

"Peter!"

Luke looked to the north and froze. Then he turned back to the wolf.

There's the chance that there's the soul of a person in that wolf.

His thoughts hurtled from the wolf to Peter's comments to the Tears.

"You're in there! Whoever you are, you're in there!"

Ahooooooooooo.

The wolf rose to her feet and barked.

Luke scratched his head, pacing. "But how in the world do I get you out?"

It takes a great power, and a desire of the soul to come out.

"Great power I've got … and you sure seem to want out … but that still doesn't tell me what to do." Luke kicked at a clump of grass. "Agh! How do you do something you don't even know how to do?!" He looked at the wolf. "It's never gonna happ—" He froze and his mind shot back to an afternoon spent in a clearing with Samech a few weeks earlier and a buckler that would shimmer and vanish.

Focus on what you want the disciplines to do, and believe.

Hoooooouuuuuuuuuuuuu!

He whirled around and looked at the wolf. "Can't hurt to try, girl … well, hopefully not." He marched over and shoved his hand into his pocket. The wolf whimpered and whined and barked, feet dancing back and forth. "Here goes nothing … Now be still." He focused on the blue of her eyes and then closed his own. Light and heat exploded out of his closed fist as he pulled the Tears out of the pouch.

Help me not screw this up ... please.

I am here, Luke.

Luke started at the voice and then smiled. He felt warmth wash over him and his shoulders relax. Pain drained from his body and his mind watched as blue light drifted out of the bane wolf. He felt the Algid slow and then stop a hundred yards away. Lightning bugs flickered and paused in midair. A rabbit's nose twitched and stilled. The blue light pooled near Luke's feet and then rose like mist over a pond. He waited, the woods around him, hesitating. He drew a breath.

AHOOOOOOOOOO.

The Tears dropped from his hands and the heat and yellow-white light winked out. He felt his pendant warm, but a chill swept through his body. Blue mist swirled to his side, and the bane wolf's head pointed up into the night sky. Luke stumbled backward as she lowered her head and looked at him, gold eyes gleaming.

"Ohhh no."

Grrrrr ...

The wolf snarled and crouched.

Reeeeeeiiiiiiiii!

The scream splintered the air in the clearing and Luke crumpled to the ground. The wolf yelped and raced away into the darkness, the blue mist twisting and fleeing along the path behind her. Luke lay on the ground staring up at stars and the shadows of leaves. He held his breath for a few moments before exhaling. When he sat up, the sound of his breathing was the only noise in the woods.

Guess trapped souls aren't exactly ones to stay around and talk. Probably pretty mad at the bane wolf, too. At least you didn't get eaten by a bane wolf, Rayburn, or chased through the woods by an angry soul. It's still early, though … or late … or …

He stood up and arched his back and rolled his shoulder.

Ahooooooooooo.

Hooooouuuuuuuuuuuuu!

He turned to the north, the howls drawing closer. *Kaleva. Peter.* "Now, how do I make sure I run into Peter first and not the wolves?"

"I wouldn't worry too much about that, boy."

Luke whirled around. His breath fogged in front of him and the pendant grew hot under his shirt. Shadows passed in front of his eyes as he turned in a circle. "Who's there?"

A cruel chuckle sounded in the darkness. "Oh, boy, you should know who I am by now."

Orange eyes appeared in front of him. Tree branches creaked and moved aside as if by the hands of invisible giants. Blackness thickened into a body as the creature stepped forward. Luke trembled, his mind stuttering. Light poured out from the Tears. It intensified and the creature winced. A blackness surrounded the glow, but light still pushed through the darkness enough to illuminate a few yards in each direction. The Tears rose off the ground, floated through the air, and settled into the creature's claw. The body of the creature billowed for a moment like a flag in the wind and then settled. "Hmm … never liked touching them. Always feels so unsettling."

Luke raced toward the river, crashing through rose hedge and saplings and tripping over fallen tree trunks. Laughter followed him through the woods.

"Ha, ha, ha … you can't hide from me in the night, boy!"

Luke slid to a halt near the river. Coldness seized him and his back arched, muscles spasming throughout his body. A hiss sounded in his ear.

"*He* may want you alive, but I *don't*. You have caused too much trouble, boy, and for that *alone* you need to die." The voice moved farther away. "But ... you did bring me the Tears, and I couldn't have gotten them without you, so perhaps I won't prolong your pain."

The world spun in front of Luke until orange flames filled his vision.

"Good-bye, Luke Rayburn."

Pain exploded in Luke's chest. "Ahhhh!"

HOOOOOUUUUUUUUUUUUUU!

He fell backward, flailing through the air, as cold and darkness wrapped around him.

TWENTY-ONE

Blue Eyes & the River

Luke coughed and sputtered. His stomach cramped and water spewed out of his mouth.

Pat, pat, pat.

"That's it, boy, come on now … I don't have … long," the voice overhead said.

Luke felt thumping on his back and heard the rustling of grass. Half his face lay in wet dirt, his clothes sopping. Aches awakened throughout his body and his throat was raw.

What … happened?

In his mind, he saw orange eyes and himself falling backward. He heard whining behind him and cringed. He heaved himself up, rolling to his hands and knees, and his stomach cramped again. Convulsing, he dropped to his elbows and panted. Eventually, he was able to sit on his knees, hands resting on his hips. A grove of trees surrounded him. As he scanned the patch of grass and shelter, his eyes latched on to two lumps to his right.

Peter.

Luke crawled over, mud and muck sticking to his hands, and pulled himself up beside the man and his hound. Lying with her head on her paws, dark spots caking her fur, Kaleva whined and nudged Peter. She glanced up at Luke and then back at her master. Peter lay on his back on a grass-covered mound rising to the base of an oak tree wider than Luke was tall. Luke looked up to see that the moon was either hidden behind branches or had set already, grayness chasing the dark of night to the west. An orb the size of a holding coin winked into existence near Peter's face. His skin was ashen and his complexion sallow, and his chest barely rose. Dark stains covered his legs and abdomen. When Luke touched a dark patch, it left his fingers red.

"Sir?"

Peter's eyes fluttered open and a smile flickered across his face. "Ya made it, boy."

"Yes, sir."

"Good." Peter's face contorted and he coughed and closed his eyes. "Couldn't let that beast have ya."

Luke felt a sting in his eyes. "Sir, we've got to get you back to the holding. I … I don't know how to heal … and … and I lost the Tears."

Peter coughed. "No, boy, I'm done. I'm not going nowhere now … Now ya listen to me." He searched for Luke's hand and clasped it with both of his. Luke felt his hand engulfed by callused fingers. "Kaleva will get ya back to the holding. She'll get ya back safe." Peter shivered and closed his eyes. "Cold …"

When Kaleva growled, the hair on the back of Luke's neck stood up. A breeze swirled around him and he frowned. "Salt water?"

A low rumble rose from the hound's throat as blue light seeped into the oak grove.

"Oh, my love."

Luke whirled around. The ethereal figure of a woman floated a few feet away. Mist along the ground shrouded her feet and seemed to blend into a gown that rose to her shoulders and billowed in the wind. Her hair flowed out behind her and a cloud crossed her face as she drifted toward Luke. Her blue eyes flashing at him, she smiled. "Ah, do not be afraid, young one. I will not hurt you."

Luke swallowed, dropping his hand to Peter's leg. Kaleva crouched closer on the other side of her master, her lips still quivering at the woman. "I'm sorry, but I'm a bit short on trust tonight, ma'am. Who … *what* exactly are you?"

Laughter washed over the grove like small waves and Luke relaxed. "I am a spirit—a ghost, some would call me. A soul is the most accurate, though. I am she whom you freed from that fiend of a wolf." A storm passed over the woman's face, lightning in her eyes, and Luke shrank back. "I am Anora, and that man you are protecting is my husband."

Luke's mouth dropped open. The woman giggled and glided toward them. Kaleva stopped growling as the woman's hand touched her head. She knelt beside Peter, and when she placed her hand on his chest, his eyes flickered open and recognition dawned on his face. "Mmm … Anora."

Anora gave a tight-lipped smile. "Yes, my love … I'm … I'm so sorry."

"Ssshhhh." Peter's eyes flickered again and his chest became still.

Her shoulders trembling, she spoke in a whisper that sounded like the sea trapped in a shell. "… will see you soon … remember to whom you give trust. *He* will carry you home …"

Luke's heart ached as the night faded around them. The chirping of crickets, the last night song of tree frogs, even the stars in the sky disappeared behind a gray curtain. Light welled up in the east. The branches of the oak trees above swayed with Anora's muffled sobs, and a drop of blue light rolled down her cheek and fell toward Peter's chest.

Just then, a hand darted in and caught the tear as it fell, causing the light to ripple.

"Mr. ... Mr. Roberts?" Luke said.

Mr. Roberts lifted Anora's chin toward him with hands covered in scars and calluses and brushed a second tear away. Anora's face glowed where his hand touched her and he smiled.

"There will be no more tears for you, child ... It is time to go home."

Turning from her, Mr. Roberts bent down, grasped Peter's hand and pulled. A sigh rushed through the trees and Luke shivered as a blue glow was drawn from Peter. Moments later, a ghostly blue form floated before them. It was Peter, glowing and translucent just like Anora. He was dressed like the pale body lying on the ground, but there were no scars or wounds to be seen.

Mr. Roberts smiled, his eyes dancing as if he knew some joke or secret hidden from the rest of the world. "Well done, Peter ... well done."

Peter bowed. "Thank ya, my Lord."

Mr. Roberts pulled Peter's hand across to Anora's and clasped them firmly together before releasing both. "Follow the Dawn Star. He will meet you and lead you the rest of the way."

Peter bowed again. Anora curtsied but then, in a rush, threw her arms around Mr. Roberts's neck and kissed him on the cheek. Wrinkles formed around his eyes as he smiled, and then he motioned with his head toward the west. Peter winked at Luke and patted Kaleva on the head, his hand leaving sparkling light there. He took his wife's hand again. Turning, the pair walked away hand-in-hand, melting into the woods and the fading night.

Luke's heart was heavy in his chest as the blue light vanished. Kaleva turned her head toward the sky and a keening howl broke from her throat.

Hooooouuuuuuuuuuuuu.

"Come."

Warmth washed over Luke and he turned around. Mr. Roberts was squatting next to a crackling fire, rotating a brace of rabbits as grease dripped into the flames. Luke's stomach rumbled loudly as he sat across the fire from him. Kaleva plopped down with a sigh and Mr. Roberts chuckled. As they sat by the fire, gray light seeped into the stand of trees and the chirps of waking birds sounded in the woods. A breeze rustled the branches on the outside of the grove. When the meat was done, Mr. Roberts pulled a knife from his belt, sliced off strips of it, and handed them to Luke. He tossed one of the rabbits to Kaleva, who snatched it in midair and set to crunching on it. Luke blew on the strips of meat and tossed them between his hands. After a few biscuits that Mr. Roberts had pulled out of a sack and some more strips of meat, Luke leaned back and wiped his mouth with the back of his hand. When he looked at Mr. Roberts's green eyes, he saw a combination of sadness and anger and something else he couldn't put his finger on. When he looked deeper still, he saw the reflection of his heart in the man's eyes and turned away.

"I should have listened to you," Luke said. "I shouldn't have gone after the Tears ... I was so sure that I could find the Tears, that I could beat the hunter and his wolves, and now I've lost them and ... my friends!" He started to stand, but Mr. Roberts held his hand up.

"Easy, Luke, your friends are fine, thanks in no small part to you. Help arrived when you drew the band of dark creatures away. We must leave soon, though, for they are unaware that you are safe."

"The hunter and darkness—they wouldn't have been able to get to the Tears without me, would they, sir? That's what the dark one said anyway."

Mr. Roberts pursed his lips. "Perhaps. There were other ways to get to them. They may have learned one of them eventually, but trusting the words of a dark one is never wise, Luke. Those are creatures born of lies and deceit, and they take pleasure in nothing so much as causing pain and destruction. Even the truth of their words, when there, is twisted."

"Why didn't you tell me what would happen, make me listen to you, sir?"

Mr. Roberts cocked his head and smiled sadly. He sat there as pinks and oranges spread from the east and Kaleva snored softly.

Why is he just staring at me? Heat rose to Luke's face. "You could have told me again, done something ..." Mr. Roberts arched his eyebrows, and Luke turned away. "But I wouldn't have listened, would I?" An image of snow whirling through the air and green light fading into the night passed through his mind. "I never saw you after that night at the ball. Is that why you went away, because I wouldn't listen to you?"

Mr. Roberts shook his head. "No, Luke, I went away because you asked me to"—he leaned over and poked Luke in the chest—"in here. *But,* I never really left you." He winked.

Luke felt his heart tighten and he looked in the direction

in which Peter and Anora had gone. "Where did they go, sir? What happened to them?"

Mr. Roberts smiled and looked to the west. "Somewhere they have both wanted to go for a long time. Somewhere they will be together, and happy. As to what happened to them" — he turned back to Luke — "that is something you must learn. It is not something that can be told alone."

That's not much of an answer. "Were they really ghosts?"

Mr. Roberts chuckled. "What you call something does not change what it is, Luke. You may call them ghosts if you like."

That's an even worse answer.

Mr. Roberts laughed harder, and Luke couldn't help joining in. Kaleva opened an eye, looked around and closed it again with a sigh, her breath fanning the flames and sending sparks flying into the air. Luke laughed until moisture pooled in his eyes. He reached over and ran his hand along the dog's back. Though Kaleva's eyes remained shut, her tail thumped, snapping a sapling in half.

"What will happen to Kaleva, sir, now that Peter's gone?"

"She will go to Father Woods. He was one of the few who knew anything of Peter, though still not much, and accepted him … a true friend."

Luke sat there for a moment petting Kaleva as the fire faded and light grew in the sky. Mr. Roberts stood up and a cloud the size of a basketball formed above the fire, sending rain drizzling over it and dousing it. He looked north and two hawks launched into the air, trailing sparks and light behind them. When he turned to Luke, his face had gone flat. "And now, we must be going … We have one task remaining."

Luke trudged along next to Mr. Roberts through the woods, Kaleva bounding alongside them, sniffing every few feet.

"Where are we going, sir?"

"North, near where the Algid leaves Granite Lake."

Luke stopped in his tracks. *Granite Lake!* He hobbled to catch up with Mr. Roberts again. "That ... that's on the other side of the holding, sir." He looked around at the trees and shrubs and limestone boulders. "And are we even in the holding anymore?"

Mr. Roberts remained silent. Luke sighed and plodded forward. To his right, a red bird flitted through the branches of an oak tree. The tree shimmered and Luke halted.

The tree had disappeared.

"Uh, Mr. Roberts, sir ..." Luke turned and saw that he was standing in the middle of a meadow, trees and shrubs growing behind him and a sea of grass surrounding him. In front of him, beyond the grass stretching into the distance, the surface of Granite Lake sparkled silver, orange, pink, and blue.

Mr. Roberts smiled at him.

"How ... but ... we were just ... huh?"

Mr. Roberts winked, his green eyes dancing. "There are other ways to travel. They just seem a *bit* harder to learn." He grinned and walked to the east, toward the rising sun.

Luke had to trot to keep up at times. *Now that's a trick I need to learn!*

Clouds evaporated with the morning sun as the brown waters of the Algid churned nearby, a stench wafting into the air. Between Luke and the river, a granite rock protruded from the ground, half as tall as the nearby sycamore trees. Mr. Roberts waved his hand across the rock and the stone shook.

Pop! Crack!

Chunks broke off and plunged into the darkness in the

center of the rock. A few seconds later, the stone disintegrated. Brown water and darkness gurgled up as if from a mud pit and crept toward the river.

"Is that what's polluting all the Algid, sir?"

"Yes. There is a stone at the bottom of this spring, a gem called a dark stone. This gem and those like it are formed by combining the disciplines, twisting them and filling them with darkness. In this case, darkness was mixed with water and used to fill the gem. In order to clean the river, that darkness has to be overcome."

"But, sir, we don't have the Tears anymore. Won't we need them to clean the river? Was that why darkness wanted them, just to keep us from cleaning the river?"

"No. You wouldn't be able to clean the river of this sickness even with the Tears, Luke. They're just objects. It's the power within them that's useful, but you must know that power— you must be able to reach it." Mr. Roberts smiled. "Luckily, you have that same power within you. As to why darkness wanted the Tears … well, there are other reasons for that greed and desire."

"Like the gate, sir?"

Mr. Roberts snorted. "You are familiar with the line about curiosity and the cat aren't you, Luke?"

And then there are some things that need to remain hidden.

Mr. Roberts's voice floated through Luke's head and he felt his face warm. "Yes, sir."

Mr. Roberts laughed and clasped Luke's shoulder. "Nothing wrong with wanting knowledge, Luke, or asking the questions. Just make sure you think about what that knowledge will do and be willing to accept what the answer is … even if it denies you the knowledge. You understand?"

"Yes, sir … I think."

"Good. And yes, like the gate. Now, let us be about our business."

Luke looked back down at the brown muck. "What will we do, sir?"

"We will fill the gem with the Flame." He narrowed his eyes. "You will watch me and then you will draw on what I do and repeat it. You will never be able to do this without me, Luke."

"OK ... sir."

"I do not have to be beside you, but I must always be here and here," he said, touching Luke's head and chest with his finger.

Luke felt his heart still. The sounds of bird calls and the wind vanished, along with the sound of water gurgling up out of the ground. Green light poured out of Mr. Roberts's eyes and Luke's mind filled with it. A tingle raced from his head down his spine and legs all the way to his toes. Mr. Roberts grinned, and the world came crashing back around Luke.

"Now ... *watch*."

Luke turned and stared as Mr. Roberts put his hands near his waist and then pulled on the air around him. A strand of light twisted down out of the sky and around him and curled toward the mud. Dirt rose from the earth and twined about the light. Droplets of water fell from the sky and formed another thread. Flames appeared dancing on the wind and twisted around the light as well. A shimmering rope of air like thick spider's silk joined the twisting lines. Leaves sprouted from the ground, forming a vine that wrapped around Mr. Roberts's leg and twirled into the other disciplines.

What about time?

Ripples coursed through the twisting disciplines. As a ripple moved toward the end of the cable, the disciplines wound together faster and faster. Luke squinted toward the front of the rope near the stagnant water as the light intensified. He put his hand in front of his eyes and turned his head.

Whoosh!

Air rushed toward the cord and exploded back out in a flash of light. Luke staggered back, whiteness flooding his vision even with his eyes squeezed shut.

"Mr. Roberts!"

"Luke, it's OK. Here I am."

Luke felt a hand grasp his elbow and ease his body forward. "What happened, sir?"

"The disciplines have combined to form the true Flame, the power that this world and everything in the universe are made of."

Luke felt his heart relax and a grin spread on his face. *Now that is cool.*

"You will have to feel the disciplines until you are able to shield your eyes. Though you will never be able to look directly at the Flame, you can work with it. Now, stay in my shadow, close to me, and feed the disciplines toward me."

Luke shuffled forward, hands fumbling for Mr. Roberts. When they found him, Luke leaned against his back and thought about the twining disciplines. He didn't have to think long, though, before energy spread through his body, making him quiver. The sounds of water crashing over a falls and fire raging through a forest filled his ears. He drew on light and earth, fire and water, air, life, and, finally, time. His head spun and then, as the sound faded, energy bled from his body and the light dimmed. Panting, he opened his eyes and stared at Mr. Roberts, who smiled and pointed toward the springs where the mud had bubbled up.

"Well done, Luke … That will do it."

Luke grinned. The darkness was gone, the water so clear

that he could see the rocks at the bottom of the pond. A gem the size of his fist pulsed white light in the deepest part of the pond. The light spread, chasing darkness out of the spring and down the river. Luke followed the clean water with his eyes until it flowed around a bend in the river and south.

"It worked?"

Mr. Roberts nodded.

"I don't understand. Why couldn't anyone else do it—the council or the women's circle?"

"They were trying to fix the river by cleaning it from within using what was already in the water, but in this case, darkness could only be cleaned from a power outside the river and the holding—only with the Flame."

"But what about south of the falls? Some of the water was clean there."

Mr. Roberts's smile faded. "Yes, but only temporarily. Pain and discipline can clean darkness away, but if there is nothing to fill the void once it has been there, it will find its way back in and be even the worse for it. In the case of the falls, the *pain* caused by the water's colliding with itself separated the darkness from the water, but as you saw farther downstream, it came back."

Luke rubbed the sides of his forehead.

Mr. Roberts chuckled. "It will get easier to understand over time, son."

Luke sighed. "It's worse than the headaches from Ms. Lisantii's vocab tests." He whirled around at the sound of horses' hooves pounding the ground.

"Luke!"

"Dad!"

His father dropped from the back of a brown mare and ran

toward Luke. Luke raced to meet him, and his father crushed him in an embrace.

"Boy!" His father leaned back and held him at arm's length. "You come talk to me next time! Whatever it is, *whatever*! We'll do it together, you hear me?"

Luke smiled, his eyes stinging. "Yes, sir."

Luke's father jerked him back, squeezing him into his chest and holding him there for a minute. He relaxed his grip and turned to Mr. Roberts. "Jeremiah."

Mr. Roberts's eyes danced, as he settled his cowboy hat on his head. "Your boy did good. His heart's in the right place … most of the time." He winked at Luke. "You've at least set an example in that way, Joe."

Luke's father swallowed and nodded, his jaw clenched.

"What about the gnomes, sir? Won't they just poison the river again?"

"It's not that easily done in the first place, Luke, but I think they'll find that much harder in the next day or so." He looked at Luke's father. "Joe, tell your father that there are dark clouds gathering on the horizon. They are distant still, but gaining in strength."

Luke's father nodded as Mr. Roberts turned and walked to the north, Kaleva padding along beside him. Luke watched until they vanished into a cluster of cypress trees, branches swaying in the wind on the shore of the lake.

TWENTY-TWO

Friends & Enemies

On their way back to Rayburn Manor that morning, Luke's father paused near the edge of Westcliffe Forest and turned to him. "Suppose I ought to let Mom and the others know you're all right. Might not go over too well for me if I waited until we were back at the house." He whispered a word on the wind and a silver orb appeared near his face. "Sara, Luke is fine. We're on our way back to the manor. I love you." The ball spun and, trailing silver, streaked into the trees to the south.

"Awesome," Luke said.

His father remained silent most of the way back, only occasionally asking Luke about the night and his experiences. Luke told him about meeting Peter, getting the Tears and running from the falls, swimming across the river, freeing Anora from the wolf, and losing the Tears.

"She was in the wolf the whole time ... and Peter was alive still. But I still don't know where they went to."

His father chuckled. "Nor I, though I have my suspicions. We'll have to see if we can figure that out ... together."

Luke ducked his head and grinned. "Yes, sir."

As he went on to tell his father of the journey north, his father's eyes widened at the mention of traveling with Mr. Roberts. And he stopped dead when Luke told him about using the Flame to clean the river.

"You used the *Flame*?"

"No, sir. I just helped feed Mr. Roberts the disciplines. I don't think he really even needed me, and he told me I wouldn't be able to do it without him, but—"

"Grandma will be fascinated"—his father chuckled—"and jealous. You aren't going to get a moment's peace for a while, son."

They walked in silence then for a time. The sun rose higher, filtering through the arched canopy above the trail. Birds flitted from branch to branch, and a rabbit bounded past in front of them. Luke's father turned to him as the trees opened onto a meadow, his horse dipping its head toward the knee-high grass.

"I'm very proud of you, Luke. I want you to know that. I would suggest listening to Mr. Roberts more often. And talking to your father more often as well wouldn't hurt, but you were very brave, and you put your friends before yourself. That is a quality to be valued above almost all others."

Luke felt heat rush to his face. "I didn't do so good, Dad … I … I left my friends surrounded by gnomes and wolves."

"*Tsk.*" His father smirked, his steel-blue eyes narrowing. "Luke, humility is valuable, but you must learn to discern between humility and self-pity."

"Yes, sir."

"Your friends told me why you ran, and in what manner you left them. Even the cowardly dryad, Bros"—his father's face contorted—"spoke of your bravery."

"What happened after I left, Dad. Do you know? Mr. Roberts said everyone was OK."

They waded through bahiagrass and Indian blanket flowers.

"Matt will be able to tell you more when we get back, but yes, everyone is all right. From what I garnered through the night, most of the dark creatures took off after you. Matt, Marti, and Samantha managed to fight off the remaining few … And Bros helped them some, so they say." He spit the words out. "Seems the darkest of the creatures were desperate for the Tears, though Matt did manage to take down two of the darkmen. The Guard picked them up when they got there and apparently had a pretty good time of laughing at two grown men getting bested by a boy." He chuckled and arched his eyebrows. "Though I'm not sure after talking to Uncle Landon about Matt that the guardsmen should be so surprised."

Luke smiled. "They shouldn't."

"I have to tell you, though, Luke, Mr. Thompson was pretty furious about Samantha going running off into the night with y'all. I was getting a bit hacked off, to tell you the truth, but" — he chuckled — "I think his daughter … convinced him that you were not wholly to blame."

"I shouldn't have dragged her along … or any of them, but I wouldn't have been able to get the Tears without them. Of course, then the Tears would still be safe."

"But you wouldn't be, Luke. You have friends who are very loyal and care about you a great deal. They were very proud to help." He sighed and smiled. "And Trent is *not* very happy to have been left out."

Luke grinned. "Maybe next time."

His father glared sideways at him. "Excuse me?"

Luke wiped the smile off his face. "Just kidding, Dad. I'm just kidding."

"Hmm …We'll see."

The sun hovered overhead and sweat beaded on Luke's forehead as the manor came into view. Jake and another of the servants stopped and waved to Luke, and Luke waved back. Then Ricardo stepped out of the stables and shooed the boys on.

"Luke!" Luke's mother ran out to meet them as they walked into the north garden. She was followed by Trent, Uncle Landon, Mr. Acharon, Ms. Nichols, and Matt.

"Mom!" Luke ran to his mother, and she squeezed him until he coughed and sputtered. "Mom … Mom …"

His mother leaned back, wiping at her eyes with one hand, and then pulled him back tightly as the others walked up. Smiles, hugs, and pats on the back came from every direction.

Matt glared at him. "You pull that stunt again and I'll punch you square in the face, Rayburn."

"Yeah, me, too," Trent said. "Why'd you leave me out?!"

"*You* will not be going anywhere, Trent Alexander Rayburn, and neither will your brother!" his mother said. "Chasing around bane wolves and darkmen and Lord knows what else. Ew" — she shivered — "and those creepy little gnomes."

There were laughs of relief all around.

They spent the rest of the evening on the back patio around a fire pit. Mr. Robinson grilled hamburgers and sausage, and bowls of steaming cheese and colorful dips lined a wooden table set up on the patio flagstones. As darkness fell, Luke and Matt sat in the center telling their tale until at last, eyelids drooping, they stumbled up to bed.

Gray light crept in through the three arched windows on the east wall the next morning. On a bed under the center window was a mound covered in blankets. Luke squinted at the bed, leaning forward a few inches.

Creak.

Luke froze.

"You may come in, young one."

Luke jumped as the voice sounded and the shadow sat up in the bed.

"I have been hoping I would get to speak with you today, though I am surprised you are up so early."

Luke shuffled in and eased the door closed behind him. "I didn't sleep very well last night, ma'am."

Light bloomed in two sela'or above the bed. Smiling green eyes looked up at Luke from the bed. Mayeem chuckled. "Indeed." She reached a hand out and took Luke's in her own. "I must thank you, Luke. I am indebted to you. You saved my life."

Luke's face flushed and he ducked his head.

Mayeem squeezed his hand, pulling him down into a slat-backed wooden chair beside the bed. "I do not like to think about what would have happened had you and your brave friends not come."

Luke swallowed. "You're welcome, ma'am. I did have a bunch of help from Marti, Matt, and Samantha."

"So I've heard. I'm very sorry I wasn't awake when you arrived yesterday, but my body is still very weak."

"How … how long were you down there, ma'am?"

The mermaid sighed and arched her eyes. "As best I can tell, the sun set three times while I was frozen in that cave."

Luke nodded and sat silently for a few moments. Gray light brightened to purple, and a mockingbird called outside the window. "Did you know what was going on?"

Mayeem frowned. "A bit. It was much like a dream of which

the memories fade quickly upon waking. I remember bits and pieces, but even those flee from my grasp."

"Were you hungry?"

"Ha ha ha." Mayeem's voice filled the room like the sound of a gentle stream tinkling over rocks. "Not while I was in a frozen state, no, but once I became aware again, *ravenous!*"

Luke grinned. "I would've been."

The mermaid grinned, too, and the sound of feet striding down the corridor carried through the wooden door.

Luke's smile faded. "Ma'am, how come when you touched the box, you were … frozen … but I wasn't? Was it because we used the key?"

Mayeem sighed. "I'm not sure, Luke. I've given it a good deal of thought since waking and … I just don't have a good answer. It may be that once the trap was sprung, it would not reset itself, or that as long as I was frozen no one else would be, or perhaps it was because you and your friends so thoroughly defeated the guardians placed there." She chuckled. "I will have to talk with those in my clan who sent me, but your reasoning is as sound as any other I've thought of."

"It just doesn't make sense still, though, ma'am. If that was true, why didn't the hunter just come in and use the key himself? He sure seemed to know where the Tears were for a while."

"That is another question I have been mulling over, young one. I believe the answer to that is in the wards, or traps, set around the Tears. Besides the guardians, there were a number of 'dormant' traps surrounding the Tears, ones that never activated when I was there nor, from what I gather, when you were there. I think the traps were set for darkness alone. The hunter needed you to go in and get the Tears. It would've been almost impossible for any creature of darkness to do so."

Luke bit his lower lip and nodded. He was about to speak when he felt the vibration of feet running down the hall, and then the door opened. One of the servants poked her head in. "Ms. Mayeem, if you please," she said breathlessly, "Mr. Rayburn said you would be interested in something outside. He sent me to help you out, if you're willin'?"

"Of course, Anabelle, thank you." The girl dropped a curtsy and stepped into the room, but she paused a few feet from the bed and looked back and forth between Luke and Mayeem, her face flushing.

"Oh, sorry," Luke said. "I'm … I'll … thank you, ma'am. I'll talk to you again later … if you can."

Luke stood and stumbled out of the chair and back toward the door. He bowed out of the door, red-faced and to the sound of giggling. The door shut and Luke sighed.

Smooth, Luke, smooth.

He walked down the hallways of the east wing. Servants scurried by as purple and pink blossomed to orange outside. He stopped near the north stairs, and two girls darted past him laughing.

What's going on?

He watched them hurry out the side doors to the ground-floor passageways.

"Luke!"

He jerked around and smiled as Jon and Amy bounded out of the stairwell and bumped into him.

"Luke, come look!"

"Come see!"

He laughed as the twins tugged on his arms, pulling him through the doors. Crisp air filled his lungs and fog lifted off the ground in the light of the rising sun. Laughter and the sound of voices carried from behind the garden walls as he trotted along with his brother and sister.

"What is it? What's going on?"

"Grandpa says the sprites have come back!" Jon said.

Luke's eyes narrowed as they passed under an archway of red-tip photinia. House servants and some of the field hands not yet out for the day joined them as they weaved through the maze of roses, shrubs, and trees. Running under the hanging branches of a willow tree, Luke pulled to a stop.

Thirty yards ahead, near the far north edge of the gardens, a pool shimmered in the sun. To the east a stream ran from the spring pool, and to the west spread the branches of a pecan tree. The tree towered over the pool, its branches forming a canopy over it, and all through the branches Luke's eyes followed the darting movements of light. He shuffled forward with Jon and Amy as they giggled and pointed. Creatures the size of his hand flitted in and out, darting behind leaves and down to the water, skimming the surface and leaving ripples spreading behind them. Colored light glowed wherever they touched; sprouts grew on the tree, and bubbles danced under the surface of the water.

One of the creatures darted over and hovered inches from Amy's face. Voices hushed and heads turned to watch the sprite. Clear wings beat rapidly behind it as its round eyes regarded Luke's sister. A green-and-purple dress shifted around the sprite, glistening like droplets of water on string. After a couple of seconds, she floated toward Jon.

"*Hee-hee-hee!*" the sprite laughed, and with a twist she touched Jon and Amy on the foreheads and whizzed away back over the water. Spots of light glowed on their faces where the sprite had touched them, fading as they spun around toward Luke.

"Did you see—"

"Luke, Luke, did you see—"

Luke laughed as his parents and grandparents approached. Luke's grandfather knelt and took his grandchildren's hands. "Now that, my dears, is not something that happens every day."

Voices and laughter rippled through the crowd, and Luke smiled as Jon and Amy beamed in their grandfather's embrace.

A few days later, Luke knocked on a towering wooden door in the servants' quarters.

"Come!"

He turned the flowered knob of the door and stepped inside. Ms. Lucy looked up and her eyebrows arched. "Young Master Rayburn. And what brings you down here today?"

"Well, ma'am …"

Thirty minutes later, Ms. Lucy walked Luke to the door, grinning. "And a fine, fine idea it is, young sir, a very fine idea indeed. I will make sure to talk with Mr. Acharon once he hears word back … I'm sure even *that* old grouch-puss will not deny her this."

She hugged Luke and then coughed and pushed him out the door. "Now off with ya!" Luke grinned as she bustled back to her desk and the door swung shut.

The sun crept up earlier and stayed longer as summer days galloped closer. Wagons brought onions and new potatoes to the house and the first cuttings of hay. Calves raced around the meadows, stopped for no reason in particular and then kicked and bucked and raced around again, their mothers chewing slowly and ignoring them. Summer corn in the fields reached to Luke's chest, and martins darted through the air chasing bugs. With the return of Mayeem's strength also came the return of sprites to some of the fields and hills of Countryside.

Near the end of the second week of summer vacation from school, Luke found himself bouncing along in the back of a wagon next to Matt as the sun climbed toward its peak. Ricardo urged the horses south back toward the manor, and Luke wiped sweat from his face with the long sleeve of his work shirt. As another wagon lumbered along behind them, field hands shouted and laughed, calling back and forth to each other. As Luke and Matt talked and kept posts from rolling down onto them, Luke's thoughts turned back a year to sand and the taste of salt in the air.

Twenty minutes later, the wagon rolled to a stop near a shed just south of the stables. Luke and Matt heaved posts and rolls of barbed wire out of the bed of the wagon and dropped them with a thud to the ground. When the wagon had been cleared, they helped Ricardo park it and stable the horses again. Trudging up to the front of the house, they saw Trent and Grandpa Rayburn at the far end of the lawn tossing a baseball. The ball arced through the air and Trent extended his leather glove to snag it before waving to Luke and Matt. Trent fired it back, and Grandpa Rayburn flicked his wrist and snatched the ball.

"Pretty good for an old man," Matt said.

Luke chuckled. "Trent keeps throwing it harder and harder, but it doesn't even seem to faze Grandpa." He frowned. "And don't let him hear you say the 'old man' part. He can throw hard enough to make your hand sore … and I'm pretty sure I've never seen him throw as hard as he can."

He and Matt turned at the sound of gravel crunching beneath buggy wheels. Father Woods grinned and waved as he pulled up on the reins.

"Good afternoon, boys!"

"Good afternoon, Father Woods!" Luke and Matt chimed back.

The wheels stopped and the priest stepped down from the seat.

"Are you here for the party, sir?"

Yip, yip.

In the carriage, a crate a couple of feet across sat on the floorboard.

"No, no, I'll be back later for that," Father Woods said. "I was actually looking for you two." He dipped his forehead and looked at the boys over the rims of his round glasses, his smile fading. "I'm running some errands for Peter."

He had Luke's full attention. "Sir?"

Father's Woods's voice dropped, though not another person was within thirty yards. "I met with Peter a few times while he was alive, and he left some … requests for me to carry out when he died, some of them quite recently."

Luke's eyes darted to the crate, from which emanated a distinct whining sound, and back to Father Woods.

"It seems he wished to have some items preserved, and he mentioned you two as well as Marti and Samantha in regard to a few of them."

Luke exchanged a narrow-eyed glance with Matt as Father Woods stepped back to the buggy and hefted the crate out. He placed it on the ground with a grunt and set to work on the latch.

Yip, yip, yip.

"I spoke with your parents already and they gave their

consent, assuming you want them. They'll have to be left with their mother for a while longer, as the hunter and his wolves are still out there somewhere, and they'll hunt for the pups once they find out about them with almost the same tenacity they did for the Tears. But"—he winked—"I thought you would like to see them."

Father Woods opened the lid and Luke peered over the edge. In the box, two stone-gray puffs of fur cowered in a corner. The puppies were about as long as Luke's forearm and blinked up at him with eyes of a lighter gray than their fur.

"Go ahead," Father Woods said. "There's one for each of you. Pick one up."

Luke turned to Matt. "Which one do you want?"

Grinning, Matt scooped up the one on the right and cradled it as it whined and squirmed. Luke reached in and picked up the second ball of fur and rested it in the crook of his arm.

"Rock hounds are very rare," Father Woods said, "and they are only born in sets of twins. These are the first pair that Kaleva has birthed, and she will likely not have any more for another decade or so." Luke's eyes widened at the priests words. "Rock hounds grow very slowly, and generally stay with their mother for quite some time. Kaleva will have to approve, obviously, but Peter seemed to think she took a liking to you on that dark night, so I imagine she'll let you keep them once they're weaned."

"But, how—" Luke's eyes widened again. "You mean you saw Peter that night, after he …"

Father Woods grinned and arched his eyebrows as Trent appeared with Grandpa Rayburn.

"Luke, whatcha—" Trent's mouth dropped open. "Puppies!" He rushed over. "Can I pet him? Is it a him?"

Luke shrugged and held the pup out for Trent to pet.

"They're both boys ... and that's unusual," Father Woods said. "Generally, a pair is one of each."

The boys held the puppies for a few more minutes and then Father Woods bundled them back into his buggy and pulled himself up into the driver's bench. Grandpa Rayburn used his hand to shade his face from the afternoon sun. "We'll see you in a few hours, Wade?"

Father Woods smirked and tilted his head. "There will be food, will there not?"

Luke's grandpa chuckled along with the boys.

With a click of Father Woods's tongue and a flick of the reins, the dappled mare started off.

If there were only two puppies ... "Father Woods! What did Marti and Samantha get?"

The priest glanced over his shoulder and hooted. "You'll have to find out yourself!"

A couple of hours later, the sun hung a few fingers above the horizon. Luke looked into the mirror on his bedroom wall as he buttoned up a blue dress shirt his mother had given him that morning. The Rayburn brighthawk rested on the left side of his chest and a silver chain peeked out from behind his undershirt. Creased blue jeans and polished brown boots reflected back up at him. He sighed.

Oh well.

"You won't get any prettier no matter how long you stare at that mirror, you know, man."

Luke picked up a book from the writing table beside him and chunked it at Matt, who was lounging in a chair.

Matt ducked. "Besides, if she hasn't noticed how ugly you are by now, today's not going to change it."

Luke tucked his shirt in and turned toward the door. Matt's and Trent's laughter followed him into the family quarters. His mother smiled as he walked past. "You look very handsome, Luke."

Jon and Amy looked over from a pair of books.

"Thanks, Mom," Luke said, embarrassed.

He worked his way through halls and down stairs until he walked out the main doors to the entrance hall. Mr. Acharon nodded to him as he walked up to the open door of the blue carriage. "You ready, Luke?"

Luke swallowed. "No, sir."

Mr. Acharon gave a wicked grin. "Good."

Luke frowned, but the estate manager just motioned with his head toward the carriage and chuckled. Luke stepped in and the door closed. Ms. Lucy beamed over at him as the carriage jolted forward. "This is so *exciting!*"

Butterflies woke up in Luke's stomach as he leaned against the window. *This was a horrible idea, Rayburn.*

An hour later, Luke stood fidgeting in the entrance hall of Heatherfield Park, the Thompsons's residence, with Ms. Lucy and Mr. Acharon on either side. Mr. Acharon's eyes narrowed and scanned the room. Voices sounded on the other side of the south doors, and the butterflies in Luke's stomach became a whirlwind. Mr. Thompson pushed the door open.

"But, Father, the party isn't for another three hours. I still don't understand—"

Samantha stood in a yellow summer dress with her hair over one shoulder and a purple gem an inch across hanging around her neck. Luke took a shaky breath.

Frowning, Samantha looked at Luke and then at Ms. Lucy and Mr. Acharon and then back at Luke. "Father?"

"It seems Mr. Rayburn would like the ... *pleasure* of your

company for a while before the party. *If … you would like to go?"*

Samantha turned to Luke and narrowed her eyes. Mr. Jefferson pushed into the room behind the pair, and Luke held his breath until she nodded. "Yes, Father."

His face twitching, Mr. Thompson nodded and looked at Mr. Acharon and then glared at Luke. "I will arrive at seven."

Luke nodded. "Yes, sir."

Mr. Thompson smiled at Samantha. "Be safe, dear." He whispered something else and leaned over and kissed her on the cheek before turning toward the doors. Mr. Jefferson walked alongside Samantha as she stepped toward Luke.

"I don't think we'll be needing any help along this afternoon, Phillip," Mr. Acharon said.

Mr. Thompson turned and looked from Mr. Acharon to Mr. Jefferson.

"I just thought I should go, sir," Mr. Jefferson said, "to make sure Miss Thompson is safe."

Luke saw Samantha cringe and give a tiny shake of her head. Her father pursed his lips. "No, I will need you here tonight, Nathan. Even if not the other two, I trust Ms. Lucy. Samantha will be fine. Let us go now; the day is waning."

Mr. Thompson turned and strode through the doors into the house. Mr. Jefferson glared at Mr. Acharon for a moment, quivering. Mr. Acharon smiled, but his eyes remained ice. Mr. Jefferson snarled and wheeled around and toddled off after Samantha's father.

Luke sighed as Samantha stood beside him.

"Whew," she said.

Her eyes danced as they walked past a servant in the brown livery with the wolf emblem of the Thompson household and down the stairs toward the carriage. She paused as Luke handed her up into the carriage, her hand clasped in his. "Where are we going, Luke?"

Luke swallowed. "You'll see." He winced as his voice cracked.

Samantha smiled with narrowed eyes and stepped in. Luke handed Ms. Lucy up next and then climbed in opposite them as Mr. Acharon closed the door.

Twenty minutes later, the blue light of a traveling tunnel sparkled in the early evening air. The face of the dryad Bros, now healing nicely, leaned in through the window of the carriage, smiling. Two other male dryads, who looked like guards, stood behind Bros, glaring at his back not as if he *had* some dread disease but as if he *were* that disease.

"She'll be there, in the cove near the edge of the holding."

Luke nodded. "Thank you, Bros."

The dryad nodded sheepishly. "You're welcome. I'm glad … I'm glad I could help."

Luke glanced back at the two dryads behind him. "Can you not go anywhere without them?"

Bros glanced over his shoulder and chuckled. "Not for a long time. What I did, Luke … it was inexcusable for one of my kind." He winked. "It could've been"—his countenance darkened—"and probably *should've* been much worse." A smile lighted his face again. "Besides, it's just kind of like being stuck at home, really, with friends. Egoz there on the right is my cousin."

"Egoz!" Luke exclaimed. *The one who was under the manor that night.*

Bros frowned. "You know him?"

Luke snorted and shook his head. "No, just … heard of him."

Bros shrugged. "Hmm. Oh well." He hopped down and waved. "Have fun, Luke!"

Luke smiled sarcastically. "You, too." The carriage rolled forward and white light enveloped them.

Pop!

The taste of salt and the sound of waves rolling onto the beach filled the carriage, and Luke looked at Samantha. A smile spread across her face as she stared at the window. "The ocean!"

Luke grinned. "It's a holding near the island of Shalloke, where my family came last summer."

Samantha clasped the windowsill and leaned out, drawing a deep breath and closing her eyes. The horses clopped down a cobblestone path toward the shore, stopping a few dozen yards from where the waves rolled in. Luke hopped out and helped Samantha down and then Ms. Lucy. Samantha clasped her hands together and grinned.

"Come on," Luke said. "I want you to meet someone."

Samantha slipped her sandals off and followed Luke over a dune to a still cove a few yards away. As they neared the water, a fountain bubbled up, filled with blue light. Samantha gasped as a face and a body formed in the water. "An ocean nymph!" She clapped her hands as the nymph dipped her head.

"Yes, child, my name is Josephine."

Luke stood and listened patiently while Samantha and Josephine talked for the next thirty minutes. As colors painted the clouds overhead, Mr. Acharon cleared his throat behind them, and Luke and Samantha turned to him.

"I am sorry, but we need to make sure we are back at the house by the time your father arrives, Miss Thompson."

Samantha smiled and dipped her head. "Yes, sir." She

turned back to the nymph and grinned. "It was very nice to meet you, ma'am."

Josephine inclined her head. "It was a pleasure, young one. I will look forward to it again someday." With a glance at Luke, the nymph sank with a twirl back into the cove.

Samantha watched the ripples for a moment and then turned. As she and Luke started up the dune, she put her arm through his, and Luke felt his heart jump. When they reached the carriage, Samantha stopped and looked at him. "Thank you for bringing me here, Luke." She studied his face, her green eyes making the rest of the world disappear, and her voice dropped to a whisper. "You are sweet, and kind, and I am very happy I came here with you." With a smile that made his heart ache, she turned and stepped into the carriage.

He took a deep, shaky breath. *Maybe not such a horrible idea, Rayburn.*

People flowed into Rayburn Manor and lights floated all along the driveway. Carriages rolled past and others pulled up, servants dashing from one to the next. Luke stood at the top of the stairs, his stomach roiling again as the black carriage halted below. Warmth spread across his chest. Samantha stood next to him, along with his parents. Mr. Thompson stepped out of the carriage and walked up the steps, eyes latching on to Luke. As he set his foot on the top step, Samantha ran to him and wrapped her arms around him and kissed him on the cheek. His lips quivered as he set her down.

"We got to see an ocean nymph!" Her voice bubbled over as she pulled her father into the house. Mr. Thompson looked over her head and nodded to Luke.

Well, it's not a smile, but at least it's not a curse.

A few steps behind, Mr. Jefferson tromped along, glowering at Luke and his parents. His father rested his hand on Luke's shoulder, but the man still made his skin crawl.

Thirty minutes later, Luke's parents released him from the duty of greeting guests and he bounded off to the back patio. Samantha, Matt, Trent, and Marti sat around a table as Luke weaved his way over with a plate of stuffed sausages, cheese bread, and roasted corn.

"What took you so long, man?" Matt said as Luke sat down.

"Keep it up and I'll convince your mom you need to be out there with me!"

Matt snorted but held his hands up. "OK, OK, jeez."

The laughter at the table mingled with music from a guitar and fiddle nearby. Luke listened as Marti and Samantha talked about their gifts from Peter.

Marti pulled a brown leather book stamped with the letters *PMR* out of a cinch sack beside his chair. "It's a book containing everything f-f-from his life. I mean, it's almost two h-h-hundred years of stuff, from here, from other h-h-holdings. Half of it is in sh-sh-shorthand I can't figure out yet, b-b-but just what I've r-r-read is unbelievable."

"It's like the grand champion of old dusty books." Matt shook his head and turned to Samantha. "What about yours?"

Samantha held her necklace out, light pulsing inside the purple gem as a plum bird flitted to the table and hopped toward her. "Father Woods said he wasn't sure of its origins, but he said he didn't think Peter would've given it to me if it was dangerous. He said he could tell it was powerful, some unique combination of earth and life. All I know so far is that it gives me a cool kinda tingly feeling when I put it on." Samantha wrinkled her nose and gave a little shiver.

As children raced by chasing a rabbit that left glowing paw

prints, conversation turned back to the Tears. Marti frowned and looked at Luke.

"They h-h-haven't found anything?"

"Nope. And I doubt they will. The Tears are long gone."

Matt pursed his lips, his voice low. "But they still have to get three more objects, right? I mean, we can beat them to those."

Luke sighed. "I'm … I'm not sure we should. I mean, maybe we should just leave it alone. If I wouldn't have gone to get the Tears, they would probably still be there, safe."

"I don't think so, Luke," Samantha said. "They would have found another way. Even Mr. Roberts said so, right?"

Luke shrugged. "Well, even if we were going to, we have no clue about what the other objects are or even where to start looking."

Marti grinned. "Hey, we f-f-figured out where the Tears were even though no-no-nobody had seen them in, like, forever. We'll f-f-figure this out."

Trent, Matt, and Samantha nodded, and Luke felt a grin fight its way onto his face, but then he noticed Samantha's face fall as she looked behind him. He looked over his shoulder to see Jennifer walking by looking straight ahead.

"She still won't talk to you?" Luke said.

"No."

Luke sighed. "I'm sorry, Samantha."

"Yeah, that s-s-sucks."

Matt glowered toward the crowd, where Jennifer had disappeared. "I still don't understand why in the world she hangs out with Jon David and his goofballs anyway."

Samantha smiled, but her lips trembled.

"Excuse me, Luke," a voice boomed over his head.

"Mr. Volf!" A smile came back to Luke's face at the sight of Mr. Volf in jeans and a button-down shirt hanging loosely past his middle, with a toothy grin on his face and coarse black hair curling on his head. Next to him stood a girl reaching a bit above his waist and looking down at her feet.

"How are y'all doing this evening?" Mr. Volf took in the expressions around the table and sniffed, his smile slipping from his face. "Well, those are some dark looks ... Didn't mean to interrupt if I did."

"No, sir. It's good to see you," Luke said.

A half-smile returned to the man's face. "You, too, lad. Very glad to hear that you managed to give that hunter the slip ... so to speak." He leaned down and his voice lowered to a whisper that sounded like a steam engine. "Don't go it alone against them, next time, though, ya hear?"

"Yes, sir."

Mr. Volf nodded and glanced around the table. "And that goes for the rest of you, too. Too dangerous by far, and there isn't any point. You've help here in Countryside, you understand?"

Heads nodded.

Mr. Volf reached for the lapels of his pharmacist's coat that weren't there and settled his hands behind his waist instead. "Hmphf."

"Sir?" Samantha coughed and nodded toward the girl next to Mr. Volf.

Mr. Volf frowned and glanced beside him at the girl, looked back at Samantha, and then jumped. "Oh, yes ... yes! Sorry, dear. This is my niece, Zeeva Volf." He patted the girl on the shoulder as if he were handling china.

Cream-colored skin peeked out from under a purple sundress, and straight raven-black hair with a streak of white fell around her face. The girl nodded and looked up. Luke heard an intake of breath from Matt.

"Whoa ..." Trent's voice carried from the other side of the table.

Bright purple eyes the color of the plum bird blinked, and the girl dropped her head again.

Samantha stood up and stepped toward the girl, extending her hand. "Hi. I'm Samantha Thompson." Luke smiled at the sound of her voice, lost in thoughts of sand and a pair of green eyes inches from his face. As his thoughts lurched forward a couple of days to when his family was scheduled to leave Countryside for summer vacation "outside" of the holding, he sighed. *Three months sure is a long time not to hear her voice.*

Zeeva's head rose and a tight-lipped smile played across her face. "Hi." She reached out and shook Samantha's hand.

Samantha turned toward the table. "And these *rude boys*" — Luke jerked his gaze away from Samantha and sprang out of his chair—"are my friends. This is Trent, Marti, Matt, and Luke." Luke stepped forward and reached out a hand. Zeeva smiled and a couple of pointed teeth slipped past her lips.

"Luke Rayburn. It's very nice to meet you, Zeeva."

Zeeva's eyebrows arched. "So this is *your* house."

Luke chuckled. "My grandparents', yes, and Trent here" — Trent jogged around the wrought-iron table and chairs—"is my little brother. My other brother and two sisters are running around here somewhere."

"You have *four* brothers and sisters?"

Luke nodded and stepped out of the way as Marti stepped forward to say hello. Then six pairs of eyes turned toward Matt.

"Matt!" Luke hissed, but Matt didn't move. Luke punched him in the side and Matt blinked and lurched to his feet, knocking the chair over backward. Samantha and Zeeva giggled and Luke frowned at his red-faced friend.

"Hi ... um ... Matt ... Nichols ... It's nice to meet you, Zeeva."

Mr. Volf narrowed his eyes at Matt. "Well, just thought maybe you lot could show Zeeva around town this summer. She's going to be starting high school with y'all next year here in Countryside."

Samantha took Zeeva's arm and pulled her toward the table. "We'd love to, Mr. Volf. We were just about to go look at the tree sprites, actually."

Zeeva let herself be led away, and Mr. Volf nodded as they walked toward the north garden. Trent and Marti followed, and after a moment of staring at him, Luke slapped Matt on the back of the head.

"Ouch."

"Come on, man, what's wrong with you?"

"Sorry. Nothin'." Matt shook his head and jogged a few paces with Luke to catch up.

Halfway to the gardens, Luke glanced to his left and froze as Matt went ahead. A shadow pooled in the corner of two holly bushes and his mind flashed back to a corner of a falling-down house. Red eyes filled his mind and a hiss that made his skin crawl sounded in his head.

"Well, Luke, I see I can't even trust you to find and bring back a single simple item."

Luke's limbs were stiff and cold, as if gripped by the hand of a giant snowman. "It wasn't simple … and I shouldn't have been looking for it anyway. All I did was get people hurt."

Shadows thickened around Luke, pressing into his sides.

"Sometimes people have to get hurt. The Tears could have given you the power to protect thousands. Only a fool or a coward refuses a gift of that power that's right in front of them. I practically laid the Tears in your lap, and yet still somehow you lost them!"

Luke felt himself shake his head. "There were tests to pass, and traps ... the water and the key and—"

"Excuses! I gave you help ... information, seekers. I even pointed out what was right in front of your face!"

Ice stabbed into Luke's heart and he quaked.

The voice softened. "I can't protect you, Luke, if you don't help me. As I told you, betrayal often begets betrayal and you should be careful how much you trust those around you. There are some out there who desperately want to hurt you, and we need more ... power to stop them."

"Who wants to hurt me? You've never told me *who*."

"You'll know soon enough ... For now we will try and locate the other objects."

Luke gritted his teeth as orange eyes flashed with flame and cold seeped through his chest and into his legs. "No. I'm done. I won't go looking for anything else ... All it does is cause problems." His teeth chattered.

Contempt filled the voice as it receded. "Fool. We shall see. You will change your mind, and when you do, *I* will still help you." The shadow thinned and the eyes faded. "If it's not too late."

Orange light seared Luke's eyes and he felt his muscles slacken. He stumbled forward and bumped into Matt.

Umphf.

"Hey." Matt looked at Luke's face. "What happened?"

Luke shook his head at the sound of boots clomping on the stones behind them. "Later."

"Well, boys, and how are you tonight?'

Luke felt warmth surge into his body again, washing away the cold and the fear. He turned back to see smiling bright green eyes.

"Mr. Roberts!" Luke said.

"You boys going to see the sprites?"

"Yes, sir," the boys said.

"Mind if I join you?" Mr. Roberts leaned down and rubbed his hands together. "It's been a long time since so many of the sprites have returned openly!" He snapped his fingers and strands of blue light shot out and twisted, curled, and weaved down the stone path, chasing shadows into the night. Luke's mouth fell open and Mr. Roberts laughed. As the three of them began walking, the cowboy leaned close to Luke's ear. "Once started, some things must be seen through to the end, Luke," he whispered, "but when knocked on, the door will always be opened."

He winked, and they all walked into the clearing beside the spring a few paces behind Samantha, Trent, Marti, and Zeeva, the blue light swirling and dissipating into the garden.

Luke shuffled to a stop. Servants and guests laughed and walked around the garden in pairs and larger groups. There were several tables covered with white tablecloths, but unlike in the rest of the garden and the house, no lights shone. All through the air and weaving in and out of the branches of the pecan tree, sprites darted, their colored light leaving trails in the air behind them and causing plants to glow. Samech waved, standing at the edge of the water along with Mayeem, who dipped her legs into the pool. Luke's parents, Uncle Landon, and Matt's mother sat at one of the tables smiling toward them. As Luke stood gaping at the sprites, watching the people walk around the clearing and listening to the laughter of his little brother, his friends, and Mr. Roberts, contentedness filled his chest.

Two days later, Luke settled into a seat in the train-car cabin.

An image of a bare-chested sprite in blue shorts flying toward him flashed through his head. He pulled three items out of his backpack and set them on the cloth-covered bench. He picked up the first item, a letter creased and folded multiple times into a rectangle. Glancing out the door of the cabin, he listened to Trent laughing and darting around with Jon, Amy, and Jodi and then slid the wood-and-frosted-glass cabin door shut.

> *Luke,*
>
> *I was relieved to hear you survived your adventures recently — word travels pretty fast, especially among the darker creatures. They are a little scared, to be honest ... there are very few who can say they have escaped the grasp of a hunter ...*

Luke snorted. *For now.*

> *At any rate, the sprites are who I have been using this year to get messages to you.*

Luke's mind flashed back to the tiny footprints on his writing desk and a green glow that floated out the window as he fell asleep one night.

> *They are very trustworthy messengers and have agreed to get word back and forth between us. I have a new lead on my niece ... I feel like I'm closer than ever right now, but time will tell. My sister's mood is darkening and she seems to be giving up hope.*
>
> *You need to know that someone there in Countryside is still feeding information to darkness out here, and that someone seems to know an awful lot about your family — and you. I'm trying to learn anything*

I can about who it might be, but obviously you can't just walk up to one of the soulless or a dark-man and say, "Hey, you know that Rayburn kid in Countryside?" Just be careful.

I received your last letter but I'm afraid I'm not much help on the gate or what the other three objects might be. I will tell you this, though, whatever that gate is, if it takes a lot of power to open it, the objects are probably filled with the Flame. There aren't too many objects left like that in this world, so ... I'll keep looking.

In the meantime, keep yourself safe. Have fun this summer traveling and if you need something just get me word and I will do what I can.

Take Care,

J.

Luke folded the letter and put it back in his backpack. He reached over and picked up the second item, a gold oval flattened to the thickness of a coin. He waved his hand over the coin and laughter filled the room.

"Luke, we thought you might like to listen to this every once in a while this summer."

He closed his eyes and smiled at Samantha's voice.

"Whatever—it was her idea, man."

He chuckled at Matt's voice in the background.

"Oh, whatever, Matt."

"H-h-have fun, Luke. Bring us back s-s-something cool."

"Yeah, something better than glowing beach sand this time!"

Luke shook his head.

"Anyway, have fun and write if you can. We'll …"

The boy's taunts and laughter faded into the background and Samantha's voice dropped to a whisper. "I'll miss you … Bye, Luke."

Luke took a deep breath and his heart swelled. He opened his eyes, put the coin in his jeans pocket, and sat up. As the train lurched forward, he heard steps outside the cabin and then a knock at the door.

"Come in."

The door slid open and his father poked his head in. His eyes latched onto a rolled-up parchment next to Luke and he grinned. "You busy?"

"No, Dad, I was just going to look at the map Professor Lewis gave me. You wanna help me?"

His father stepped inside the cabin. "You bet!" He pulled a wooden trunk away from the wall and sat on the bench across from Luke. Luke rummaged around in his backpack and pulled four leather map weights out as his father unrolled the map. They set the weights down and looked at the lines sketched onto the map depicting trees, villages, mines, and other features of the landscape. Across the top of the map were the words *Holding Silver Creek, Trapper Mountain Quadrant*. The train picked up speed and the whistle blew outside.

"So you think we might actually be able to find the abandoned mine Professor Lewis talked about?" Luke said.

"Not sure, but I'm sure we'll see some stuff not on the map, and that's the fun part, adding to it!"

Luke grinned as his father pored over the map. The train car curved to the south and out of town, and after crossing the Algid, they climbed out of the valley. When the town of Countryside and the lighthouse on Sandy Isle had passed from view, Luke's thoughts shifted from the sparkling water of the

Algid to the Redwall Cliffs and then south to Clearwater Falls. Matt, Marti, and Samantha's faces flickered through his mind like darting tree sprites. As the whistle blew, he thought he heard howling in the distance and he grinned as he pictured two gray puffs of fur yipping and jumping up and down.

Blue light glowed outside the window and the clickity-clack of train wheels echoed through the hills. Luke looked to the north toward his grandparents' home and sighed. Leaning over, he turned his attention to a set of tracks on the map that his father pointed to and nodded.

Home ...

J.T. Cope lives in Texas with his wife and three girls. Their little corner of the world also contains chickens, rabbits, turkeys, and a pair of occasional bobcat visitors who meander through the orchard across the creek.

You can visit him online at www.jtcopeiv.com.

ACKNOWLEDGMENTS

I'm grateful to the staff at TED for support and encouragement. Jane Ryder, Liz Felix, and Morgana Gallaway for keeping me sane and directing me to answers for the multitude of questions I come up with. Doug Wagner for extensive comments and a seemingly unending supply of patience. Mark Korsak and Christopher Fisher for jumping in with both feet and doing a rather fantastic job. Karinya Funsett-Topping, Julie Miller, and Lori Alayne for paying attention to the myriad details I so often neglect. I am grateful to the students, librarians, and friends who have asked for more and helped to keep my spirits up. My parents, who have been ever interested and inspiring. And most of all my insuppressibly heartening wife Katie and our three who allow me time to visit and explore Countryside.

This edition was prepared for printing by
The Editorial Department, LLC.
7650 E. Broadway, #308, Tucson, Arizona 85710
www.editorialdepartment.com

Original illustration and cover design created by Mark Korsak,
with interior design and typography directed by Christopher Fisher.
The Managing Editor was Doug Wagner; the Continuity
Editor was Karinya Funsett-Topping;
proof editors were Julie Miller and Lori Alayne.
Print production directed by Morgana Gallaway.

The text is set in Chantelli Antiqua, designed by Bernd
Montag, and Palatino Linotype, created by Hermann Zapf
and named after 16th-century Italian master of calligraphy
Giambattista Palatino.

The cover art was created traditionally with water colors
on acid free board. The interiors are a mix of traditional ink
drawings with digital embellishments.

CPSIA information can be obtained at www.ICGtesting.com
Printed in the USA
LVOW12*1518200116

471538LV00014B/199/P

9 780996 050067